She had t[...] no matter what she saw.

No matter what happened.

And yet she managed to observe as Liam stood there naked, stretching his body, flexing those amazing muscles of his...and more. Making her insides react in ways they absolutely shouldn't right now.

But scolding herself didn't help.

He accepted a vial of clear liquid from Patrick and drank it. He seemed to shoot one more look toward her. Then Denny lifted a large light from where it had been in his backpack, turned it on and aimed it toward Liam.

She knew what to expect—kind of. But she still couldn't help feeling amazed as his face lifted and its features began elongating into a muzzle, and his body grew smaller, furrier, more slender, shrinking closer to the ground.

And in a very short time, handsome, naked Liam had turned, as anticipated, into a wolf.

VISIONARY WOLF
&
CODE WOLF

LINDA O. JOHNSTON

AND

LINDA THOMAS-SUNDSTROM

HARLEQUIN® NOCTURNE™

Recycling programs
for this product may
not exist in your area.

ISBN-13: 978-1-335-21999-2

Visionary Wolf & Code Wolf

Copyright © 2019 by Harlequin Books S.A.

The publisher acknowledges the copyright holders
of the individual works as follows:

Visionary Wolf
Copyright © 2018 by Linda O. Johnston

Code Wolf
Copyright © 2018 by Linda Thomas-Sundstrom

This edition published by arrangement with Harlequin Books S.A.

For questions and comments about the quality of this book,
please contact us at CustomerService@Harlequin.com.

HARLEQUIN®
www.Harlequin.com

Printed in U.S.A.

CONTENTS

Linda O. Johnston loves to write. While honing her writing skills, she worked in advertising and public relations, then became a lawyer...and enjoyed writing contracts. Linda's first published fiction appeared in *Ellery Queen's Mystery Magazine* and won a Robert L. Fish Memorial Award for Best First Mystery Short Story of the Year. Linda now spends most of her time creating memorable tales of paranormal romance, romantic suspense and mystery. Visit her on the web at www.lindaojohnston.com.

Books by Linda O. Johnston

Harlequin Nocturne

Guardian Wolf
Undercover Wolf
Loyal Wolf
Canadian Wolf
Protector Wolf

Back to Life

Harlequin Romantic Suspense

K-9 Ranch Rescue

Second Chance Soldier
Trained to Protect

Undercover Soldier
Covert Attraction

Visit the Author Profile page at Harlequin.com.

VISIONARY WOLF

Linda O. Johnston

Visionary Wolf is dedicated to all
Harlequin Nocturne readers, especially those
who have enjoyed my stories about Alpha Force.

And yes, as always, my thanks to my fantastic
agent, Paige Wheeler of Creative Media Agency,
and to my wonderful Harlequin editor, Allison Lyons.
There may be no further Alpha Force stories, but I
look forward to more Harlequin Romantic Suspense.

Also, as always, I thank my dear husband, Fred,
for being there, and for inspiring me.

Alpha Force.

Chapter 1

Good thing he was at Ft. Lukman, Lieutenant Liam
Corland thought. At any other military facility, he
would never feel comfortable walking calmly with his
dog, Chase, across the nearly empty grounds, in his casual camo uniform, later in the morning than he should
be reporting for duty. In fact, he wouldn't feel comfortable working at any other military facility, period.

But this was where Alpha Force was stationed. He
had just left his apartment in the bachelor officers'
quarters. Now he headed toward the building across
the compound that contained so many important func-
tions—mainly laboratory, cover dog kennel and offices,
including his own.

Sure, he should have started his important assignment of this day an hour ago, so he didn't want to make
his lateness too obvious. He avoided the most used path-
ways, hustling along behind buildings occupied by units

other than Alpha Force. Chase and he would be picked up on security cameras when they sneaked in through a back door of the appropriate building, but no one would do anything about it, since they belonged there. Besides, he had a good excuse, and he probably wasn't the only one who slept in a bit. Not that he had gotten much sleep anyway.

There had been a full moon last night. He had shifted, of course—pretty much on his own terms, thanks to Alpha Force.

And thanks also to the help of his aide, Sergeant Denny Orringer, who now waited for him in the kennel and lab building. Covering for him, if necessary.

He'd talked to Denny earlier, and—

There. Chase and he had reached the back of that building, near the doors leading into the kennel area. The shapeshifters' cover dogs like Chase were kept there frequently, along with other dogs that helped this military base look like it had a lot of well-trained canines living here all the time.

Of course Alpha Force members who had cover dogs also kept them with them a lot as well, both at Ft. Lukman and when they were traveling—as long as there were some living here, too, to keep up appearances.

Liam, a tech expert, used the key card he had programmed himself to open the back door. He slipped in and enclosed Chase in one of several fenced areas, joining three dogs that resembled him.

Of course, Chase looked wolfen, resembling Liam himself while he was shifted...

"See you later, guy," Liam whispered to his canine companion, who was already being greeted by his fellows.

Heading for the stairway down to the most important floor of the building, which contained offices and the laboratories where the very special Alpha Force elixir was brewed, Liam walked slowly, figuring he was likely to run into someone else dressed like him.

But fortunately, he saw no one—so no one saw him, either, as he again used a key card to open a door, this time to the stairs.

He heard raised voices from down the hall when he slipped carefully into his own office. They sounded excited. With his special senses, even when he was in human form, he could easily have eavesdropped had he wanted to.

But what he wanted was to get to work.

First, though, he shot a quick text message to Denny to let him know where he was. Then he booted up his computer, a highly sophisticated desktop that was the epitome of today's technology.

A good thing, since it was used for such a critical purpose.

His phone made a text ping. Denny was probably just acknowledging what Liam had sent. He'd check it later.

A sudden urge for a cup of coffee shot through Liam but he ignored it. He'd get one later when he went to the meeting, but right now he needed to check his usual social media and other sources.

His job at the moment? Look for any and all mentions online of people claiming to have seen shapeshifters last night, in this area first of all, then other locales in this country and the world where Alpha Force members were stationed. And, finally, everywhere else.

He'd undoubtedly find some mentions. Perhaps a lot.

He always did, and most appeared to come from people who loved what they considered paranormal—fiction lovers who wanted to see if others, unlike them, had spotted shifters during a night of a full moon. They were easy to deal with.

But Liam needed to deal with the reality of those who didn't have the kinds of backgrounds to have been introduced to Alpha Force and what it did, but had caught glimpses of possible Alpha Force shifters on that night of the full moon—or claimed to.

Liam had to find their posts, then kid around online. Make them look foolish to the rest of the world, and maybe even to themselves.

That was one of the things Liam, vying, at least in his mind, for tech champion of the universe, did best. But he wasn't a geek. Oh, no. He loved being a member of the military. Of Alpha Force. He both looked and acted the part.

Except at the computer.

Using one of his many false identities, he logged on to a favorite social media site—and gasped. "No!" he exclaimed aloud.

He read the post more carefully, then jumped onto several other sites—and got the same results.

Existence of a strange military unit of shapeshifters was mentioned more than once on this day after a night of a full moon. That wasn't unusual.

But claims of damage, destruction—and injuries to real people? The extent of what was described on so many sites was horrific.

And did not bode well at all for Liam's vision of shifters' acceptance someday by other people. Those lies were more of the reality now, though.

"I need to let the others know." Liam was barely aware he was talking aloud. He picked up his phone, then realized this was critical enough that he wanted to tell his superiors in person. One in particular—Major Drew Connell, their commanding officer who had begun Alpha Force and remained in charge.

Drew's office was on the opposite side of this floor, past the lab areas, and Liam immediately headed there. If he hadn't had this important assignment, that was where he would have gone first, since nearly all Alpha Force members present on the base attended informal meetings in Drew's office the morning after a night of a full moon. Liam would have headed there eventually anyway to let the others know what he found.

But with these horrible allegations… Liam had to let his unit members know right away. Then he had to dig further online to learn their truth—or, hopefully, not.

If not, though, how had so many unheard of references and accusations been put out there?

He put his computer to sleep, then hurried out his office door, down the halls whose plainness would never suggest the amazing things that went on in the laboratories beyond them, to another hall lined with closed doors. The last one was to Drew's office.

Without knocking, Liam burst in, expecting to see Drew there holding court with the other shifters and their aides.

But though the room looked busy, he didn't see that officer in charge. Nor did he see Captain Jonas Truro, Drew's close friend and aide, a medical doctor like Drew, but, unlike him, not a shifter.

That was strange for a post–full moon meeting in

Drew's office. Did they know what Liam had learned online? Were they trying to deal with it themselves?

But Liam might just be allowing his own angst over what he'd seen on the computer to lead him to false conclusions. Drew and Jonas could be down the hall in the restroom. Or checking something in the lab. Or—

"Oh, there you are, Liam." Denny, in a folding chair near the doorway of the small, crowded office, stood and looked at him. "I'm glad you read my text." Which Liam didn't always do quickly, and he wasn't about to tell his aide he hadn't this time, either. Denny was younger and shorter than Liam, and he had a slight growth of facial hair. Liam kept his own dark hair closely shaved—when he was in human form.

He wondered what Denny had said in that text, but he wasn't about to check now.

"Come in, Liam," Captain Patrick Worley said, also standing. He was tall, dressed in camos like the rest, and the expression on his face looked grim. Had he heard about what the Alpha Force shifters were alleged to have done?

Had Alpha Force shifters actually done any of it? Any of them in this room?

"Glad you're here," Patrick continued. "Have you checked out any online references to shifters yet?"

"Yes, and—"

But Patrick didn't let him finish. "Good. We'll want to hear about it. But first there's something you need to know that we've been discussing. Something bad."

Liam swallowed hard. "I definitely want to hear about it." Hopefully, none of it was true and he could find a way to calm all the comments that had shown up online. Or—

"It's about Major Connell," Patrick said. "Something went wrong with Drew's shift. Really wrong. He hasn't shifted back from wolf form yet, and he's not doing well. Right now, Jonas is with him at the veterinary clinic in Mary Glen. Drew is being cared for by Melanie."

Drew's wife, a veterinarian. Not a medical doctor.

This was definitely bad. Very bad. Certainly more important than the false claims Liam had seen online.

What was Alpha Force going to do?

"How is Drew now?" demanded Dr. Melanie Harding Connell. Dr. Rosa Jontay's boss faced her at the back of the Mary Glen Veterinary Clinic's main hallway, arms crossed, head tilted.

Rosa understood her concern, of course. Major Drew Connell wasn't just the head of that highly special military unit known as Alpha Force. He was also Melanie's husband. Father of her adorable four-year-old daughter, Emily, and two-year-old son, Andy.

"He seems tired," Rosa said softly, looking into Melanie's sad but pretty blue eyes. "I just came out of the room for a short break and to get coffee, but I'll be heading back in there soon. Jonas is still with him."

That was Captain Jonas Truro, also part of Alpha Force, and from what Rosa understood Jonas was additionally a medical doctor—and Drew's aide when he shifted. She had seen him a few times in the year or so she had been here, but, as with most of the Alpha Force members, she didn't know him well. Jonas had apparently been hanging out with his superior officer earlier that night—and later.

"Thank you. And thank Jonas." Melanie also seemed tired. Stressed. But that wasn't surprising.

As the only veterinarians at the clinic, they both wore white lab coats. Rosa was the taller one. They both had brown hair pulled up in back by clips, with Melanie's darker than hers.

Not that she was comparing herself to Melanie, Rosa thought. She considered them both exceptional vets, and that was what really mattered.

But she did wonder what it was like to have as strange a relationship as the one between Melanie and Drew. Committed and deeply caring—but yes, strange, since Drew was a shapeshifter.

"Everything okay with the rest of the clinic?" she asked Melanie. "Do you need me for anything else?"

"Fortunately, we're not very busy today. What I need you to do is—"

"I'm going back into that examination room right now," Rosa finished. "But with this kind of situation… it's so different, and other than to keep an eye on him I'm not sure what to do."

"That's all I want you to do. Having Jonas there helps, but the kind of medical assistance Drew might need now—"

"Is veterinary. Right. I understand."

The door to the reception area down the hall opened, and the senior receptionist, Susie Damon, came out and looked toward them. "Our eleven o'clock Yorkie appointment is here for an exam and shots," she called. "Okay to bring him in?"

"Fine," Melanie responded. "I'll be right there."

Melanie was handling all the cases that came in, for now at least. She was clearly upset, and Rosa assumed she feared breaking down if she was the vet to spend time with Drew.

And that might make things worse with him.

Melanie looked back toward Rosa. "Just so you know, I did get a call a few minutes ago. So far…well, I gather there are no more answers from Ft. Lukman yet, but one of the Alpha Force members is on his way to relieve Jonas. Maybe whoever that is can shed some more light on what's going on there, and when…"

She didn't have to finish. Especially not with the newest look of pain that flashed across her face.

"That's fine," Rosa said. "I'll still hang out with Drew, but I'll also see what I can learn from whoever that is and report to you if it…if there's any indication of what they're doing and how long it will take."

"Great. And maybe Jonas can help more by doing something at the base. I'll check back with you soon." Melanie headed down the hall toward the reception area as Susie led the tiny Yorkshire terrier and his not-so-tiny owner toward one of the closest exam rooms.

Which left Rosa to go grab two cups of coffee from the break room at the end of the hall and take them with her to another exam room, the one where Drew had been brought by Jonas and Melanie early that morning, before anyone else had arrived—but after dawn had broken.

Rosa looked around the hallway once more, but it was empty. Then she slipped into the room.

It was a fairly ordinary exam room for a veterinary clinic, with the back wall covered by a cabinet containing shelves for supplies like bandages, exam gloves and disinfectant, and a sink in the middle for washing hands and more. There was a closed trash can nearby, and a couple chairs sat along the outer wall. In the middle was a substantial metal table.

One of the chairs was occupied by Jonas, who stood when she entered. He was a large guy, dark-complected and dressed in a camouflage uniform. He was around her own age of thirty, she figured.

"Here's some coffee." Rosa handed him one of the cups.

"Thanks," he said as he accepted it.

Rosa turned then. On the table with legs adjusted to keep it close to the floor lay a large canine that resembled a wolf. And he was a wolf—of sorts.

That canine was Major Drew Connell of nearby Alpha Force, its lead officer, from what Rosa had heard.

She had also heard that Alpha Force was a highly covert military unit of shapeshifters, which was fascinating to her. There had been a full moon last night, and Drew had shifted into his wolf form. But he hadn't shifted back at dawn or beyond.

He'd been home when the sun rose, and the Connells' home was next door to the vet clinic. Melanie had brought him here after taking their daughter to preschool and making sure the sitter was there for their son. Rosa could only guess what Mommy had said to their kids about where Daddy was, and about the wolf in their house.

Or maybe the kids were shifters, too…

Melanie had also called Jonas, who had arrived at the clinic even before Drew and had stayed with him, along with Rosa, from early morning. It was around ten o'clock now.

Rosa realized she had been standing in the doorway after closing the door behind her. The wolf on the table hadn't moved—before. Now, he made a soft growling sound and, moving slowly, carefully along the towels that had been secured around the metal top, repositioned himself into a canine sit. His fur was long, an almost silvery brown, with patches of darker coloration. His eyes were amber, and he seemed to stare at her over his long, pointed muzzle.

"It's okay, Drew," Jonas said. "It's just Rosa."

In his current situation, Drew looked a lot like Grunge, a wolflike shepherd-malamute combination that Rosa had been informed was his cover dog. That meant, she'd been told, that Grunge could be pointed out to people as Drew's pet, the canine they supposedly saw when he was changed, not him. She assumed Grunge was hidden at home at the moment, or maybe at the base.

"Hi, Drew," she said. "How are you feeling now?"

He couldn't answer by speaking to her, of course. But from what Melanie had told her, the members of Alpha Force took some kind of medicine—an elixir, they called it—before they shifted that helped them keep their human cognition. He most likely understood what she said.

But they also were supposed to turn back into human form once daylight began after a night of a full moon, unless they had drunk that elixir and chose not to shift back then. She gathered that Drew hadn't chosen to stay a wolf when daylight arrived that morning, but still hadn't regained his human form. And judging by the reactions of Melanie and Jonas, that wasn't good.

He apparently did understand her, though. Maybe. But he aimed his gaze down at the table and shook his head slowly, as if communicating to her that he wasn't feeling well.

"I'm so sorry," she said.

And she was. The fact that she had known about shapeshifters, and had, in fact, helped to treat some shifted wolves and other creatures at her home in Michigan, had been the main reason Melanie had hired her here. Apparently the shifter community kept in touch with each other, or at least some did, and Melanie had been hunting for someone like her. And Rosa had been thrilled by the offer of this kind of job.

"Is there anything I can do to help?" she asked, not for the first time, looking from Drew to Jonas and back again. She had sat in here with the two of them pretty much since she had arrived at work that day. Melanie had tearfully explained the situation, including her request that Rosa stay with Drew and make sure he wasn't suffering.

Or, even better, report to Melanie when he finally started to shift back to human form.

But that hadn't happened. Not yet, at least.

Right now, Drew didn't even look at her, let alone attempt to communicate something he wanted her to do. Jonas didn't offer any suggestions, either.

"Would you like some water?" she asked Drew.

He looked at her and nodded, so she removed a clean metal bowl from the sink, filled it partway and placed it on the table in front of him. He lapped up maybe half of it.

A knock sounded on the exam room door.

Rosa glanced at Drew, who was once more lying on the towel-covered table, head between his paws in a fully canine position, the bowl off to his side.

"Come in," she called.

The door opened and Susie popped her head in.

"There's a guy here from Ft. Lukman who says he's come to help out."

To take over for Jonas, Rosa assumed, from what Melanie had said before.

She figured that Susie and the others who worked here had some knowledge of the ties Melanie and her husband had to Ft. Lukman, and probably even knew there were shapeshifters there—and possibly that Drew was one of them.

But they'd also been instructed to remain totally discreet, even among themselves. To Rosa's knowledge, they never talked about it—or at least they'd never done so around her.

"Thanks, Susie. Let him in."

In a moment, a tall guy dressed in a camouflage shirt and slacks like Jonas entered the room, and Susie shut the door behind him.

Jonas rose again. "Liam," he said. "Glad you're here." He turned to Rosa. "This is Dr. Jontay, one of the vets here. Rosa, that's Lieutenant Liam Corland."

"Hi, Dr. Jontay," the guy said in a deep, masculine voice. He held out his hand and gave hers a quick, substantial shake. The contact made her feel fully aware of this man's presence. He was wide shouldered, and his face was angular—and gorgeous. His hair was black and military short. Dark brown eyes looked straight into hers, but only for a moment.

"Hello, Lieutenant Corland," she said as matter-of-factly as she could manage, considering how oddly her mind was reacting to this guy.

"Liam," he gently corrected, making Rosa regret she hadn't done the same. He turned to Jonas. "I'm assigned to relieve you here."

"Got it. Thanks. I'll run now, and keep you informed about how things go at the base." Jonas bent toward Drew, who was sitting up once more on the table, and said something into his ear, which twitched canine style. Then he exited the room.

"Well," Rosa said, not exactly sure how to handle this. What was this Liam going to do here?

As if she had spoken aloud, he looked her directly in the eyes once more. "Do you know and understand the full situation?" His tone was demanding. She didn't like it, but she did understand.

"Yes, I think so," she said. Then, more brazenly, "Do you?"

"Of course. I'm a member of Alpha Force, too. One of its…special members." Again, he caught her gaze, as if attempting to ensure she knew what that meant.

"Then you're like…" She tilted her head toward the table, where the canine Drew remained seated, clearly watching them and presumably understanding. "Like Drew," she finished.

"That's right. I'm here to help Drew out as much as possible from the…from the military angle. Watch over him while members of our unit try to figure out how to help him in their way." Something to do with that elixir that helped shifters? Something else? Maybe she would find out more. "And discuss if you think there's any veterinary way to help him…help him get over his current condition."

"I see." This seemed so odd—and yet, since Rosa had grown up with both real wolves and shifters in her area, she could deal with it. Right?

Of course. But the part of all this that made her somehow feel worse at this moment was that she couldn't help focusing on how this Liam had admitted to her right away what he was.

And she felt terrible to think that this gorgeous hunk of a military man was also a shapeshifter.

Chapter 2

"Hi, Drew," Liam finally said.

There his commanding officer was, in canine form, sitting on a bunch of towels on a lowered table in the middle of this veterinary examination room. Watching them. And now he nodded his head as if in greeting.

Liam turned back to Dr. Jontay. Rosa. This vet was fairly special, from what he had been told before he left Ft. Lukman. She had apparently been found after a long hunt for a good, smart backup by Melanie Connell, who'd been seeking a vet who knew about shifters, had provided medical care to them in the past and would keep her mouth shut about working with more in the future.

Rosa was one pretty, hot woman, to boot.

But checking her out wasn't why Liam was there.

Seeing, taking care of his friend, his mentor, his superior officer—that was his reason for coming to this clinic.

Sure, he'd told his fellow Alpha Force members at Ft. Lukman about the accusations he'd found online. That was important, of course. But not as important as ensuring that Drew returned to normal. Fast.

And when the topic of needing Jonas to get back to the base to help find a solution arose, Liam volunteered to hang out with Drew here for as long as it took to get him cured.

The rest of the team had argued, since the idea of having so much garbage out there online about shifters and Alpha Force was horrendous, and Liam was the best tool they had for countering it. But he'd told them he had taught Denny how to start his critical counter-social media games. Plus, he would work on it himself as Drew's condition here permitted.

They'd finally agreed, since most of those at the base would be focused on how to deal with what had happened to Drew, and keeping one of their own with him was critical, too. But if what Denny accomplished, with Liam's backup, wasn't enough, they would send Denny to trade places with him so Liam could focus on his job—which was now ridiculing all the ridiculous, and not so ridiculous, claims that had appeared on the internet.

So Liam's giving a damn about his mentor and wanting to do something about it had worked out—at least for now.

"Okay if we sit down?" Liam asked Rosa. "I've got a few things to update for Drew." Assuming that the elixir Drew had first developed, and had worked with over the years of Alpha Force's existence, still allowed him to keep his mental acuity—his *human* mental acuity—hours after he should have shifted back. And his nod before had indicated that, at least, hadn't been affected.

"Would you like a cup of coffee before we talk?" Rosa asked Liam.

Nice lady, or at least polite.

Or did she have an ulterior motive?

"Yeah, thanks. I'd love one." But he'd love finding out what was on her mind even more.

"It's just down the hall." She motioned toward the door with graceful fingers. Probably skilled fingers, too, since she used them to cure animals around here.

He wondered what those fingers would feel like on him… Heck, just because she was a pretty brunette with shining brown eyes and full lips didn't mean he should allow himself to feel any attraction toward her. She wasn't a shifter. She might work with shifters, but he had no idea how she felt about them.

He followed, as she apparently wanted. Well, he wanted it, too.

A guy in blue scrubs walked past them in the fairly long hall—probably a vet tech, Liam figured. He waved to Rosa. "Everything okay?" he asked.

"Everything's fine, Brendan," she replied. "Are all our patients being handled okay?"

Liam assumed she asked that because she wasn't caring for anyone besides Drew right now, or at least it looked that way.

"Sure. Melanie's got it covered, and Dina and I are helping." The guy waved and walked through one of the doors off the hall. Liam assumed Dina was another vet tech.

"Good," Rosa said softly. Then, more loudly, she

said, "We've got coffee brewing in the break room, right here." She walked a few more steps, then opened a closed door and motioned for him to follow, which he did.

"Coffee's fine with me," he said right away, "but why am I really here?" He looked around. The room was a bit larger than the exam room and had a few small tables clustered in its center, a fridge on one side and a counter on the other where a large coffee maker sat.

The smile she sent up to him was pretty, as well as ironic. "I'm that obvious? Well, you're right. I don't want us to leave Drew alone for long, but I wanted to ask how things are going at Ft. Lukman. Does anyone there know why Drew hasn't shifted back? What are they doing to help him? I figure that, since they wanted Jonas there, they must be working on that elixir, since I know he's a medical doctor and has helped Drew before with that stuff."

"You're right, and I know they're hoping to come up with some new formulation of the elixir that'll help." But from what Liam had heard, no one had any good ideas yet about why Drew hadn't shifted back despite clearly wanting to, or what kind of adaptation could be made to the elixir to help him. They'd even given him some more of the current version of the elixir to lap up, but that hadn't helped.

"Okay." Rosa turned her back and headed to the coffeepot, where she poured some into two foam cups that she got out of the cabinet below. She handed one to him. "Milk? Sugar?"

"Black," he said. "Thanks."

She went to the fridge and added a few drops of milk to her cup. She turned again toward him. "We'd better get back to Drew." She seemed to hesitate. "Do you know anything about the formulation of the main elixir?"

"Just generally," he said.

"Then what do you do in Alpha Force? For one thing, I assume from what you said before that you're a shifter."

She said that very matter-of-factly, as if she knew about and accepted their existence, as she'd implied earlier, which fit with the little Liam knew about Melanie Connell's assistant vet.

"Yes," he said. "I am." He thought he caught just the tiniest hint of a reaction in her expression. Maybe he was wrong, and she was good at hiding what so many regular humans who knew that shifters were real actually thought about them. Just to bug her, he asked, "Are you?"

Her brief laugh sounded genuine. "No, though I've worked with quite a few over the years." She paused. "Do you do anything special for Alpha Force? I mean, do you handle some of their special ops–type assignments, or do you do something besides train for the future at the base?"

Somehow, he wanted to impress her, which made no sense. He had no intention of flirting with her. But it wouldn't hurt to tell the truth. "Well, I do train for the kinds of special assignments we're sent on," he said. "But I'm also the chief technology officer."

Those pretty brown eyes of hers widened. "Really? What does that entail?"

He didn't want to tell her about the stuff he had seen online making claims of injuries and worse, caused by shifters last night during the full moon. From the little he'd seen here in Mary Glen it had all been false, anyway—he hoped. If all was going well, Denny was continuing with the solution.

So instead of being fully honest, he said, "I just scout around to see what technology is out there that Alpha Force may be able to use to enhance its already fantastic and covert abilities." That probably sounded good, and it wasn't entirely false, since he did that along with the rest.

"Interesting." Rosa pulled her gaze away from his face. "Now, let's go back and check on Drew."

Checking on Drew was exactly what Liam wanted to do. And he was glad to see that the wolf with the silver-tipped, thick brown fur sat up on the towel-covered table as they entered and began observing them with his wide, golden eyes.

What was he thinking? Liam would try to find out.

"Hi, boss," he said. "Rosa and I just got some coffee, but the caffeine wouldn't be good for you right now. But I want to bring you up-to-date on what was going on at the base."

That everyone in Alpha Force was scrambling around trying to figure out what happened to him. Liam would tell him that, but word it a bit differently.

Also, as the commanding officer of their unit, Drew would be the first person Liam would normally tell about the kind of online social media fiasco he'd discovered—under other circumstances. He wouldn't now, of course. Giving Drew further information that would torment him wouldn't help him shift back any faster.

And would it do any good at all for even a tech expert like Liam to do research online about what had happened to Drew? Shifters weren't likely to post anything about problems in their shifting, let alone what to do about it.

Plus, Alpha Force had its own unique take—and elixir—that would render most comments inapplicable.

Just in case, though, Liam would take a look later.

"How are you feeling now?" Rosa moved around Liam as if taking charge. She approached Drew and patted him gently on the head between his pointed, moving ears as if he were a pet canine. That irritated Liam a little—although he had a passing thought that if she wanted to touch *him* that way, or any other way, he probably wouldn't mind at all, shifted or not.

Drew actually did seem to try to communicate with her some, growling slightly, then shaking his head.

"Do you feel bad physically?" Rosa asked. He stopped moving. "Or are you just frustrated that you haven't changed back?" He nodded.

Good. At least he seemed to be using human cognition and showed no sign of growing wilder, wanting to attack. He was a human in the guise of a wolf, but for a much longer time than Liam was aware any shifter had remained that way without choosing to stay shifted.

So how were they going to bring him back?

Almost as if he heard Liam's thoughts, Drew gently pushed Rosa away with his head. He lay down on the table and stared at Liam.

"I think he wants you to bring him up-to-date, as you said." Rosa looked at Liam with a wry grin on her lovely face, her brown eyes looking both interested and sad. She seemed to really care about her veterinary patient. She probably knew him as a person, too, since she worked for his wife. Liam wished he had something to say that would make her smile.

And Drew, too. Wolves could smile, after all. At least shifters could, somewhat, while in wolf form.

"Okay." Liam sat down on one of the chairs. Rosa remained standing beside Drew at first, her eyes examining him as the wolf regarded the other man in the room. "Now, here's the situation—and if you have any ideas we'll have to figure out a way for you to convey them to me."

Drew nodded as he continued to lie there. Rosa moved to the chair beside Liam.

"First," Liam said, "Jonas and Melanie—and maybe Rosa, too—" he looked at her for an instant and saw she was regarding him steadily "—may already have asked you this, but do you know why you haven't shifted back? I gather this wasn't your choice. Was anything different this time from one of your regular shifts?"

The response was no, based on the low, grumbling noise he made and the slight shake of his head.

"Okay, then. Here's what I learned from the conversations at the base before I left."

Liam started talking about all he had heard and participated in once he had joined the meeting in Jonas's office. No other shifter had had any problem, so they didn't believe it was the elixir—the most current version of the tonic that Drew had begun brewing with the changes that had been suggested and tried by other shifters and seemed to work best for everyone. It allowed for all-important human cognition while shifted. There were slightly different versions now being used outside the full moon to give more choice about when to shift into wolf form and when to shift back. A version that wasn't being used much, if at all, allowed for shifting back to human form when the moon remained full, but it had never been as perfected as the unit members hoped for.

"So," Liam said, "did you drink the regular elixir we're now using during the full moon?"

Drew nodded.

"And did Jonas use the light on you?" That was still preferred by Alpha Force members even under a full moon to ensure the timing.

Again, Drew nodded.

"I assume the elixir looked and tasted like it always did, right?" Rosa asked. Liam was impressed that she was jumping into the discussion, as if she knew what she was talking about. And most likely she did, considering who her boss and her boss's husband were, as well as her own apparent background of at least knowing about shifters.

Shifters other than those in Alpha Force also sometimes attempted to develop their own formulas to help them change when they wanted to. Even some members of Alpha Force besides Drew, including second in command Captain Patrick Worley, and Lieutenant Simon Parran, had brought their own versions when they had joined the unique military unit, or so Liam had heard.

Rosa might have known something about that even before joining this clinic as a veterinarian.

Liam, though, hadn't brought anything like an elixir with him when he'd joined the unit. As always, he'd been focused on his technological skills. He had been online when he'd first learned such stuff actually existed, beyond the stories and legends, and so did a special, covert military unit that used it.

That was how he had learned about Alpha Force, and the rumors about what and where it was. Why he had shown up at Ft. Lukman one day with a résumé in hand, and had asked to speak with the officer in charge, who happened to be Drew.

Drew had apparently been as impressed by him and his techie skills as Liam had been impressed by Alpha Force. The result had been Liam enlisting and joining the unit—and being taught and mentored by the man before him, the shifter who now couldn't shift back.

Liam had to figure out how to help him, by assisting the others working on the same problem to succeed or otherwise.

"Well, it would be easier if I could report back to the rest of the gang that you admitted to drinking something besides, or in addition to, our regular elixir," Liam said, pursing his lips a bit. "But I know they're all trying hard, without knowing what they're looking for, to research how this could happen."

"I'm trying, in my own way, too," Rosa said, standing again. "I gave him a brief physical before, but would like to do more now, although under these circumstances I'm not sure a regular veterinarian, even with some knowledge of shifters, can help."

"But we appreciate your trying." Liam also rose and looked at her. This, at least, was a different angle. "What do you want to do?"

"A blood test, for one thing. And I'd like to take a closer look at Drew's body to see if there's something visible, a cut or growth beneath his fur…anything that may be different. Maybe an X-ray, too."

"Great," Liam said. "I'll help."

Drew appeared to be okay with it as well, since he just stayed limp on the table, which Rosa adjusted to be closer to her waist level. She did the exam first, saying she would draw blood when they were done, then take it into the clinic's lab to analyze.

"Many vets send blood out to a specialized laboratory for analysis," she told Liam. "But with this kind of patient I've learned to conduct the analyses myself. It's safer that way."

Liam wanted to hug this attractive, smart, careful vet, but of course he didn't.

Instead, he helped her work with Drew, moving him on the table so she could use her stethoscope to check his heartbeat—normal for a canine, she indicated. Also to feel his chest, his limbs, his back, his skin, seeking any kind of lump or other abnormality, but she found none.

With Liam's help—and also that of Brendan, the vet tech he had seen in the hall before—they moved Drew into another room where the X-ray equipment was kept, but once again nothing unusual was discovered.

Brendan took charge of the move back to the same exam room. There were others in the hall then, including a woman also dressed in blue scrubs like Brendan, whom Liam assumed was the other vet tech Brendan had mentioned before.

Melanie, too, came into the hall just as Brendan got Drew inside the room. "How is he doing?" she asked in a thick voice.

Rosa, who'd been following them, said, "We haven't found anything yet. He seems tired at times but he—" her voice lowered "—he seems to know what's going on and communicates with us when we ask questions."

"That's good," Melanie said. "I just wish…" She didn't finish, but instead hurried away from them, down the empty hall.

Liam looked into Rosa's lovely brown eyes. She looked sad. No, worse, tormented. He had another urge to hug her in empathy. Better yet, to come up with an immediate answer.

He did neither. But he also didn't look away from her.

Odd, but he felt they'd somehow bonded over this difficult situation. They both wanted to resolve it. Fast. For similar, but not identical reasons.

Alpha Force needed Drew back the way he was. And Liam needed his friend and commanding officer.

His wife, head vet at this place and Rosa's employer, mother of Drew's daughter and son, undoubtedly needed him most of all.

Brendan came out the exam room door. "Okay, he's situated on the table again. He looks tired."

Rosa immediately pulled her anguished gaze away from him and Liam felt a pang of…sorrow? "Thanks, Brendan. I'm going to draw some blood now."

Which was what she did, after entering the room again accompanied by Liam, who helped to keep Drew resting despite the prick of the needle.

But there wasn't a lot he needed to do. Drew appeared exhausted.

What was wrong with him?

And how were they going to fix whatever it was?

Chapter 3

In a way, Rosa appreciated the break from hanging out with Drew and using her veterinary skills to watch over him for any illness symptoms that the wolf he was now might evince.

She was of course happy about his apparent understanding of what she, and other people, were saying. That tended to be true with shifters she'd had as occasional patients around here, unlike before she moved here, when the shifters turned fully into the animals they were. And despite his apparent exhaustion, Drew seemed to be doing all right.

But of course he wasn't.

So, after drawing his blood using a needle, she said, "I'll be back soon. I need to analyze this." She waved the tube containing the red liquid just slightly. She felt sure that both Drew and Liam understood what she meant even without saying so.

But notwithstanding the pressure caused by her worry, she felt even more concerned as she left the room. Drew was her patient, and as a veterinarian she was always anxious about her patients, who generally couldn't tell her what their ailments were.

In Drew's case, she might not know all he was feeling, but she knew what his most important condition was.

Plus, oddly, she felt a bit apprehensive about walking away from Liam at the moment. Not because she thought leaving him with Drew was inappropriate in the least. But she recognized that, in the short time since she had first met him, she was relying on him to at least acknowledge, and possibly approve, what she was doing with his commanding officer to make him well.

"Ridiculous," she muttered, as she reached the door to the lab, next to the room where Drew's X-rays had been taken. She was the vet. Liam just worked—and shifted— with her patient.

Yeah, and probably had more knowledge than she did about how to deal with this situation. But Rosa would do all she could.

As she'd told Liam, if blood work was needed for most patients of the vet clinic, they sent the sample to a nearby lab for analysis. But the blood of shifters in wolf form was different from that of other canines.

Rosa had learned those differences where she had first obtained her veterinary license and begun practicing, in an area of Michigan where wolves of both types were prevalent.

That was one of many reasons why she had fit in when Melanie had conducted a hunt for the right type of vet—one with knowledge of what, in shifters, remained the same and what didn't.

Not that Rosa was a doctor for humans, but from what she understood, shifters' blood and other characteristics remained the same as other people's when they weren't shifted.

Now, as she entered the lab, someone was already in there: Dina, the clinic's other vet tech besides Brendan. "Hi, Rosa," she said. "Anything I can do for you here?"

"Not now, thanks," she responded to the short young woman in the typical blue scrubs.

"Let me know if that changes. I just checked out the discharge from a wound of one of our canine patients. Fortunately, the bacterial count was low."

"Great," Rosa said, as Dina left the room.

Sometimes Rosa did have one of the techs handle the blood work, often preparing it to be sent to the official lab. Other times they analyzed other kinds of liquids or discharges from the animals.

But the very rare times there were samples from shifters in animal form, either Melanie or Rosa handled it herself.

Not that the techs or other people who worked here didn't know, or at least suspect, that some of the patients were not exactly regular pets. Still, though they talked about it a little, everyone around here seemed to understand the need for tact and confidentiality. Now, at least. Rosa had heard that there were some rumors after Melanie had taken over this clinic, as a result of the death of the former veterinarians—parents of one of the officers at Ft. Lukman, Captain Patrick Worley, who happened to be a shifter.

Not wanting any interruptions, after placing the tube of blood carefully on the table, Rosa locked the door and muted her phone.

She then washed her hands carefully once more, as she'd done before extracting the sample.

Finally, using a microscope and other appropriate equipment, she began the process of analyzing the contents of the sample, including the red blood cell count and the blood type. As anticipated, both were quite different from a normal canine's—even though canines had more blood types than humans did.

But there was more that she didn't anticipate. She had done only a few analyses of shifters' blood, since they generally remained in shifted form for only a short while. She figured that those around here might have extra chemicals in their blood thanks to their imbibing the elixir to help them with their shift.

That didn't explain, though, the additional contents in Drew's sample. Stuff she couldn't really analyze. It seemed a darker red than usual, somewhat thicker than the blood cells surrounding it.

She was knowledgeable but not an expert in chemistry, and what she saw might mean nothing.

But she realized that, whatever it was, this might be the evidence of whatever was keeping Drew in his shifted form.

She needed someone else to check it out, though. Someone more skilled in this than she was.

She placed the samples into airtight containers for now. Then she hurried back to the exam room that contained Drew—and Liam.

She slipped in without knocking, which was a good thing. Drew was asleep.

Liam had his smartphone in his hands and seemed to be concentrating as he typed something into it. He heard her, though. He probably would have even with normal ears, not just those of a shifter in human form. He looked at her right away.

She gestured for him to follow her, which he did after aiming a glance in Drew's direction. Evidently he thought all was well, since soon they were out in the hall together with the door shut.

Fortunately, the hall was empty. Rosa looked up at Liam, into his face. Her concern must have been written on hers since his handsome masculine features tightened into a frown. "What's wrong?" he asked quietly.

"I guess my worry is obvious." She kept her voice low, too. "Are any of your Alpha Force people experts in chemistry? I assume they are because of putting together your elixir, right?"

"I think so, but since that's not my area I can't tell you much. Why? Is there something wrong with Drew's blood?"

The guy was apparently smart and astute. But then again, he'd known she had drawn blood and gone off to try to analyze it.

"I'm not sure, but there's something different about it. I still don't want to send it to the standard outside places, so I wonder if anyone at your base could take a look and figure it out."

"Let me check." He walked to the closest end of the hall, which was a good thing, since Melanie exited one of the exam rooms, and a couple followed her, the man holding the leash of a good-sized boxer. Melanie aimed a quizzical glance in Rosa's direction, and Rosa just smiled back.

She didn't have anything to tell Melanie except to report her question.

When she turned back, Liam was just pressing a button on his phone, evidently ending a quick call. "Yes, a couple of our guys, Jonas Truro in particular, may be able to help. Let me take the sample you have to him. I've already got Sergeant Noel Chuma, one of the Alpha Force aides, on his way to relieve me here." He looked up, over Rosa's shoulder.

Rosa realized she must have looked worried to Melanie, or maybe her boss was just curious—or wanted to see her shifted husband. But from behind her she heard, also in a soft voice, "What's going on? Why are you both out here?"

She didn't want to alarm Melanie—or give her false hope that they were about to find any answers. Turning, she said, "I just need a little advice about Drew's blood test. And Liam checked and found that some of the guys out at the base might be able to help. Unless you'd rather I didn't do it…"

"No, I'd rather you do it. How is Drew?"

"Sleeping," Liam said. "But I think we need to wake him up, at least briefly. My contact said to bring the samples you already have, Rosa, but also another one that hasn't been separated or analyzed at all."

"Fine," Melanie said. "I'll go in with you while you draw that sample and wait with Drew till Noel arrives." She looked pale, but the expression on her face appeared…well, a little hopeful, if Rosa was reading it right.

"Good," she said. "And I'm going to the base, too, to talk to your guys there." She looked at Liam, half expecting him to object.

"That'll work," he said. In fact, was that a touch of relief on his face? Admiration? Or was she reading too much into it? "You can tell them what you found and your take on it, and they can do their own kind of analysis."

"Good," she said again. "Now, let's go get that other sample."

Liam wanted more information about blood tests in general, and this one in particular.

At least that was the reason he gave himself, and Rosa, as he told her he would drive her to the base and back.

He had no other reason to be alone in this smart vet's presence for the twenty minute trip to Ft. Lukman, or the return trip. She could drive herself, of course.

But she seemed okay with the idea of riding in his black military-issued sedan. Maybe she wanted to talk more about the blood test. Or maybe she felt uncomfortable with the idea of appearing by herself at the military facility.

Or maybe he was reading things into her attitude.

They were on their way now, just exiting the town of Mary Glen on the way to Ft. Lukman. The distance was only about five miles, but it always felt longer, thanks to the two-lane roads lined by tall trees of the surrounding woods.

Liam figured the site of the military base, with its particularly covert unit, had been chosen because of the obscure location.

"So you said you're not a shifter," he began, aiming a brief glance at her in the passenger seat, a box containing the carefully wrapped blood samples on her lap. That statement didn't address the blood tests—but he'd get there. He had other questions he hoped to get answered first.

Their eyes met for an instant before he looked back toward the road. The grin on her face looked wary. Even so, she was still one pretty lady.

"No," she said, "I'm not. But where I grew up in Michigan there were quite a few wolves, and I learned early on that a few of my school friends and their families happened to be shifters. The existence of real wolves in that area gave them a bit of cover."

"Makes sense. My family lived in Minnesota for the same reason. But not being a shifter yourself, how did you end up learning that your friends were?" All the shifters he knew were taught from a young age to keep that critical fact to themselves.

"Well, I always wanted to become a veterinarian. I love animals. I always had a dog or two, visited the nearest zoo a lot and—well, I realized at a fairly young age that I heard more wolf howls in the distance on nights of the full moon than otherwise." She leaned toward him a little. "Did you howl then as you were growing up? Turned out my friends did. One of them, a guy I guess I had a crush on in seventh grade, hinted to me about where to show up at sundown on one of those special nights. He knew I was there, hiding behind a tree, when his family and a couple of others went out into the forest together. It was really amazing to watch when the four of them went from being a regular human family to a small pack of wolves. I never forgot it, of course, though that guy stopped talking to me. Guess his family caught my scent and bawled him out."

"But you knew then," Liam stated. He couldn't help smiling. It must have been quite an experience for a young non-shifter.

"I knew then," she confirmed. "I hardly ever talked

about it—but I just happened to snoop around on more nights of the full moon and saw that a few other friends shared that characteristic."

"And did they stop talking to you, too?"

"I tried to be a lot more careful. If they knew about me, they never said so, and I never said anything to them, either."

"But you still wanted to help them as a vet?"

"Sure. When I went to veterinary school I made sure to learn about all canine anatomy as well as volunteering to help the vets who worked with the local zoo. And then, as I learned enough to help, I visited that first guy's mother one day—he was off at a different college by then—and told her what I knew about them, and how I was learning a lot about working with feral creatures like wolves, in case anyone needed medical help while shifted. She pretended not to know what I was talking about, but—"

"But sometime near then she called on you in her wolf form to come help another shifter who needed medical help that night, right?"

"Exactly."

Liam could hear her big smile in the tone of her voice. He looked over and grinned back at her. "And from then on they knew you were there to help."

"Yes, I was. I helped them and myself, and they were the ones to give recommendations about me to Melanie when she put word out—very discreetly, I might add—about how she was a regular veterinarian with... interesting contacts who sometimes needed medical assistance. Since the shifters around me made a point of not admitting their true nature, I thought that the type of organization Melanie hinted about—the US military, of all things—might be a fascinating group of potential patients."

As he was growing up, Liam had known a couple local people who seemed to recognize what he, his family members and others in the area were, but although they were mostly polite, they didn't attempt to get to know any shifters better.

He was impressed with this lovely lady who not only accepted the idea of shifters in her life, but actually seemed to appreciate them. Worry about them. Want to heal them.

"I'm sure Melanie is really glad to have your help," he told her, then shared a brief smile with her before he made another turn on the twisty road.

"And I'm really glad to help her. And the others." A tone he didn't quite recognize modified Rosa's voice.

"Especially Drew," Liam guessed.

"Especially Drew," she agreed. "But... I just hope we really can help him."

"We will," Liam asserted—hoping it was true.

Chapter 4

Even though Liam had asked her to ride with him so he could ask questions about blood and blood types, Rosa was somewhat amused that they never really got into that topic much. And when they did, all she needed to do was go over a bit of what she had already been thinking about.

Yes, she told him when he finally asked, the blood types of people and regular canines had differences. So did the blood types of wolves in general from shifted wolves. People and their unshifted counterparts, not so much.

And the differences she saw from the blood she had drawn from Drew? Well, she didn't exactly know what they were, except for the odd consistency and darker coloration. That was why she hoped for someone else's advice.

She didn't let him know how concerned she really

was, although since she was looking for guidance he probably gathered that.

Would those at Ft. Lukman know whether that blood issue was the cause of Drew's not changing back? If so, would they know how to fix it?

Liam didn't seem inclined to talk much more about it, which was fine with her. It allowed her to avoid revealing how inadequate she felt, and instead gave her time to ask him about what he did as a technology expert for Alpha Force.

That got him going immediately—and what he had to say about the online claims worried her, too, as someone who had friends and patients around here who were shifters.

Sure, she had met actual shifters at home when she was young. She had also seen sites on the internet, mostly blogs or social media posts, that speculated whether there actually were such things as shapeshifters, as depicted in horror movies and otherwise. Sometimes people claimed to have seen the real thing, and maybe, like her, they had.

She had even found some references to oddities that had allegedly gone on here in Mary Glen a while back. But she'd also seen posts about how all that got resolved when it was discovered that one member of an offbeat group of people who claimed shapeshifters exist had made unsubstantiated claims for his own benefit. Discovering who it was and stopping him had helped quiet things down in this area—at least as far as the rest of the world was likely to know.

But what Liam was describing could be a lot worse for the ongoing peace of shapeshifters—and Alpha Force in particular. Rosa now lived near downtown

Mary Glen, not far from the vet clinic. She had heard nothing at all regarding the claims Liam described about how shifters around here, under the last full moon, had hurt some regular people in this area—badly.

Neither had Liam, he assured her. It was simply untrue.

And it was his job to make sure that anyone who saw those ridiculous posts didn't believe a word.

He'd already checked on how his aide, Denny, had started dealing with the situation, and believed he was doing a good job. But Liam would take over himself later that evening.

After driving through the thick woodlands, they finally arrived at the gate to the military base. Even Liam had to provide his ID to the guards despite being stationed there, and of course Rosa had to provide hers, as well. Then Liam drove across the base to a building she had visited once before to check on an injured animal Melanie had explained was a cover dog, resembling one of the shifters in canine form.

Most of the time, those cover dogs that needed shots or exams were brought to the veterinary clinic, like all other pets in the Mary Glen area. That was how Rosa got to meet and treat them.

However, they'd chosen not to move that dog, Spike—Seth Ambers's cover dog—without getting him treatment first. Fortunately, though he'd been bleeding profusely, he'd had nothing worse than a fairly minor cut from a broken bottle he'd stepped on.

When Rosa had arrived, Spike was in a special fenced pen by himself in the upstairs area where the cover dogs were housed when not on duty, his leg bandaged, and one of the aides continuously changing the dressing. Rosa had been able to follow Drew as he carried Spike downstairs to what he'd referred to as the base's primary lab area, where she'd been able to snip off fur from around the cut, wash it well, soak it with disinfectant and wrap it in sterile bandages after providing topical anesthetic, a few stitches and a larger cover bandage and temporary cone collar to make sure he didn't chew too close to it. He'd healed just fine.

The poor dog's injury had given Rosa not only the opportunity to see part of the military facility that housed the amazing Alpha Force, but also to increase her already good reputation, thanks to Melanie's verbal recognition of what Rosa additionally did to help those shifters who needed medical assistance while in their animal forms.

Liam parked his car and used a key card to get them both inside the building. The guy was either a gentleman or he didn't trust her not to drop the critically important box containing Drew's blood samples, since he carried it inside. He then led her to the stairway to the area where Rosa knew the labs, and some offices, were located. He unlocked that door and she followed him downstairs.

A lot, maybe all, of the members of Alpha Force were gathered in a room past the labs where Rosa had been before.

"This is Drew's office in this building," Liam told her, "although he's got another one in the main admin building at the other side of the base."

It wasn't a large room, but there were many chairs in rows facing the desk, all occupied. Rosa recognized a few of the people there who'd sometimes brought their cover animals to the vet clinic or had come to visit Drew and Melanie in their home next door.

Even so, Liam introduced her to them all—and most important to her now were Captain Patrick Worley and Captain Jonas Truro, whom she'd already met. They were both medical doctors, but only Patrick was a shifter.

Then there was Lieutenant Seth Ambers, also a doctor, Staff Sergeant Jason Connell, who was Drew's cousin as well as a member of Alpha Force, aides including Staff Sergeants Ruby Belmont, Piers Janus, and more. Rosa hoped she would remember names, but even if she didn't right away, she would try to have as good a relationship as possible with all of them, easiest if a solution was found quickly for Drew's problem.

When he was done with the introductions, Liam told Rosa to join him standing behind Drew's desk facing the group. "Rosa has come here to give a rundown, especially to everyone who's a medical doctor, regarding what she found when she conducted Drew's blood test. I've mentioned that to some of you." He gestured toward the box they'd brought, which now rested on Drew's desk.

Rosa wondered if the entire group needed to hear this, since she figured only a few would know anything about blood and blood tests and the different blood types of regular people and shifters and all. But considering the fascinated and concerned way they stared at her, she assumed they were all highly worried about their commanding officer and what was going on with him. They wanted him back, as normal for his type as he'd been before.

Plus some of them were shifters, too, and would want to ensure, if possible, that the same thing didn't happen with them. And fellow Alpha Force members who were aides would need to know how to help the shifters they worked for.

So, yes, for their own reasons they all needed to be there.

She first described how she had been put in charge of Major Connell by the head veterinarian at the clinic—his wife. "Melanie did her own exam first, of course, and I've been keeping her up-to-date. But I'm sure it was hard on her to have to check out poor Drew in this situation."

Rosa then talked about how she had examined Drew, had kept him under her care, had looked for any abnormalities in his canine form—and had, of course, taken a blood test.

"I don't know that I need to get into much detail here," she told the group. "I did find what appears to be some irregularity in the consistency and color of the fluid and, not being a chemist beyond the skills needed to be a damn good veterinarian—" she smiled a bit sadly at that, realizing that her own fears of inadequacy were showing in her irony "—I wanted to see if anyone here could help analyze Drew's blood and determine if it's the cause, or an indication, of what's going on with him."

"We'll take a look." Patrick was the first to stand, then Jonas did. "Come into the lab area with us, Rosa, and we'll start checking things out, okay?"

"Of course."

She glanced toward Liam, who nodded. He apparently wasn't joining them, but he was her ride back to town. She suspected she'd be able to find another one, though, if necessary.

Patrick picked up the box. She wasn't surprised when

Seth joined them. It wouldn't hurt to have all the doctors who knew human patients' traits getting involved, or at least that's what she surmised.

Patrick led Rosa next door to the lab areas, where he asked Seth to start the analysis process, getting slides ready for the microscope and more.

"We really appreciate this," Patrick said, standing with Rosa in the middle of the main room, which was lined with shiny metal cabinets with glass doors. Some had equipment on top—a lot of microscopes, for one thing.

Patrick was a tall guy, dressed in camos like all the people around here but Rosa. His hair was light and short, his face long and nice looking, with a cleft in his chin.

He didn't resemble Liam except for his height and outfit—and for an instant Rosa missed Liam's presence. Ridiculous.

"I appreciate it, too," she said to Patrick. "I just hope you can figure this out."

"I'm sure you know we want to," he replied. Seth was already removing the various vials of blood from the padding in the box. Rosa had labeled them with the time collected and whether she had done anything to attempt to examine each particular sample, so she figured they at least wouldn't have any questions about that.

But what they all really needed was answers.

She hung out in the lab for a while, mostly watching the others, listening to them discuss what to do next. Then Patrick said, "You know, Rosa, this is going to take a while. Why don't you go back to your clinic, and we'll let you know what we find, okay?"

In other words, her staring wasn't making them go faster, but might be causing them some discomfort.

She didn't want that. Besides, back at the clinic she'd be able to bring Melanie up-to-date, such as it was with no answers so far, and maybe do something helpful there before the day ended. "Sounds good," she said.

She just hoped that Liam was ready to leave.

Liam was champing at the bit.

He had gone to his own office, upstairs in another part of the building, but only briefly to check on how Denny was doing.

He'd promised to return Rosa to town, and though he figured he could get someone else to do it, he wanted to be the one.

He also wanted to get on his own computer and get busy doing his own thing to start fixing all the absurd and detrimental rumors.

"Here's what I've done," Denny had told him, and good guy that he was, Liam's aide had followed his prior instructions and started with one of the social media sites where the posts were among the most awful and accusatory against shapeshifters the night before, including an unnamed military group containing shifters. Oddly, as Liam had previously noted, a few had signed their posts with the names of Greek or Roman gods, like Zeus, Hera, Orion, Diana and Poseidon, and even Cerberus, the three-headed dog. They could be a group of anti-shifters, or just one person pretending to be a bunch. Which frustrated Liam. He hadn't had the time to start figuring that out yet.

Still, Denny had used one of his own fake identities to make fun of the stupid stuff. That needed to be started even before they attempted to figure out the sources of those posts.

"Good job," Liam had told him, making his short, young helper grin widely.

"Thanks. You want to take over?"

"Soon," Liam assured him. "Meantime, keep up the good work."

He returned to Drew's office, where some of his fellow Alpha Forcers remained. Could he text Rosa to see how much longer she'd be? He felt a duty to do as he'd promised her.

He also felt eager to see her again, and not entirely to get her update on what the others were doing to assess Drew's weird blood.

He was delighted when she came back almost immediately after his reappearance. "They're working on it now," she told Liam and the others in the room. "Not much I can do to help, so do you think…" She looked at Liam, who just nodded, reading the question in her eyes.

"Yep," he said. "I'll take you back to the clinic now. Right?"

"Thanks." She smiled at him.

He got a promise from the clearly worried Jason that he'd keep Liam informed about anything the doctors found and revealed about his cousin Drew's bad blood. Then he told Rosa, "I've a stop to make before we leave."

"Oh. Okay." The way she looked at him, he assumed she thought he meant the restroom.

"Pit stop first is fine," he agreed, "but that's not what I meant."

In a few minutes, he met her to go upstairs. Instead

of heading for the door out of the building, he turned and said, "Time for some cover dog attention."

"Really?" She sounded delighted. "Then you're going to get yours?"

"Yep, that's my Chase."

"Is Spike there, too?"

He knew that was Seth's dog. "Sure. That's right—you took care of his wound, didn't you? I've heard a lot about it."

"He's still okay, isn't he?"

"He sure is."

They'd reached the door to the large room where the cover dogs were in enclosures. For fun, Liam let out a brief howl as if he was shifted, and several of those inside responded in kind. He grinned at Rosa's pleased smile.

"Gee, these guys sound a lot like wolves," she said, "and so do you."

"I wonder why."

He asked her to wait outside while he went in for Chase. She agreed, but asked to peek in the door and see all the canines hanging out there behind the low fences.

When he returned with Chase, her smile was even broader.

"So this is how you look when you shift?" she asked.

"Yep, that's me—or close enough to me for now." He asked what she knew about cover animals. From what she told him, Rosa had already learned from Melanie that the shifters in Alpha Force all had cover animals who resembled them when they were shifted. That way, if a non-shifter happened to see them while they were in shifted form and claim they must be werewolves or whatever, they could later bring out their cover ani-

mal—mostly wolves here at Ft. Lukman these days—
show the non-shifter, and tell them they'd simply seen
the Alpha Force member's pet. That seemed to work
well, Liam thought, since Alpha Force members didn't
need to wait till a full moon to shift.

Now Rosa and Liam walked outside toward his car,
then into the warmth of the midday air, and he soon
tethered Chase in the back seat. His look-alike cover
dog-wolf sat up and looked around expectantly. Chase
always enjoyed attention and was probably eager to see
what the rest of the day held in store for him.

There'd be one stop he might enjoy. After they
dropped Rosa off at the vet clinic, Liam had promised
a visit to his family in town—his brother, Chuck, and
sister-in-law, Carleen. They had moved from Minnesota to Mary Glen just a few months ago and bought an
existing restaurant that was a franchise for the Fastest
Foods chain, planning to stay here a while.

That was the result of Liam learning about a possible experiment that would involve allowing limited
individuals related to Alpha Force team members to occasionally use the elixir on nights of a full moon, with
results to be examined by the unit. Those people had to
be shifters, close in both relationship and distance, although if all went well, the program might be expanded.

Liam's family were shifters like him, and were eager
to have more access to the elixir. That's why they had
considered their move here worth it, even if they wound
up only being closer to Liam. But of course they hoped
things went better than that—and they had, at least
somewhat. His family members had been allowed to use
the elixir once now, during this most recent full moon,

as part of the experiment. And more? That remained to be seen, but the ongoing experiment might help.

Liam had received a text message from Chuck a short while ago, as he waited for Rosa. He hadn't seen his family since their shift last night, nor had he had a chance to speak with the Alpha Force member who'd acted as their temporary aide for the occasion, Sergeant Kristine Parran. Though he'd talked to them briefly on his way downtown before, and they'd sounded thrilled, he wanted to know more about how it all went, and apparently they wanted to talk to him, too. But he couldn't stay long at the restaurant.

So first he'd take Rosa back to the veterinary hospital and dash in with her to see how Drew was doing. Then he'd stop to see family—quickly.

And finally, he would fulfill his obligation—and do what he really wanted to. He'd hurry back here to get on the computer at last.

As Liam pulled his car past the base's front gate and onto the road secluded by trees, Rosa took her phone from her purse and looked at it. "I was hoping to get a call right away saying they'd figured out how to help Drew."

"That would be a nice thing." He looked at her briefly and nodded. And had an idea.

He could easily drive past the restaurant on the way to the clinic. That would give him a great excuse to keep his visit quick. He trusted Denny, but the aide was too new at this to fully accomplish what Liam needed to do. If he stopped with Rosa to buy a fast-food burger and coffee—and ask in more detail how his family had enjoyed last night—he could leave quickly to return Rosa to her clinic.

Besides, he would get to stay in her presence just a little longer. That wasn't important, of course—no matter how much he knew he'd enjoy it. But the idea seemed to work well in all ways.

"I'd like to stop to pick up a meal to go, from the Fastest Foods shop," he told Rosa. "My treat, if you'd like anything."

The look she shot at him was one of surprise. "Good idea," she said. "You don't have to treat, but I'll pick up a few things for the clinic staff…and also get Drew a burger to help keep his spirits up."

"Good idea," he said in turn. "We'll be there soon." Then he had to ask. "Did you get a sense that my superior officers knew what they were doing when it came to analyzing Drew's blood and determining if that had anything to do with his non-shifting?"

"I liked those guys," she hedged. "And I'm hopeful… but not sure. I just wish there was more I could do."

He hated to hear the sad tone in her voice, and to see the dejection in her expression when he managed another glance toward her.

"I've got a feeling," he said to cheer her up, "that there is more you can do, and you'll figure it out."

He looked at her again briefly as she shifted in her seat. "Really? I can't make any promises, but I sure hope you're right."

Me, too, he thought, then made the turn from the woodsy road into town.

And if she figured it out—well, that would give him a good excuse to kiss those now happily smiling lips of hers in thanks.

Chapter 5

"There we are." From the driver's seat beside Rosa, Liam pointed just ahead along one of the town's main streets. Sure enough, a familiar large neon sign that resembled those in lots of other locations jutted over the sidewalk: Fastest Foods.

"Yes," Rosa agreed, trying to sound excited. And to her surprise, she was—a little.

A stop for a meal?

After all that had gone on today, Rosa wasn't really hungry, but the stop would give her a little more time in Liam's presence. Despite being in the same places a lot that day, they really hadn't spent much time together.

On the other hand, she barely knew the guy. Plus he happened to be a shifter. Not that she disliked shifters.

Quite the contrary…but she certainly couldn't be attracted to one, no matter how caring and sympathetic he happened to be about his commanding officer's medical—or whatever—problem.

The restaurant stood alone in the middle of a sizable parking lot that also had a drive-through line. "Are we going to go through there?" Rosa pointed toward the stream of cars slowly inching forward.

"No, we'll go inside, though we'll order takeout."

He fortunately found a parking spot right away in the busy lot and opened his door. Rosa opened hers, too, and hopped out. "I assume you'll roll down the back windows a bit for Chase," she said, looking into the back seat at the wolflike dog, who was now sitting up, panting a bit. Fortunately, the outside air was cool.

"No need," Liam said. "He'll come in with us."

"Into the restaurant? Is that allowed?"

"Of course. He's a soldier dog—and he's also kind of my service dog." Liam's grin, as he stood beside her near the car on the black paved surface of the lot, seemed proud.

"Oh. Okay." Rosa loved dogs, and other animals, enough that she wished they were all allowed into all restaurants and other places that served people.

Of course, shapeshifters were allowed anywhere— as long as they were in human form, as Liam was now.

And Rosa realized it was okay to bring Chase, too, when they walked in the door of the crowded, noisy restaurant and Liam was greeted right away by the people who seemed in charge.

A guy who'd been behind the service counter came out the door beside it and hustled toward Liam. They shook hands, then hugged each other. Was he a relative? The guy was about Liam's height, with similarly dark hair and angular features. He wasn't in a camo uniform, of course, but a blue denim shirt and jeans, with a white apron on top.

He looked down then and grinned at Chase, leashed beside Liam. "Can't pet him, bro, though I know he's family. You know that's why we keep our Louper out back, too, when he's here."

"Right. Not sanitary when you're on duty. But let me introduce you to someone." Liam turned toward Rosa and gestured for her to join them.

As she did, a woman who'd been cleaning tables in the busy place dashed over. She was dressed similarly to the man who'd hugged Liam. She was slender, with long, silver-blond hair pulled into a clip at the back of her head, a very attractive woman—who also hugged Liam.

Rosa knew she shouldn't feel jealous about that—especially when she looked down and saw a ring on the woman's finger.

"So good to see you, Liam," the woman said.

"I'll say," said the man.

Liam once more looked at Rosa. "I want to introduce you both to someone I'll bet you'll be very happy to know one of these days. This is Dr. Rosa Jontay, one of the town's veterinarians. Rosa, this is my brother, Chuck, and his wife, Carleen. They own this place now—and they're also owned by Louper, a dog who stays either in the enclosed backyard behind this place, or at home. He's home today with a dog walker visiting him. Louper resembles Chase."

Liam looked at her and grinned, and she read in his look the fact that these two people were also shifters who happened to have a cover dog, even though they weren't military.

"Very nice to meet you." She shook hands first with Carleen, then Chuck. "And I would be delighted to meet your dog sometime when he's here or otherwise, though I hope he has no need of a vet."

"My sentiments exactly," Carleen said. "Now, you two come over here and sit down, and we'll get you something to eat."

"Oh, but—" Rosa began, but fortunately, Liam took over.

"We just need some takeout right now," he said. "Rosa's going to get some extra stuff for some of her veterinary staff, and she needs to get back to her clinic."

"Great," Carleen said. "We'll get our staff moving on it right away. Just let them know at the counter what you want."

There were several people ahead of them in the line, and Rosa didn't want to butt in. "We'll take our time," she said. "But thanks."

Liam nodded his agreement, though he said, "It helps to be related to the owners when you're in a hurry. I agree with being polite to their customers, though. And if you don't mind standing here a few minutes to hold our place, I'd appreciate it. I've something to ask Chuck."

"Fine," Rosa said, and agreed to keep Chase with her. She watched Liam talking to his brother by the wall nearest the door into the order area and kitchen. It was one of the few times she wished she had a shifter's abilities—not to shift, but to hear things better than a normal person. The two brothers seemed to be talking animatedly, and she was curious about what they were saying.

The teenage guy at the front of the line stepped aside

after placing his order. Rosa was glad to move ahead a little, particularly for the sake of the animals that might be needing her care back at the clinic.

Including, perhaps, Drew. She'd at least check on him, no matter what Melanie and the Alpha Force guy who'd taken over for Liam said about how he was doing—though she'd be absolutely delighted if he'd changed back during their absence.

Unlikely, though, or Melanie would have called her.

At least now there were only three more people ahead of her in line, and two appeared to be a couple. Rosa bent and patted Chase's head. The dog was definitely behaving well, leashed at her side.

Liam rejoined her. "Everything okay?" she asked.

"Real good," he responded, without more detail. In fact, he was quiet for a while.

"How long have your relatives owned this place?" Rosa asked finally, to make conversation. Besides, she was interested in his answer. "Did they follow you to Mary Glen?"

And did they want to become members of Alpha Force? she wondered. She figured that a lot of shifters might want to do so if they knew of the reality of Alpha Force, and its special elixir. With their relative, Liam, now a member, she had no doubt that Chuck and Carleen were well aware of the nature of that military unit.

She'd ask Liam more about them later, as she couldn't here, in public.

"They've been here about four months," Liam said. "They bought this franchise from the former owners and just took over. And yes, they followed me here."

"Got it." She looked around again. The restaurant was filled with customers—and with the aroma of grilled meat. Even she could smell it, and she figured it must be many times stronger to Liam, even in his human form. Or at least that's what she'd heard from shifters in her past—and now. They all had enhanced senses.

And of course Chase stuck his nose in the air and sniffed, off and on.

The next person moved out of their way in line. As they started to edge forward a woman rushed out the door from the kitchen and threw herself against Liam, giving him a huge hug. "Liam, so glad to see you," she exclaimed.

"Good to see you, too, Valerie," he said, although his not-so-inviting expression, and the way he moved back, suggested he was fibbing a bit.

Somehow, that made Rosa feel a bit better about the woman's highly effusive greeting. But who was Valerie?

She found out right away as Liam introduced them. "Rosa, this is Carleen's sister, Valerie. And Valerie, Rosa's one of Mary Glen's wonderful veterinarians."

Carleen's sister—a sort of sister-in-law to Liam. That made Rosa feel somewhat better, although since they weren't related by blood that connection wouldn't keep Liam from getting into a relationship with her.

But that wasn't Rosa's business, though he hadn't appeared to care about Valerie in that way.

Valerie resembled Carleen. Her silvery blond hair was shorter, though, and loose. She had deep brown eyes like her sister.

"Welcome to town," Rosa said, to be polite. "Do you work here, too?" She gestured around the restaurant.

"I do right now," the other woman said. "Look, you go ahead and place your orders, and then we can talk."

She must have said that because Liam and Rosa had finally reached the front of their line. But Rosa didn't want to take the time to talk to Valerie, and hoped Liam felt the same way.

Fortunately, Valerie disappeared, heading back into the kitchen—but then reappeared behind the counter, next to the guy who'd begun taking their order. She was the one to start entering things on the computer, and her counterpart, a twentysomething guy with a scruffy beard, didn't look exactly thrilled about the help.

Rosa wasn't surprised that Liam's order consisted of a double burger, rare—lots of red meat. She asked for several sandwiches, including burgers and a couple containing chicken. The one with the most beef she intended to provide to Drew in his canine form.

When they were done ordering, Rosa immediately handed her credit card to Valerie over the counter. She'd already gotten it out and didn't want to argue with Liam about it. She didn't even look at him and was glad when Valerie took it from her and began to ring up their order.

"I'll pay you back," Liam growled from beside her. She just waved in a neutral gesture. This was another thing not to get into a discussion about here.

Valerie soon handed them the plastic bags containing their food. "Come back anytime, Rosa," she said. "Bye, Chase. And Liam—when are we all getting together again? You know I'm only planning on being here for a fairly short while, so I'd really like us to see each other as often as possible while I'm in town."

"I'll talk to Chuck about it," Liam said.

"Talk to Chuck about what?" said a voice from behind Rosa. Liam's brother was there, maybe to say goodbye.

"Having a family get-together," Valerie replied. "Soon, I hope."

"Sounds good to me," Chuck responded. "We'll invite you over to our condo soon, bro. You, too, Rosa."

She couldn't help but cast a sideways glance toward Valerie to see what she thought about that invitation. Carleen's sister remained smiling, and it didn't appear forced.

Maybe Rosa was wrong about this woman flirting with her kind-of brother-in-law. Maybe she just intended to keep the family in contact as long as she did stay in town.

"Thanks," Rosa said, not committing to anything.

But somehow the idea of spending more friendly time with Liam, not related to veterinary or Alpha Force issues, sounded good.

For now, though, she was glad when Liam said goodbye to Chuck, then Carleen, who also joined them, and waved to Valerie behind the counter.

Time for them to get busy with everything they each needed to do for the rest of the day.

Liam refused to feel embarrassed or uncomfortable about the attention Valerie had leveled on him. The woman was attractive, sure. She was also a shifter, like her sister. She'd made it seem that flirting with him was second nature to her, though he had never encouraged it.

But he always remained friendly toward her. She was, after all, a member of his family.

"Nice people," Rosa said from beside him in the car. Behind them, Chase shifted in his seat, clearly wanting to get into the bags of food that sat on the floor near Rosa's feet.

"Of course they are," Liam said. "They're family."

"Like Chase?" Rosa wasn't exactly jesting. She'd told him she considered pet dogs to be family, and she assumed the relationship between a shifter and his cover dog had to be strong.

"Yeah, kind of. Chase and I are pretty damn close these days." Hearing his name, Chase sat back on the seat and made a low sound that made Liam laugh. "Glad you agree," he said.

As they continued on, Liam thought a bit about his brief discussion with Chuck. Yes, both he and Carleen had loved the way their shift went. Yes, the Alpha Force person who'd acted as their aide for the night had been just great: Sergeant Kristine Parran. The elixir had been amazing. As far as he knew, all had gone well from Alpha Force's perspective. And, yes, both Carleen and he would love to do it again. Soon.

Almost as if she read his thoughts, Rosa asked, "Are your brother and sister-in-law shifters, too?"

"Yes," he acknowledged.

"Do they get to use your elixir?"

Good and appropriate question, he thought. Without saying too much, he told her they were involved in an experiment being conducted by Alpha Force, in which they could be given occasional doses of the elixir on nights of a full moon.

He was glad that Rosa and he had reached the vet clinic, since he didn't want to answer any further questions she might have. Liam parked along the street. He intended not to just let Rosa out of the car. He planned to go inside and check with Denny about how things were going. And most especially, he wanted to see for himself how Drew was doing.

He opened his car door at the same time Rosa opened hers. Her expression seemed to register surprise as she turned back to look at him. "I thought you were just dropping me off so you could get to work."

"Not till I check on Drew. Besides, we can wolf down our sandwiches together." He grinned at his own pun, and she laughed.

"Fair enough." She bent down to get the bags as Liam got out to leash Chase and let him out of the back seat.

As Rosa headed toward the clinic's rear door, bags in hand, Liam let his dog sniff the curb and driveway, and when he was ready, hurried him to the entrance.

The street had been fairly well lined with cars, so Liam wasn't surprised, as he entered the waiting room, to see a lot of people there with their pets—everything from an English sheepdog to a couple mewing kittens in carriers.

They all carried scents of their own.

Since he didn't see Rosa there, he figured he'd better let the receptionist behind the desk know he needed to catch up with the vet. But Susie, whom he'd met before, smiled and motioned Chase and him through the inner door.

Rosa approached him from down the hall. "I just put our food in the break room, but let's go check on Drew."

"Great." Liam followed her to the room where he had last seen his superior officer. Rosa opened the door, but motioned for him to enter first, which he did, Chase right behind him.

The place looked the same as before, with wolfen Drew sitting on the towel-covered top of the lowered table. With him, on one of the chairs against the wall, sat Staff Sergeant Noel Chuma, who was an aide to whichever Alpha Force shifter needed him.

And no one needed help now more than Drew.

Noel wasn't a big guy, but he was strong, smart and dedicated to Alpha Force. He rose, and the expression on his deep-toned face worried Liam.

He couldn't ask detailed questions now, though. Not in front of Drew.

"So, how's our patient doing?" Rosa asked. She approached Drew, who regarded her with stony eyes that, on some canines—whether shifters or not—would have made Liam worry that he was about to attack.

He knew Drew wouldn't do that. But Drew's expression did indicate that he wasn't happy.

That he probably didn't have a sense he'd be shifting back anytime soon—and it was getting to be late afternoon on the day he should have retaken his human form early in the morning.

"He's mostly been resting," Noel answered for him. "We've been for a couple of walks and he seemed happy enough to be out of this room, but, well—*happy* isn't the best word. I think he's really frustrated."

"Understandably," Liam said.

Drew made a growling sound that didn't seem threatening, but might've connoted frustration. It was enough to get Chase, who had sat beside Liam, to stand again and watch his sort-of counterpart.

"Tell you what," Liam said. "Drew, are you okay with being here on your own for a few minutes? Dr. Rosa and I brought lunch back and we need to sort it out, but one of us is going to bring you a really good burger very soon."

Drew answered by making a noise that this time sounded like a sigh, then lying back down.

He didn't seem overly excited about the late, tasty lunch he'd get.

And Liam could understand why.

Chapter 6

"I don't want to leave him alone for long," Rosa said quietly, once they were back in the hall with the door shut behind them. "But we do have a sandwich for you, too, Sergeant Chuma."

"Noel," he corrected. "And I'm sure you want to talk with me about our CO and what went on while you all were gone."

Rosa watched the two military guys trade glances. She figured Liam would hear a lot more than she would, but not while they were all together.

And she appreciated that the sergeant had come here, to ensure that Drew was nearly never alone. His condition was such that no one knew what needs he might have, or when he might have them. And he certainly wasn't in any condition to grab a smartphone and call for help.

They all headed the short distance along the hall to the break room. Rosa motioned for the others to enter first, glad to see that Brendan had just come into the hall, ushering a young woman with her standard poodle mix from another exam room. Rosa waited long enough for Brendan to ensure that his charges entered the reception area, where the owner could pay her bill and they could leave. But when Brendan turned again, Rosa was right beside him.

"Is Melanie in that room?" She gestured to the room he'd just come out of.

"Yes. Want me to get her for you?"

"Please."

Brendan once more went through that door, and almost immediately Melanie, in her white lab jacket, strode out and faced Rosa. "You're back. Do they have any answers yet at Ft. Lukman?"

"They're working on it. I gave them the blood samples and discussed what I'd seen, and my concerns. They got right on it, so hopefully they'll figure it out soon."

"Yes. Hopefully." Melanie's hair wasn't pulled back as neatly as usual. Her pretty face seemed to be aging minute by minute. Rosa just hoped she was providing adequate care to their patients, despite the stress she was under.

"Meantime," Rosa said brightly, "Liam came back here with me, but I assume he'll be leaving Noel here, since he has to get back to the base right away. Or almost right away. We brought a late lunch from Fastest Foods, a few sandwiches. That includes a really nice big, rare burger for Drew." Rosa made herself smile broadly, then motioned for her employer to follow her as Brendan reappeared in the hall, followed by a large man hugging a moderate-size golden cat.

She was glad when Melanie did as she hoped and joined her, Liam and Noel in the break room. Given a choice, Melanie picked out a chicken sandwich among those laid out on one of the tables in the middle of the room, as did Rosa. That left burgers for the guys.

Including the large one for Drew, which Liam was holding. "I'd like to go say hi to Drew, if that's okay with you," he said to Melanie. "I can give this to him then."

"Of course. And thank you both so much for bringing Drew a burger from Fastest Foods. It's one of his favorite places when…when…" Her voice started to drop off, and Rosa recognized her signs of sorrow.

"When he's not shifted," she finished brightly for Melanie. "And when he is shifted. I get it. Let's give him what we have now, and I promise that, when he's back to his unshifted self again, I'll go get him even more burgers there. Okay?"

She looked at Melanie's brave smile and almost broke down herself. Rosa had had a few relationships now and then, but hadn't met anyone she wanted to spend her life with. Melanie had, and she'd even gotten past whatever confusion she might have felt about falling hard for a shapeshifter.

She was clearly, deeply in love. And the man she loved was in distress. Ill. In the middle of a condition that no one knew anything about, so no one knew how to fix it. Fix him.

A wonderment about how she'd feel if Liam somehow became her veterinary patient flashed through Rosa. Ridiculous. Yes, she found him good-looking as a human. Kind. Sexy… No, she wasn't going there. She wasn't going anywhere with him, or with these ideas. She glanced at him, though—and saw that, for some reason, he was watching her.

She turned away and quickly stepped toward Melanie,

then gave her a hug. "We'll figure it out," she promised, hoping she wasn't lying about something as important to her employer as that.

"I know," Melanie said hoarsely. "And thanks." She turned to where the two men stood behind her, eating their sandwiches. "And thanks to both of you, too."

"No problem," Liam said. "Noel, you said you'd give us a rundown of how Drew's been doing while you've been with him."

"Sure." The muscular guy chewed briefly, then described how things had been since he'd gone into the room. "Drew slept a lot. When he was awake, he seemed mostly comfortable but unhappy, getting off that table and pacing around the room, looking me in the face as if he wanted to tell me something, then shaking his head and lying down again. I wished I could understand what he wasn't saying."

Maybe this wasn't such a good idea, Rosa thought, even though it might be helpful in trying to figure out what was wrong with Drew, how he was reacting.

But how Melanie was reacting...that was hard. Sad.

For many reasons, they needed to get this all straightened out. Fast.

But what else could Rosa do?

She would continue pondering that till something came to her. Something useful—she hoped.

For now, though, she looked at the others and said, "Great. Thanks, Noel. Now, let's all join Liam and go present Drew with his nice, meaty hamburger."

Liam, with Chase fastened in the back seat, was on his way back to the base—and felt somewhat bad about it.

Because he'd seen that his friend and mentor, his commanding officer, Drew, hadn't improved.

Because he was also leaving the woman he'd spent the last few intense hours with, attempting to help Drew—and becoming impressed with her tenacity and knowledge and caring. Not to mention her sexual appeal…

Enough. He needed to concentrate on the real issues. "Got it, Chase?" he called into the back seat, as if his dog would tell him to get his mind back on track.

He had seen most of his fellow shifting Alpha Forcers in their wolfen or other modes such as cougars and hawks while he was still human. They were always involved in training sessions and drills in both forms. Testing the elixir in its current standard mixture and in variations.

He'd been a member of Alpha Force for only about a year, but he knew that the brew of their special potion was always undergoing potential changes.

Fortunately, Drew, who'd been the originator of the elixir, was continuously thinking of ways to improve it, as had the others who'd come up with their own versions before joining the covert military unit. Drew and those others seemed always amenable to attempts to improve it even further.

But what would they do now, with Drew unable to even be human, let alone work to improve their elixir?

Liam was glad that wasn't his area of expertise. But he still wished he had answers.

Well, he hadn't any—but hopefully he would help Alpha Force get them. He'd received a call from Patrick earlier—and had agreed to be the subject of a test tomorrow night.

A test that involved shifting with a modified version

of the elixir, in an attempt to help determine what had happened to Drew.

Liam had immediately agreed.

He also figured that the intensity of what was now going on with Alpha Force was likely to put at least a temporary halt to their experimenting with allowing family members to use the elixir sometimes during the full moon. The intent was to observe them now and perhaps eventually use them as extra assistants on limited unit assignments while they were in shifted form—and had more cognition thanks to the elixir. He liked the idea of his brother and sister-in-law being able to participate, but he'd understand if their one-time experiment remained just that, and knew they would understand, too.

And Liam and his membership in Alpha Force? Well, in addition to being a possible guinea pig tomorrow— guinea wolf?—he'd soon be right by that amazing contraption that was his area of expertise: his computer.

He'd take care of his own work as well as he could, and as fast as he could.

Then he might attempt to do some further digging into what was going on with Drew.

Yeah, right. As if the internet would, despite its vastness, have detailed answers to flawed shapeshifting. Thanks to his background and love of technology he'd done a lot of research on many subjects, particularly shifting. And though its various aspects always seemed to have at least a reference or two, nothing really addressed this issue—at least nothing he'd seen so far.

As usual, there wasn't a lot of traffic in Mary Glen, so his drive back to the base wasn't taking long—a good thing. En route, Liam continued pondering what was next. Maybe he could figure out the answer to the non-shifting question himself somehow. While shifted. Thanks to the elixir, he could choose the time—like tomorrow night.

Tonight would be too soon, since he had work of his own to do. Plus he needed to undertake some preparation. He wanted to talk again to Melanie first, get her rundown about what Drew had been doing yesterday before moonrise. He'd rather do that in person, a good excuse to return to the clinic tomorrow. And if he happened to see Rosa there? Well, he could also ask about her latest insights into Drew.

He could further request that she hang around when he accomplished his shift, in case he needed a veterinarian's help this time because of the likely changes being tried.

He'd also check with the aide Jonas, who'd helped Drew with his shift into wolf form—and had been there to try to help him shift back.

By now, Liam had completed the winding drive through the forest and reached the base. He pulled out his ID, and as he handed it to the entrance guard, immediately started pondering what he needed to accomplish now.

Time to get on the computer.

Rosa exited the exam room where she had just given a fourteen-year-old shih tzu her annual checkup, including a few shots.

She always enjoyed caring for senior pets, making sure they were as healthy as possible for their age so they could hopefully remain with their owners for a nice, long time.

Younger pets, too.

All pets. And other animals, of whatever type…or origin.

Almost automatically, she turned away from where the owner was carrying the shih tzu to the reception area, and headed toward the room that housed Drew for the moment. The clinic's technician Dina walked out of it, staring at the door as she shut it behind her.

Uh-oh. Did that mean there was a problem? Rosa hurried in her direction, and Dina nearly bumped into her. Dina was shorter than her male counterpart, and older—late thirties, Rosa believed, compared with Brendan's early twenties. Brendan was thin, and Dina was heftier, but both were strong and muscular, as was best for carrying ill animals when necessary. Of course, they both wore blue lab jackets.

"How are things?" Rosa asked immediately, shifting her eyes toward that now closed door and back again to Dina's face. She was a pretty lady, prone to smiling, but she looked serious now.

"They're okay, but that wolf-dog seems to be getting more distressed all the time when he's not sleeping." Dina kept her voice low, but Rosa figured she knew who and what that animal was, and that if he was awake he'd hear what she said and understand it.

"I'm not surprised." Rosa considered making some kind of optimistic statement when she went in to see Drew, to cheer him up a little, but what could she say? Sure, his coworkers in his military unit were working on it, and even she hoped to come up with something more than just taking blood tests, but for now she didn't know what or how.

Maybe Liam would figure something out. If so, she hoped he'd let her know. Perhaps even allow her to participate. For Melanie's sake in particular, she wanted to make sure things worked out well.

And also so the other shifters, including Liam, would know what to do if such a problem ever arose with them.

"Anyway," she said to Dina, "I was planning on stopping in to see him now, too. I assume Noel's still with him, right?"

"Right. I think his presence helps."

"Glad to hear that," Rosa responded, not surprised. Hopefully, an Alpha Force member experienced at being an aide would know how to behave in the presence of a shifter in animal form—even one with a problem. "I'll go check on them both now. Thanks for looking in on our patient."

"Sure." Dina turned and hurried down the hall.

Rosa opened the exam room door and peeked in before entering. Drew was lying down and appeared to be asleep. But as she glanced toward Noel, seated on one of the chairs looking at his cell phone, Drew rose on his haunches to a seated position and stared at her expectantly.

"No news yet," she told him, as if he had asked a question. Then she did add something optimistic, as she'd been considering. "But everyone is still hard at work on finding you an answer."

Or so she hoped.

Liam had been on the computer for an hour now. *His* computer. Or at least the top-of-the-line system owned by the US government that had been assigned to him for his work.

He loved it. He also liked being alone here now, with Chase, in this solitary, quiet office in a remote area of Alpha Force's main building at the base. A small room, sure, but one with a comfortable desk chair, high quality shelving and even a large screen television mounted on the wall in case some of his technological research could be assisted by tuning in to news or other useful shows.

It was getting late. He had spent quite a while with Denny going over all the posts his aide had found about shifters anywhere, and particularly those with alleged military connections.

They were generally consistent with what Liam had already discovered and informed Denny about as a basis of his search. There weren't as many as Liam had feared, which was good.

But those that existed had been viewed many times, according to those sites, especially those alleging misconduct by the shifted wolves. They had collected a bevy of fascinated comments despite the general consensus, still, that it was all fiction, since shapeshifters didn't really exist.

As directed, Denny had used a couple of the fake identities Liam had helped him create to jump in and make fun of some of the nastiest comments.

Liam was about to do the same with as many others as he could. Grinning, he began. Let's see. Who should he be first?

He opened one of his favorite social media sites and signed in as Mite T. Maus. *Maus* was the German word for mouse. Several of his assumed identities used implied animal names, which worked well while he attempted to make fun of anything posted that suggested shapeshifters were real.

"Okay, now," he said aloud. "Let's see what we can do." He immediately asked for the supposedly injured townsfolk to contact him, let the world know how they were doing, and how much fun they had attempting to fight off weird creatures who supposedly were part human. Hey, he—or rather Maus—claimed, he'd done that once as a kid and now treasured the scar on his right arm. But, gee, that doggy had remained in his neighborhood and tried biting him again after the moon was no longer full. That was one reason he really tried hard to find proof of shapeshifters.

He got a response almost immediately—but the person, using the name Cerberus, only posted a picture of a bloody raised finger.

Hopefully, that would just make other readers laugh. It certainly didn't suggest proof of shapeshifters.

Liam did something similar under another name on another site, and the early responses there were more belligerent, suggesting there was something wrong with him for not believing in shapeshifters. Other people responded by apparently laughing at the believers. Interestingly, as he'd seen before, some of them also used the names of Greek or Roman gods—Hera, Zeus, Diana and Orion.

He also checked out similar social media posts by Denny. They, too, made fun of the whole idea of shapeshifters.

Did all this help quash what the suggestion of attacks had begun last night?

At least it was a start, and Liam kept it going for a while. Some names, like Orion, seemed to pop up a lot.

He wondered more than once what Rosa would think of all this. Her job was saving animal lives. His was protecting shapeshifters in this quirky way.

"Hey, Rosa," he said aloud, after finding her picture on the Mary Glen Veterinary Clinic website. "What would you think of this?"

Maybe he'd actually ask her. But at the moment, he needed to work.

Finally, though, he'd had enough of this—for now. But his night wasn't over.

Nope, next thing he'd do would be to check out who'd done the original posts, attempt to learn their real identities. That could take a tremendous amount of time. But somehow, he had to get at least some sleep that night.

He wouldn't be able to sleep all day tomorrow. No, he would need to report in to his current commanding officers about what Denny and he had learned, and what they'd done about it.

Then he would need to do that additional checking to see if he could learn more about Drew's day before his critical, and faulty, shift.

Which would, as Liam had already figured, involve going to the vet clinic. Get what info he could from Melanie. And Rosa.

Rosa. She was on his mind too much.

But for now she had to be. He definitely wanted her present when he shifted tomorrow night. Melanie might be too emotional. Besides, she had her kids at home.

And Liam was relatively certain that, however he decided to conduct his shift, it wouldn't hurt to have a veterinarian in the background.

And it certainly wouldn't hurt if that vet was as kind, caring—and sexy—as Rosa.

Chapter 7

"So how are you feeling this morning?" Rosa asked early the next day.

The shifted wolf who was Drew sat on his table-bed and looked at her, ears erect. He'd been alone when she walked in. Melanie must have been okay with it, as he had apparently spent the night by himself here in this room.

Rosa felt certain Melanie would have popped in on him now and then as she sometimes did at the clinic when they had patients staying overnight, especially if they were badly ill. But then Drew was always around to watch the kids. Not last night. At least their house was next door, but Melanie wouldn't have spent much time away from the children.

And though Melanie sometimes had Rosa visit those ill animals instead, she hadn't asked her to come here last night, either.

"I gather you're as okay as possible under these circumstances," she continued, knowing Drew wasn't going to answer—at least not by talking to her. He did move his head a little, as if in a nod. That was good. He apparently still maintained his human cognition despite the time that had passed.

Melanie hadn't arrived for the workday yet. Of course, Rosa's boss had to follow her usual routine of taking her daughter to preschool for the morning, after the babysitter arrived for their son.

Rosa had beat the two vet techs to the clinic, too. Susie, at the reception desk when Rosa arrived, had confirmed that so far she was the only staff present. Rosa could have gotten here earlier than Susie, too, but had somewhat taken her time getting ready.

She was up early, hadn't slept well that night.

Too much on her mind.

At least she didn't have to worry about shapeshifters running around under a full moon, as she had the night before. But she did have to worry about at least one shapeshifter—this one, who was her patient.

"So," she said, "are you hungry? We don't have any fresh burgers here that I know of, like we did yesterday, but I'm sure we have some good, premium dog food. Or if you'd prefer people food, we can work that out, too. I'm not sure what you ate yesterday besides that burger."

Was that a touch of amusement on the wolfen face? Rosa knew she was blathering a bit. The two techs, when they arrived, might have a better sense about what Melanie had told them to feed Drew. The visitors from Ft. Lukman who'd hung out with him probably did, too, especially Noel Chuma, who'd been here for quite a while. Was he awake at his quarters yet? Should Rosa call him?

Almost as if she had actually called him, there was a knock on the door, which opened immediately. Noel entered, followed by Liam. Chase wasn't with them.

"So how's our patient today?" Noel approached Drew, who stood up and nodded as Noel stroked his head.

Liam, closing the door behind him, looked at Rosa, his head cocked at a slight angle. "How's our patient?" he repeated. "And how's his excellent veterinarian? You're here early this morning, Dr. Jontay."

"So are you, Lieutenant Corland. In fact, that's even more surprising. I work here. But why have you come?"

"Well, that's somewhat obvious, since we have a common issue here." He looked toward Drew. "We're going to figure this out, sir. Soon. But I do wish we could get your input."

The expression on the wolf's face darkened. Rosa had the impression that he was upset, certainly. But she also believed he would have done something else to try to communicate with them if he actually had answers.

Which in a way made things worse. His optimism, if he'd had any, might be waning. And, she'd gathered, he was the number one expert on formulating that elixir in its various permutations over the past few years. As a medical doctor, would he know anything about why his blood was different while he was shifted?

Were there answers to be found?

There had to be, even if Drew himself couldn't participate in fixing things.

"But don't worry about it." Liam must have read the same emotion on the wolf's face. "We're making progress on working on a solution. It'll come soon. I promise."

Rosa glanced at him, and saw that the large smile he

sent toward his commanding officer didn't look exactly happy...or promising.

But keeping Drew optimistic was vital. "We trust your Alpha Force team on that," she said, "and we'll be doing everything here that we can to help and support them, to make sure what Liam said comes true."

Liam looked toward her, and for a moment his smile did appear genuine. She felt a warmth circulate through her that had little to do with the hopefully true promise she was backing. He was clearly appreciative of her support—and more, she believed. She had a sudden urge to go shake his hand. Well, hold it, and draw him closer for an encouraging hug, and—

Ridiculous. Sure, they could, and should, work together for this important common purpose. But the fact that she found the guy appealing, despite his being a shifter, was totally foolish.

Yes, they could reinforce each other in what they were saying to this man-wolf who needed to hear it. And for it to happen.

But that was the only thing they should do together.

"Well, this is quite a crowd." The door had opened again, and Melanie walked in. Like Rosa, she was dressed in her white lab jacket. Her pale face barely contrasted with the color, and the dark circles beneath her eyes, despite the makeup she'd put on, didn't disguise that she mustn't have slept well, if at all. "I assume you're all here to give my husband a new elixir formulation or whatever that will bring him back to human form."

She looked first toward Liam and Noel, then at Rosa.

"Soon," Liam said, but despite his upbeat tone Rosa assumed he was just attempting to cheer Melanie. "We've a few questions first, though. Could we go to your office?" He looked at Melanie. "All of us, including Noel."

"Fine." Melanie didn't sound especially agreeable, and Rosa assumed she was trying to not only do as Liam apparently wanted, but also attempting to be nothing but positive in Drew's presence.

Rosa followed the others out the door and down the fortunately still-empty hallway to the office. Although Rosa figured it was late enough now that Melanie could have one of the other staff members hang out with Drew, she didn't stop in the reception area or break room to set that up.

Liam closed the door behind them. Melanie remained standing behind her desk, and though Rosa wanted to sink into a chair, she didn't choose to be the only one sitting down. She was between Liam and Noel.

"Now, what's really happening?" Melanie's tone was sharp, almost accusatory. Rosa hardly ever heard her boss be anything but pleasant and encouraging.

But this wasn't a usual situation.

Liam sat in one of the chairs facing the desk, as did Noel, and Rosa was glad to do the same.

"I wish I had some really great news for you, Melanie," Liam said. "But so far all we have is ideas—and, well, a little more. Before we can stir them together and implement a cure, we need more information to be sure we're not missing something. Noel, we've already talked, of course. You weren't Drew's aide that night. Jonas was."

"Right," he agreed.

"Thanks to Jonas, I've received nearly a minute-by-minute rundown on all Drew did before and during his shift, till he headed home still in shifted form." Liam turned toward Melanie. "Did you see him that evening before his shift?"

"No," she said dejectedly. "I didn't even have the chance to wish him a good time while shifted. And then when he came home when the sun rose... I wondered where Jonas was, Noel. Did you see him?"

"Yes, he was trying to find Drew. Drew started out on base, of course, and the shifters were just doing a few maneuvers that night. Nothing particularly stressful. I was just observing and helping generally. We all had an early dinner, then got the gang together in a secluded area, had them undress, and the aides shone the lights on them—nothing unusual for the night of a full moon or other nights when shifting was scheduled."

"That's right," Liam said. "That was how it worked for me, too."

Rosa pictured the scene in her mind—and forced herself not to think too graphically of how Liam might have looked nude after taking the elixir so he could have more control over his shift and maintain his human cognition. She'd heard that was their standard procedure.

Including getting undressed to have those lights turned on the shifters... She sighed silently.

Her purpose here was all she should be thinking about regarding shifters.

Including that handsome, smart—and sexy—Liam.

"Okay," Liam said. "That's what I figured, or you'd have told us otherwise. Just so you know, our medical guys don't have answers about the unusual quality of Drew's blood. They're still working on it. They're also working on modifying the elixir, and we're going to test a new formulation tonight—one that should make me remain in shifted form longer than usual—as well as a possible antidote that'll let me shift back when I want to. Those will be variations on some of the formulas used before, and if the one letting me shift back works okay, then they'll enhance it and give it a try with Drew."

"Really? That sounds great!" Melanie's sudden grin also suggested she was optimistic.

Rosa not so much. Still… "Yes," she said. "But in case you have any issues while shifting—"

"You go with them, Rosa," Melanie said, "in case they need any veterinary help."

That wasn't where she'd been going with her comments—was it?

Well, maybe so.

If she did as her boss said, she'd get the opportunity to watch Liam's shift.

All of it.

"That's okay," she said. "Although I know you can't go, Melanie. But I doubt that Alpha Force will want someone who's not a member of their military unit to barge in that way."

"It's not barging in," Liam contradicted, "and I was planning on asking if you would come along, just in case, since we'll be playing some unusual games here."

Games? He considered it a game?

Maybe so—from his perspective.

From hers? It was serious.

And what if he really did need some veterinary care as a result of what they'd be doing that night?

"Okay," she said. "Count me in."

This had to be a mistake, Rosa thought a short time later as she drove her car to the base, following Liam.

But it promised to be a fascinating one—and maybe helpful, too.

After some discussion, they'd left Noel at the clinic to watch Drew again and provide more food to him, since Melanie would be busy taking care of the day's veterinary patients. The knowledgeable aide would be useful during what was going on that afternoon at the base—and night—but Noel could catch up with them later.

Was she going to learn a lot more today about Alpha Force—and its shifters' methods, even outside of a full moon?

Was she actually going to see Liam shift? He'd said he'd be doing so that night as a test. That way, his fellow Alpha Force members would be around to help him shift back after attempting to imitate, somehow, what Drew had done.

Was she going to need to use her vet skills to help him while he was in wolf form, if whatever the test they were conducting ran into glitches?

Just in case, she had brought her veterinary bag filled with essential items in case she needed to examine, and possibly treat, Liam for illness, injuries or whatever.

She felt a bit guilty leaving Melanie on her own to care for patients, but her boss was one very good veterinarian. Plus the two techs would be able to help out with the general stuff, particularly after being given instructions.

Part of a day away from her beloved job—and for a very good cause, to help her boss's husband—should be fine.

After reaching the gate, Rosa figured that Liam had informed the guards about who was in the car behind him. Getting their okay to go through was quick.

She followed him to a parking lot and got out as Liam also exited.

He strode toward her, somehow looking all handsome, proud soldier. His camo uniform didn't hurt, but Rosa had a sense that anticipation of what was to come helped to ramp up his attitude.

"You ready for this?" he asked, as they met on the pavement near the building's back entrance.

"Sure," she asserted, with as much confidence as she could muster. And in actuality, she was ready—to see how things worked out.

To actually see a shift today? Heck, yes! She'd known shifters for quite a while, but this promised to be a first for her around here.

As they reached the building, Liam brought a key card from his pocket and swiped it in, then opened the door. But before either of them entered, he took her hand.

Somewhat startled, she looked up into his amazing deep brown eyes. "We'll figure this out," he said. "We'll help Drew."

"I know," she said, but she had the sense that he was asserting that aloud to try to make it come true. Well, that was fine with her. That assertion made her feel even more confident, too, than she had before. Liam was, after all, a shifter and a technology expert and a military man. He had to know what he was talking about.

She hoped it wasn't just the way her insides warmed as they exchanged glances that was revving up her confidence.

He squeezed her hand tighter, drawing her closer. Was he going to kiss her? She hoped so and remained looking up at him in readiness.

But then he released her. "We're going to go visit

Chase first, then head downstairs to see how the gang is progressing with playing with the elixir formulations."

"Right." She stepped back, all business once more—or at least she hoped she appeared that way despite the regret inside her.

He preceded her into the low-slung building, leading her down a hallway to the really nice kennel area she'd visited before, where the cover dogs were housed when not with their closest allies—the shifters they resembled. There were only four present now, and a couple started barking when Liam opened the door. Rosa just laughed at their eagerness to be noticed.

Chase was in the closest fenced-in area with one other wolflike dog. Nice, fluffy bedding lay on the tile floor for them, and the place looked almost elite enough for military officers to hang out when not on duty.

Maybe these dogs were considered officers of sorts.

"Hi, guy," Liam said, after letting Chase out of his enclosure. "Miss me?"

The dog's tongue came out and licked Liam's arm as if he'd understood what his master had said and was answering affirmatively.

"Good." Liam didn't leash him, but gave a gesture that told Chase to come with him. He then led Rosa back out the door. As he shut it, she stroked Chase's head.

She would see tonight, she believed, how much Chase resembled Liam when he was shifted.

And would Liam fail to shift back like Drew? Would he remain looking like, being like, his cover dog for a longer time than just that night—as Drew continued to look like his cover dog, Grunge? Rosa had seen Grunge at the clinic sometimes, since he, too, mostly lived next door.

"Okay," Liam said, as they walked down the hall.

"Let's take Chase out for a minute, then we'll bring him back and head downstairs."

Their visit outside to the nearby small patch of lawn was quick and productive. Soon they'd brought Chase back to his enclosure and were walking down the stairs to the lab and office area. Rosa walked beside Liam, who had a hand on her shoulder as if to guide her.

She was aware of it. Very aware. Appreciative of the contact.

More appreciative than she should be.

When Rosa had been on the lab floor recently, she had mostly been in Drew's office—although not with him. Now, Liam led her into a vast laboratory area.

She had seen similar places in veterinary school and otherwise, but knew this one was amazing. There were quite a few shiny metal cabinets along the perimeter, with metal counters on top that held a lot of different kinds of equipment. Unsurprisingly, that included electron microscopes, as well as items that appeared intended to test humans for things like respiration and circulation.

Was there any apparatus to check out canines and other animals when the humans were shifted? Most likely.

Patrick and Jonas, whom she'd seen the last time, when she was here to give a rundown about Drew's blood test, stood with Denny near one of the counters on which large containers of liquids had been placed, as well as some smaller vials.

Were some or all of these that incredible and all-important elixir?

"Welcome," Patrick said, and Rosa knew from before that Captain Patrick Worley was the highest ranking officer in this small group—and apparently the second highest in Alpha Force, after Drew. He was a medical doctor, dressed like the others in a white lab coat. "Put on one of those jackets over there—" he pointed to a coat rack that had a lot of lab coats on hangers "—and join us."

Rosa complied immediately, as did Liam.

This was the group she had kind of anticipated, since she had learned that Lieutenant Jonas Truro was also a medical doctor, and Sergeant Denny Orringer was Liam's aide while shifting.

All of them, except maybe Denny, would be appropriate to attempt to modify the elixir for its current purpose, and Denny would need to be there for Liam's test shift that night.

Assuming she was correct about the skills of each of them. But in the day since Drew's problems had begun, and based on her visit here before, she believed she was accurate in this, at least.

But what had they been doing?

And had they come up with the necessary answers to allow Liam to test their latest brews—and ensure that they could get Drew shifted back to human form soon?

She hoped she would find out.

Chapter 8

Liam had been watching Rosa's face—her lovely, animated face—since they arrived down in the lab.

He wanted to read Rosa's mind right now. What questions did she want to ask those who were now redoing the elixir? But he'd find that out soon.

In a way, he was relying on her. Sure, he was a member of Alpha Force and these guys would have his best interests in mind.

Sort of. Drew's best interests would come first, and that was fine. As long as Liam wouldn't wind up unable to shift back for any prolonged period of time, like his poor commanding officer.

"So," he began, looking at Patrick. "Can we talk about—"

"I know the elixir's formulas, all of them, are confidential," Rosa interrupted, leveling a quick glance at him before turning toward Patrick. "I don't need to know much. But could you tell me in general what you've been working on—what formulations will help Liam shift into wolf form, and how he won't be able to shift back right away, and, most important, how you intend for him to be able to shift back soon? Oh, and where are you with figuring out what was in Drew's blood? Is that a factor in what you've done?"

Great questions, Liam thought. And he liked that Rosa was sort of taking over, as he'd hoped.

She would be the vet in charge when he was shifted, of course. He hoped he wouldn't require her services. But it would be better if she was fully informed, just in case…

"You're right," Patrick said. "We've been working on all of that. And we'll tell you what you need to know. Thanks for coming, although we hope it'll just be a waste of your time."

"Me, too," Rosa responded. "But just in case…"

"Of course."

As the officer in charge of Alpha Force with Drew out of commission, Patrick was worth quizzing—and listening to. He gave the appearance of being in charge, too, Liam thought. His eyes, a light shade of brown, looked determined and assessing under his furrowed brow, as though he was attempting to figure out how much he could trust Rosa with. He stood right beside one of the shiny metal counters that held lines of microscopes with vials of liquid between them, probably the most important location in the lab today.

Liam just hoped what was in those vials had been mixed and vetted and perfected as well as possible before any of it was finally tested—on him.

"First of all," Patrick said, "most test work so far was

done in our inner lab over there." He cocked his head toward the side of the room, where a small area was se- cured behind a metal wall—not someplace Liam had ever been invited into, but he knew what that room was. "If we're going to talk, though, let's go sit in the lounge area." That was another part of this large room, also be- hind walls, but glass ones.

"Good idea," Liam said, and after seeing Rosa nod, too, he followed Patrick, as well as Jonas and Denny, to that area. Denny might be his aide, but he seemed to be doing a good job of toadying up to the officers in charge here. That was fine. Maybe he'd learn more than Liam did and be able to use it that night.

They were all soon seated on the couches in there, and Patrick started talking, with occasional input from his other colleagues. Apparently they still had no an- swers about the change in Drew's blood, but were still working on it. The conversation about the development and constant updating of the original elixir was long, but didn't really give much in the way of detail, since it was primarily confidential.

Rosa continued to acknowledge the confidentiality— mostly. She did ask some specific questions at times and received a little more information.

Finally, they got to the crux of what was important today.

"Yes," Jonas said, "the elixir has been modified a lot since it was first used by Alpha Force, sometimes because new members bring their own versions with ingredients that are then incorporated. We've experi- mented with it for specific kinds of shifts or issues, and we're always working on more. Like now." As a medi- cal doctor as well as an Alpha Force aide, he was bound to know a lot of the details, maybe as much as Patrick, who was also a doctor. Jonas leaned forward on the sofa, clasping his hands in front of him. He appeared concerned, ready to do what was necessary both to answer questions and to attempt to fix the situation. He was, after all, not only Drew's chief aide, but also his friend.

"So what you've been working with now is just variations of formulas you have already developed?" Rosa asked.

"Pretty much so," Patrick acknowledged. "We can't discuss the various contents, which are sometimes derived from human or canine bodily fluids and are other times chemicals we purchase, but you get the general idea."

Rosa nodded. "I don't want or need to know what those contents are, but I understand you've been working with them for quite a while and test those permutations on shifters both during full moons and otherwise, right?"

"Exactly." Patrick nodded as he settled in his seat, as if feeling less stress now with this conversation.

"And I gather that part of your research includes attempting to come up with formulations that allow shifters to remain shifted for long periods of time."

"Yes. We've had something like that for a while, but it always allowed the shifter who drank it to choose to change back at will. What we're working on now won't give the shifter that choice, but will definitely give his or her aide the ability to trigger the change back."

"And that's what you'll have Liam test tonight?" There was a catch in Rosa's voice. Liam wasn't sure that the others would have heard it, and he certainly didn't know her well, but it still made his insides warm a bit. She gave a damn.

But maybe not about him. Maybe about the issues with all shifters.

In any case, he appreciated her caring.

"Yes," Patrick said, "and before you get too worried, we've worked with it as much as we could over this brief period of time. We're pretty certain it'll do what we need it to."

Pretty certain?

Rosa caught that, too. "Are you certain enough to really test it on an actual shifter this soon? What happens if Liam winds up like Drew?"

Jonas laughed aloud, which surprised Liam—a bit. But the medical doctor/aide had been a member of Alpha Force for a while and had seemed to give a damn about the unit and its members for as long as Liam, more of a newcomer, had known him. "We've considered that in our preparation, and if anything, erred on the side of caution. Our concoction will definitely allow us to bring Liam back to human form. But even so we won't be certain about Drew until we test it on him afterward. We don't want to try it on Drew first, though, since we don't know for sure what caused his failure to shift back, and we feel we have more control about testing this first with Liam."

Rosa seemed to hesitate, then said, "I have to assume you guys know what you're doing—even without the assistance of the person who, I've heard, has done the most to create and modify the elixir, Drew. But—"

"But I'm going to let them give it a try," Liam said, softly but firmly. "I appreciate your concern, but I trust these guys." He had to, if he wanted to remain a member of Alpha Force. And he'd been the one to volunteer to shift that night, with the intention of helping Drew.

"It's of course up to you." But Rosa's gaze remained on him for only a few seconds before moving on to Patrick, Jonas and Denny in succession. "I just hope you're right. Otherwise, I suppose I'll have the veterinary fun of treating another shifter in wolf form for a while."

There wasn't anything she could do about it, Rosa realized, but fret and worry.

They remained sitting there, talking in generalities about the very specific issues they could run into that night with Liam using those new elixir formulations for shifting—and shifting back.

Would she be so worried if someone else was going to be the test subject?

Sure, she told herself. Yes, she had come to know Liam a little over the past short while, liked the guy, admired his intelligence both as a shifter and as an apparent computer and technology whiz. She also liked the way he seemed to really care about his commanding officer, enough to risk his own life, or at least its stability, to try to help him out.

But now, as Liam engaged more in the conversation about techniques they would use—apparently not much different from normal—she enjoyed watching the good-looking, serious yet droll shapeshifter trade questions, information and barbs with his fellow Alpha Force members.

And when they finally were through, Liam looked at her. "You know, Dr. Jontay, this may wind up being the only time I can give you a tour of this base. I'd like to show you around. Okay?"

The expression he leveled on her looked mostly amused—yet she somehow caught a hint of pleading in it. Maybe he just wanted to get away from this gang for now, before he had to meet up with them again for a test that hopefully would go well, yet could instead go very bad.

What could she do?

What did she want to do?

"Sure," she said, meaning it.

The group made plans to meet at the base's cafeteria for dinner in a few hours—all of them, for a final yet discreet discussion about what would happen afterward. Then, somewhat relieved for the moment, Rosa followed Liam out of the lounge, through the lab and up the stairs to the building's main floor.

She felt as if she could breathe better then. And when Liam told her his first target for their current outing, she could only grin.

They were going to visit the area where the shifters' cover dogs were housed—again. And not just to see Chase.

"A bunch of our dogs should be around today. I want to introduce you to some you haven't met yet, let you say hi to those you know." Liam spoke with an almost evil grin, stopping in the hall with the door to the stairway closed behind them. "I think they're all healthy, but it wouldn't hurt to have a quick vet check for each of them."

"It also won't hurt to kill a little time there so we don't have to think about our...plans for tonight," she added.

"There's that, too." Liam's voice had changed from teasing to almost gloomy.

"You don't have to do it, you know," Rosa said

quickly. "They can figure out another method to test their new formulas. Or—"

"They need to try it on a shifter," he said. "I'm one of the lowest on their wolfen totem pole, one of the unit's newest members."

"But I thought they asked you to enlist in Alpha Force because of your special technological skills. You're the chief technology officer? Surely it would be better to have someone who doesn't have your abilities be the one to take chances tonight."

"Well, I've taught my aide enough to have him follow up on the social media stuff that's so important to deal with right now—although there are aspects that I'll need to take care of. After I've shifted back."

"But—"

He put a finger over her lips to keep her from continuing. And then, strangely, he glanced around the hallway.

What was he looking for?

Rosa figured that out nearly immediately, when he replaced his finger with his warm, sensual lips.

But only for a moment—long enough to shut her up, though.

When he pulled back she felt speechless—and disappointed that the kiss had ended so soon.

"Now," he said, "let's change the subject." He turned his back and strolled down the hall toward the room containing the dog enclosures.

Okay, maybe that hadn't been the wisest thing to do—although it was really, really enjoyable.

Including viewing the sexy look on Rosa's face as he backed away.

And it had accomplished what he'd wanted to do just then: keep her, for that moment, from addressing the subject of his upcoming shift.

Oh, he wanted to talk to her again, hold conversations on animal health and her take on shifting and—well, nearly anything…tomorrow. After he had shifted back.

And hopefully without needing Rosa to take any critical steps as a veterinarian to deal with his health while shifted.

They'd reached the door to the large kennel room and he pulled it open without looking at Rosa. Of course, the wolf-dogs inside began barking, and Chase stood up on his hind feet behind the fence enclosing him.

"Hi, guy," Liam said to his cover dog. Rosa, beside him, petted Chase briefly but caringly, then started visiting with some of the other dogs in their enclosures.

"Oh, hi, Spike," she said to one of them. "How are you doing?"

"Far as I know, he's doing fine," Liam said. "Your treatment of his injured paw did the trick. He's been acting just fine here and also when brought out to do his duty as Seth Ambers's cover dog. I know Seth's happy about his quick recovery."

"That's great. And how about the rest of you?" Rosa's intense gaze ranged over the other fenced areas. "Everyone feeling okay?"

As far as Liam could tell, they were. They all moved around excitedly on their bedding and regarded Rosa and him as if they wanted even more attention than the acknowledgment they were currently getting.

And why not? Rosa and he had a while before dinnertime. "I think they're all fine, but eager for walks.

Let's do it, okay? Short ones. We'll leave Chase here for now."

"Love it!" Rosa grinned at him, making him feel all gushy inside. He turned and headed to the wall where leashes were hung.

They had some time to kill that afternoon, so they wound up taking their time on the walks, just for fun. These walks really weren't necessary, since the dogs were well cared for and often spent active time with the people they worked with. But in the afternoon, like now, usually those people were doing other things, so the idea was that these dogs could bond together here in their own kind of pack.

But aides and others came in often to talk to them and walk them.

Grunge, though, was a different matter. Drew's cover dog spent afternoons here, but was generally the only one to pretty much live off the base, at the house next to the veterinary clinic with Drew, Melanie and their kids.

Grunge was here now. Liam assumed that was because Melanie chose to let him stay here while she dealt with Drew's issues. Rosa clearly understood the situation, for as soon as Liam handed her a leash she went over to where he was enclosed with Shadow, the cover dog of Staff Sergeant Jason Connell, Drew's cousin.

"I'll get Shadow," Liam said. "You take care of Grunge. I'm sure he knows you from the clinic and next door."

"He does," Rosa agreed, kneeling to pat the wolf-dog she had taken from his enclosure. He nuzzled her, clearly recognizing her and liking the attention. "Poor guy." Rosa gave him a hug, then stood. "Getting Drew changed back is important for many reasons—and

Grunge's best interests are among them. I'm sure he'd rather be home with his human family."

Telling them all, particularly Chase, that they'd be back, Liam motioned for Rosa to walk Grunge out the door while he followed with Shadow.

Both dogs seemed excited to be outside on the base's nearby grassy grounds, and Liam was glad that Rosa seemed perfectly happy running with her charge, as he did with Shadow. They spent around twenty minutes giving the dogs, and themselves, some exercise.

Returning to the building, they put the two canines back in their enclosures. Rosa chose to walk Spike next and seemed delighted that the dog whose injured paw she'd treated seemed as well now as Liam had told her. Liam elected to take Rocky, Lieutenant Ryan Blaiddinger's cover dog, out this time.

And when they brought those two back, Liam told Rosa, "It's time for me to show you around more. I'll just bring Chase along with us."

"That sounds great." Rosa smiled at him. "It was delightful to hang out with these dogs for a while, and in case you're wondering, though I did no formal checkups, I saw nothing wrong with any of them. Looks like they're well cared for here."

"Of course. They're not just wolf-dogs. They're our alternate personalities."

Rosa laughed. "Of course."

With Chase leashed beside him, Liam took Rosa on a nice, long walk around the base, pretty much sticking with the narrow driveways. He pointed out where he lived, in the bachelor officers' quarters at the far side of the property, with the main office building nearby. "I don't know whether you've ever met our highest-up commanding officer, General Greg Yarrow, but he maintains an office in that building. He mostly hangs out at the Pentagon, but visits us here often. I know he sticks up for Alpha Force with the higher-up muckety-mucks, though he's good at maintaining our secrecy where it matters."

"I don't know him, but I've heard of him."

Rosa seemed to have no trouble keeping up with Chase and Liam. She of course wore civilian clothing, not too casual but not particularly dressy, either. And she fortunately had on athletic shoes, although perhaps she always wore comfortable shoes, as a vet who'd likely be on her feet a lot during the day.

The May day was warmish, but not too hot. Liam enjoyed the walk and he hoped Rosa did, too. She seemed to. She often pointed to something she saw, such as the base's auditorium, where programs were sometimes held with outside military folks, or even those stationed on base who weren't part of Alpha Force. It was small and attached to the rear of the main admin building.

They discussed Alpha Force in low voices. They discussed Liam and the work he'd done before joining the unit—technologically oriented, of course. And the work he did now that was a natural follow-up.

He turned them around eventually, took Chase back to his enclosure with the other cover dogs and steered Rosa toward the cafeteria. "We're meeting the gang here for dinner right around now. You ready?"

"Sure." But the look she leveled on him was worried. "Are you?"

He knew what she was referring to. They would discuss his upcoming shift as they ate.

"Of course," he lied. He preceded Rosa into the small

cafeteria and looked around. Sure enough, Patrick and the gang already occupied one of the tables. Other tables had men and women in camouflage uniforms sitting at them, too. The place was more than adequate for this relatively compact military base. It contained a salad bar at one end, as well as a nice-sized area where workers dished out some prepared food. There was also a beverage station and a grill. Nice place with an excellent smell, even for a shifter in human form.

Liam was prepared for this. He really was. He got a steak dinner, of course, while Rosa just picked up a salad. They sat down at the empty seats that had been saved for them.

And then they all began discussing, in low voices and generalities so non–Alpha Force people wouldn't know what they were talking about, what they would be doing later that night.

What *he* would be doing later that night.

He wished that their beverage bar served alcohol, but it was better that it didn't. That could affect how the elixir worked, of course.

And then, much too soon, dinner was over.

It was growing dark outside.

It was time.

Chapter 9

Rosa could tell after dinner that the guys, shifters or not, were gearing up for what would soon take place.

What would soon happen with Liam.

Everyone rose from around the table and picked up their dinnerware to take to the counter where used items would be dealt with by the staff. "So," Patrick said, "let's all head back to the building for now."

And then what? Rosa had some idea as she picked up her things. The Alpha Force members didn't pay much attention to her, but appeared to share glances filled with anticipation. And concern?

Looked that way to Rosa. Maybe that shouldn't worry her, since they all should be concerned because of their dedication to ensuring that everything worked out as well as they'd told her.

But it worried her nonetheless.

"Let me handle that." Liam, beside her, reached for

her plate. Somewhat startled, she let him take it and place it on top of his own, although she still held her iced tea glass.

"Thanks, but you don't need to," she said softly. He didn't need to do anything but...well, prepare, at least mentally.

But maybe doing something mundane and useful would help him with it.

"You're right." The smile he aimed at her appeared all Liam—cocky and happy and teasing. And yet there was something in his deep brown eyes that told her she was right.

He wasn't entirely himself. Not that she really knew him all that well after interacting with him for just a couple of days. But she'd been considering the concern of his fellow Alpha Force members.

It wasn't any surprise to her that he would be concerned, too. He should be—even more than all the others.

He was their experiment. Their potential scapegoat if things didn't go well—instead of Drew.

And she needed to stop thinking like that.

"So, I'm not sure where any of this is going to take place," she told Liam after they left their things on the counter. Then, side by side, they began walking through the still busy cafeteria and followed the others outside. "Patrick said we were going to the building, which I assume is the lab building, right?"

"Yes, but they'll be gathering up...what's needed. Our shifts around here..." He lowered his voice so she could hardly hear it, even though she figured that the other military people stationed here had to know at least something of what Alpha Force was about. "...

are generally held outside, in an area toward the north of the building."

"Got it," she said. They'd headed slightly in that direction to walk the cover dogs when they'd taken them out before. There was some lawn there, with woodlands abutting it. Maybe shifts were done best under the cover of trees.

And maybe that was a good thing, since surely if they thought things would go wrong they'd want to conduct their test inside, in the lab area, where they'd have access to chemicals and whatever.

Or was she just being too hopeful?

"So, I'm pretty excited about all this," Liam said. They were outside now, still following the others, this time along one of the narrow roadways toward the area of the base containing the lab and kennel building. "And I trust these guys. Things will go fine."

Rosa glanced toward him as they revved up their pace and saw he was striding quickly and determinedly, yet he once again aimed his smile at her. Sort of. Was he doing this to make her feel better—or himself?

No matter. He was a good guy. Brave. Intending to risk his own well-being not just because he was under orders, she was sure, but because he intended to help his friend and commanding officer.

She had an urge to reach over and grab his hand. In support and possibly comfort, not to show she had any feelings for him except as a fellow human being—and more—facing a potentially challenging situation.

But she swallowed that impulse. And soon they reached the building.

Liam stepped behind her as she followed the other guys inside. "You can wait here," Jonas said to her.

"We're just grabbing the necessary supplies, but we'll bring them outside for the shift."

Rosa wasn't sure whether they were telling her to butt out for this moment or just saving her the walk down, then up, the stairs. It didn't really matter. At least they hadn't ordered her to leave.

Then again, they were concerned they might need her.

She watched as Liam moved around her, nodded, then began talking to Denny as they hurried down the stairs after the others.

She fought the urge to follow, but since the current commanding officer had told her to wait, it made sense to listen to him.

What if she breezed down this hallway and stopped in to see the other cover dogs again while she waited? She didn't think Chase would accompany them to where Liam shifted. There shouldn't be any need for a cover dog when that shift would occur right here on the military base, and presumably where they'd go to accomplish it would not be near where non–Alpha Force members stationed here were likely to be.

All she would do, therefore, was potentially get Chase and the others stirred up, not a great idea.

Having nothing better to do, she pulled her phone from her pocket and began scrolling through email messages. There were a couple from the owners of veterinary patients, but when she opened them she saw that Melanie or one of the vet techs had already looked and responded. She'd just been copied on them, and for now her input wasn't needed.

Maybe she should—

"Here we are," called Liam's familiar deep voice.

The door to the downstairs lab had opened. Liam was the first to exit, followed by Denny, who held a large backpack in his arms. He shoved it over his shoulder.

Rosa had a good idea what that pack must contain. She knew that the Alpha Force elixir, at least in its prior formulations, required that the shifter drink some, then have an artificial light resembling a full moon directed on him or her.

Not that she'd ever seen that, but she had learned about it in discussions about how Drew had shifted but not changed back.

With the elixir, they used the light even when the moon was full. When the moon wasn't full, it was even more necessary.

But changing back? Some of the elixir's formulations allowed it despite the moon being full, but all the shifters could, and generally did, change back when the moon went down at dawn. And when the shift was done outside a full moon using the elixir, the shifter apparently could just elect when to change back.

Before.

The others—Patrick, Jonas and Denny, all still in their camo uniforms, as was Liam—had exited that doorway and Rosa now followed the group outside. Most of them also carried backpacks—more lights? Different elixirs?

Would she ever know?

And did it matter?

A car drove along one of the base's nearby roads, but fortunately didn't head in their direction. Rosa followed as the Alpha Force group headed over the adjacent lawn, then into the woodland beyond.

The night was dark now, although there were some

lights here and there on the base, but no bright ones nearby. The cool air washed over Rosa, but her slight shiver wasn't because of the cold.

No, she was anticipating what was to come, and it worried her.

She remained with the group—and was unsurprised when they stopped in a fairly large clearing.

This had to be it.

Sure enough, the guys pulled the backpacks off their shoulders, lowering them to the ground.

"I think this is overkill," Patrick said to his subordinates, motioning to all those bags, "but we'll have some alternatives if anything doesn't work quite right."

Meaning if something went to hell during Liam's shift. Rosa didn't even want to think about that.

But she was glad they were prepared. She just hoped that, whatever they had, it would actually do what they wanted it to.

And then it was time.

The other team members flocked around Liam, sort of shielding him from her gaze, Rosa supposed. But she still managed to see in between them as Liam began taking off his clothes.

And aiming a glance, off and on, in her direction. He knew where she was—and that she was observing.

Yes, she was definitely observing. And getting aroused despite herself and the situation as muscular, gorgeous, sexy Liam was soon nude.

Heck, she was here as a doctor. A veterinarian. Her patients never wore clothes, although a lot of them had fur. And at the moment, she was here in her professional capacity in case a shifted wolf happened to need a vet.

She had to remain professional, no matter what she saw.

No matter what happened.

And yet she managed to observe as Liam stood there naked, stretching his body, flexing those amazing muscles of his...and more. Making her insides react in ways they absolutely shouldn't right now.

But scolding herself didn't help.

He accepted a vial of clear liquid from Patrick and drank it. He seemed to shoot one more look toward her. Then Denny lifted a large light from where it had been in his backpack, turned it on and aimed it toward Liam.

She knew what to expect—kind of. But she still couldn't help feeling amazed as his face lifted and its features began elongating into a muzzle, as his body grew smaller, furrier, more slender and shrank closer to the ground.

And in a very short time, handsome, naked Liam had turned, as anticipated, into a wolf.

His shifting was complete.

Did he feel different than usual? No, despite knowing that the elixir he had swallowed was at least a slightly modified formulation from the one he was used to. It tasted the same. Under the light Denny had shone on him, it acted the same.

And, fortunately, that meant he still retained his human cognition while shifted, perhaps the largest plus in using the elixir—in addition to having the ability to shift outside a full moon, of course.

Now, he just sat, resting his tail on the ground in the glade among the trees, looking with wolf eyes from each of those around him to the next. Letting the discomfort of his shift ease away. Waiting to decide what to do next.

His gaze lit for the longest time on Rosa. She had

watched him shift, and this was probably the first Alpha Force shift she had observed, despite possibly seeing some shifts during her childhood.

She had also seen him, in human form, completely naked before his shift began. He knew that, if he were still in human form, just thinking about having that lovely, sexy lady watching him would have caused the pertinent parts of his body to grow and ache and yearn for more.

But he was now in wolfen form. He looked away from Rosa and toward his current commanding officer, Captain Patrick Worley, to see if there were any orders pending.

What should he do next?

Attempting to shift back was the challenge he was to address, even knowing he was not supposed to have control over it now.

He wasn't about to try to shift back again this soon. A lot of the reason for this shift was to test the new formulation's resistance to any determination on his part to become human again on his own terms, at his own time. But he needed to let his body bask in this form first.

And let that pain and discomfort that went with the twists, turns, size reduction and change of a shift to ease, then end.

"Okay, Liam," Denny said. "How are you feeling?"

Liam looked at his aide and nodded his head, moving his canine ears to listen to the forest sounds as he did so.

He enjoyed being wolfen, hearing small creatures on the ground, in the trees, perhaps aware that there was now a large potential predator on the loose in their area.

But he wasn't about to hunt squirrels or birds or anything else right now. Not even people.

He had a lot more on his mind than pretending to act like the animal he now was. A wolf.

"Good. I'm glad you're okay." That was Patrick, who appeared to watch him the way a military officer observed cadets in his charge, making certain he was following orders.

The only order Liam was aware of for now was to shift on cue, as he had done. The next order he anticipated was to attempt to shift back—which was most likely to be unsuccessful, since that was the way his shift this night had been planned.

It would then be up to those here, his fellow Alpha Force members, to ensure he became human once more.

"Is there anything you would like me to do for you?"

He turned his head abruptly to regard the source of that question. Rosa. She had approached and now stood almost in front of him, closer than any of the other humans around, his fellow Alpha Force members.

Yes, was the initial thought that came in response to her question. Hold me. Be there for me. Make certain that I will be able to shift back soon, as promised. He liked being wolfen, certainly, but remained fully aware of what had happened with the leader of his pack, Drew Connell, and he did not want that happening to him.

Had he still been in human form, he would also have chosen to misinterpret Rosa's question as an attempt at seduction, one he would have gladly agreed to.

But now?

She remained a few steps away and he moved toward her, raising his head to keep staring into her eyes. Soon, he edged against her, feeling her warm legs against the fur on his body. Inhaling her sweet, human, womanly fragrance. Listening to the increased pulse of her breathing.

Was that because of her concern?

"I'm interpreting that to mean yes," she said, and he saw her look at the human men around her. "It won't hurt for me to give him a quick exam."

No one objected. He believed she would not have accepted that answer if they had.

For the next few minutes, she knelt on the ground beside him, staring into his eyes, his opened mouth, his ears. Touching his back, then his chest as she had him roll over.

He wished once more that he was in human form, to have her stroke him and caress him—and examine him—that way.

Oh, yes. He retained his human cognition.

Soon, she was done. She stood. "He appears to be in good canine health," she said. "I don't find anything wrong with him, from my veterinary perspective."

Those around her expressed their relief.

"How soon should we have him try to shift back?" That was his caring aide once more. Denny was also the only one there who had no medical skills, plus he was talking to his military superior officers.

"Let's move a little deeper into the woods," Jonas said. "No reason, other than to swallow up a little time."

"I assume that won't do anything to hinder his shift back," Rosa said.

"As we told you, we don't think his initial attempt will work, anyway. We modified the elixir we gave him to prevent his shift back from being as easy as usual so we could then try the other new formulation prepared *for Drew on Liam first. This is just to prepare for it, not try it too soon."*

"I get it."

And so Liam obeyed, enjoying the prowl into another part of the woods around them. He flexed his legs, his tail, his ears, considering how they would feel when he finally attempted to shift back.

Wondering how he would truly feel when, as anticipated, that vital act would be out of his control.

He allowed Jonas to lead the way, knowing that under other circumstances he would dash far from these humans, allow himself to use his swifter legs to get away, utilize his keener senses while shifted, as well. Hunt. More.

But not now.

Soon, Jonas stopped, as did the others. Liam turned to ensure that Rosa remained with them. She did, following the rest.

"Okay," Jonas said. "It's time. Liam, shift back to human form."

He sat on his haunches again. He closed his eyes. He sensed those parts of his body that needed to change, as he always did while shifting back. And using his thoughts, instructed them to modify themselves into the way they needed to be now.

There was no reaction.

He looked toward Jonas, attempting to convey his thoughts and his acceptance—temporary—for now.

"No change?" Jonas asked.

Liam shook his head slowly in the manner humans considered to mean "no."

"Try again," Patrick said.

Liam stood, turned in a circle—and looked toward where Rosa stood, watching him.

"Are you okay?" she asked him.

He nodded his head in human fashion to indicate he was, not conveying his concern. His fear, despite how he had anticipated this.

His gratitude that she asked—and appeared to care.

But now...how long would they wait before allowing him to truly shift back again—or trigger the attempt themselves?

He had known this was coming.

All would be well. He hoped. Eventually.

But he hated that it was out of his control.

Linda O. Johnston   119

where it all about watching him.

"We are." Clavel, the owner, not.
...

Chapter 10

Rosa stood back, outside the small circle of military men who surrounded the member of their team they were focused on. Watching him in the beams of several large flashlights they'd placed on the ground beneath the trees, aimed toward him.

Waiting.

She hated this.

Yet…not entirely. She also found it fascinating.

And frustrating.

And, well, hate was too strong a word. Or maybe not. Rosa didn't hate that Liam was a shapeshifter, only that there were questions remaining unanswered. Provocative questions.

When would he be able to change back into human form?

Would he be able to change back, under these circumstances? Or would he be like Drew Connell, no matter what the others said? If that was a possibility, how could she help?

She didn't really know much about shapeshifters except for potentially being able to treat them medically while they were in shifted form.

But helping them get that way, or out of it? She had no skills, no knowledge, of that.

All she knew was that she would hate it if Liam was unable to get back to being… Liam.

Now, she watched the expressions on that canine's face as he continued to sit on the ground in the middle of the humans observing him. Discussing him, as if he wasn't there—or couldn't understand.

But from his expressions, and reactions, as he watched their faces, listened to them, she knew that Liam the shifter had retained his human cognition the way she'd been informed that Alpha Force members who drank the elixir would.

Apparently other shifters did not.

"Okay," Jonas was saying, confirming what Patrick had stated. "You're right. Our modified version of the elixir worked the way we planned it. That's a good thing—but it's time to use the other, secondary formulation, the kind that we created to do the deal—get a stuck shifter to change back no matter what happened to him or her before."

"Right," Patrick said. He held his large backpack in his arms, as he had before. Now, though, he set it on the dirt in front of him, knelt down and started sifting through its contents.

"You got it?" Jonas asked. "If not, I brought some of that special concoction along, too."

"I've got it." Patrick pulled out a large vial whose

clear liquid contents sparkled in the artificial light. The container appeared full.

What did it contain?

Rosa didn't really need to know, although chemistry was an important part of her profession and she had always been reasonably good at it.

But she also recognized and acknowledged that there were plenty of things about the covert military unit Alpha Force that nonmembers weren't told. And despite her possibly being of assistance to them, she was definitely a nonmember.

Hopefully, after tonight, she wouldn't even have a reason to want to know those contents and how they blended together. If Liam—no, *when* Liam—changed back, it would demonstrate that the stuff worked. Plus it would also work on Drew.

"Okay, then." Denny had pulled his smaller sack off his back and now held it in front of him.

Good aide. Liam, in his current form, would have a difficult time lapping up liquid from a glass vial like the one holding the shift-back formula, or whatever they called it.

But Denny had removed a metal dog bowl from his bag and held it out in front of him. Patrick immediately pulled the plastic lid from the top of the vial and tilted it till some of the liquid poured into the bowl.

How much was needed? How much would Liam drink?

Hopefully, these experts knew how to handle this— even though this aspect of shifting apparently was new to them, too.

"Okay," Patrick said a few seconds later. "That should be enough. Put it down in front of him."

"Right." Denny bent and positioned the bowl on the ground where Liam could lower his muzzle and begin lapping.

"Anything we should tell him first?" Patrick looked toward Jonas, who must have been involved in this new formulation.

"Just drink," Jonas responded, looking at Liam and not Patrick. "We'll use the light on you, although it might not be necessary. In any event, make the assumption that after you drink it you can shift back the way you usually do—by choosing to, willing your body parts to go back into their human form. Got it?"

Rosa was glad to see Liam's immediate nod. *Work, please work*, she thought. Sure, she remained concerned, even if these more knowledgeable men felt convinced things were in order.

What if they were wrong?

Or what if they were just putting on an act for each other and for Liam, hopeful that all would go well... but not certain?

She watched as Denny once again removed the large light from his backpack where he had stowed it. He turned it on and aimed it at Liam.

Liam sat still for a moment, staring away from the light. Staring away from all of them, into the trees and, perhaps, beyond.

Was it working?

Damned if she knew.

But he started moving, twisting a bit, beginning to move his paws, his legs. He shook his head, aimed his gaze downward.

And then—and then his limbs started elongating. Slowly but definitely. His fur appeared hazy, seeming to be sucked inside him, again slowly. His ears moved sideways and started to change shape, even as his muzzle began retracting. He moaned.

"Is he okay?" Rosa heard herself whisper. This was astounding to watch, though she had seen a shift before. But she hated to see or hear an animal in any kind of pain, and Liam appeared to be hurting.

"Yes, this is normal," Denny replied softly. He remained standing right beside the wolf-man to whom he acted as aide. "He's changing back!" Denny sounded excited, perhaps a bit surprised. Maybe he hadn't really thought that what they had done here would be effective, would allow Liam to shift back.

But it did appear to be working, and Rosa glanced first at Patrick, then Jonas, to see their reactions, to determine if they, too, believed Liam was changing again as he should. Both were nodding as they watched.

But it looked so strange to Rosa. It looked so wonderful. Liam groaned some, first in a throaty wolfen growl, and then sounding like a man in pain.

Even as he continued to extend, to grow, to change, to somehow absorb his fur.

And then, in the dim but steady light, Rosa could see the man who was Liam—perfect, muscular, gorgeous...nude.

What the Alpha Forcers had done had apparently worked.

Exhausted.
Ecstatic.
Liam was both.
He continued to lie there on the ground, arms be-

neath his head, as Denny came over to cover his body with a sheet. First, though, Liam turned onto his back.

He knew Rosa was there, standing in the background, watching him. He liked that she was staring at his naked body, despite how limp he was all over after that intense but oh, so wonderful, shift.

His breathing was deep, labored—and all human, a good thing. He smiled, closed his eyes as he was shrouded in that sheet—and when he opened them he was looking straight into Rosa's face.

"Are you okay?" she asked. Somehow, she had imposed herself in front of the Alpha Force guys nearby to check on him. He appreciated it. He appreciated *her*.

Not that he would tell her or anyone else, at least not now. "I'm fine," he said, hearing his own voice rasp. He turned his head toward the others. "Can we go back to the lab now? I want to talk this over, find out what you all thought about this—and learn how quickly you'll be trying your new formula on Drew."

"Fine," Patrick said. "Tell us when you're ready to sit up, then stand. We'll help you back to the building."

Liam did feel somewhat like an open sack of flour, ready to collapse and flow back onto the ground as, with Denny's help, he began to stand.

But once he was on his feet, covered by the sheet, he felt like himself once more—himself after a usual shift back to human form, which meant he was achy and uncomfortable, but basically himself again. And given a little time, that discomfort would disappear.

"You want to get dressed now?" Denny asked him. His aide had helped him remove his clothes before and remained in charge of them for now.

"Sure," Liam said. That would give him a little more time here.

It would also give him a little more time to be naked in front of Rosa, as his body returned to normal. He hid his smile as Denny turned to retrieve his backpack, which contained the camo outfit Liam had been wearing.

As he stood straighter, squaring his shoulders, he glanced in Rosa's direction. She was watching him. Good. But he couldn't interpret her expression. Was that relief he saw? Maybe. She caught his gaze and smiled wanly. "Good to see you back, Lieutenant," she said.

Denny lowered the sheet then, holding out Liam's clothes with his other hand. He took his time accepting the items, slowly leaning over to don his briefs, then his pants, and finally his shirt.

All the time shooting glances toward Rosa, but not just her. He needed to get dressed—but he liked the idea that she continued to observe him. And the others were watching him, too, undoubtedly to make sure he was doing okay.

"Good job," Patrick finally said, when Liam was done.

They hadn't returned to the lab building when Liam was finished shifting back. Rosa found that interesting, since that had been the plan. But there apparently was no need right now.

What Liam apparently needed was rest. And so Denny left them for a while, then drove up in a car and helped Liam inside. "I'm taking him to his quarters in the BOQ," he explained to her.

The others apparently knew that. None apparently intended to accompany Liam and his aide.

Rosa wished she could—to make sure that Liam rested well, returned to normal. Didn't shift back or need a veterinarian.

Didn't need a hug, which she felt like giving him.

In support of him…and herself.

She kind of needed a hug after that. It had been an amazing experience to watch him shift—both ways.

To examine him in shifted form.

To see what he looked like when he returned to being a man. All man.

So maybe it was best that she stayed far away from his residence that night. She might be somehow turned on by seeing him that way, but clearly they would never do anything about it, particularly not tonight.

She walked back to the lab building with the others, since her car was parked near there. She talked with them about the experience she'd just had.

"Thanks for letting me watch," she said. "And I'm so glad Liam didn't really need my help as a veterinarian."

"We're all glad about that." Patrick looked down at her and smiled. She had noticed before that he was a nice-looking guy. He seemed a bit older than the others, which made sense. He was a senior officer, in charge for now. And he appeared to know what he was doing, as well as care about those who reported to him.

Something occurred to Rosa. "I'm sure you'll be talking to Melanie, right?"

"Yes," Patrick said. "We'll let her know tomorrow how things went, tell her we intend to use this new formulation to help Drew."

"You're sure it'll work for him, too?" she had to ask.

"We've every belief it will," said Jonas from her other side.

"Great. Is it okay if I tell her what I saw here with Liam? I'll let her know when I see her how well this went, although I won't make any promises to her. That's up to you." She sent a grin toward both guys, hoping it appeared real. She still had her misgivings about Drew.

But she really, really hoped the stuff worked as well for her boss's husband as it had for Liam.

"Yep," Patrick said. "It is. But sure, if you talk to her first you can tell her how things went today, and tell her I'll be in touch."

"At least we all have reason to feel optimistic."

"Yes," Jonas said, "we do."

And on her drive back home that evening Rosa felt more than optimistic. She felt happy.

But she wondered when she'd see Liam again, and under what circumstances.

She decided to stop at the clinic, partly to make sure all was well there, partly to talk to Melanie if she was present and partly just to check on Drew. She wouldn't say anything to him about what had gone on this evening, with Liam's shifts that first prevented him from changing back to human form, and then allowed him to choose. The wonderful result—Liam was once again in human form, as he'd wanted. As they'd all wanted.

But telling Drew was up to the Alpha Force people. She didn't want to provide Drew with any hope that could be dashed because of circumstances she didn't know about.

It was about nine o'clock when she parked on the nearly empty street in front of the place and, after walking to the back door, used her key to go inside. Melanie was unlikely to be there that night, with her young kids at home, unless she happened to drop in quickly to see Drew.

As far as Rosa knew, there were no other animals besides Drew who were staying overnight and might need some additional attention before morning. Even so, she walked through the hospital and stopped at the room considered to be the infirmary, which contained crates where overnight patients were kept. It was empty. Good. She breathed deeply, glad she didn't have to handle any treatments that night.

She heard a whine from down the hallway, though— in the direction of the exam room where Drew was staying for now. She headed there. Was Noel Chuma hanging out there tonight? The aide hadn't been with them at the base for Liam's test shift, and Rosa had assumed he was still hanging out here with Drew.

But Noel wasn't in the room. Drew had clearly heard her walking around, since he was sitting up on the towels on his table, watching the door. "Hi, Drew," Rosa said in an upbeat tone. "How are you doing tonight?"

Not that she really expected him to answer, but he clearly understood what she said. He nodded his head slowly, but this time the sound he made was more like a loud, snorting sigh.

"I get it," she told him. She wished she could do something, say something, to make him feel better. But she again worried about giving him hopes that could turn out to be false. "Anything I can get for you? Anything I can do for you?" She confirmed there was a bowl filled with water on the floor that he could easily access, and she felt certain he'd been given his dinner earlier by Melanie. A burger? That was more likely than dog food.

Surprisingly, Drew stood up on his hind legs and braced his front paws on the wall of the exam room for support. He looked at her, nodding, then let go and danced in a canine circle.

"That looks like human actions to me," she said. "I'm delighted that you still know who you are." As Liam had, although his timing was far different from Drew's.

And Rosa, at the time, couldn't wait till Liam changed back again, too.

Drew uttered a low woof as he lowered himself back to the floor in a more canine position. He looked beyond her, moving his ears.

Did he hear something? Someone?

In a moment Rosa heard footsteps in the hallway. Drew must have heard them when the person was farther away.

No—persons, plural. A few seconds later the door opened. Noel came in first, then Melanie, carrying her son and holding her daughter's hand. Andy and Emily both wore pajamas and looked tired, as if they had just been awakened, but the adults appeared full of energy.

The grin on Melanie's face was huge, and Noel appeared happy, too. Rosa believed she knew why.

They must have talked to the Alpha Force folks, learned of their success with Liam that night.

But could they—would they—reveal to Drew what had happened?

She found out quickly. Melanie let go of Emily's hand and knelt down, carefully placing their son on the towels beside the wolfen creature there before giving him a big hug. "We've got some reason for optimism at last, honey. Just wait till you hear."

"Yeah, good news, sir," Noel said to his canine

charge who was also his superior officer. "Are you going to tell him, Melanie?"

"Oh, yes." Melanie sat on the floor after picking up Andy again, and their young daughter joined her, on her lap. "Emily, you can tell your daddy that his friends did an experiment this evening, and it went well."

"Daddy, friends," began the child, but she was interrupted by Drew's bark, which somehow sounded ecstatic. He stood and nuzzled first Emily, then Melanie and Andy.

"You were there, weren't you?" Noel asked Rosa.

Busted. She nodded. "That's right, but I didn't think I could discuss it in front of Drew. I figured the Alpha Force guys would want to be the ones to let him know."

"Very appropriate." Melanie stood once more, holding their son and looking at Rosa. The sorrow and pallor Rosa had seen before on her boss's face had disappeared. "But Patrick phoned Noel and told him to go to my house to take a call there."

Then he'd changed his mind about waiting until morning, Rosa realized.

"I was so afraid at first…" Melanie didn't finish that sentence, but Rosa could guess what was on her mind. If Noel had been told to be out of Drew's presence for the call and had told Melanie that, she'd possibly anticipated bad news.

"Well, I don't know how these things are supposed to go," Rosa said, looking down into Drew's intense eyes. "But I saw Liam drink something, then shift into wolf form and not be able to shift back at first, then drink something else and change back." Oh, yeah. Into human form. Very human form.

"That's fantastic," Melanie said. "And since Patrick

told Noel and me that in the phone call and didn't tell us not to let Drew know—well, that sounds like a good sign to me."

Rosa hoped that was true…

"Me, too," Noel said. "I gather that tomorrow night will be when they'll give it a try." At Drew's canine glare, Noel amended, "They'll do it. Everything will be fine tomorrow night."

Rosa definitely hoped so.

She didn't imagine she'd be there to watch, which was fine with her. If Drew needed some kind of veterinary attention before he shifted back, his wife would undoubtedly be there to help.

Liam would probably be there, too.

Once more, she wondered when she would see him next—for surely, sometime they'd be together for something relating to Alpha Force.

She couldn't help hoping that it would be soon.

Chapter 11

He was back at his apartment in the BOQ. Denny had left after driving him there and helping him inside.

Liam's energy was returning. His feelings of being human were all there.

It had worked! He had an urge to grab a bottle of beer from his fridge to celebrate, but knew better. Too soon after a shift wasn't any better than drinking before it, especially since some of the potions he'd imbibed undoubtedly remained inside him.

And so he decided to get his high another way.

Not at first, though. He got a bottle of water instead from his refrigerator and turned on his computer. For a while, he checked online. There weren't many new posts at his usual sites about shifters and damage they'd done under the recent full moon, and he was glad about that. Some did have added mentions of shifters more generally, and he assumed one of his false identities

once more to add his own posts to make fun of them—
pretending to be someone who was so excited about
the idea of becoming a shifter he was willing to eat
wolf poop to give it a try. Oh, that wouldn't do it? Gee,
that's too bad.

And he quickly got some responses including LOLs—
laugh out loud.

But he slowed down soon. It was nearly time to go
to bed.

He had something he wanted to do first—the high he
had considered before, sort of. This near eleven o'clock
might be too late to call Rosa, but he did it anyway, sitting on top of his bed in his underwear. It was almost
time to go to sleep, after all, and he was especially tired
after this unusual evening.

As he picked up his phone, he noted he'd missed a
call from Chuck. It was too late to call his brother back,
especially since they opened the restaurant early in the
morning. He'd pop in there tomorrow to see him.

Then he pressed in the number for Rosa.

"Hi, Liam?" she answered almost immediately. "Are
you okay? Do you need any medical treatment or—"

"Not from you," he said. "I'm still in human form, or
I wouldn't be talking to you this way. No, I just wanted
to say good-night and thank you again for being there
in case I did need some veterinary assistance before."

"Anytime," she said, and he heard a noise, with his
intense canine hearing, that might have been a swallow, as if she'd just realized what she'd said. She'd sort
of offered to always be there for him if he needed her
while shifted.

Now maybe he could get her to make a similar offer
while he was in human form...

No. She might accept the existence of shifters, but she probably had no interest in getting more involved with one.

Although she had seemed quite interested in seeing him naked while he was shifting—but that didn't mean anything other than the fact she was one sexy, non-shifting lady.

"I'm just calling to let you know I'll be at your clinic tomorrow morning to talk to Drew about how things went," he said.

"Melanie already did. She and Noel heard from Patrick, and they let Drew know about it, too."

"Well, I assume he'll want to hear it direct from this source, too. So maybe I'll see you tomorrow at your clinic."

"I'll certainly be there," she said, "so I'll see you tomorrow."

As they hung up, though, Liam ignored an urge to see her tonight. Really see her tonight.

As they both got naked…

Not going to happen tonight or any other night, he told himself, ignoring the beginning of a somewhat inappropriate, very human erection.

But the idea remained in his mind till he finally fell asleep.

Rosa had been reading in bed when Liam called, a detailed veterinary journal that usually wound up blurring her vision and relaxing her enough so she would eventually fall asleep. But after she heard from Liam she was wide-eyed once more.

She could no longer concentrate on the magazine, so she stopped trying. As she lay there with her eyes closed, what kept going through her head was a rehashing of all that had happened around her that day.

Amazing stuff—watching a man shift into wolf form and back again.

Unnerving stuff—wondering if he would, in fact, be able to shift back.

And much too arousing stuff, seeing that sexy shifter nude in human form.

Still, she fell asleep eventually and woke up the next morning bright-eyed and ready to head to work.

Now if she only knew what time to expect Liam…

She arrived early and after putting on her white lab jacket went to check on Drew right away, as she had last night. Brendan was in the room with him, not Noel, and Rosa figured the Alpha Force aide might actually be back at his quarters getting some sleep.

"How's he doing?" she asked the young, thin vet tech in the standard blue scrubs. She watched Drew's reaction as he stretched on his bed of towels and looked at her. Was he irritated that she'd acted as if he wasn't in the room—or didn't understand her?

"He seems tired but okay," Brendan said from across the room, where he appeared to be reorganizing some bandages and other supplies in a metal cabinet. He responded in a way that also didn't acknowledge Drew's background.

The wolf-dog stood and moved toward Rosa. He sat and reached one paw out as if he wanted to shake, but as she reached down to oblige he batted her hand and growled.

"I get it," she said. "But if all goes as well as we hope, you'll be…yourself later today." She didn't want to go into too much detail despite being sure that Brendan knew who and what Drew was. But since they didn't really talk about shifters around here, based on Melanie's preferences, Rosa chose to follow their employer's opinion and keep things discreet.

He nodded, then turned away.

The exam room door opened and Melanie came in. "Oh, good, you're here, Rosa. We need to talk about one of our patients."

Which was fine with Rosa, even suspecting that patient was Drew. "Okay," she said.

Melanie did her usual thing these days and knelt on the floor to hug her wolfen husband, which Rosa found both endearing and sad. When she stood again she faced Brendan. "Dina is at the clinic now, so since we've got a tech on duty I'd like you to stay in here for a while, okay?"

"Fine." Brendan patted his pants pocket and Rosa figured he was checking to see if his cell phone was there, since she doubted he'd hold any ongoing conversation, one-sided or otherwise, with Drew.

Rosa followed Melanie. Before they got to her office, the clinic's receptionist, Susie, entered the hall, followed by a large woman with a small and fuzzy Yorkie mix in her arms. "I'll show her into the exam room right there." As always, the senior greeter was dressed like the vet techs, but she had a choice as to what color lab jacket she wore. Today's was bright pink. She pointed her long fingers with nails matching her shirt toward a door across from them.

"Very good," Melanie said. "One of us will be there in just a minute." She smiled at the patient's owner, whose tense expression softened into what appeared to be relief.

Rosa wondered what was wrong with the little dog and hoped she would be the one to find out. Then she would do her damnedest to make sure the pup recovered from whatever it was fast.

Sure, she cared what was going on with Drew, but he appeared okay for now, and there was nothing she could do for him but make an attempt to keep him cheerful. Melanie would be better at doing that, although she needed to treat patients, too. Brendan seemed to have things together, so they could rely on him, at least for now. And maybe Noel would return after getting some sleep.

Before the rest of the Alpha Force people came to do as they'd done with Liam the night before...

Liam. He'd said he would be here this morning, but maybe he'd meant when the others came, late afternoon or evening.

She'd look forward to seeing him, of course, and convincing herself that he remained well—and in human form.

Whenever he got here.

They were in Melanie's office now, and her boss closed the door, motioning for Rosa to take one of the seats facing her desk. She did so, but was eager to leave so one of them could go examine their small dog patient outside.

"I guess there's nothing really new to discuss right now about Drew and what to expect." Melanie stood beside Rosa rather than sitting down. "We discussed it all last night—or I assume you didn't have any more to add about what you saw with Liam."

Only that he had a gorgeous naked human body, but

she certainly wasn't going to mention that. She wished she could forget it…didn't she?

But she understood what Melanie really wanted—or thought she did. Rosa stood again and faced her boss. "I wish I could guarantee that Drew will easily slip back into his human incarnation tonight, Melanie. And I did see Liam struggle before he got that new Alpha Force drink, then succeed in changing back after he received the new formula they developed for this. I don't know much about it—and you're aware of that. I don't know what will happen tonight. But, hey, boss, at least there appears to be a good chance all will go well. We all certainly hope so."

Tears welled in Melanie's gleaming blue eyes. Rosa stepped forward and gave her a hug.

"Thanks." The word came out in a rasp, and Melanie hugged Rosa back. "Will you be here to watch this time?"

"If you want me to, and the Alpha Force folks let me."

"I do, and they will. Now—would you please go take care of our patient? I need to have a few minutes to myself right now, but I can assure you I'll be ready for our next patient."

"Sounds good." One more quick hug, and Rosa left the room.

It turned out that Nutsy, the little Yorkie mix, had been running around in his family's yard and started limping. His owner had swept him up into her arms and brought him right here after stretching his legs and touching the bottoms of his paws, but not finding anything to explain the limp.

Rosa, on the other hand, discovered the cause immediately after first gently squeezing those paws, then examining them using a flashlight. "Burrs," she said. "A couple of them between the pads on both paws on the right side. No wonder he was limping. That had to hurt."

It could have been discovered by his now relieved, hugely smiling senior owner, but it hadn't been. She'd have to pay for the visit, plus some antibiotic to ensure the areas didn't become infected, but she seemed thrilled that Rosa had rescued her little Nutsy.

Nutsy was just Rosa's first case that day. She gave shots and an annual exam to a cat who was a long-time patient. She provided another exam, this time to a six-month-old mixed breed puppy. She checked an older Great Dane with a heart murmur, and a much too young cocker spaniel with hepatitis.

Fortunately, they all left with happy owners and the likelihood of having happy lives for quite a while longer.

As Rosa entered the reception area after sending the cocker and her family on their way, she was surprised—well, not too surprised—to see Liam entering from the outside. It was now late morning.

"Well, hi, Doc," he said, then told Susie he was there to see their patient in the exam room. He didn't mention Drew's name in the crowded reception area—a good thing, since locals might know Melanie's husband's name but not his background.

"Fine," she said. "Go ahead back."

"Great. Doc, I've got a couple of questions. Could you come with me?" He aimed an innocent, large-eyed expression at Rosa that she didn't trust a bit.

But she wanted to know what was on his mind. Besides, there was only one patient waiting in the reception area, and Rosa knew Melanie was nearly done with her current patient. "Sure," she said, but nevertheless looked toward Susie. "Let me know, though, if I'm needed right away."

"Of course, Doc. But we're good for now."

And so Rosa found herself walking into the rear hallway with Liam. She was happy to see him—even though he was fully dressed, in his usual military camo uniform.

"So how's our patient?" he asked, when the door was closed behind them.

"In good health, as far as I can tell," Rosa told him, looking up into Liam's amused brown eyes, "though I have to admit I wouldn't necessarily recognize symptoms common to shifters that regular canines don't get."

"Oh, we're pretty much like regular canines when we look like them," he said.

"Except for your minds. And your abilities to shift back. And—"

"Okay, you have us pegged."

"I assume that was your first question," Rosa said. "Do you have any more?"

"That's the most important one."

The hallway seemed shorter than usual, since they reached the door to Drew's room quickly. Or maybe it was just that Rosa was enjoying being in Liam's company. He reached around her and opened the door into Drew's exam room.

The wolf-dog was sitting up, watching them enter. He'd obviously heard them. Noel was on the floor beside him with a bunch of bandage pads arranged in rows. Some had *X*s on them and others had *O*s. "We're playing a modified version of tic-tac-toe," he told the others. "Drew's using his nose and doing a pretty good job."

Rosa laughed, and Liam clapped. "Good job—and good way to pass the time till you can do it all again with your fingers," Liam said.

The wolf who was Drew barked softly, and all the others laughed.

"Okay, looks like you need a reward, sir." Liam looked at Drew. "It's nearly lunchtime, and I've got an urge to go visit my relatives and their restaurant. Care for a hamburger or two?"

Drew barked even louder, nodding his wolfen head.

"And I'm going to need help carrying food for everyone back here." Liam looked at Rosa. "Care to accompany me?"

"Why not?" she said, though she figured there were plenty of reasons not to. But unless a new, urgent patient came in or Melanie wanted her here, she would ignore all those reasons for now.

Good. Drew was doing well, and he would do even better tonight. Liam felt sure of it—as sure as he could be. Their initial triggering shifts for taking the new elixir formula had been different from what Liam was used to, of course, so no guarantees.

But after requesting a few minutes alone in the exam room with Drew and telling Rosa he'd meet her in the reception area shortly, Liam described for his mentor what he had gone through last night and assured him that he'd be among the Alpha Force members who'd be there for him that night.

It wouldn't hurt for Drew to be jazzed and optimistic.

"We'll celebrate in advance," Liam concluded, then told Drew he'd be back soon with his burger.

Drew nodded and shot him a wolfen smile. Then Liam left to find Rosa.

They were soon in his car driving to the Fastest Foods shop. "I almost brought Chase along today," he told Rosa, "but my cover dog was scheduled for some training with a few of the aides, who were going to pretend he and some of the others were actually us, shifted. It's good practice for our cover dogs to continue lessons so they act like regular canines even when they can tell via their senses that we aren't regular."

"Sounds interesting," Rosa said. "Maybe I should watch that kind of thing one of these days to ensure the wolf-dogs are treated at least as well as their human counterparts."

"As far as I'm concerned, you're welcome anytime." He paused to make a turn onto the street housing the restaurant—and couldn't help asking, "So what did you think of watching my shifts?"

"They looked pretty painful to me."

When he glanced at her, she was watching his face. There was a gleam in her eye that suggested she was remembering not only his discomfort, but what else he'd done during shifts—like, getting nude.

"Yeah, there's some discomfort involved, but it's worth it."

"I'd like to hear more about that," she said, as he parked the car. "Why do you like it? Although I guess you really don't have a choice, even as a member of Alpha Force, right?"

"I've got more choices relating to my shifting thanks to my military unit, but no, the shifting just comes naturally under a full moon."

They were soon inside the restaurant. As always, it

was busy. Liam looked around for his brother, wondering again why Chuck had called him last night. Well, he'd find out soon.

He got into the line along with Rosa, and found they had to raise their voices a bit to be heard in the crowd. Once more there were a bunch of people ahead of them. This time, he didn't see his family, but figured he'd run into them before they left.

The person who hurried toward them first was Valerie, popping out the kitchen door in her dark blue shirt and jeans with an apron on top, and stopping right beside them. "Welcome," she said, looking only at him. Liam had gotten the sense often that his sister-in-law's sister wanted more than a flirtation with him, but he didn't even want the flirting. Friendliness was fine, though.

"Thanks," he said. "Right, Rosa?"

She raised her dark brown eyebrows when she looked at him, but then turned toward Valerie. "Yes, thanks," she said.

At least Valerie was polite enough to look at her and smile—for maybe an instant.

"Looks nice and busy today," Liam continued.

"As always," Valerie said. "I'm really impressed with all Carleen and Chuck are doing here. I may even stay a while longer than I originally planned."

Liam wasn't thrilled to hear that, but it wasn't really his business. Although maybe he'd have to actually talk to Valerie one of these days and let her know he had no interest in her beyond being a distant relation of sorts. "Speaking of them, are they nearby?"

"Always. I think they're both in the backyard giving Louper a treat. I'll let them know you're here, if you'd like."

"That would be great." But almost before Liam had finished speaking those words he saw Chuck heading out the same door Valerie had come through. His brother made a beeline in their direction, and Liam couldn't help grinning. "Hi, bro," he called.

A moment later, they shared a man-hug. "Good to see you, bro," Chuck responded. "Everything okay?"

"Sure. And with you? I didn't see until too late that you'd called last night, and you didn't leave a message."

The people in front of them in line moved a bit forward. Liam glanced toward Rosa, who also moved ahead. Valerie was still there, too, but ignoring Rosa, who glanced at her, then shrugged.

"Well, yeah, I just wanted to talk to you a little about—well, stuff. Can you come back later, maybe dinnertime? We could talk then."

"No, sorry. I've got things going on tonight." Just as a teaser, Liam said, "And the reason I didn't get your call last night was...stuff." Chuck was being a good boy and not even hinting at the word *shifting* in his nice restaurant crowd. But they both knew what the other was talking about.

But a look of shock and—was it anger?—came over Chuck's face. "You did? Last night? Without telling me? That's not right."

Liam blinked. He looked away and met Rosa's gaze. She looked puzzled. And, almost beside her, Valerie, too, appeared confused.

Once again the line moved, and Liam watched as first Rosa and then he kept up with it. He said to Chuck, "It's very right. You know what—what's going on in my life. I can discuss some of it with you, but not all. And not here. And definitely not tonight. Maybe tomorrow."

"Yeah. Maybe. Well, you're almost at the head of the line. Carleen's taking orders. I need to go back and help her. Let's talk tomorrow. I'll give you a call—assuming you'll answer next time."

"Make it tomorrow, and I will."

Liam watched as both Chuck and Valerie headed back to the kitchen door.

"Everything okay?" Rosa asked.

"Sure," Liam asserted. Then he added, "Maybe."

"Oh, dear," said Rosa. "Anything I can do?"

"Not now, but—"

Somehow, smiling at each other, they both said at the same time, "Maybe."

Chapter 12

They'd given their order to the person behind the counter—Liam's sister-in-law, Carleen. Rosa had seen his interactions just now with his other family members and wondered why his brother seemed upset, unless, of course, she had misread his actions. She'd met the guy only yesterday.

But the way Liam watched him and Valerie as they went back to the kitchen area convinced Rosa that she was right. Liam's good-looking face was marred by what she interpreted as a possibly puzzled and even a bit angry expression.

Chuck wound up talking briefly to his wife behind the counter, then disappearing, probably to somewhere else in the kitchen. Rosa and Liam soon reached the head of the line and placed their orders with Carleen, for themselves and the others at the clinic, including

Drew. If Rosa was reading it correctly, the woman acted polite, but as if she and Liam were strangers.

Because of her brief conversation with Chuck?

Strange. But it really wasn't Rosa's business—except that she felt bad for Liam.

While they waited for their order, after splitting the bill in half as they'd agreed while driving here, Liam walked away from the order counter between the nearly filled tables. Rosa thought about joining him, but one of them needed to be nearby to pick up their food when their number was called. Looked as if that had to be her.

As she stood there, glancing now and then at the number on the receipt to ensure she recalled the right one—which, of course, she did—she couldn't help wondering what all these customers would do if they knew the owners of the place were shapeshifters.

Probably just laugh at the idea, as most people would. Not her, though—not since she was a kid and first heard of such things. Literally heard them, since she often was awakened during the nights of a full moon by howls. Still—

"Sorry it's taking so long."

Rosa felt a little startled not only about the comment, but by who'd made it: Valerie. She'd had the impression that Carleen's sister didn't like her, possibly because she'd come in here with Liam, and the woman—probably a shifter, too—kept attempting to flirt with him.

Rosa was glad, though, that Liam didn't seem interested. Not that she wanted him to be interested in her, either—except as a friend and veterinarian to the cover dogs and shifters.

Now she responded, "I'm glad, for your family's

sake, that the place is busy. As it should be. Even though it's fast food, it's really good."

"Even for a…regular person?" Valerie lifted her eyelids beneath her silvery bangs in a way that suggested complete innocence, but Rosa knew exactly what she was alluding to.

"Absolutely." Rosa made herself grin. She definitely found this woman—or whatever—rather annoying, mostly because of what she said. Or so she assured herself. It couldn't be because she didn't like the idea of anyone flirting with Liam—anyone else, that is.

Not that she was flirting exactly…

"Glad to hear that. And of course most of our customers are regular people."

Rosa didn't like that Valerie had said "*our* customers." That implied that she was in business with her sister and brother-in-law. Although in some ways she was, since she clearly was working here while in town. Or at least appearing to help out. She was even wearing an apron like the others sometimes did, over her regular clothes.

"I figured," Rosa responded, just as one of the people behind the counter called another number. She glanced at the receipt again. It still wasn't their order.

"Look," Valerie said in a low voice, sidling up so close that Rosa felt a little uncomfortable. "I'd really love to talk to you one of these days about what it's like to be a veterinarian who works with—well, you know. Some of the animals associated with Ft. Lukman."

At least she was being somewhat discreet. There were, after all, real wolf-dogs hanging around there who were the cover dogs.

Rosa kept her voice soft, too, as she responded,

"They're good, healthy canines for the most part, at least from what I can tell. And Melanie Connell, the head veterinarian at the Mary Glen Clinic, is the one who tends them the most."

"Except for now, I heard."

It wasn't surprising that someone associated closely with Liam would know what was going on with his commanding officer, and therefore, to some extent, Drew's family. Though Rosa understood that the Alpha Force people hadn't wanted that kind of information to be made public in any way. Still—

"Number 94," called a youthful male voice from behind the counter, and Rosa breathed a small sigh of relief. That was their number.

Liam must have recalled the number, as well, since he joined her quickly, despite the crowd noise that clearly didn't prevent him from hearing the call. Rosa wasn't certain where he'd been, though it couldn't have been far away. But after holding her ticket up and shooting a small smile toward Valerie, she was the one to move forward and collect the plastic bags of food.

"Glad it's ready," Valerie said, but the expression on her pretty face suggested frustration. She apparently wanted their conversation to continue.

"Me, too," Rosa said, meaning it. She was ready to go back to the clinic, both to provide lunch to the others who worked there and Drew and his aide, but also to get out of here—and end this potentially uncomfortable conversation with Valerie before it got very far.

But she wasn't surprised when Valerie didn't stop there. She edged up to Liam. "So glad you came in. Two days in a row. Is this becoming a habit? I'm sure that Chuck and Carleen are happy to see you…and I am, too."

Rosa had no doubt about the latter. But Chuck? He hadn't seemed happy to see Liam—or at least to talk to him.

"Oh, you'll see me back here, I'm sure," Liam said, "though it won't be to pick up lunch every day. And you can tell Chuck, since he clearly doesn't want to chat with me right now, that I will be in touch, and I'll answer some of his questions."

Which implied he wouldn't answer all his brother's questions, Rosa noted.

She wondered what those questions were—and if they'd led to the apparent disagreement she'd noticed before.

"I noticed that you and Chuck seemed to have some kind of disagreement," Rosa said from beside Liam as he began driving them back to the clinic.

He'd first taken her behind the restaurant and said hello over the fence to his family's dog, which resembled a wolf. Rosa said hi to Louper, too, then remarked she was glad to meet him this way and not professionally.

Now, Liam's car smelled really good once more, since the aroma of all those burgers, and a bit of chicken, too, wafted around them despite the food's enclosure in plastic bags. He had an urge to stop and grab one, rather than getting into the pending conversation with Rosa.

But she was right, and it would have been hard for her not to notice the way his brother stomped away from him almost as soon as they'd arrived.

"Yeah," Liam therefore answered, but added truthfully, "although I'm not exactly sure what it was about."

"Well, what did he say?"

Did it make sense to tell Rosa anything about it? Apparently, Chuck wasn't thrilled that Liam hadn't returned his phone call, especially because the reason was "stuff"—in other words, he was shifting outside the full moon, and hadn't let Chuck know in advance. But that certainly wasn't the first time, nor would it be the last.

So what was on his bro's mind?

"Actually," he finally said, "I'm not sure. For some strange reason, I wasn't able to return his phone call last night, and I figure that has something to do with it."

"Yes," Rosa laughed, "a very strange reason. And from your Alpha Force's perspective, and Melanie's and probably Drew's, a very helpful reason."

She got it, then. In fact, this smart, beautiful—and sexy—veterinarian seemed to get nearly everything, including the good and bad things about his shift last night.

Did she get that he had some interest in her beyond her healing capabilities? It would likely be better if she didn't, but he nevertheless hoped she did.

"Well, I'll talk to him about it soon," Liam said. "Or at least what I'm able to discuss with someone outside Alpha Force and not connected by necessity, the way you are." *And by your smarts and caring and all that,* but he wasn't going to mention it now. "I'm sure he'll be okay about it, especially if I'm able to report that all went well tonight and a difficult shift that didn't change back has been resolved."

Rosa didn't say anything for a minute. And then, from the corner of his eye, he could see her look at him. "You mentioned before that your brother and sister-in-law are part of an experiment that lets them drink elixir on some nights of the full moon. That lets them keep their human cognition then, right?"

"Right," he agreed, pulling onto the street where the veterinary clinic—and Melanie and Drew's house—were located. "It's definitely an experiment so far and only a few close family members can participate. Since Chuck and Carleen relocated here recently, they were a natural fit for trying it out, though they didn't necessarily have to be chosen. I'm glad they were, but I'm afraid that Chuck now is making assumptions about his ability to use the stuff, and if not, whether I should have the same restrictions he does."

"Well, I'm not a part of all that. But in a way I can understand why a regular shifter who knows about Alpha Force's capabilities might feel jealous."

"But he and Carleen should feel delighted to take part at all." Liam knew he shouldn't take it out on Rosa, not even a little, so he calmed his voice. "I know what you're saying, though. Maybe, if they hadn't bought the restaurant, so have nearly all their time taken up by it, one of them could join Alpha Force."

"But then only that one would be able to enjoy the ability to use the main elixir regularly, right? And even then, it would be limited to military orders and use and all that."

"You got it," he responded. "But they don't get it, and they don't get the opportunities to use the elixir as I do." He sighed. "Maybe it wasn't such a good idea for them to participate in this initial experiment after they joined me here."

"Maybe not," Rosa answered. "But they're here and so are you. I'm sure you'll figure out how to make sure things work best for them, for you and for Alpha Force."

Liam continued to consider Rosa's words as he parked and they went inside the clinic and shared lunch with Melanie, Drew, Noel and the rest of the veterinary hospital's staff.

"You ready for tonight?" he asked Drew, in the room that had become his, just before he prepared to leave.

Drew nodded his wolfen head. Of course he'd be ready.

Liam just hoped that everything went as well with Drew as it had with him.

Rosa felt somewhat sorry when Liam left, but not too sorry.

He'd checked with the powers-that-be at Alpha Force. And yes, they wanted her to be there that night during their attempt to bring Drew back from being shifted.

No, she told herself. She needed to be optimistic. It wasn't just an attempt.

They would bring Drew back, just as Liam had once again shifted into human form.

She'd said goodbye to Liam after lunch and confirmed she would come with Melanie to Ft. Lukman a little later.

"Do you think it's a good idea for her to be there?" she asked Liam at the back door before he left. "If things don't go as planned—"

"She's been affiliated with Alpha Force longer than either you or me." His deep brown eyes looked down on her understandingly. "I know she's expecting to be there, and I mentioned her to Patrick when I confirmed they want you there."

"Well, that's good, then."

"Very good, since if anything goes wrong while

Drew's still in wolf form you'll be there to help. I doubt
that Melanie would be able to stay detached enough
to do it."

"Probably not," Rosa said. "So, we'll see you tonight."

The expression on his face appeared very welcoming,
and very sexy. "Yeah," he said. "See you tonight."

She had an urge to reach out and hug him. Maybe
even do the unthinkable and give him a kiss—just in
support, nothing else.

But she did neither.

She had to remain professional.

Especially considering all that would go on that
night.

Patrick, not Liam, drove the SUV that went to pick
Drew and Melanie up late that afternoon, as well as
Noel Chuma, who'd still been at the veterinary hospital.

Liam was told, though, that he could go pick up Rosa
a little later. He was happy to do so. Very happy.

Was Rosa happy? He wasn't sure, although she
clearly wanted to help out in the event something didn't
progress as it should and Drew needed veterinary help.
She had seemed to accept Liam's shifting without res-
ervation, so she was unlikely to freak out about Drew's
doing the same thing—assuming he did shift back, as
they all hoped.

When he reached the clinic, Liam parked and tried
to open the door of the waiting room, which generally
was unlocked during business hours and beyond. But
not today, and he understood that they'd closed early
because the veterinarians would not be available. He
pulled his phone from his pocket to call Rosa, but as

he did the door opened and there she was, dressed in a casual shirt and slacks—no medical jacket. But she was carrying a medical bag. He, of course, remained in his military camos.

"Thanks for coming," she told him. "I was listening for you and heard you try the door."

"Hey," he said, "that's pretty good. Do you have the hearing of a shifter?"

Her face was the picture of lovely innocence as she said, "Sometimes I wish I did."

He laughed, then bent his arm and gestured with his other hand for her to grab it so he could guide her down the walkway to the sidewalk. He'd parked against the street's curb, as usual.

She hooked her arm in his and grinned. He liked having her that close for the short walk. He liked having her close to him anytime, he realized.

But after tonight, if all went well, he was unlikely to see much of her in the future. He might as well make the best of this short time.

"So how does everyone feel today?" Rosa asked, when they were both in the car and he pulled onto the street. "I mean at Alpha Force. I know how Melanie and Noel feel, and, to some extent, Drew, too."

"He's the most important in all this," Liam said. "How is he doing?"

"Just reading his actions and facial expressions, I had the impression of one very stressed canine." She hesitated. "How likely is this to work?"

"Very likely," Liam said, meaning it. "You already know it worked for me."

But he realized that didn't guarantee the same results for Drew. After all, he and others had shifted normally on the same night Drew ran into trouble, and no one knew what caused the difference.

They soon arrived at the gate to Ft. Lukman and followed the usual routine to provide credentials to the guards. "Things will be done somewhat differently today," Liam told his passenger. "It'll all take place in the lab."

"I wondered about that," Rosa said. "Drew is clearly already in wolf form, although I'm not sure that was the full reason why both your shifts were done out in the woods. But I thought that if something…er, if creating any changes to the formulation is necessary, or—"

"Or if something goes wrong." Liam parked the car in the lot near the Alpha Force building and looked over at her. "We're all concerned about that and, yes, I gathered that it'd be better to be near the lab in case they need to play with the elixir or with Drew, or anything else."

He reached beside him to open his door, but felt Rosa's hand on his other arm. He turned toward her and saw a look of concern—fear?—on her face. He grasped that hand as she said, "Liam, I— Things have to go well tonight. I don't have half the knowledge you do about any kind of shifting, let alone what Alpha Force does. But I care about Melanie and Drew, and you and all the others who are being affected by what's going on with Drew. I want you to know that I do care."

"Thanks." He heard the rasp in his own voice. Then he couldn't help it. He stretched from his side of the car to Rosa's, bending over the console and reaching over to gently pull her head toward him.

And then he kissed her.

Briefly, yes, but for those few heated seconds, he felt

as if his entire body had been captivated and engaged—
and sexually stimulated.

"Wow," he said, as they mutually ended it.

"Yes, wow." Rosa's voice was low and raspy.

But she opened her car door and got out. And he
did the same.

They had a highly important shift to observe.

The tension in the air was as tangible as if a veil of
some kind had been lowered in the lab area. Rosa figured
that if it was that obvious to her, the Alpha Force members, particularly the shifters with all their extra-acute
senses, must be able to hear it and smell it and more.

But everyone sat in chairs set out at one side of the
room—everyone but Drew, who sat on the floor in front
of the rest. The seats had been brought from Drew's office, and Rosa assumed they all wanted to be closer to
the counters and lab areas in case immediate modifi-
cation to the elixir or something else scientific had to
be accomplished.

Her mind returned often to that latest kiss from Liam,
both reassuring and sexy. But the latter was totally inappropriate. She might like shapeshifters but it wasn't
a good idea to be attracted to one, no matter how appealing Liam was while in human form. And she didn't
feel entirely reassured, either.

Still... Patrick had left the lab area after greeting
Liam and her. They appeared to be the last people expected. Everyone there talked quietly, allowing their
conversations to include Drew, who sat in the center of
them all, looking around with his wolfen eyes.

Appearing tense, or at least that was Rosa's official
veterinary opinion.

"You okay?" Liam asked at her side. He'd been talking with Melanie and Noel. Melanie appeared anything but okay, so Rosa was glad she was at least talking to the other humans. Once again, she had left their children with a sitter. Rosa hoped that when Melanie returned home next, it would be with their dad, looking like himself.

"I'm fine," she responded firmly. She had to at least appear that way. But she was worried about what would happen if Drew didn't shift back.

Patrick returned to the room then. He immediately walked over to what appeared to be a large refrigerator and extracted a glass vial.

With great ceremony, he poured some of its liquid contents into a metal dog bowl, then turned to look down toward Drew.

"It's time," he said.

Chapter 13

Liam felt Rosa's eyes glance toward him. He swallowed the urge to reach toward her and take her hand in reassurance that all would go well.

First, he couldn't be certain of that.

Second, they were in a crowd who might misinterpret any indication that he gave a damn about how she felt. Or maybe it would be a correct interpretation. Either way, it was inappropriate.

For now, he just shot her a smile, then turned back to watch Drew eagerly lap up the formula in the bowl.

Would it work?

It had to.

The room was quiet as everyone watched, waited. Liam inhaled, his intense senses allowing him to catch a whiff of the specialized, important elixir. He recalled it, of course, from last night. Had it been modified at all since then? He didn't know.

He had felt his phone vibrate in his pocket soon after they had gotten in here and sat down. It vibrated again now.

He assumed it was Chuck calling, but he could be wrong. He would check later. He had already told his bro he'd be unavailable to talk that night, anyway.

He'd make time for Chuck tomorrow—and give him whatever update on the "stuff" happening tonight seemed appropriate and not under a high security alert.

One of these days he'd schedule a date with his brother to go someplace where they could talk and not be heard, where he could listen and respond to whatever was bothering Chuck.

Someday. Not now.

For the moment, he cast aside anything outside what was in his vision: Drew. Sitting on the floor as Patrick lowered the lights a bit.

Jonas Truro was acting as Drew's aide. The medical doctor who had been working with Patrick and others on the various formulas for the elixir now was the one to shine the bright light on Drew.

And now it was time to wait. To hope. To watch the shifter in wolfen form and hope that this time he would in fact shift—back to being Drew in human form.

To his surprise, Liam felt Rosa reach over to squeeze his hand where he'd rested it on his knee. Maybe it was okay now, since the lights around them had been dimmed and no one would be paying much attention to them, anyway. He turned his hand over and squeezed hers back.

They both needed some reassurance—even though everything that might or might not happen now was far from being anywhere in their control.

Still, he shot Rosa a quick, comforting glance, saw her smile slightly and turn back to watching Drew.

He did the same thing.

Drew moved his legs. Did that mean anything other than discomfort, frustration?

Yes! His rear legs began to firm up, elongate, grow larger. His front legs then started changing as well, back into the form of arms. At the same time, his body began taking his wolfen fur back inside. He grew larger, his head changing its form into one that was human. All of him was becoming human.

It was working!

Around him, Liam heard gasps of happiness, words of support, sounds of delight. Rosa squeezed his hand even more as she moved closer to his side, calling out Drew's name encouragingly. Liam did the same, catching her glance yet again, sharing happy smiles before again looking down toward the floor where Drew, naked except for a beach towel placed on him by Jonas, writhed, grimaced—and grinned.

Liam looked toward Melanie then. Her voice was perhaps the loudest, shrillest, happiest, and tears of joy ran down her face.

"Go, Drew," someone called—Noel? It turned into a group chant. "Go, Drew."

"Go, Drew."

That towel changed shape around him. Drew changed shape beneath it. And after a few minutes, the chanting still going on, Drew grabbed the towel with his now completely human hands, clutched it around himself as he stood and looked around, smiling broadly.

He was a tall man with hair that resembled his wolfen fur—dark, highlighted by silver. He appeared somewhat unsteady, yet he continued to stand, to smile, then to gesture with his hand that wasn't grasping the towel.

"Hi, everyone," he called. "I'm back!"

The celebration was beyond anything Rosa had ever seen before. Better than a family happy to retrieve an ill pet whose health had been restored at the veterinary hospital—or at least most families. Better than a major birthday party. Better than a wedding celebration, or milestone anniversary festivity.

Well, maybe her mind was exaggerating a lot, but everyone had gone upstairs to the main floor of the building, let the cover dogs out of their enclosures and entered an area Rosa hadn't seen before, a paved, high-ceilinged inside courtyard not far from the kennel.

She wasn't sure where the music came from, but it resounded throughout the room. It was upbeat, definitely danceable. Everyone watched and cheered and clapped as Drew took Melanie into his very human arms and led her around the improvised dance floor.

Two people, in love, dancing joyously. Lovely, Rosa thought. And appropriate. Even for a military unit? Well, why not?

At their feet, the wolflike dogs roamed the room, accepting pats from the other people there and acting as if they, too, were happy.

For the moment, Rosa was the only other woman there besides Melanie. She half hoped Liam would ask her to dance—but it was Patrick who requested that she join him.

Of course she did, as part of the ceremony. Besides, she'd heard he was married. But his wife, Mariah, was a well-known wildlife photographer, and Rosa gathered that she was off on some kind of research assignment. As far as Rosa knew she wasn't a member of Alpha Force, either, so she probably wouldn't have been there that day even if she was in town.

The song ended. "Thank you, m'lady," Patrick said to her, bowing at the waist.

What else could she do but curtsy? "And thank you, sir," she said.

"Hey, everyone," Liam called. He stood near the entry door, and Denny, beside him, held up a can of beer, with a case on the floor beside him.

Apparently, that was what Liam's aide had been up to, under the assumption that all would go well that night. He'd brought back drinks for the group to share, probably in a toast.

"Come on over here and grab a beer," Liam continued. "We're celebrating."

And in human form, Rosa thought. No chance of any of them shifting that night, at least not as far as she understood the process. She didn't know if drinking alcohol was ever good for shifters. She certainly wouldn't want to treat an inebriated dog.

But the celebration was clearly ongoing. As a result, she followed the others and picked up a can from the case. It felt cold, and she looked forward to drinking it.

"Let me propose a toast," Liam called, confirming what Rosa had anticipated. "To Drew, our amazing commanding officer, who's undoubtedly ready to command us once again."

"Hear, hear," everyone responded, lifting their cans in unison. In moments, they all had taken a swig of their beer—all except Drew, if Rosa was correct. He just held the can up and grinned widely, then waved it in the direction of Patrick, Jonas, Liam, Rosa and, finally and happily, Melanie.

He had, of course, drunk something else of great potency not long ago, so he was being smart, Rosa thought.

The crowd didn't stay together long, though. "I need to get this guy home for a good night's sleep," Melanie called out. "In his own bed, for the first time in a few nights." She wiggled her dark brown eyebrows in a suggestive manner that caused everyone to laugh.

Rosa figured, though, that the idea of a good night's sleep worked, but she doubted that Drew would be ready to take on any other enjoyable challenges in his bed that night. Not that she'd ever know.

Liam took hold of Chase's collar. "I'm taking my buddy home with me tonight," he pronounced. "How about the rest of you?"

The other Alpha Force members with cover dogs also took control of their own canine doubles—including Drew. He bent to hug Grunge, who had been among the others that evening. Melanie was the one to take control of Grunge, though. "Hey, guys, it's time for us to go home and see the kids," she told both shifter and dog.

Which made Rosa smile. She recalled then, though, that she had ridden here with Liam, and his BOQ unit was right here, at the other side of the base, from what she understood. "Would you mind dropping me off at my place?" she asked Melanie.

"No need." Liam was beside her now. "They need to head on home. I'll be glad to be your chauffeur again."

"Oh. Thanks." Though that might not be the most efficient thing, Rosa agreed that she didn't want to interrupt the married couple's attempts to get back into their routines now that Drew was himself again.

The entire group then dissipated. Rosa walked with Liam, Chase at his other side, as they headed to his car.

"That was amazing," she told him. "I anticipated that things would go well, of course, after all that went on with you last night. But since I'd been helping to keep an eye on Drew for the past couple of days I'm even more impressed that he's back in human form again. And that I got to see him shift. Shifting is—well, I don't know what to call it other than amazing."

"Yeah, it is. It's also a thrill for those of us who do it. Fun. Uncomfortable, sure, but well worth it."

"I'll bet it is." They'd reached Liam's car in the parking lot near the building, and Rosa got in while he leashed Chase in the back seat. When Liam got into the driver's seat, Rosa found herself asking, "Did you ever wonder what it would be like not to be a shifter? I mean, that's clearly so much a part of your life, what would you do if you lost the ability to shift?"

"Well, in our society, I'd rather get stuck in human than wolf form," Liam replied. "Especially after our little experiment, when I couldn't shift back as usual. I rather like being who and what I am, though. Shifters aren't fully unique, but we're definitely different from what's considered normal by most people. Good different. Really good different."

He hadn't started driving yet, and now he looked over at her, grinning. The expression on his handsome face did look smug, as Rosa anticipated. But there was more. The way he looked at her suggested heat and sexiness, as if one reason he was glad to be in human form at the moment was because of what he could do with his hard, muscular—and damnably sensual—body.

Which made Rosa wonder what it would be like to

make love to him, and the very idea—not for the first time—ignited her insides and moistened her in her most vital area.

Their eyes met and Rosa saw heat and desire in Liam's gaze, too, which only turned her on all the more.

But no. That was wrong. Inappropriate, no matter how good it might feel.

She forced herself to yawn, covering her mouth as she looked out the windshield. "Boy, this has been quite a day, hasn't it? I'm looking forward to going home and heading to bed."

Uh-oh. Dumb way to put it, since that only seemed more suggestive.

But maybe it was all in her own head, since Liam started the car and said, "Yeah, I'm tired, too. How about you, Chase?" He glanced in the rearview mirror, and his dog barked softly. "Right. Time to go get some sleep soon, boy." And then he drove out of the parking lot.

Okay, he had to be imagining things. But he thought he'd seen heat and even desire in Rosa's gaze. Where had that come from?

Yeah, his own desire for her, he figured. Driving her home was a good idea. They needed to leave each other's company, the sooner the better.

Unless… No. He needed to think rationally. Act rational. Get his mind off his yearning to strip the clothes off her curvaceous and tempting body.

He was just feeling like celebrating even more after the Alpha Force success of this day—and yesterday with him. That was all.

He had to calm down, though.

It dawned on him then that he was heading in the

direction of the veterinary hospital, but he wasn't sure where Rosa lived. Because they had previously discussed how things would go today, Rosa had taken a car service ride to the clinic that morning, after being told she would be driven to the base, and then home that night.

They were on the same wavelength, though—as they seemed often to be. "I figure you're driving us toward the clinic, and I do live near there," Rosa said, "so going this way is just fine. We're just about to cross over Mary Glen Road. But instead of turning left onto Choptank Lane, where the clinic is, make a right. I live on Porter Street."

"I was about to ask," he said, nodding. "I'm not familiar with Porter, so you'll also need to direct me when we get there."

"My place is a duplex, only about a block away from where we turn onto Porter."

With her instructions, they arrived at the place she designated in about five minutes. The street appeared entirely residential. Cars were parked along it, as well as in many of the driveways. Streetlights lined it, and most of the homes appeared to be single or two-family structures. Rosa's place was one of three duplexes in a row. It was two stories high, attractive, with a redbrick facade decorated by a large white front door and white window frames.

"Nice," Liam said.

"I like it. In fact, if things go as I think they will, I'm going to offer to buy the whole building. My landlady lives in the other unit, but she's been talking about moving. If so, I'll rent her place out."

"Great idea."

And it sounded like Rosa had every intention of staying here in Mary Glen. That was good. At this point, Liam had every intention of remaining in Alpha Force.

Not that he wanted her to stay in his life or anything. But it didn't hurt to have another skilled veterinarian besides Melanie in the area—

Who was he trying to kid? Himself?

He liked the idea of having Rosa in his vicinity. Too much.

Then again, he was in the military. He wouldn't remain at Ft. Lukman all the time, even though his main responsibility was using technology for the unit's good and therefore hanging out in his designated office. But having Rosa somewhere in the area was irrelevant to who and what he was. It had to be.

Still, he might as well enjoy her company for now.

He parked in front of her house, and she opened her door. Chase stirred a little in the back seat. Did he need a bit of exercise, or a walk for another reason?

He was at least a good excuse. Liam got out of the car, too, unsecured Chase from the back and put his leash on. "Care to go for a short walk with us?" he called to Rosa, who was watching them.

"Sure." She had been carrying the medical bag she had brought along earlier, and now hurried to place it on the stoop by her door. Then she joined them on the sidewalk below what appeared, in the muted light, to be a neatly trimmed lawn.

Liam walked slowly, watching as Chase sniffed the grass and pavement. Rosa stayed with them.

"He's a good dog," she said softly, "no matter what his background or responsibilities are working with you."

"Yes," Liam responded. "He is." Chase also appeared ready to go back inside. Time for them to head back to Ft. Lukman. But Liam didn't feel in any hurry. Still—should he ask Rosa if he could have a drink of water?

Tell her he wanted to discuss more about what happened that evening with her, in private?

Those could both lead to spending a little more time with her. Bad idea or not, he wanted to do so.

Before he said anything, though, she once again demonstrated their thoughts were somehow synchronized. "Would you like to come in with me for a little while—you and Chase? I could use another drink, and you seem sober enough to join me and still drive home safely. And maybe we could go over again what it really feels like to do…what you do, and Drew. It might help me in case I ever need to provide any veterinary treatment to the Alpha Force crew."

"Sounds good to me," Liam said. "And, yes, I'm sober. Maybe too sober. I'd love another drink, but I promise not to overdo it. I need to make it back to the base tonight in one piece, with Chase safe, too. And now that what happened tonight actually happened, I need to get up early tomorrow to dig back into my real work."

"All the more reason to have a drink together." Rosa had stopped walking, and in the light from the nearest streetlamp Liam could see that the expression on her face as she looked at him was somewhat sad. "We probably won't be seeing much of one another now that things are resolved."

"Maybe not," Liam said, "but since they were resolved favorably I'd be happy to toast it all again."

Chapter 14

Okay. Maybe Rosa wouldn't be seeing as much of Liam from now on, and maybe that was a good thing. It would mean there weren't any cover dogs—or shifted people— around Alpha Force who needed veterinary attention.

As she led Liam and Chase into her front hallway, she considered thanking him and telling him to leave. A few more minutes in his presence might only make her feel worse.

Although…maybe, if they talked over their drinks, she'd come up with a way to keep him nearby, at least for the immediate future.

"My kitchen is over here." She gestured beyond the open living room to their left toward the door just beyond it. "I'm much better at uncorking a bottle of wine or grabbing a beer bottle from the fridge than I am at mixing an honest-to-goodness drink, so I hope that's okay with you."

"Beer pretty much always works for me," he said, and she led Liam and his sweet wolf-dog down the hall.

Fortunately, Liam liked the ale she happened to enjoy and keep around. Rosa also put a bowl of water on the linoleum floor for Chase, then watched for a long minute as he began lapping it up. She felt enthralled and somewhat sad to see the dog refresh himself in her kitchen. Though Rosa didn't currently have any pets of her own, she of course adored animals. Why else would she have become a vet?

She had recently lost her only pet, a cat who'd lived a nice, long life and then left it peacefully. She missed having Rally around, but it had hurt so much to lose him that she had been waiting to rescue another.

When she finally looked up and took a sip of beer from the bottle she held, she saw that Liam was watching her instead of his dog. She felt a little embarrassed. Was her sadness obvious—or was he watching her for another reason?

"Let's go into the living room," she said. Not that sitting at her small kitchen table would be a bad thing, but they'd probably be more comfortable on her couch. Although maybe allowing Liam to get comfortable wasn't a good thing. Even so, she gestured to him and led him back down the hall in the direction from which they'd come. She didn't have potato chips or other snacks to share, but maybe that was okay. Maybe he would just drink his beer quickly and leave.

She sat on one side of her rather ordinary light green couch, and he sat at the other. She had end tables on both sides, so there were places for each of them to rest their beer when they weren't drinking.

She decided to start their conversation on a neutral

note—though it wouldn't be something most people would discuss. "So what's next with Alpha Force? I know your group is secret and there are things you can't talk about, but do you have any missions or whatever coming up?"

"You're right that it's secret, and I probably couldn't answer you if I happened to know something, but I don't. Best I can say is that some of our teammates aren't at Ft. Lukman right now, so I assume they're either on some kind of mission or engaging in practice maneuvers."

Liam's expression appeared wry—why did that wryness look so appealing?—and he lifted his bottle to his lips. His very sexy lips...

If Rosa had considered his presence here a possibly bad idea before, now she felt sure of it.

Or maybe it was a really good idea.

"Okay, then what can you tell me about Alpha Force and shifting that ordinary citizens like me are allowed to know about?"

"It's preferred that ordinary citizens not know anything," he responded, "except in very limited circumstances, like somehow getting involved in one of our operations, or being related to an Alpha Force member, or taking over veterinary care of one of us while shifted, that kind of thing."

"I definitely know part of that. And you know I'm fully aware of the existence of shapeshifters. What can you tell me about shifters that I probably don't already know?"

He laughed. Then he grew more serious. "Want to know why I'm really here tonight, Rosa?"

Her insides suddenly caught fire—with hope, she

realized, not necessarily because of what he was about to say. "Yes, I would."

"I wanted to have another opportunity to get together with you after all our meetings and whatnot this week. I figure we're both going back to our normal lives now, which is a good thing because it means that Drew will also hopefully get back to normal. But I've liked our discussions and… Well, you know."

She did know. But she wanted to tease him—especially since he happened to be describing exactly how she felt.

"No," she lied, "I don't know."

"Then let me remind you." Liam's beer bottle was suddenly on the table beside him, and he had moved his butt—his firm, sexy butt—closer to her on the sofa. Really close. He took her beer and put it down on the other table. And then Rosa was in his arms.

His kiss this time was the most erotic she had experienced with him, not just the generally friendly, though suggestive, lip contacts he had given her before. Somehow, he repositioned her so her back lay on the sofa, her head on its arm, with both his hands behind her—one gripping her behind.

His mouth was hot, and his tongue imposing in a delightfully sexy way. What could she do but kiss him in return?

His hands soon moved forward, first to touch her breasts, and then down to grasp her most sensual areas outside the slacks she was wearing—giving her a hint of what it would be like for him to really touch her there.

"Oh, Liam," she whispered against his mouth. They were supposed to be talking, weren't they? But this was much more fun. And then, impulsively, giving no thought to what she was saying—or was she blurting out exactly what she was thinking?—she said, "Let's go to my bedroom."

In reply, he gently rolled off her, and for a moment she missed the bodily contact. But he grabbed her hand, as if he was going to lead her, but instead said, "Take me there."

Which she did, out of the living room and to the end of the hall toward the stairway to the unit's second floor. She walked slowly up the stairs, still clasping his hand with one of hers and the railing with the other to keep herself from falling, thanks to her weakened knees, the way she kept turning to look deeply into Liam's dark, luminous, infinite brown eyes.

She heard the sound of Chase's paws as the dog followed them up the stairs, which were carpeted only in the middle. Soon they reached the second floor, which held two bedrooms and a bathroom. The master bedroom's door was around the landing, toward the front of the house, and Rosa led Liam there.

She hadn't had a relationship that encouraged her to bring a guy home since she'd started working here in Mary Glen. Now, after she turned on the lights, she looked at the room from the perspective of how seductive it was.

Not very, perhaps, with the mirrored dresser at one end and another chest of drawers at the far side of the closet door.

But the queen-size bed was in the center. Pillows were stacked at the end against the headboard, and the blue-and-green-patterned comforter covered the rest.

Sexy? Maybe not—but that bed absolutely looked inviting to her now in a way it never had before.

She glanced at Liam beside her. His eyes weren't on the bed, but on her. Eyes that spoke of desire. Eyes that appeared to strip her of her clothing as they slowly ranged down her.

But he didn't grab her or begin removing those clothes. Instead, he said softly, raggedly, "I want you, Rosa. You seem to want me, too. You know what I am, so before we do anything I want to make sure you——"

She grabbed him, pulling his head down so his mouth was on hers again. At the same time, she reached behind him and began tugging his camo shirt from his uniform pants.

Want him? Hell, yeah.

He maneuvered so he was soon unbuttoning her shirt. He pulled it off before she got his off, and in moments he took her breasts into his hands, massaging them roughly, but not uncomfortably, before removing her bra.

Her breathing turned ragged, her body heat became totally centered in her most sensitive areas—and soon, somehow, they both were naked and on top of her bed.

His hands were everywhere, on her nipples, below, all places on—and in—her that made her desire more than his fingers inside her.

At the same time, she took his hard, long erection into one of her hands, teasing it with her fingers, rubbing it up and down as it somehow seemed to grow even harder, more elongated.

"Rosa…are you ready?" His voice was even raspier now. Sexier.

"Oh, yes," she said, though she realized she might be making a big mistake. She had no protection here, or anywhere, since engaging in sex hadn't been part of who she was for the longest time.

She moaned as Liam suddenly pulled away, wondering for an instant if this was all a joke on his part—a very heated, sensual, unfunny joke. But as she watched in the dim light from the hallway, he moved off the bed and reached for his pants, which were on the floor beside Chase.

His dog moved his large, wolfen head from the area rug and looked at Liam as if taunting his master. Oh, yes, Rosa's imagination was on overdrive. Chase was an actual wolf-dog who didn't have human thoughts, yet she was ascribing mental acuity to him as if he was a shifter.

But she didn't think about the dog for long. She was relieved, happy—and admiring—when Liam extracted a small package from his pocket. He had brought a condom.

Good, smart, well-equipped guy, in more ways than one. His personal equipment outshone any Rosa had ever seen, in reality or fiction.

In moments, he'd sheathed himself and lain back down beside her. He began stroking her gently, as if she needed to be restored to sexual desire. At the same time, she rubbed his sheathed arousal.

And then he pulled himself up by his arms on the bed as if about to do a pushup—but instead held his body up by one arm while he used his other hand to aim his amazing sexual organ toward her own aching area.

The lovemaking act was every bit as incredible as Rosa had anticipated. She reached climax nearly immediately, as Liam apparently did, too.

Both breathing irregularly, they lay side by side for

a short while, holding hands, laughing, discussing what they had just accomplished.

And teasing one another. Rosa was delighted, and not at all surprised, when they did it again. And again.

She was also amused—and delighted—to realize that Liam was prepared for each act.

He stayed the night. She was glad.

And when she woke in the morning, hearing Chase moving on the floor, she hoped that all they had done that night was an introduction, not an ending, to their being together despite not needing to work on an Alpha Force issue together any longer.

Rosa wasn't exactly the domestic sort, but she still managed to make Liam and herself some breakfast—nothing fancy, though. Toast with butter and marmalade, coffee and an orange.

"Thanks," he said, as he sat at her kitchen table peeling the orange. "This is a great, sweet ending to a great, sweet time."

She had to laugh. "That's almost poetic."

"Yeah, it is, isn't it?"

They had both taken Chase for a short walk first, after showering and touching one another again and—well, taking more time than Rosa had anticipated to start their day.

But when they finished eating, she locked her home behind both of them as Liam fastened Chase into the back seat of his car. Her car was in the garage, since she'd left it there purposely yesterday and relied on a local ride-share service.

And so there was no more need, for Drew's sake or

Alpha Force's or any wolf-dog's, for them to stay in each other's presence any longer, at least not right now.

She stood near Liam's car and ignored the fact that neighbors could be watching when he took her into his arms and gave her one final kiss. "Hey," he said. "Looks like we'll need to plan to get together just for fun one of these days, right?"

"Right," Rosa replied, then initiated the kiss she figured would be their final, at least for a while, since Liam seemed interested in seeing her again. "Keep in touch." And then she walked away as Liam drove off.

And ignored the moistness in her eyes. It was better this way. Sure, the guy was damn sexy, but he was a shifter. A healthy shifter. One she had no reason to see anymore—except for fun? Or maybe just if one of the Alpha Force dogs needed some vet care.

Well, she would just have to see if he meant that he wanted to get together again. But he'd have to call her, since she wouldn't be calling him.

Care for him? Yes. But have an ongoing relationship with a shifter? And what if something happened and he became like Drew and didn't shift back right away?

Could she live with that? Did she want to find out?

She just wasn't certain.

A few minutes later, she was in her car driving the short distance to the clinic. It was difficult for her to drive.

For one thing, she felt exhausted. After all, she hadn't gotten much sleep. And she still remained aware of every inch of her body, which had been touched so sensually, so often, by Liam. Her usual white scrubs almost felt too constricting.

And those kisses this morning, despite being enjoyable, hadn't been too heated out in the sunlight of the early day. Even though she doubted she wanted anything long term with him, she missed Liam's erotic touches already.

Besides, this was the beginning of a new day of sorts. She was on her way to work, to do her job, to take good care of animals that needed veterinary care. Including a couple of spayings she'd been warned about by Susie, since the receptionist also kept the schedule.

Drew wouldn't be at the clinic. If he felt well enough, he'd probably have headed right away to Ft. Lukman to take charge again. And if he didn't, he'd stay home and rest in human form now.

Either way, Melanie would be thrilled. As she should be.

Would she want Rosa to take over more patients while she celebrated? Before, she had wanted to spend all her time as a veterinarian, possibly to keep her mind off how her husband was doing. Now, she might want to spend more of her time with him—although if he was at the military base that wouldn't work.

And their kids? Rosa figured little Emily and Andy would be delighted to see their daddy as much as they could now.

Rosa reached the clinic and parked her car. She entered, as always, via the back door, then went to wash her hands at the sanitary sink before letting Susie know she was here.

Melanie was in the back room washing her hands, as well. "Good morning," Rosa said. "And how are you today?"

Her boss's grin lit up her entire face. "A whole lot better than I've been for a while, that's for sure."

"I figured."

"Which is a good thing, since we're going to have a busy day. We'd scheduled a couple of dog spayings today before…well, before we got sidetracked."

"I know. Do you want me to take care of both?"

"No, let's each do one. Brendan can work with you, and Dina with me."

And so Rosa's day began. Both spayings were to take place that morning, and along with those patients were a few annual physicals, inoculations, a skin issue on a cat, an injury on a dog's paw.

A standard day at Mary Glen Veterinary Clinic— without a shapeshifter wolf in one of the exam rooms.

And no reason to believe that Rosa would hear from Liam any more that day.

Chapter 15

"So, any more social media posts about violent or murderous shapeshifters that we need to deal with?" asked Denny.

Liam had been sitting at the computer in his private tech office for an hour and felt a little stiff as he turned to look at his aide, who stood in the doorway.

"Nothing new posted within the last twelve hours," Liam said. "I've stopped having a good time making fun of all the dumb allegations, for now, at least, as well as the ones about shifters in general that make sense. I'm focusing on trying to find the sources of the original ones that contained all those false accusations."

"Any luck?" Denny came in and bounced into a seat beside Liam, scowling at the computer screen. The young Alpha Force helper, in his camos like the rest of them, appeared to have a lot more energy than Liam that day.

But it wasn't the seven-year difference in their ages that did it. No, Liam had engaged in lots of exercise and little sleep the night before—a very good thing.

Except it wasn't too helpful with his work here.

Neither was his regret that new posts had pretty much tapered off—nor his expectation that there would be more.

"Not so far," he said to Denny. "I gather that whoever did it might have some of the same skills that I do, the kind I taught you. They managed to create identities that make no sense if you dig into them, and the sources so far aren't clear. At least some of them are related, though."

"Yeah, like the ones who signed with the names of Greek or Roman gods. Well, knowing you, you'll figure it out." Denny popped up again, a grin raising the slight beard on his face. "I'll leave you alone for now, but I'll look forward to your showing me in more detail how you approached it. You're one damn great techie teacher!"

"Thanks. And now that you've complimented me like that, what can I do but comply and teach you more?"

"That's the Alpha Force spirit," Denny chortled, then left the room.

Liam hadn't wanted a distraction like that, but now he was glad it had occurred. He didn't feel like he was getting anywhere that day, and he was really frustrated.

But at least he was back on the job he was supposed to do, not just researching how a shifter could be denied the ability to shift back.

Still, even now that Drew was back almost to normal—they'd had a short meeting earlier where their commanding officer showed off how he looked and how his mind was working—Liam wondered how it had happened in the first place.

Not that it was in his job description to find that out, as it was the doctors like Patrick who'd figured out how to bring Drew back.

But even so… Instead of returning to his research on who'd really made those social media posts, he did some additional research of another kind: shapeshifter sorts of websites and all, those few that appeared to take it seriously, to check at locations he hadn't looked at before whether anyone suggested problems with shifting in either direction.

He had already discovered a site or two that sounded somewhat realistic, but even if they talked about things like different light emanations from a full moon or other triggers to shift or not to shift, nothing seemed potentially applicable to what Liam was looking for.

But he fully intended to make sense out of it somehow. Alpha Force had not only had its existence plastered somewhat over social media, but its members had been made to look like killers when they were shifted.

Sure, he'd laughed at the whole idea online on a number of sites, made jokes out of it, and got more people to agree with his foolishness than to seem to buy into the idea.

But it still wasn't good for Alpha Force.

He wanted to help his military unit now—and in the future. To envision, and help to bring about, everything the members could do to help their country. Change the world.

But to do that, they had to remain covert.

Which was difficult. Somewhat impossible. Yet Liam

intended to do all he could technologically and otherwise to accomplish that.

"Hey." Another voice called to him from the doorway. One most recognizable, and most welcome, especially now.

Drew's.

Liam turned. "Well, hi, boss. How ya doing?"

"A whole lot better now, partially thanks to you. You're probably the only other one around here who knows what it's like not to be able to shift back on schedule, though your circumstances were a lot different—despite being somewhat intentionally alike."

In his human form, Drew still resembled himself as a shifted wolf—at least a bit. He was slightly taller than Liam, and his dark hair was highlighted with silver—the way he'd looked at the veterinary clinic. Like Grunge, he had gold-colored eyes. His eyebrows were dark.

"Very true." Liam paused. "Do the guys have any idea yet why you didn't shift back naturally, let alone long after the moon wasn't full anymore? Something wrong with the original elixir?"

"Still checking into it. But—well, it doesn't hurt for you to know. The suspicion now is that somehow the elixir I drank wasn't the same as the one the rest of you had, or I was otherwise treated differently. But so far there's no evidence as to what it was or how it happened."

Liam looked into his commanding officer's face. "I've been checking the possibilities online, too, but nothing has stood out enough for me to even mention it."

"Well, keep at it." Drew walked up to Liam, slapped his back lightly and looked over his shoulder at the computer screen. "Anyway, thanks for all you did. I've asked Melanie to thank Rosa for participating in attempts to cure me, too. You can second that for me when you see her next."

Liam took a deep breath, then looked into Drew's face. His CO was grinning broadly.

"Not sure when that'll be," Liam said honestly. "Or if I'll see her again, since I'm not the one who takes ill cover dogs to the veterinary clinic or anything."

"Well, I maintained some of my human cognition, and I gathered that you two had something going on, or might someday. And speaking from my own experience, there's nothing wrong with getting involved with non-shifters if they happen to be veterinarians who believe in shapeshifting."

Liam laughed. "Maybe not." But then he grew serious. "I do like her. But not all women, or women veterinarians, are like the really great one you found." Although Liam had a sense that Rosa was even better. Still… "I'm just not sure about getting involved with anyone, shifter or not. There's just too much going on around here."

"I get it," Drew said. "Anyway, it's all your call. She's a nice lady, and you're right. I happen to have a particular affinity for veterinarians."

Drew then asked about what Liam had been up to, what he had found, and they discussed the online social media stuff dealing with shifters, some of it possibly correct and some of it clearly wrong.

And in a while, Drew thanked Liam again and left. "Time for you to do some more of your unique research," he said. "Let me know if you find anything interesting. Oh, and forget what I said about Rosa—unless you decide not to." He laughed, then left.

Liam figured he wasn't going to forget anything about Rosa. Not any time in the foreseeable future.

At least he had no reason to believe she could have been involved in what happened to Drew.

Although with her background knowing about shifters, her ability to access Drew and the rest of Alpha Force thanks to Melanie…

No. Surely it couldn't have been her, even if she had the knowledge and skills to mess with the elixir. He saw no motive for her to do such a thing. She seemed to like shifters. A lot.

Unless she was a damn good actress and had some reason he didn't know about to harm them. Maybe she'd even become a veterinarian to gouge at them more easily.

But why?

No. Couldn't be.

Yet if he was still going to seek answers, since the idea had now crossed his mind, it wouldn't hurt to see her under the pretense of dating…just to be sure.

And after last night—well, she would probably not be surprised if he happened to ask her out for dinner. Maybe even tonight.

Really?

Heck, yes.

Rosa sat at her desk in her small office, finishing up some records on the computer. She needed to finish fast, yet still do her usual thorough job of noting details, as well as questions, regarding the patients she had seen that day. She first reviewed her prior notes on the spayings, then began adding her most recent exams and treatments.

That's when she'd felt her phone vibrate in her pocket, and pulled it out.

Liam. His text message? Join him for dinner. Where?

No trouble guessing that: at his family's fast food place.

Well, that allowed him to kill two birds with one stone, though Rosa the animal lover always grimaced when she thought of that expression.

Even so... Rosa pushed the buttons to call Liam, smiling as she stared at the computer page in front of her where she'd been describing how she had treated that dog with burrs in his paw. The dog might still be limping a little now with that paw treated and bandaged, but should be fine soon.

"Hi, Rosa." The deep voice at the other end of the phone sounded pleased. And sexy. But then it always had sounded sexy to her, even before that aspect of their knowing each other had come true.

"Hi, Liam. Got your text. I'd love to have dinner with you tonight."

She considered suggesting someplace other than Fastest Foods. But she liked what they served, and she figured Liam always enjoyed the excuse to see his relatives again.

Well, for tonight—again—that was fine. But their dinner conversation would include some suggestions of other, nicer restaurants in town. She would be glad to pay her share, if that was the issue, or even treat him.

Assuming they continued to see each other...

"Wonderful. I'll pick you up at the clinic at—what? Six o'clock?"

"Sounds good. See you then."

That was only about an hour away.

And of course Liam was right on time. He called her on his phone from the clinic reception area, where he was waiting for her. "Susie is watching me. I don't see any ill animals out here, so I assume you can come now, right?"

"Right," Rosa said. "On my way."

She figured Susie was about to close the office, since Melanie had already left, saying goodbye first and letting Rosa know she was on her way home—to relieve her afternoon babysitter. Besides, though Rosa had hardly thought about it, today was Sunday and their workload was supposedly lighter—though that always depended on how many patients were brought in. Rosa was supposed to get a couple days off a week, but rarely took advantage. Melanie almost never took time off.

Right now, Rosa wondered when Drew would be home from the military base, if he wasn't already. As far as she could tell everything seemed normal, finally, with the Connell family.

Which made her feel very happy.

She shut down her computer and headed down the hall to the reception area. And sure enough, there Liam was.

He stood by the desk as if he'd been chatting with Susie. The room was empty except for them, a good sign that the clinic would be closed soon till early tomorrow. Unless, of course, an emergency called in.

"I'm ready to go," Rosa announced, looking first at Liam, then toward the receptionist. "Unless you say otherwise, of course."

"Hey, Doc, you're in charge here, not me," Susie said

with a laugh. Then, looking from Rosa to Liam and back again, she said, "And I'd imagine you're going to have a good evening whether or not I wish it for you, but… Have a good evening."

Laughing, Rosa wished her the same, then strode up to Liam's side. He was one good-looking tall, muscular guy, and tonight he was wearing a nice beige shirt over dark slacks—no sign of his military affiliation right then, unless she counted his short hair. "You have a good evening, too," Rosa told him.

"I'm planning on it." He held out his arm, and Rosa grasped it.

"See you Wednesday," she called to Susie as they exited through the outside door. Susie's days off this week were Monday and Tuesday.

Rosa had grabbed Liam's arm as part of the show, but didn't release it till they got to his car.

Chase was fastened in the back seat, and Rosa finally let go of Liam to open the rear door to give the dog a greeting pat. By then, Liam had opened the passenger door, and Rosa approached to get inside.

First, though, Liam pulled her close and gave her a quick but sexy kiss. Then he said, "That's just to ensure I'll have a good evening, like you told me."

In response, Rosa got close to him again and they shared another kiss. "My turn to ensure I'll have a good evening," she said, and then got into the car.

Yet on the drive there, she wondered how good her evening would be. Maybe it was her own mistake, since she'd asked Liam how his work as chief technology officer was going.

He had pulled onto one of the main streets on the way to the restaurant. The sky wasn't completely dark, so she could see the look he leveled on her then. "Not as good as I'd like it to be," he said.

"Really? Why not?"

"Maybe you can help," he countered. "Admit to me if you were one of the people who posted online about all the shapeshifters during the night of the full moon and all the horrendous misdeeds they accomplished."

He had to be joking, but his expression remained blank. He was focused forward while driving so she wasn't able to meet his glance as she responded as if he'd meant it, "You know I'd never do such a thing. I like and respect shifters. You've seen that."

"Just kidding," he said, though he didn't sound that way.

And Rosa kept quiet for the next part of their drive.

Chapter 16

Was it frustration that led to Liam's bad mood—frustration at not completely solving the puzzle that was his job, finding the identities of those who had posted those vile social media comments about shifters a few days ago?

He knew it hadn't been Rosa. He'd already given her a few moments of blame in his mind for causing Drew's difficult shift. And now this. Dumb. And wrong.

Heck, he had what he wanted for the moment: Rosa's company. His job, his responsibilities, his concerns—whatever the reason he was worried, it could all be put on hold.

"Hey, you know what?" he said.

"What?" Rosa's tone, unsurprisingly, sounded wary, and she didn't look at him. Which made him feel miserable. Having that beautiful lady look him in the eye—when he wasn't driving, at least—and smile at him, give him one of her sexy stares…well, despite his not-so-great state of mind, the idea aroused him now where the sun didn't shine.

"I could use your help," he replied. "One of the things I'm trying to do on the computer, in addition to figuring out who posted some really nasty and incorrect stuff about shifters, is to make it all into a joke. We'll be at the restaurant soon, but for now would you help me come up with some new ways to make fun of shape-shifters—so I can stick them up on the web and make people laugh at the whole concept?"

Rosa was the one to laugh. "In other words, you want this ordinary human being who just happens to know that shifters exist to help you convince others that it's all just a big joke?"

She was looking at him now. He had pulled onto the street where Fastest Foods was located and slowed down. "Exactly," he replied. "For example, one of the posts on a major social media site said something like the person heard so many howls under the full moon that he grabbed his phone to use as a camera. Sure enough, when he got there he claimed to have seen a bunch of wolves that, catching his smell, began to stalk him. He snapped a picture before running away, but when he looked there weren't any photos. He was convinced of what he'd seen, but mad they'd gotten away without his being able to prove they were werewolves. I figure it should be easy to make fun of him, since he can't substantiate what he saw. I've got some ideas, but what would you say?"

This was actually a situation he'd run into frequently after responding to people who'd claimed to have seen shifters, but hadn't captured any pictures.

Sure enough, Rosa came up with almost exactly what he'd replied sometimes—dumb, corny, yet cute enough to make fun of the supposed shifter-viewer. "Easy," she said. "Just reply 'Were' and when they follow up reply something like 'Were? Where! Where are the weres?'"

Liam laughed. They'd unfortunately reached the restaurant parking lot and its long line at the drive-through. He considered driving around the block to give them more time to create answers to the posts he could describe to her, but figured this wasn't a good time for that.

But it would give them something else to talk about in private, in the future, when fellow diners wouldn't be eavesdropping.

"Hey, I think you'd be good at my job, too," Liam said. "One of these days I'll make a list of some of the idiotic posts that claim there are werewolves around, and get your input before I respond to them." Except for the ones that claimed shifters had hurt regular people around here—possibly shifters connected to the military. Those he didn't want to talk to her about.

Those he would deal with himself.

After pulling into one of the few vacant spots in the crowded lot Liam opened his car door and wasn't surprised when Rosa did the same. In fact, she was the first to open the back door to unhook Chase from his safety constraint.

Rosa was a veterinarian. A woman in charge. Someone who could take care of herself.

Just another reason he couldn't help feeling attracted to her—which he had to tamp down before it slugged him even harder in the gut.

Rosa might be a woman in charge—but she wasn't

Melanie Connell, not only knowledgeable that shifters existed, but willing to hook up with one permanently.

Although the sex he had shared with Rosa...

"Hey, Chase," Rosa said, as Liam got close to them on the smooth asphalt and held out his hand for his cover dog's leash. "Wouldn't you rather walk inside with me tonight?"

She reached down to pat the wolf-dog's head, and Chase leaned into her touch, clearly happy for the attention.

Which made Liam wish for a little attention, too.

"Okay," he said. "You've got him for now. But remember, boy, you're my cover dog, not hers." Liam had kept his voice low despite not seeing anyone with them in the lot. When he looked at Rosa, she grinned at him, then turned to lead Chase inside the back door of the restaurant.

As always, the aroma of cooked meats permeated the air. A good thing. And as he'd expected, the place was packed. He considered suggesting to Rosa that they go someplace else. In fact, one of these days he would ask her on a real date, where they could dine well without running into his family.

Although at the moment, eating here was the best way for him to find the time to see Chuck and Carleen.

"Hi, guys!" They were greeted nearly immediately— by Valerie. "Come on in. Are you eating here? I'll find you a table right away."

"Thanks," Rosa said, then glanced back at him. "I take it you do want to stay."

He nodded. "As long as it won't hurt the place's business."

"Anything but, since you've got your dog here, too,"

Valerie said. "Customers like dogs. Too bad Louper's at home today." She winked at him then.

The woman wouldn't quit, would she? But Liam hadn't ever faced off with her and made it clear he didn't really want to flirt with her.

And he certainly didn't with Rosa around.

Rosa had clearly seen the wink, since although she appeared to be scanning the full restaurant for a table, her body seemed to freeze for an instant. Chase, sitting beside her, stood as if he sensed her tension.

Maybe Valerie's actions were a good thing for triggering Rosa's interest in him, Liam thought. But did he really want her interest?

And if so, did he want it this way?

"Hey, bro." It was another feminine voice speaking from off to their side, this time Carleen's. "Glad to see you. Hi, Rosa, and Chase, too."

Hearing his name, Chase looked up. Rosa looked sideways and said, "Hi, Carleen. Good to see you."

Did she mean it? Rosa was a nice, polite lady, so he wasn't sure about her feelings regarding his family. But she never objected to coming to Fastest Foods and she undoubtedly knew she'd see them there, so she must be okay with it.

They soon got in line and despite the number of people ahead of them received their food—a hamburger for him and a salad for Rosa—fairly quickly. They'd left Chase in the corner at the table Valerie had found for them among the crowd of noisy patrons, and were soon sitting there eating.

But not alone, as it turned out. "Can we join you?" Carleen asked. She held a tray containing a couple sandwiches. Liam assumed he would see his brother behind her, but instead of Chuck she was accompanied by Valerie.

He looked toward Rosa, across from him, for her opinion and she nodded. "Sure," he said. And then, as they sat down, he asked, "So where's Chuck?"

"In the kitchen," Carleen said. "Where else? He's helping our main cook, since one of our assistants called in sick. I'll go spell him there soon as we're through."

"Great," Liam said.

Valerie started a conversation then about Rosa's veterinary practice, asking the number of dogs she worked with versus the number of cats, what other kinds of pets came to the clinic and that kind of thing. It seemed like a pleasant conversation. At least Rosa appeared happy to respond.

At a lull, Carleen asked, "How long have you been here in Mary Glen?"

"About a year," she responded.

"How did you happen to end up here?"

Rosa shot a somewhat pleading, somewhat exasperated look toward Liam as if asking for his help. He knew the story, but also knew she didn't want to talk about it, even to shifters—especially in public.

"From what I gather," he said, "Dr. Melanie Harding Connell was in need of a new vet to help her and Rosa just happened to fit her criteria." There. That was true, but it was general enough not to make any waves.

"That's right." Rosa sounded relieved.

The table nearest him emptied then, and it didn't take long before there were other customers seated there. The group of twentysomething men and women who were about to leave stopped near their table, though, as if to say goodbye.

One guy, with a shaved head and short dark beard, waved in the direction of Carleen and Valerie, who sat next to one another. He was followed by the other two guys, who were dressed similarly to him, and the girls who wore casual yet flowing dresses in shades of pink. "See ya soon," the first guy said. "You know we'll be back."

"Hope so," Carleen said.

"When are you getting those summer seasonal sandwich combos that you've been promoting?" one of the girls asked. She was taller than the other two, with short, blunt dark hair.

"It's still May," Carleen said. "We're starting them in June."

"Got it," the girl said. "We'll definitely be back before then, won't we, Horatio?" she asked one of the men.

"Of course."

They turned to leave at last. As they did, the girl said to one of the other guys as they maneuvered away, "But can you wait till June for that summer fruit salad combo with a double burger that they're promoting now, Orion?"

Orion? A Greek god's name? One of the names in some of the worst posts about what shifters had done under the last full moon—a writer whose real identity Liam had been trying to track down.

"Excuse me," he said, standing to follow them. He took Chase's leash, partly as an excuse to go outside, and partly in case he needed assistance from a current canine if his target recognized what Liam was after and didn't want to cooperate. Chase might be a cover dog, but he was also protective and would attack if anyone attempted to harm Liam.

He saw Rosa's puzzled glance but had no time to explain now—and probably wouldn't want to explain later, at least not as long as they were here.

But by the time Chance and he weaved their way out of the restaurant, all he saw was the suspicious group of people entering an unmarked SUV, probably a shared ride they'd called.

He noted the license number just in case, but figured that wouldn't help identify any of them, let alone Orion.

Damn.

Rosa could tell by Liam's furious expression and the way he hurried after those people that they'd said something to really trigger something inside him. But what?

She remained at the table with Carleen and Valerie, who had stared after him and then returned to eating, pretending nothing was wrong. This was pretty much the first time Rosa had been in their presence when Liam wasn't there. She had no problem being with them. She'd have been friendly and pleasant even if they hadn't been Liam's family members.

Although maybe it would have been less stressful if there hadn't been a connection—especially the possible attraction between Liam and her.

"So tell me something about your upcoming seasonal meals," Rosa said to Carleen, so they'd have something to talk about. Carleen's smile looked a bit relieved, as if she, too, had been searching for a way to start a conversation. For the next few minutes she described how their new dishes were still fast food, but would have sides like fruit and salads that were a bit healthier.

Not necessarily things that shapeshifters like them were likely to enjoy, at least not when they were in wolf form, Rosa thought. But she didn't mention that even teasingly—especially here, where they were still surrounded by a crowd of probably regular people, like her.

Valerie ate her burger and drank water with it, but only picked at her french fries. Liam had told Rosa that his family members, including his sister-in-law and her relatives, were also shifters. Rosa was curious about how the non–Alpha Force members did under a full moon around here, but clearly couldn't ask that, either. She of course knew that Chuck and Carleen, as Liam's close relatives, had been part of that experiment the military unit was trying with their special elixir. Another topic not to get into, despite her curiosity.

To everyone in town, including these people, she was merely a veterinarian at the local clinic working with animals who needed medical attention.

And she wasn't supposed to talk about how, sometimes, some of her patients were of human background.

It didn't take long to exhaust the topic of the new meals. Rosa mentally searched for something else to discuss that wouldn't lead to anything secret or controversial.

Where was Liam? When would he get back here?

As it turned out, his brother got to the table first. "Hi, ladies. I assume it's okay if I join you." Without waiting for an answer, he sat down on the chair Liam had previously occupied. Fortunately, there were a few other empty chairs around, so Liam could commandeer one on his return. Assuming he did return soon.

Rosa certainly hoped he would.

Chuck carried a burger—what else?—and a glass of water on a small plastic tray. Once again, Rosa noticed the similarity in the brothers' appearances, although Chuck, slightly older, wasn't quite as good-looking as Liam.

Rosa worried that, in her mind at least, no man, whether a relative or not, seemed as good-looking as Liam. Well, it was okay to be attracted to him, as long as she kept reminding herself that their relationship was based more on their respective backgrounds and careers than on any independent attraction. Fun, yes. Long-lasting? Unlikely.

"So," Chuck said after he was seated. "I saw Liam sitting here before. Where is he?"

"Oh, he got up a little while ago," Valerie said. "Looked like he had something on his mind."

"Like the restroom," Carleen said with a grin. Rosa wasn't about to contradict her, since that could lead to a discussion she didn't want to have. She knew what had triggered Liam's departure—those people. What she didn't know was why.

For the next few minutes, Chuck talked about how good business had been that day.

"You always look busy when I come here," Rosa said.

"Which is a good thing," responded Valerie.

Before they got any further, Liam finally returned, Chase leashed and maneuvering behind him among the crowded tables. Liam clearly saw the situation and brought a vacant chair with him.

"Hi, bro," he said, sitting down. Chase lay on the floor beside him.

"Hi back, bro." Chuck scooted the open paper wrappings that contained Liam's food toward him—half of a burger and some onion rings.

Rosa wondered if Liam would mention why he'd left for a while, and he did. Sort of.

"So, Carleen," he said, "those folks who stopped here to talk about your new menu. Sounded like you know them."

"I know them as frequent customers," she agreed. "But that's all. Why? Do you know them? Is there something…about them?"

Rosa wasn't sure if Carleen was asking if they were shifters, too, or something else. She was interested in the answer.

"I just heard recently about a guy named Orion. Interesting fellow, and if that was the same one, I wanted to talk to him. Do you happen to know where he works? Where he lives?"

"No, like Carleen said, they're customers," Chuck said. "All of them, and some others, too, who are sometimes with them. Don't know if they work together or live in the same area or what, but they seem like one big crowd."

"Got it," Liam said. "Well—tell you what. Rosa and I will be heading out of here when we're done eating, but I'd like to follow up with those guys, especially Orion. Would one of you call me next time they come in?"

"Sure," Valerie responded. "But what should we tell them?"

"Not a thing," said Liam. "I'll just head here if I can and make contact with them. Since why I'd like to say hi is a little obscure and I might just forget about doing it, there's no need for you to mention it to them."

"Okay…" Carleen said, drawing the word out as if she was confused. Rosa figured they all were.

She wanted to get Liam off alone to get an explanation. Assuming he'd give one to her, since he hadn't to the others, and they were closer to him than she was.

He changed the subject then, and soon they were laughing over some stories Chuck related about a few customers—not those—who had tried to wheedle their ways into jobs at Fastest Foods. But their klutziness with their own bags and trays of stuff made it clear they wouldn't be able to handle the work here.

In just a few minutes, though, Chuck finished his last bite of sandwich and rose. "I've got to get back to the kitchen. Carleen, you, too."

"And me," Valerie said. "I've got some cleaning to do."

They all said their farewells to Liam and Rosa. Rosa was glad. She'd thought it might take some maneuvering and even begging a bit to get this evening ended. She wanted to go home and rest—and ponder all that had happened today. Not as much as on some days recently, but she was tired nonetheless.

Although if Liam decided to come to her place to tell her what all that had been about before, she would be glad to give him a good-night drink.

And if it led to more... Well, that was hoping for too much.

Plus if he really thought she could be making absurd comments online—well, she certainly hoped he was just considering everyone and didn't really believe it could be her.

A short while later they were in his car. He had to drive her back to the clinic to get her vehicle. And maybe that would be the end of the evening.

But Rosa hoped not. And so once they were settled with Chase in Liam's vehicle and he'd begun to drive out of the parking lot, she said, "I know there's something going on, and I want to hear about it. I'll even

bribe you to let me know. Follow me to my house after
we get my car, and I'll give you an after-dinner drink."
And hopefully confirm that he didn't really mistrust her.

He pulled up at a stop sign under a streetlight and
glanced over at her. "A drink sounds good. Spending
some time talking—and maybe more? That sounds even
better."

How could she refuse?

Chapter 17

A short while later, Liam and Chase were with Rosa in her living room. She had, as promised, poured drinks for Liam and herself, a nicely aged brandy from a well-known manufacturer that she particularly liked.

They first tapped glasses as Liam toasted shifters and people who helped shifters. That made Rosa laugh, but the intense and sexy expression on his face caused her to grow more serious.

"So," she said, to change the subject that was now percolating not only in her head, but in the rest of her body. "Tell me why you chased those people out of Fastest Foods."

".I didn't chase them out of there. As I said, I wanted to catch up to them. Talk to them."

"About what? I gathered your family doesn't know them well, only as sometime customers. What's going on?"

Liam took a deep sip from his glass, then put it down on the end table beside him. He turned back toward Rosa.

"Okay," he said, "I'll tell you—because I know you can be discreet. You know the reality about the existence of shifters, and you keep it to yourself except when talking to your boss and others with direct connections to Alpha Force. Or that's the way I see it. Right?"

"Yes, that's right." She swallowed a hint of hurt at his feeling he needed to ask for her confirmation. He knew her that well, at least, didn't he?

She felt a little better as he continued, indicating he must trust her, after all. He started telling her more of what he apparently didn't want anyone else to know.

It was about his job—his real job with Alpha Force as its chief technology officer. And about what she knew he'd been doing: researching online social media posts about shifters and shifting, particularly related to the last full moon—had it been only a few nights ago?

"Those posts that all but accused Alpha Force shifters of doing some real damage, particularly against people in the vicinity of Ft. Lukman—I've found a bunch, and so has Denny. Like I described to you—and you helped me with—we've made fun of them online to help make people who don't know the reality of shifting think it's all a big joke. No way of guaranteeing that, of course, but some of the comments we get in return make it appear that a good percentage of those who aren't sure at least enjoy the jokes—and hopefully consider them more of the reality than what's actually true."

"I get it." Rosa took a sip of her smooth, intoxicating brandy. "I've seen that kind of thing online, too, and have since I was a kid and started learning about shifters. Some people just like to talk about them, although most seem not to accept their reality." The fact that Liam had suggested she might be doing that now had hurt, but at least he'd retracted it.

"Which is generally a good thing on our behalf. And fortunately, a lot of the posts seem to be about books and movies, all fiction, that portray shifters the way their creators want them to appear. But a few seem real—and those that claimed that shifters injured people this last time mostly sound genuine, but they're not. Those who posted them sound frightened, though, and afraid what will happen during the next full moon and after."

Rosa pondered that for a few seconds. "But you're sure no shifter around here did hurt anyone, right?"

"I checked with all Alpha Force members, and Denny and I both looked online for the claims of what was done and the identities of those who were allegedly harmed—and it all seemed false. I also looked for the identities of the people who posted those claims…and one was named Orion."

Rosa felt her eyes widen. "Ah. That's why you chased those folks, including the guy called Orion. And it also makes sense that you'll keep trying to find him." She paused and took another sip while looking into Liam's deep brown eyes. They looked angry. And at the same time, she got a sense that he felt pleased that she now understood. "Isn't Orion a Greek god? A hunter?"

"Yeah, which also worries me. Some of the other people who posted that stuff also had mythological names. Don't know if it's the same person or a group, or they're just imitating one another, but whoever they are, they've made it nearly impossible to track down their origins—

and I'm usually damn good at doing that." This time, Liam nearly finished what was left of his brandy in one gulp. "And by the way, one person who was out there a lot was named Diana. That could be her real name. It's a somewhat popular name. But—"

"Wasn't Diana the Roman goddess of the hunt?" Rosa pondered that. She hadn't spent much time study- ing mythology as a kid, but she'd always been interested in myths involving animals, so she'd learned at least something about it.

"That's right," Liam said. "And guess what? Diana's also the Roman goddess of the moon. Appropriate, don't you think?"

"Definitely." Rosa considered offering him more brandy, but if he was driving back to the base she didn't want to encourage him to do something dangerous, like getting drunk.

"Anyway, that's your answer. I want to talk to Orion, or at least the guy who was called that by his friends at the restaurant. He might have nothing to do with this situation. His name might actually be Orion, though I've never met an Orion before."

"Me, neither, though I've always enjoyed viewing the Orion constellation on clear nights when it's around."

"Ditto." Liam smiled at her. This time his smile seemed genuine. Amused. Caring?

She could be reading a lot into it.

A lot that she wanted to see there.

"Tell you what," he said.

"What?"

"Let's take Chase out for a short walk. That way he won't bother us."

"He never bothers me," Rosa responded, though she had an idea where Liam was leading her.

"Not me, either. But I want him to sleep later while we're…" He stood and held his hand out to Rosa. She put her glass down and grasped his warm, firm, sexy fingers.

He pulled her close, and the kiss they shared then made it very clear to Rosa where they were going that night.

And it would be a very good thing if Chase was nice and empty and sleepy, so he wouldn't bother them till they were ready to get up in the morning.

Liam stayed overnight. A good thing. A really good thing.

And over the next couple of weeks he managed to spend even more time with Rosa, sometimes volunteering to take cover dogs into the vet clinic for checkups, sometimes just asking Rosa out on a date—and not always at his family's fast-food joint. She invited him to her place often for dinner, too, which he liked. A lot.

Enough to not worry about whether he was seeing her too much. Enough to feel certain that the little hiccups of accusation his mind had aimed toward her now and then were totally false. If—when—they stopped seeing each other so much, or at all, he'd simply have to deal with that. And since neither of them wanted to call what they had any kind of relationship except for having fun…well, that was fine for now.

Meanwhile, he also popped in at Fastest Foods sometimes on his own. No one had called him to say that Orion or anyone in that group had stopped back in, but just in case…

For though he still found posts to make fun of that mentioned shifters, he remained unable to track down in cyberspace the true identities of those who'd posted the nasty allegations against shifters, especially those supposedly in the military. Frustrating. Very frustrating for someone with his vast online skills.

Each time he went to the restaurant, he spent at least a few minutes talking to Chuck. At first his brother seemed to have calmed down after being upset with Liam, but not explaining why.

As time went on, Chuck seemed more snappish again, and Liam finally took him aside and confronted him about it.

"You know what it's about." Chuck glared at him, not a particularly good thing, since they stood facing each other in a corner of the kitchen—and sharp-edged knives used to carve veggies and fruit for the June menu were on the counter.

Not that Liam really figured his brother, who so resembled him physically, was angry enough about whatever to attack him. But he still wanted to know Chuck's supposed rationale, to be sure.

"Pretend I don't, and tell me," Liam said, crossing his arms and leaning against the wall.

Chuck drew closer, so close that his mouth nearly touched Liam's ear. "Shifting," he whispered. "Are Carleen and I going to get to—you know."

Ah. Liam did know. He'd definitely suspected that was the reason, but Chuck knew Liam had no say over whether the experiment continued and he'd be able to allow his brother and sister-in-law to get a dose of the elixir under the next full moon.

The upcoming full moon. It was getting closer.

And Alpha Force intended to be better prepared for it. In fact, Liam was scheduled to engage in a practice shift tomorrow evening.

But would Chuck and Carleen be happy when they next changed naturally under that full moon because they'd gotten a dose of the elixir and kept their human cognition?

Liam could make no promises.

"I don't know," he responded. "I'm not sure where the experiment stands right now. Everyone seemed okay with how things worked out last time, but that could mean they don't need to experiment again for a while. Or it might mean you and a couple of others at other locations could be permanent elixir-drinkers. I'll check, though I don't know if any decision has been made yet."

Their conversation ended then because Carleen and Valerie joined them. "Hey, brother," Carleen said. "I've got your lunch on the tray over there. I'm going to eat now, too, and intend to join you at one of our wonderful tables. You okay with that?"

Liam was definitely okay with that. In fact, he appreciated that his kind sister-in-law must have recognized what was going on and decided to stop it.

And when he sat at the table, it wasn't just Carleen who joined him, but Chuck and Valerie, too. They had a nice, friendly conversation as if they were just regular family members without anything else on their minds.

Liam got up to refresh his water glass, needing a moment to breathe despite how well things were going. When he returned, a woman was standing there talking to the others. She was a pretty lady with short blond hair and narrow red lips, and looked vaguely familiar.

Was she one of those who'd been with Orion?

Apparently so, since Chuck said, "I just asked Johnna

here if she knew where some of the others she ate with the other day happened to be now."

"Chuck said you wanted to talk to Horatio or Orion, right?" she asked.

Not wanting to appear too eager, Liam just nodded.

"Haven't seen either of them for a week or so, but next time I do I'll try to bring them in."

"Great," Liam said, and hoped that would actually occur.

But he wouldn't hold his breath.

If the decision whether Chuck and Carleen could use the elixir again had been made, no one was informing Liam yet.

He'd spent last night at Rosa's—again. He'd told her about his frustration that day at meeting Johnna but still not learning more about Orion.

He had also told her he was about to imbibe some more of the elixir and shift outside the full moon—tonight.

"You're sure you'll be okay?" she had asked while they were lying in bed, resting after a really great bout of no-holds-barred sex, his favorite, especially now that he was engaging in it with Rosa.

Too bad he couldn't convince himself he could go there every night forever.

He couldn't convince himself of that because Rosa still seemed remote at times, concerned…and unsure whether she really wanted to be doing this with a shifter, although she never said so aloud.

But that made Liam doubt himself and his strong internal goal of someday having regular people accept shifters as they were. That couldn't happen if even someone like wonderful, dedicated veterinarian Rosa, who knew and worked with shifters, didn't necessarily want to have a long-term personal relationship with one.

"Of course I'll be okay," he'd asserted, hoping he was right.

"I assume Melanie won't be there. Could I hang out on the base just in case you…you need some veterinary assistance?"

That was sweet of her. Although, in some ways, it was just part of who she was. Part of her job.

The veterinarian that she was would care for any animal in need, no matter how he'd gotten in animal form.

Which was all the more reason for Liam to not get any further involved with her. She might care for shifters in either form—but still not completely accept them as equals.

And now he was back at Ft. Lukman, down in Drew's office on the lab floor, where Drew was telling Denny and him and the others who'd be with them that evening about the formulation of elixir Liam would be taking.

"It's just the latest regular formulation," Drew said, leaning forward with his arms folded on his desk. "Although, since it's the same formulation I took on the night of the last full moon, we're testing it again—on you. You're okay with that?"

"I was okay with testing the stuff that wouldn't let me shift back, so why not the latest good stuff that let everyone but you shift back during the last full moon?" Liam grinned at his boss, although inside he kind of wondered if he was being told the truth.

Well, he did trust Drew. And his fellow Alpha Forcers. And what good would it do any of them to lie to him?

But he was, after all, one of their latest recruits, so

he could be subject to more stressful and questionable
stuff than most of the others…

"Why not the good stuff indeed?" Drew rose and,
maneuvering around his desk, approached Liam. "And
I still appreciate your agreeing to be our test shifter the
last time, to try to make sure I was given the right stuff
to make me normal."

"Oh, you're always normal, boss," Liam said, as he
stood and they grasped hands. "Besides, I'm nearly always ready for a shift. Looking forward to tonight's.
You going to be there keeping an eye on me?"

"Sure," he said. "And since Melanie has to stay home
with the kids, I'm hoping your buddy Rosa will be there
to ensure all goes well when you're shifted."

"I'm hoping that, too." And when the meeting was
over and Liam called Rosa, he confirmed that she definitely would be present.

Which somehow made him feel more relieved about
tonight's shift.

Rosa was with them again, in the woods at the far
side of Ft. Lukman. The sky was dark, the air cool.

"You good to go?" Denny asked Liam. Those two
Alpha Force members stood side by side beneath a canopy of dark trees, while others from their military unit
hung out nearby, talking.

Rosa was closest to Liam and Denny, yet not part
of either group.

This was beginning to feel familiar to her, though.
Too familiar?

Not hardly. It was only the second time she had been
here for any shift. But the shifter, once more, was Liam.

Would this one be like last time, when his Alpha

Force teammates had purposely made it hard for him to shift back? Supposedly not…but what if they hadn't told him the entire purpose for this exercise?

Last time, she had been curious. Interested. Caring, yet not emotionally involved except for wanting to ensure the animal Liam became remained healthy.

This time—well, they had a relationship of sorts now. A fun one filled with companionship and sex. And yes, she had sort of admitted to herself that she would fall in love with him if she let herself.

Assuming she wasn't already.

No. This definitely wasn't the time to puzzle over that. Too many things to think about. Too many issues and problems and—

"You ready, sir?" Denny spoke to Liam, his tone somewhat satiric. He held a glass vial of some clear liquid—obviously that all-important elixir. And beside Denny on the ground was the large battery-operated light that Rosa understood was supposed to resemble and act somewhat like a full moon.

"Yes, Sergeant," Liam responded, his own voice also sounding somewhat mocking. "Hand it over, my trusted aide."

The other Alpha Force members who were there— Drew, Patrick, Jonas and Noel—had stopped talking and now looked at Liam and Denny. "It's time," Drew acknowledged. "Go ahead."

Nodding, Liam took the vial from Denny and drank the liquid within. When finished, he began removing his clothes—glancing at Rosa with a smile that looked teasing as he got down to his underwear.

And then he removed that, too.

One quick look at her, and then all his attention

seemed, appropriately, to focus on Denny. Denny lit the lantern and aimed it at the nude, attentive man beside him.

In moments, Rosa watched as Liam went down on his knees, his limbs began moving and shrinking, his body started to grow its wolfen hair.

His shift had begun.

Chapter 18

It had been short. It had been sweet.

And now Liam was already back in human form.

That had been the intent for this shift. A test to ensure that the elixir was still a good formulation and still did its duty. That all was well with Alpha Force, although there would be a bigger test for all of them in a few nights, under the next full moon.

And fortunately, it did appear that all was well.

Beneath the canopy of trees, Denny had helped him put his clothes back on. Liam was tired, but nothing unusual about that.

Next, Drew and the others who were medical doctors conducted a quick physical exam and pronounced him well and in good condition.

He'd made sure not to look at Rosa till he was dressed once more. And when he did, she was on her cell phone, not watching him.

Although he had glanced at her as he had shifted back and noticed her attention was fully on him. And now she seemed slightly furtive, as if she was purposely pretending not to notice him for now.

But he suspected that wasn't true.

If he hadn't been so tired, and if his body hadn't had at least some residual of the elixir's formula within it, he might even have suggested they engage in a late drink to toast what had happily occurred.

Instead, though, his commanding officer approached her. "Thanks, Rosa, for being here. But I have to say I was glad your services weren't needed."

She shoved her phone into her jeans pocket and gave a smile that Liam wished had been directed at him. "I'm glad, too. I assumed all went as well as it appeared to, right?"

"Right," Drew said, moving in Liam's direction. He motioned for Rosa to join him, which she did. "I'll be telling Melanie soon not only how well things went, but how much I appreciated your being here just in case."

The crowd began to disperse then. Denny was directed to take Liam back to his quarters, while Drew motioned for the others to join him as he walked Rosa to her car.

But the night wasn't completely over. Once Liam was back at his place and getting ready to go to bed, he called Rosa.

"Thanks again for being there," he told her.

"I'll be there again during the full moon," she replied.

"Great. And hopefully we'll get together before then."

"I'd like that," Rosa said, making Liam grin and parts of him rise to attention.

"Dinner tomorrow night...to discuss all this?" he suggested.

"Good idea," she said, and when they hung up Liam was definitely hopeful that they would do more than eat and talk.

Rosa had felt so good at Liam's test shift. Who knew that she would wind up caring so much about a shapeshifter?

Well, it was partly her job. Speaking of which, she was at work now, about a week after that shift. She was in one of the exam rooms—the one that had been occupied by Drew when he had been staying there, in fact. But today she was waiting for Brendan to bring in an aging rottweiler with kidney issues that just needed a follow-up exam after the meds she had put him on.

She had spent several evenings—and nights—with Liam since then, including his staying overnight at her place the night after his test shift. She had talked to him often in between, too.

Time had passed quickly. The moon would be full tonight.

And she had plans to go to the military base just to watch and be there and offer veterinary help if any of the shifters needed it while in wolf form.

Her phone began vibrating in her pocket. Since her latest patient hadn't yet come in, she pulled it out.

Liam. Her heart began racing. Was he okay? Was all in order for the major shifting that would go on that night?

And why was she so worried?

"Hope I'm not calling at a bad time," Liam said when she answered, which made her feel better.

"I wouldn't answer if I couldn't talk, but I can't talk for long."

"Quick question. Can you join me for dinner at Fastest Foods tonight before—"

The exam room door opened and Brendan brought in Graf, the rottweiler.

"I'll look forward to it," Rosa said. "Gotta run now." And then she hung up—smiling and looking forward to that evening, or at least the beginning of it.

Liam, sitting back on his chair in his office at Ft. Lukman, patted Chase on the floor beside him, stared at his computer screen and shook his head.

He had second thoughts after his phone call with Rosa. Not about getting together with her for dinner. Oh, no, he really wanted to see her, even spend a little time with her, since it had been a couple days since their busy schedules had allowed them to do more than talk on the phone.

Unfortunately, he still hadn't solved his problem regarding the identification of whoever had made those totally false claims against what was probably supposed to be Alpha Force, after the night of the last full moon.

And he had spent a lot of time on it, ramping up the amount and intensity over the past week—since another full moon was coming that night. Definitely frustrating.

Even so, the second thoughts he was experiencing involved where Rosa and he would meet tonight. He'd enjoyed dining at other Mary Glen locations with her.

But, his preference for that evening or not, Fastest Foods was, in fact, the appropriate place for them to go. He would see Chuck and Carleen, make sure they were ready for their shift that night.

And yes, fortunately, they would once again be using the elixir, and Sergeant Kristine Parran would be their aide for their shift. He hadn't even had to step in and argue on their behalf, although he would have tried it if necessary. No, fortunately, Drew had let him know that the decision had been made. He couldn't say how long their experiment would last, but Liam's brother and sister-in-law would at least get to use the elixir this one additional time.

And he'd kind of hinted that it was partly to thank Liam for his test shifts over the past month, including the one that had helped Alpha Force figure out how best to try bringing Drew back to human form.

Liam's phone rang and he pulled it from his pocket. It was Drew. "I've been thinking that we ought to all meet in the cafeteria for an early dinner tonight," he said. "Celebrate in advance what'll go on later. Our unit has always seemed to enjoy doing that, and I've already checked with Patrick and a couple of other members. You up for it?"

"I'm up for a get-together," Liam confirmed, "but how about doing it at Fastest Foods so Chuck and Carleen can join us, too? They're participating tonight the Alpha Force way, after all." And that way he wouldn't have to change any plans with Rosa, although he'd let her know they'd be dining with a bunch of people who'd also be anticipating what would occur that night. "I'll call and tell them to reserve a corner of the room for us."

"Sounds good," Drew said. "I'll let the others know."

The evening before their shift would be a lot different from the way he'd planned, Liam realized as he hung up. That was okay, he told himself. He would still be with Rosa, though they wouldn't be eating alone.

Well, they wouldn't have been alone anyway, dining at Fastest Foods and checking in with his brother and sister-in-law.

And there should be plenty of occasions after this when just the two of them could dine—and more—together.

Though Rosa had known she'd be joining Liam at the restaurant that evening, so there would likely be a bunch of people around them as they ate, she hadn't initially known that that bunch of restaurant customers would include a fair-sized group of Alpha Force members as well as friends—like her.

But Liam had warned her, and the early evening seemed to have turned into a bit of a party. A party of anticipation, where everyone seemed happy and optimistic. She hoped they were right.

Now, she sat at one of the small wooden tables that had been saved for the group on one side of the always crowded dining room, with white folded cards saying Reserved. The Alpha Force members who attended were in casual civilian clothes, and so was she.

Melanie was also there with Drew, and they'd brought their adorable children, Emily and her little brother, Andy. Jonas, who Rosa knew was Drew's aide and would help him with his shift that night, sat with them.

Emily, who had dark hair with shimmers of silver in it that resembled her daddy's, had a kiddie-sized burger on a paper plate in front of her and every once in a while picked it up in both hands and took a bite. Her brother, who had similar looking hair, seemed to love french fries.

As far as Rosa knew, it wasn't usual for little kids to

have shimmery hair like that. She still wondered if Emily or her brother resembled their father in other ways—like shifting—but she hadn't learned that yet.

Drew and Melanie hadn't brought Grunge, Drew's cover dog. Nor had Liam brought Chase, and Rosa saw no other dogs present, either. All shifters, including Patrick, and Drew's cousin Jason, were there with their aides.

Rosa figured that if any of them were seen while shifted, in a situation where an explanation for non-shifters would be needed, their aides would retrieve whichever wolf-dog was required, after the shift back. Maybe that was true of Louper, too, but the Corlands' dog wasn't there that evening, either.

"So everything's in order for later," Denny said, from Liam's other side at their table. Rosa was well aware that Liam's aide would be the one to hand him his elixir and monitor his shift, as well as his shift back.

They sat at a larger table—in fact, two tables that had been pushed together. With them were Chuck and Carleen, and another chair had been saved for Valerie.

Rosa had been nibbling on a salad. She would be present when the shifts all occurred, supposedly together, and she could only hope that she would remain calm. Seeing one person shift—Liam—and both he and Drew shift back individually, had drawn a lot of emotions from her. Seeing an entire group?

Heck, she could handle it. She had to—particularly because she couldn't know whether her veterinary services would be needed.

Okay. Not that she was that hungry, but she had been only picking at her salad, and mostly eavesdropping on everyone else at the table without saying much.

"I need an iced tea," she declared, unsure if anyone was paying any attention to her.

But Liam turned and leaned toward her. "I suspect you need a break from all this," he said softly, "at least a short one. Go grab that iced tea." He smiled.

She couldn't help smiling back as she stood. She had an urge to give him a big hug—and not only because he seemed to understand her current mood. But that would only be appropriate now if they were alone—and they were far from alone.

"Can I get anybody anything?" she called. A couple of the aides—Denny and Kristine—asked for a large order of fries that they promised to share, and Rosa felt just a little relieved that she had another reason to go to the order counter.

Fortunately, there was no line and she was able to grab her small order quickly. Valerie was behind the counter, which surprised Rosa a little. She had even been there earlier, putting the orders together for the Alpha Force group and others. But she'd be shifting that night, too, right? Shouldn't she be resting or something?

Rosa had the opportunity to ask her, very softly, as Valerie joined her to walk to the table, "Are you okay? I mean, I'm aware that you're going to have an...exhausting evening, right?"

Valerie did resemble her sister, with her silvery hair and dark brown eyes. Would they look alike while shifted?

Would Carleen's ability to drink the elixir make a difference in her appearance?

"That's for sure," Valerie responded, also in a soft voice. "But I'm used to it. I'll be fine."

But Rosa was curious. "I know that Chuck and Carleen will have...well, help. Will anyone be helping you?"

Valerie laughed, though it didn't sound entirely humorous. "Nope. I'm here on my own. Being Carleen's sister doesn't really connect me to that Alpha Force, so I still do things the old-fashioned way. I always know what's coming, of course, and around here I just lock myself in my room at Carleen and Chuck's house, where I'm staying. Of course, I have to lock their dog out to make sure we don't get into a dogfight when...you know."

They had reached the table, but before Rosa sat down she had to ask, "I know they're getting—I mean, things will be a little different for them, like it was last time. You're okay with doing things the 'old-fashioned way'?"

"Oh, I'm fine with it." Valerie's dark eyes shone as she glanced at Rosa. "Like I said, I'm used to it. Sure, I'm curious...but it's not like I have any choice, anyway. But come see me afterward. I'd like to hear your version of what they go through. I'd imagine that in most ways it's no easier than what I'll do."

Rosa smiled sympathetically at her, recalling how uncomfortable Liam's shift appeared. And maybe in some ways it would be better not to take the elixir that would allow her to keep human cognition. That way maybe the pain and discomfort of shifting wouldn't be as memorable.

But how would she know?

"Sure," Rosa said. "I'd like to hear your version afterward." They both sat down at the table with Liam and the rest of his family.

But almost immediately, the people Liam had followed from the restaurant the other day appeared, walking by them—and the one known as Orion even bumped their table.

"Hey." Liam rose and faced the guy. "Don't you say 'excuse me' in person when you mess up? I know you don't online."

Orion was short but muscular, and he drew himself up almost to Liam's height to face him. "What are you talking about?"

"Aren't you Orion? And don't you like to post lies on social media?"

"Yes to the first. But I don't lie on social media. I post a lot of pictures, play a lot of games, but that's all. And you? Why are you giving me a hard time?"

"Because someone calling himself Orion is giving me a hard time online. And—"

"And forget it. I don't have to talk to you. And you can be sure I won't be communicating with you on the internet."

With that, Orion, and the guy Rosa thought was called Horatio, stormed off toward the counter to order food.

"If it wasn't starting to get late I'd follow the guy," Liam said. "But at least I know he turns up here now and then. And if you can get some contact information for me one of these days…" He looked from Chuck to Carleen. "I'd appreciate it."

"We'll try," Chuck said. "But we don't see him that often, and…"

"I get it," Liam said. He looked frustrated, but Rosa certainly understood why he couldn't do much now.

The light outside had started to grow dimmer.

Rosa soon finished her salad and iced tea, while the

others also finished their dinners, including the fries she had brought back.

Then it was time for the group to leave. Many of them had things to do that night that they wouldn't want anyone else around here to see...

Chuck and Carleen excused themselves to talk to their employees, who'd be closing up the restaurant early, in about an hour.

Rosa rode in Liam's car, which was driven by Denny. She got out with Liam and headed for the familiar clearing, as did the other shifters and some of their aides, who'd also parked nearby. Some of the aides headed for the lab building, though, where Rosa understood they would retrieve the elixir and lights.

Rosa waited at Liam's side. So did Chuck and Carleen, both of whom seemed jazzed. "It's so great to really be part of this group tonight," Chuck said quietly. "If only we could get a commitment of some kind that this won't be the last time, either."

"You know," Liam began, "I can't—"

"Right," Carleen interrupted. "You can't." She shot an almost accusatory glare toward Liam in the waning daylight, and Rosa wanted to kick both of them.

She knew enough to realize that Liam had been attempting to help them remain part of this experiment, but they should feel thrilled to get any use of the elixir, not pushy about the future. And Liam had made it clear that the decision was not his.

Too bad they didn't share Valerie's attitude that the old-fashioned way was a good thing.

Soon all the aides had joined them. Jonas was with Drew, and Melanie had taken the kids home. She hoped to have a sitter come for part of the evening, but in any

event Rosa was at least currently in charge of any veterinary needs.

It was growing darker. Liam and Drew, Patrick and
Jason all seemed restless, pacing around the clearing
near each other.

And then the aides returned with their equipment.
Soon the shifters, including Liam's brother and sister-
in-law, all drank some of the elixir from their respective vials. Rosa watched from the edge of the clearing,
hoping it all went well—and in some ways eager to see
Liam naked again, even for only a short time and for
this difficult reason.

The lights were soon aimed at the shifters, even as
the sky grew darker and the full moon appeared at the
horizon.

Liam was naked now—and as Rosa watched, his
shift began.

His shift had gone well.

*He had felt Rosa's eyes on him as he'd removed his
clothes, making as much of a show of it as he could,
considering his limbs were already changing, fur beginning to erupt from his skin.*

*He also watched his brother and his wife change,
after imbibing the elixir. Their shifts seemed to go well,
too.*

*After they were all in wolfen form, Liam motioned
with his head for his relations to join him as he ran
through the woods, rejoicing in his changed form, the
fleetness of a wolf at his disposal. The earth was covered with leaves and tree branches. The smell of the
trees and other plants filled the air. But of more interest,
he scented small rodents on and under the ground, birds*

sleeping in trees—and people around, mostly those stationed at Ft. Lukman. Even though non–Alpha Force members were cautioned, without any formal explanation, to remain in their quarters on nights such as this, not everyone obeyed.

But Alpha Force shifters would not harm them. Not with the human cognition they maintained after drinking the elixir.

With his relations, he continued through the forest, sometimes in a somewhat straight line, sometimes circling areas of particular interest where other fauna had a presence—rabbits and raccoons and more. But he had no intention of attacking any of them—not with his human cognition.

Time passed. He kept note of how the moon was progressing, especially when that bright, full orb began to approach the horizon, where it would soon disappear.

Again using his head to gesture, he waved for his family to follow him. They soon reached the clearing, as had that night's other shifters.

Although he did not need to, particularly after drinking the elixir, Liam sat and closed his eyes and told his body to begin its shift back into human form.

Strange. Nothing happened.

It felt like the time when he'd been given that special elixir to prevent him from shifting back, to test the formulation developed to assist Drew in regaining his human form.

Liam opened his eyes and saw the others, unlike him, rolling on the ground.

Shifting back.

"You okay, Liam?" That was his aide, Denny, now at his side.

He nodded, determined to become human once more.

But once more, his shift did not begin.

"Is he all right?" That was Rosa, who had joined them, talking to Denny.

"I don't know. He's not shifting."

And Liam could see that all the other shifters had again achieved human form. All of them but him.

Yet again he did as he always had since joining Alpha Force—closed his eyes and willed himself to shift back. Even without the elixir to rely on, this shift would simply have occurred after a full moon, with nothing further to do on his part.

Still nothing. Not even a semblance of a shift.

He opened his eyes, sitting on the ground, head raised toward the heavens beyond the trees, and issued a loud and mournful howl.

Chapter 19

"Oh, no!" Rosa cried. "What's going on? Liam?" She began running toward him on the uneven, leaf-covered ground in her athletic shoes, unsure what she could do, if anything. But something definitely looked wrong.

She had been standing at the edge of the clearing, watching in the early light of dawn as the wolves returned and began shifting back to human form.

All but Liam.

She reached him quickly. Denny was already kneeling at his side, talking into his erect canine ears. Jonas kept looking toward them, but was busy acting as Drew's aide. The Alpha Force superior officer, though back in human form and starting to get dressed with Jonas's help, looked tired.

Rosa immediately knelt beside Denny. "Do you know what's going on? Did he accidentally get the wrong kind of elixir? Is there anything I can do for him medically?"

"Don't know answers to any of that." Rosa could tell that Denny was attempting to act amused and calm, undoubtedly to keep Liam that way, too. "Hey, dude," he said to Liam, "anything hurt? Or is there some other reason you'd like Dr. Jontay, here, to examine you? Touch you?" He raised his brows suggestively, and Rosa smiled almost involuntarily. But keeping things light was certainly preferable to all of them showing how upset they were.

Liam barked then, nodded and looked at Rosa. She made herself laugh. Maybe the only good thing about this was that he at least had apparently kept his human cognition.

But what were they going to do? Was he going to remain in wolf form for the rest of today? Longer?

A fully dressed Drew came over to them then. "Not again," he said, shaking his head as he stared at Liam. "Well, at least this time we have a solution. Let's go back to the labs."

The entire group, now in human form and wearing clothes, picked up backpacks and lights and began walking in the direction of the main Alpha Force building.

They talked to one another, and to Liam, in cheerful and even joking tones, clearly wanting to keep his spirits up.

Rosa wished she could join them and joke and feel better, but she didn't know what the Alpha Force members were really thinking. No despair was evident. No frustration or anger that they were in the same situation as before, after the last full moon, when their superior officer had failed to change back.

Were they truly happy or relieved that it was only Liam this time? But they all seemed like nice people—

when they were in human form. No, she truly believed they were just putting on an act for his benefit.

Apparently, no one even thought about including her in their banter, and she was just as glad.

Liam's family members, Chuck and Carleen, walking with them, were clearly upset. There was no way they could get completely out of Liam's hearing, Rosa figured, but after greeting him and pretending to joke with him, they headed toward the far side of the group. Their aide, Kristine, stayed with them. Not having a shifter's hearing, Rosa didn't know what they were saying, but their demeanor as they talked with her appeared angry.

Who or what were they blaming for Liam's condition? Or were they simply upset enough about the situation that they were venting?

They soon reached the building, and Drew told a couple of the aides to go take the cover dogs out for a walk, then feed them. He immediately directed Denny to take Liam downstairs to the laboratories.

Then he faced Chuck and Carleen in the hallway outside the kennel area.

"I know you have questions, and so do we. But we need to take Liam downstairs to a private area to work with him and bring him back to human form. First—were you okay with the elixir you drank? I gather from Kristine that you maintained your human cognition."

"That's right," Chuck said. "Good stuff. It worked well for us, and we really hope we can join you again."

"Assuming that elixir isn't what affected Liam—well, you know," Carleen said.

"Right," Drew said. "We know—and understand. I gather that Kristine has your contact information, right?"

Chuck nodded.

"Good. I'll have her keep in touch with you about Liam. But for now…well, the sooner you leave, the sooner we can start working with him."

Rosa had been standing off to the side during the conversation and winced at the fury she thought she saw on Chuck's face. But Liam's brother just nodded, took his wife's hand and led her down the hall to the exit. Presumably, they had driven here last night after their last conversation with their employees at the restaurant.

And now Drew looked toward her. Was he going to tell her to leave, too?

Just the opposite. "Can you join us, Rosa? We hope we won't need any veterinary assistance, but just in case…"

"Yes," she said. "I'll join you."

Denny had used a key card to open the door. Patrick held back and asked Rosa to walk with him as they went down to the lab floor. As they followed the others down the steps, he said, "We're hopeful that the formulation Liam helped with during the shift when he couldn't immediately change back, the formulation that finally allowed him, and later Drew, to do so—well, there's no reason we know of that it shouldn't work for Liam now."

No reason they knew of. But they didn't really know, did they, what had caused Drew to remain in wolf form before under the full moon, or Liam now?

Even so, she smiled as they reached the bottom of the stairs, and said, "That's great. I'll look forward to congratulating him once he's in Liam form again."

Patrick shot her a much briefer smile, then hurried to catch up with the others.

Rosa followed them into the main, vast laboratory.

She remained near the door, just watching. Liam was on the floor near the main counter, in the middle of where the cabinets lined the walls. He stood up on his hind legs against that counter and looked from one human to the next, as if attempting to communicate his command that they fix this situation for him. Fast. And Rosa was all for that.

The next few minutes seemed a bit chaotic to her, but she gathered that the medical doctors among them were retrieving the required liquids from the refrigerator, checking their consistency and getting them ready for use. The others were setting things up, grabbing the light they would use after Liam drank the stuff. Soon, they all appeared to have accomplished their assigned tasks.

"Come over here, Liam," Drew called. He gestured for Liam to follow him into a glass-walled room that contained a sofa and some upholstered chairs—a lounge of some kind.

Maybe they thought a comfortable area would be preferable for all to go as it should.

Liam followed Drew, and Denny joined them. Only the three of them went into that room. Rosa joined the others as they settled behind the glass walls, watching.

Denny first removed a seal from the top of the vial he held, then poured the clear liquid it contained into a dog bowl on the floor. Liam immediately drank it.

Next, Denny turned on the light that resembled the full moon, which was fairly bright here, downstairs, below the main floor of the building. Rosa heard no sound from anyone around her as they all watched.

And waited. As nothing happened.

Liam did not change back.

* * *

Damn.

He recalled how things had seemed when his commanding officer failed to shift back after the last full moon, and was eventually treated with the special form of elixir that Liam himself had helped to test.

And how both of them, in their respective time, had shifted back right away, thanks to that new formulation.

He knew that had to be what he'd been given now.

What had gone wrong?

And could it be fixed?

It had to be. But when?

Rosa knew she was not in a position to insist on anything, and yet after a while, when everyone's frustration was evident, she demanded an opportunity to examine Liam.

After all, the only other medical people here were human doctors.

They waited a bit longer, though, clearly hoping things would change. That Liam would shift. But he didn't.

And so Denny left the lounge room and Drew motioned for Rosa to come in.

She wasn't exactly sure how to conduct this kind of exam, but was determined to do it nonetheless. She would use all her veterinary skills to see if there was anything different, anything clearly wrong, with this wolf-dog who happened to be Liam.

She felt his entire body, one area at a time, moving his limbs, his ears, his tail, the skin along his back and elsewhere, and observing those areas as she grasped them. She opened his mouth and checked his teeth, his throat.

Everything appeared in order for a healthy dog of his size.

That was a good thing, of course. And Rosa hadn't really believed she would be able to figure out what the problem was just by examining him.

No, she hadn't believed it. But she had hoped.

She walked away from Liam for now, after seeing his eyes on hers, his head bowed as if he was depressed. Not surprising.

Moments later, she joined the group of those in charge back out in the lab area, Drew and Patrick and Jonas, as they talked very quietly about what had, and hadn't, happened.

The fact that they kept their voices low and stood in a different room didn't mean that Liam couldn't hear them. Rosa knew that, and clearly they did, too.

They didn't express any anger or frustration or any other emotion they must be feeling, the way Rosa did. They might even feel more, since Liam was their colleague, and Drew had found himself in the same situation not long ago.

But the gist of what they said concluded that members of their unit would remain here in the lab area that day with Liam, alternating who stayed when. They would occasionally shine the light on him, just in case there was a delay in when this shifting formulation worked. Those with medical and chemistry backgrounds would work once more on that formulation.

If he didn't change back by tomorrow morning, they would go through all this again.

And Rosa? Of course they didn't mention her. But

she finally stepped up to them, let them know she intended to stay here as well, although she would have to clear it with Melanie and would also need to go to her home for a change of clothes.

"That's fine with us," Drew told her. "Thanks." There was a touch of relief in his expression, so Rosa figured he was concerned about Liam's health under the circumstances.

And so, first thing, she went to the far side of the lab area, leaned on a counter with her back toward the others and called Melanie, explaining what had happened.

"Oh, no!" her boss exclaimed. Of course her emotions would be involved, too. She had also gone through this. "Stay as long as you need to."

"Thanks."

Rosa didn't head home for a few hours, wanting to spend the time with Liam to make sure that he remained okay. Eventually, though, she did go home to shower and change clothes—then returned. Still no improvement.

She lay down on the sofa in the lounge area for a nap, and was amused somewhat when she awoke to find Liam in there with her, lying on the floor parallel to her.

Not changed back.

Alpha Force members kept coming in and leaving. Rosa talked briefly to one or another of them, but no one described what they were doing to change—or not change—the shifting-back formulation.

They did shine the light on Liam now and then, but nothing happened.

They brought in meals for Liam and her, and she nibbled at them though she didn't feel particularly hungry.

And that night she hardly slept at all. Would anything good happen the next morning?

She stayed out of the way when, just after sunrise, the main Alpha Forcers returned—Drew and Patrick and Jonas, along with Denny.

Once more, they had Liam go through the procedure they had tried the previous morning.

Rosa felt tears rise in her eyes as, after he'd drunk whatever formulation they gave him, the wolf-dog who was Liam sat on the lounge area floor as the light was shined on him once more. What would happen if he stayed this way forever?

Could he bear it? Could she?

But... Yes! Liam moaned and lay down, his limbs beginning to lengthen, his fur retracting into his body.

It didn't take long, and yet it felt like forever.

Soon, Liam was writhing on the floor, all human once more. All nude human, and Rosa found herself laughing and crying in relief.

Liam spent the rest of the morning being examined and interrogated by his Alpha Force superiors.

At least Rosa had stayed for a short while after he had shifted back to his human form. Once he was dressed and could breathe normally again, he had even gotten her to join him for coffee in Drew's office, while the others remained in the lab.

"I'm so glad you're okay," she'd said, eyeing him over the cup she held to her lips.

Those lovely lips of hers. Now that he was human again, he noticed them once more. And the rest of her.

But she had shot him down nearly immediately.

"I'm glad, too," he said. "Thanks for hanging out here."

"Oh, I was just doing my job." She took another sip of coffee. "You seemed to be fine in wolf form, but I was ready to try to help if you weren't."

Just doing her job. Sure, that was the truth—and yet he'd hoped she'd also hung around because she was concerned about him.

Cared about him.

Heck, that had been his own emotions, juggled along by his somewhat frightening inability to change back even after taking that other form of elixir developed for just that purpose for Drew.

She stayed only a little while longer.

But she did hearten him a bit by saying, as Chase and he walked her to her car, "I hope we get together again soon." And then, after unlocking her door, she turned back to him and gave him a kiss. A quick one, and yet it made him feel at least a little better.

He'd nearly asked if they could get together that night. But he still felt tired.

And his superiors had already said they wanted to conduct an examination. Plus he still had his regular work to do as the chief technology guy for the unit, although Denny had told him he'd started checking social media after this latest full moon.

Sure enough, his aide had pointed out some of the posts about shapeshifters and their reality, and their alleged aggression while shifted, attacking regular people in this area. And that some of those supposed attackers allegedly belonged to a secret military force.

As a result, Liam had spent what was left of his energy getting online, assuming some of his false personas and making fun of all those nasty posts. A couple had come from someone named Orion, but the addresses and locations didn't jibe with what the guy who'd shown up again at the restaurant and finally given him some info had provided. Nor did it appear real when Liam conducted his own investigation of the source.

Could he rule out the guy he'd met? No, but he couldn't be sure that Orion was involved, either.

When he finished, he was exhausted. With Chase, he walked back to his quarters early that evening, grabbed a sandwich with fixings from his fridge—and was pleased when Rosa called.

"How are you doing?" she asked.

"Well enough," he replied.

"Good. Stay that way." Her tone sounded like a command, but then she said, "I was worried about you before, you know."

"I know. Thanks." But neither of them suggested that they get together again sometime soon—or even sometime in the future.

Therefore, he had spent that night alone...with his thoughts.

Chapter 20

A week had passed since the night of the last full moon—and Liam's failure to shift back as he was supposed to.

But fortunately, he had eventually shifted back. And Rosa had not seen him since then.

This morning she sat in her small office at the veterinary clinic, checking out the file on one of her upcoming patients of the day, Boom—a much beloved rescue dog whose family had adopted him a little while ago. He was a middle-sized dog, apparently part Irish setter and part golden retriever, who'd previously been abused—and now had a wonderful life, from what Rosa had seen.

He'd first been brought to the clinic around the time Rosa had started working there, about a year ago, by his new family, the Orcharts. This was his annual checkup.

And everything seemed to be going great with him—

pending the results of his blood test, which Rosa was
having sent out to the regular lab.

But just drawing the blood reminded her...

"So what do you think, Dr. Jontay?" asked Millie
Orchart, the wife of Bill and mother of the boy and girl
who were like Boom's siblings.

"I think sweet Boom has a wonderful family," Rosa
responded. "And as to his health? I've found nothing to
worry about. Of course, we need to wait for his blood
test results, but I'm fairly sure he's fine. This is one
lucky and sweet rescue dog."

"We think so," Bill said, as Rosa lifted Boom down
from the examination table. The two kids ran to the
dog and hugged him.

Soon the entire family left, with Rosa staying behind in the room, smiling after them. But only for a
short while.

In a minute, she was sure she would be summoned
to one of the other exam rooms, as she should be.

This was her life. Who she was. And yet...

She pulled her phone from her pocket. Time to call
Liam. Again. They'd at least spoken daily since they
had last seen each other. He sounded busy, and she definitely was.

And yet...why not at least get together some evening
for dinner? Like tonight?

"Hi, Rosa," he said into her ear, answering his phone
right away. That soft smile she had aimed at Boom and
his family now grew much larger as she pictured Liam's
handsome face—and that body of his without clothes
as he shifted back...

"Hi, Liam. How have you been?"

"Up till now, just fine since you last saw me. Did you hear what's going on, or do you have ESP?"

Her heart froze, and she stared at a spot on the metal sink at the side of the room. "What do you mean?"

"I'm going to be shifting again tonight, just as a test."

Shifting, on this night a bit over a week since the full moon. An Alpha Force shift. A test. After what Liam had just gone through.

"Oh, and in case you're wondering," he continued, "Drew has asked Melanie to be here in case I need any help. If all goes well, we plan to continue with test shifts every couple of days with all the shifters around here, not just me, so maybe you'll be asked to help out, too."

Or not. Melanie hadn't mentioned it to her. Things around here seemed to be much as they had before the full moon when Drew hadn't changed back and Rosa had had to step in to help. She'd known about the shifters under the full moon and otherwise, but hadn't truly been involved then.

And suspected she wouldn't be involved more now.

"That's fine," she said. "I hope it all goes well." She realized her tone sounded falsely bright, and ended the call by saying, "Just wanted to see if we could get together for dinner sometime soon, but I need to get to my next patient now. Maybe after this test shift of yours. See ya, Liam." And then she hung up.

Liam felt miserable, even as he decided he had to feel good. He looked forward to this next shift, determined that it work out well with whatever elixir he was given to drink.

But now, moving in his office chair, he looked at his computer screen, one reason he had been avoiding Rosa.

He had spent a lot of time online, still trying to figure out the real source of the various lies against shifters and particularly Alpha Force. Nothing conclusive so far except the name Orion now and then, as well as other Greek or Roman god names.

He had remained in touch with the guy he knew as Orion from around here—who'd conveniently been out of town.

Since Liam had been able to figure out the guy's location by hacking into the GPS on his phone, he'd seen that Orion truly had been elsewhere, in New York City, for the past week or so. Sure, he could have sent his phone with someone else—but maybe not.

In any event, more of those nasty accusations against unnamed Alpha Force had been posted. Names including Orion had been used again. And Liam still hadn't nailed down the actual identities and locations of those who posted them, but neither had he eliminated that Orion as the perpetrator.

Orion was back in town now, and they were planning to meet at Fastest Foods tomorrow night to chat.

So that meant Liam couldn't meet up with Rosa then. And for the last few days and nights he had been pretty well glued to his computer.

"I'll get away from you tonight, at least," he said, glaring at the screen in front of him. "Tomorrow night, too."

Yet if he'd really wanted to get together with Rosa, he'd have found an hour or two. He knew that. But he'd realized, when he couldn't shift back this last time, that he cared for her too much.

Why would the woman want to be involved long-term with someone like him, with his existence so different from hers? Who sometimes couldn't even shift back into human form?

He understood that, and knew he had to stay away from her as much as possible now or hurt even more when they parted for good.

But he also recognized that seeing her, however briefly, was worth the pain.

His phone rang again and he snatched it from the desk beside his computer screen. Was Rosa calling again?

But his hopeful grin disappeared when he saw who the caller was: Patrick. "Come on over to Drew's office," he said. "We need to talk about tonight."

Liam's manufactured shift last night had gone well. Rosa knew that.

But she didn't hear the news from him.

It was the day after she'd talked to him. She had spoken briefly with Melanie after that in her office, expressing her interest and a hint of her concern.

Not that Melanie was surprised. "Drew expressly asked me to be there for the shift this time," she had said, the tilt to her head and a somewhat sad smile conveying what appeared to be sympathy. "But from what I've heard, this will be the first of several shift tests they'll be conducting before the next full moon, and you and I will both be involved, with alternating ones."

"That's kind of what Liam said," Rosa agreed. She didn't bother asking why she wasn't the one last night. Drew was in charge of his gang, and Melanie was in charge here. End of story.

But she had hurried into Melanie's office first thing this morning, on hearing her boss was there. Melanie had motioned for her to sit down, and gazed at Rosa over her desk. Rosa saw no signs of stress there, which was a good thing—and what Melanie said only supported that impression.

All had gone well. Melanie had given Liam a brief veterinary exam while he was in wolf form. Then Liam had shifted back on schedule, when he had been directed to, with no problems.

"So the first of these new experiments went fine," Melanie finished. "Hopefully, the rest will, too, and they'll act as a harbinger of successful shifts under the next full moon."

"Hopefully so," Rosa agreed. She meant it. Even if she now had no relationship with Liam outside of being an occasional vet for him and his colleagues while shifted, she wished him well.

She also wished she understood why he seemed to have backed off. Or maybe he truly was under stress with his important military job, and just couldn't find time to see her...

Sure.

Still, she left Melanie's office feeling glad that Liam was okay, even if they weren't seeing each other.

Since no one was in the hall escorting an animal to one of the exam rooms, Rosa headed to the reception area to check on what appointments were scheduled that day.

The room was small but pleasant—and empty, except for the compact desk at one side where Susie sat, staring at her computer screen as she sipped coffee from a mug. But none of the six metal-and-red-plastic chairs was occupied, and all the balls and other toys there to amuse dogs while they were waiting still sat in the large wicker basket on the floor.

"So where are today's patients?" Rosa asked, and Susie looked toward her and smiled.

"We've got a busy schedule later," she said, "but right now we have just one dog scheduled, for an exam in five minutes—Grunge. He's just coming for a checkup."

That was Drew's cover dog, Rosa knew, and he mostly hung out at Melanie and Drew's house next door during the nights. But he joined the other Alpha Force dogs at the base on most weekdays.

She assumed that Drew himself, or maybe his aide, Jonas, would bring Grunge in—and was somewhat shocked when, before she left the reception area, Liam walked through the front door with Grunge on a leash behind him.

"Oh. Hi, Liam. And Grunge. Good to see you both." Rosa realized that sounded lame. What she wanted to do—sort of—was dash into Liam's arms and give him a big, sexy kiss.

But not here. Not in front of Susie.

And really? Not at all. Not the way he'd been avoiding her. Or at least had seemed to. Though maybe he really had been as busy as he'd claimed.

"Hi, Rosa." His deep voice, plus the way he looked at her—ruefully, apologetically, sexily—stirred her even more.

Or was she imagining, hoping for, all that?

She watched him for a few more seconds before shaking herself mentally. "So, how's Grunge doing? Is there anything I should know before conducting his exam?"

"He seems fine, or so Drew told me. It's just time for him to get his annual exam, Drew said."

So why were you the one to bring Grunge? But

Rosa didn't ask that. Didn't say anything at all, except, "Great. Let's take him into an exam room."

"Number three," Susie said, after looking again at her computer.

"Okay." Rosa led Liam and Grunge down the hall. "So how's Chase doing?" she asked, as they entered the third examination room.

"Fine. He'll be due for a regular exam, too, one of these days."

"Let's get Grunge up there." Rosa gestured toward the tall metal table.

Liam lifted the wolf-dog, and Rosa helped by grabbing him behind his front legs to guide where he would be deposited. While doing so, she accidentally touched Liam's warm, bare skin. He was wearing his usual military camos, but the long sleeves had been rolled up.

That jolted her a bit, but she determined not to let it show.

Only—well, maybe it had jolted Liam a bit, too, since the moment after they both carefully let go of Grunge, Rosa found herself in Liam's arms.

The kiss they shared was exactly as she had wanted it to be—hot and hard and sexually exciting, particularly since their bodies melded together.

It was a nice, long kiss, too—but eventually Rosa ended it. She was here on duty. A veterinarian with a dog patient to examine.

And this was a highly inappropriate place for a kiss.

"Well," she said, stepping back. "It's good to see you, too. Now, let's take a look at Grunge."

She turned her back on Liam and began a very thorough and professional examination of Grunge.

In a short while, she was able to say with assurance,

"He seems to be doing just fine. No problems that I can see, although I'll want to draw some blood and have it checked."

Since Grunge was a regular canine, despite being part of Alpha Force, she would be able to have the sample sent to their laboratory, as she had yesterday with Boom and others.

She stepped into the hall and saw Brendan. Good. She asked him to come in and hold the large animal to make sure he didn't bite when he felt the needle. Which he didn't.

And that ended the exam. Brendan left the room first with the blood sample, and Rosa was alone once more with Liam and Grunge.

"So," she said to Liam, "good to see you." *And to kiss and touch you.*

"You, too, Rosa." The way he said her name only made it all worse—soft and, again, sexy and…did she really sense a hint of longing? No, that had to be her imagination.

If he really wanted to be with her, why hadn't he called her, let alone set up a time for them to get together?

But he continued, "I've missed you. And—well, I'll be eating at Fastest Foods tonight around seven. Will you join me then?"

Yes, yes, she wanted to shout. But instead said, "I think so. In fact, count on it unless you hear otherwise from me. My schedule around here has been a bit crazy these days." Which it had, though her evenings had mostly been free, except for two nights ago when she'd been handling an emergency.

"Got it," he said. "I'll look forward to seeing you there... I hope."

Then, with Grunge, he preceded Rosa out the examination room door.

Before he left the vet clinic, Liam told Rosa that he had a meeting set up with Orion at the restaurant that night. He saw her expression grow chilly.

Maybe it had been a bad idea. Maybe he should have asked her out on a genuine date, with just the two of them, on another night. His invitation had, after all, been somewhat impulsive.

He did want to see her.

But he had to talk to Orion, and this was the first opportunity he'd had since the guy returned from his trip.

Now he drove to Rosa's house to pick her up, since she'd called earlier to confirm she would join him. She had then gone home after her day at the clinic. This did feel like a date, at least somewhat. And that was good.

Oh, yes. When she greeted him at her front door, she was clad in a really pretty pink dress with a skirt that revealed a lot of leg. Plus she'd traded her usual casual athletic shoes for dressy black ones with narrow heels.

Definitely date attire. Good thing that he, too, had dressed up a bit—not in his usual camo wear, but a nice blue button shirt over navy slacks and loafers.

"Glad you could join me," he said, once they were in the car. He'd left Chase at his quarters on base, so the back seat was empty.

"Me, too. And—well, I know it's not my business, but why are you meeting with that Orion?"

"Because, though I've made some progress narrowing things down in my online search regarding posts about shapeshifters—and you know I can't tell you more than that—I think he may have some answers."

A while later, Liam was certain of it. His family, including Valerie, had joined Rosa and him at the table where they'd taken their usual burgers and sides. That gave Liam a good opportunity to grab his cola and join Orion when the guy strode into the restaurant and got his own food order. Now they sat in a different corner.

"So what did you want to accuse me of this time?" Orion said, taking a big bite of his burger as he shot a cynical glance toward Liam.

"As I've said before, I'm trying to find the real source of some posts that were written by someone named Orion. Now, from what I've learned about you, your real name is Ellis Martoni and Orion is your middle name. And you use that name more than Ellis, including online. And—"

"Enough," Orion said. "You're right. I gather you've got some pretty good online research skills. Well, so do I, though I'm actually a CPA working for an accounting firm."

Liam already knew that about him, too.

Orion leaned toward him. The guy was beefy, with short hair and a long face, plus glaring green eyes. "I also play a lot of online video games, and that's when I mostly use my Orion persona. Anyway, I've done my own research and found what I figure you did—that there are a lot of posts on various sites that are really pretty stupid because they seem to think shapeshifters, werewolves and such, are real. And a whole bunch of them were supposedly posted by someone named Orion. So that's why you came after me. But why do you give a damn about them?"

"Like I told you before, I'm a member of the US military and some of my superior officers think the references in some of those posts to a supposed military unit of shapeshifters needs to have the source tracked down and stopped. Stupid stuff, but it's a matter of policy, so I have to do it."

That was somewhat true—as true as he could admit. But he certainly couldn't refer to the fact that shapeshifters themselves were true.

"Okay. Got it. And just so we're square on this, first, I didn't do those posts. Second, though I don't know who did, I used some of my own resources and came up with some online sites that are really good at hiding sources and making it look like stuff was put out there from all over the world. Secret sites, of course. But here." He slid an envelope he'd pulled from his pocket toward Liam. "I wrote down some websites you can look at, along with passwords I made up for this situation. Check 'em out. You'll see that a lot of the supposed sources are actually local—but they're not me or the company I work for. Maybe they'll help you. But don't bother me with this again."

"Thanks," Liam said simply. He would check into this, of course. It didn't sound like something he hadn't done himself. But there were an infinite number of websites out there in cyberspace, so maybe this guy's information would help.

He hadn't narrowed it all down to local people posting, either, though Liam had always figured that those who made claims about shapeshifters around here, and seemed to stick those posts online from faraway countries, had to be playing some pretty skillful games. In any case, it was high time he figured out exactly who those people were.

This Orion guy could still be one of them, but Liam would at least look into what he'd given him.

The man rose, picking up the wrappers from the sandwich and fries he'd finished, along with his soda cup.

"You're welcome," he said to Liam, as he started walking away. "Now, leave me alone."

Maybe so, Liam thought.

And maybe not.

Chapter 21

Rosa had been having quite an interesting conversation with Liam's family—Chuck, Carleen and even Valerie.

They'd secured a table in a corner, as it was their privilege, as owners of the place, to do.

Apparently they had enough staff on duty that all of them could take the time off to eat dinners together, and talk to her.

She'd picked up her food and they'd joined her. Keeping their voices low, they began to grill Rosa about shapeshifter things within her knowledge—like, how did she conduct veterinary examinations of those in shifted form.

They knew she had examined Liam when he had failed to shift back. What had he been like then? Had she been there when he had actually managed to shift back? Had the stuff he had drunk, that elixir, helped or hurt?

Ah. That was a good reason to get the topic off Liam, at least for a short while. Rosa was well aware by now that Chuck and Carleen had, as part of that experiment being conducted, gotten to drink the elixir both during the most recent full moon and the one before that.

When, both times, someone had failed to shift back... Drew and Liam. But apparently Chuck and Carleen had both shifted again, right on time, back to human form.

"We did just fine," Carleen told her, when she asked how things had gone. "It was really fun both times— getting to maintain our human cognition while shifted. Most shifters don't, you know."

"That's what I've been told."

Rosa hazarded a glance toward Valerie, who simply changed like other shifters under a full moon—in this case, into a wolf with only a canine's cognition. Valerie was watching her sister and brother-in-law as she ate her own burger, and didn't even glance at Rosa.

And then came what Rosa figured was their goal in spending time with her.

Carleen, who was sitting at her right side, leaned toward her, a cup of coffee in her hand. "We gather that you have contact, at least sometimes, with the people in charge at Liam's military unit. We know he doesn't have the authority to make their elixir available to us during every full moon, let alone at other times. And you surely don't, either. But—well, they must think a lot of you to have you be their sometimes veterinarian, which is important to them. If you could put in a good word for us, we'd really appreciate it. Maybe they could conduct more experiments, for example, with other shifters outside their unit."

"We heard that Liam did get to shift again this week when the moon wasn't full," Chuck added. "He can't say a lot about what he does with the military, but he mentioned that. We're not part of his Alpha Force, of course, but they are recognizing somewhat that we're his family. Maybe you could mention—"

"Maybe Rosa could mention what?" Liam was suddenly there, standing right behind Carleen. He dropped down onto the chair across the table from Rosa and glared at his brother and sister-in-law. "Look, we've gone through this before." He kept his voice down, but there was still a note of anger in it. "My ears are always open when my superior officers talk about expanding their experiment, and I've made it clear you want to continue being part of it, if possible, and I'm happy with the idea. But I have no control, and Rosa certainly has none, so—"

"I'm sure they understand," Valerie interrupted. The expression on her face, which looked so much like her sister's, was sympathetic. "At least they've had the opportunity to try that elixir, and hopefully will again. I'm jealous, of course." She smiled almost sadly. "I'll be leaving Mary Glen soon, so I'm not asking to be included in that experiment, anyway. But if there was only some way to ensure that they could continue, well— Liam, you know how much it means to them."

"I do," he said. "And I'll keep doing what I can to help them continue. But you need to understand my lack of authority, and certainly Rosa's."

"But they apparently do think a lot of Rosa, right?" Valerie asked. "You've mentioned that the other veterinarian at that clinic, the one who's that officer's wife, is highly respected not just because of being married to the guy, but because of all she does to help them while shifted. And now that Rosa does that, too—well, surely they respect her and like her, right?"

"Definitely," Liam said, looking at Rosa. She had to smile, even though she recognized that, as far as Alpha Force was concerned, she was a sometimes asset but otherwise a nobody. "But look. If you want the possibility of another opportunity to use the elixir—" he looked from his brother to his sister-in-law, then back again "—you need to just go along with things as they work out. Neither of you is military, but in a way you need to follow orders and listen to what you're told. If they continue liking and respecting you, you have a better chance of getting what you're asking for. Understand?"

"Yes," Chuck said, looking Carleen in the eye. "We understand." He turned to Liam. "And we appreciate your being on our side, speaking up for us when you can. We'll listen to you, bro. We promise."

"One thing you should know, though," Liam said, then stopped. Rosa looked at him when he didn't continue right away. He was looking down at the sandwich he held, as if communicating with it in some way.

"What's that?" Chuck prompted, his tone curt, as if he expected Liam to say something bad.

Rosa expected it, too, since he hadn't finished what he'd begun.

"Once again," he finally said, "I don't have control over any of this—and you of all people, Chuck, know how nasty I can get when I don't have control." The lopsided grin he shot toward his brother didn't change the scowl on Chuck's face.

"Yeah," Chuck said. "I've experienced that now and

then." At least his response was somewhat light, despite the clear frustration he was feeling.

"The thing is, with my not changing back on time, and my commanding officer not changing back right away during the prior full moon, the unit's attention will be focused on that. My understanding right now is that other experiments, such as the one with you, will likely be put on hold till they figure that out."

"And there's nothing you can do about that?" Carleen asked, also clearly upset. "None of your technological expertise or whatever can resolve that situation?"

Rosa saw Valerie reach over and grasp her sister's hand on the table sympathetically.

"If I could understand it, fix it at all," Liam said, "I would have by now."

Their conversation was pretty much over. Rosa joined in for the final words, unfunny jokes and clearly unhappy goodbyes.

Goodbyes. Standing, collecting her trash to dispose of, she anticipated just heading home on her own. After saying goodbye.

Well, good-night, at least. She intended to talk to Liam again tomorrow, as she'd been doing.

But that was all.

Liam was friendly enough to all of them, of course, particularly his relatives. But he clearly was through talking and listening and explaining his position— and what he could talk about regarding Alpha Force. It seemed clear, after all. He might care for his family, but all he could do was explain the position he had to take as a member of his military unit. Not only did he have to refrain from making promises, but it seemed as if he also had to wrest away most vestiges of hope they might have for continuing their experiment, at least for now.

Even if Rosa wanted to, she couldn't cheer them up. Any hope they might have certainly couldn't be encouraged by her.

She knew Liam well enough to recognize he wasn't particularly happy about having to shrug off his brother and sister-in-law's wishes and pleas, but he was a military man as well as a family member and shapeshifter.

He was doing what he had to.

She decided to let him know that she, at least, understood, as they both headed out of the restaurant. He walked ahead of her through the usual noisy crowd. She wondered what he, with his extraordinary senses, thought about the conversations around them, the usual aroma of cooking meat and more that even she could smell.

They'd talked about that before, and she figured he still simply accepted it, even if his mood wasn't as happy as it sometimes was.

She followed him out the door and onto the empty sidewalk. Cars drove by on the downtown Mary Glen street, and they both turned right toward the parking lot.

"I'm sorry you can't give your family better news," she told him, now at his side.

"I'll bet you are." He looked down at her, his blank expression, his irritated tone, not altering the gorgeousness of his sexy, all-masculine face. "Do you want to kick me in the butt, too, for not being able to accommodate them, to tell them they can drink the elixir and shift my way whenever they want?"

"I of all people understand that sometimes things we really want to do are out of our control. In your case, that means that your relatives, right about now, aren't happy with you. In my case, if things are out of control, that sometimes means I can't save the life of a sweet pet who deserves to live. Not the same thing, but both can hurt."

That expression softened, and he looked human again—sympathetically, caringly human, at least for this moment. "I'm sorry. I'm being pretty selfish, aren't I?"

"Maybe," she said with a smile, as she looked him in the eyes. "But I figure you're just being self-protective. You're kind of in the middle of your work and your family, and at the moment they're both giving you a hard time."

"Boy, do you understand." Instead of smiling back, he bent down and took Rosa in his arms.

She hadn't paid attention before, but now wondered if they were the only people in the parking lot.

Well, who cared? She stood up on her toes, flung her arms tightly around Liam's back and pulled him close.

Their kiss was outstanding. Maybe even more so than many others they'd shared. Maybe not. But it certainly roused Rosa. Made her want more. More kisses? Sure. But really…*more.*

She pulled away after a minute and looked up at him. "You know," she rasped, "I like this restaurant, but one thing I don't like about it is that it doesn't serve alcohol. Care to take me home now and come inside for a drink?" *And more?*

Maybe he read in her eyes what she wasn't saying.

Maybe he simply wanted a drink himself.

Either way, his response was just as she'd hoped. "Let's go," he said.

* * *

Liam wound up spending the rest of that night at Rosa's. Drinking beer—yes. And doing more. Much, much more that stimulated him to wish for even more than what they did overnight.

Hot, incredibly arousing sex hadn't been his initial goal of the evening when he'd asked her to join him for dinner.

Not that he hadn't considered the possibility.

But as he drove back to Ft. Lukman the next morning he couldn't help thinking even more about it.

He appreciated Rosa understanding about how he had to essentially slap his closest relative, his beloved bro, Chuck, in the face, telling him that he still had no control over Chuck's or Carleen's use of the elixir.

Liam hated that, but it was the way things were, and at least Rosa got it and sympathized.

He had been trying to stay away from her on a personal basis, since there really could be no long-term relationship between them, not like Drew and Melanie.

They both wanted more.

And yet...

Well, he would just take each day as it came.

That became his ongoing mantra for the next couple weeks. He kept busy with his online stuff, but still came up with only a few answers to who had posted critical allegations against shifters after the last full moon—not all the answers by any means. Although his commanding officers were understanding and encouraging, claiming they were happy he'd been able to accomplish as much as he had, he was beginning to feel like a failure.

Him. Liam, who'd always considered himself one talented guy in online skills, and had received substantial recognition for it, including this job in the military. It almost felt as if someone as skilled was purposely attempting to outwit him. And had, so far.

But not forever. He would figure it out. Definitely. He'd promised himself...and Alpha Force.

At least his state of mind was helped by his talking to Rosa every day, sometimes more than once. He saw her several times in her veterinary capacity, on days Melanie was unavailable, when Alpha Force members worked outside a full moon to continue testing the elixir and shifting back—even though the two issues they'd experienced had been only during full moons.

So far.

He visited her at her home a few times, too. Not every night, but often enough to make him feel addicted, wanting more, knowing that, in the long run, it might wind up being bad for him.

Especially when, now and then, he hinted at the possibility that they were developing a relationship, and she turned it into a joke.

Which, despite how it hurt, he understood. She might understand that shifters existed, and be willing to help them medically. But she was a regular person with a life to live, outside of what most humans considered "woo-woo" and weird.

And now it was approaching the night of the next full moon. Rosa called to invite him to join her for dinner, preferably somewhere other than at Fastest Foods, but that would be okay, too. They'd eaten at a few other restaurants in Mary Glen besides his family's, and that might have been the better choice that night when he accepted her invitation.

And yet…well, he did have some news to convey to his family, and it wasn't good. At least not entirely.

But it wasn't all bad, either.

And having Rosa around for comfort when he related it sounded damn good.

Back at his family's restaurant.

Maybe Rosa should have insisted on someplace else this time. Sure, eating the food they served was fun, even if it wasn't always the healthiest stuff.

Worse was the atmosphere when Liam argued with his brother and sister-in-law, or wound up teasing them, thanks to what Alpha Force made him do.

But…hey, this night actually wasn't so bad, after all.

Once again Rosa sat at the same table as Liam, Chuck, Carleen and Valerie, in a corner where they could keep their voices down.

And when they all had their meals in front of them, Chuck turned to Liam.

"So what is it you wanted to tell us tonight, bro?"

From what Rosa saw, Chuck seemed to cringe, as if he expected to be kicked in the teeth by Liam's news.

Instead, though—well, it might not have been exactly what Chuck and Carleen wanted to hear, but it could have been a lot worse.

"Here's what I understand," Liam began. "The experiment that includes you has been put on hold, as I thought it was."

Carleen started to rise. "We understand," she said, although her tone was chilly. "Thanks for letting us know."

Valerie stood, too, putting her arm around her sister's shoulders. "It's okay," she said. "Shifting the old-fashioned way is just fine. I can vouch for it."

"Sit down, please," Liam said. "I'm not finished."

And then he informed his relatives that, as long as none of the shifters failed to shift back on the morning after the next full moon, the experiment would restart the following month.

Rosa felt tears of happiness in her eyes as Liam was hugged and thanked by his relatives.

But how were they sure there'd be no problems shifting back this time?

Chapter 22

Rosa talked to Liam on the phone the next couple evenings. She was pleased that he did all the calling. They made plans to get together at least one more time for dinner—and maybe more—before the next full moon occurred, which now was only four days away.

Rosa had been asked to make herself available to help out in case any of the shifters needed veterinary care while in canine form. Of course, she'd planned on it, anyway.

In fact—well, it was midmorning now, and Melanie had asked Rosa to pop into her office for just a few minutes between patients. Rosa was on her way there.

She knocked and waited for Melanie's "Come in." She soon was sitting across the desk from her boss and friend, whose pretty face looked concerned.

"What's wrong?" Rosa asked right away.

"What do you think?" countered Melanie. "We've

already talked about our duties during the upcoming full moon. Has Drew contacted you about it?"

"Yes," Rosa said. "Of course I let him know I'll be available. I didn't bring that up with you because I figured you knew it was a foregone conclusion."

Melanie's expression softened. "Yes. And it just gives me another reason to feel sure I hired the right assistant vet."

"Well, of course." Rosa attempted to sound insulted, but instead she laughed. "Okay, boss. Let's both hope that none of the shifters, especially those we like best, have any problem shifting back this time."

"Definitely," Melanie agreed, and then she led the conversation into a discussion of a few of their veterinary patients with particularly challenging medical issues, and who would do what to help them.

Susie knocked on the door and let them know that a couple more patients had come in, as scheduled, which ended their conversation.

The rest of the day zipped by, thanks to Rosa's treating a cat that had been vomiting because of dehydration, and a dog she diagnosed as being pregnant—fortunately a purebred Westie whose owner showed the breed and had planned for a new litter. Then there were a couple other canine patients who needed an exam or shots, and soon the regular day was over. Rosa was free for the night except if notified of an emergency.

Which, unfortunately, was exactly what happened. And the source particularly worried her.

The call came in on her cell phone, not the office line. "Rosa? It's Valerie. Sorry to bother you, but I really need help. No, Louper needs your help."

Valerie sounded panicked, and she kept on talking, not entirely making sense.

"Hold on," Rosa said. "Slowly. Please tell me what's wrong with Louper."

There was a moment of silence, perhaps while Valerie got her mind under better control. Then she said, "We're at home. He was playing with a ball. He carried it to the top of the basement steps and began shaking it, then seemed to drop it down them intentionally. He started to follow it and… Oh, Rosa, he fell down the stairs! He's just lying there. He's breathing, though heavily, and I'm afraid he broke some bones. Can you come check him out?"

"Of course," Rosa said with no hesitation. Too bad it was too late for her to get assistance from one of the vet techs, and Melanie had probably already left to go home to her kids.

Well, Rosa would go check Louper out. Hopefully, it would be safe to move him, and if she needed help carrying him to the car to bring him here to the clinic, she'd call someone.

Liam.

"Give me your address," she told Valerie, realizing she had never visited Liam's family's home. "I'll be there as soon as I can."

The front of the clinic was already locked for the night, and Rosa made sure to lock the back door behind her as she raced into the parking lot, her bag of medical equipment in her hand. She had a general idea of where the Corlands lived, thanks to getting the address, but she programmed it into her phone's GPS anyway. She definitely didn't want any delays in her arrival there.

What kinds of injuries had poor Louper suffered?

Broken bones? Which ones? Concussion? External wounds? A combination of those and possibly internal injuries, too?

She would find out soon.

She drove through downtown Mary Glen and in the general direction of Ft. Lukman, but turned off at a major intersection into a nice residential area. She didn't know much about architecture, but believed most of the houses were forms of Craftsman styles, with two stories, wide porches, mostly stone with wood trim. The Corlands' house resembled many of the rest. Rosa quickly parked her car in front of it and jumped out.

She ran up the walkway to the porch, hurried up the steps and quickly knocked on the wooden front door.

It opened nearly immediately, as if Valerie had been waiting there for her. Was that a bad sign regarding Louper's condition?

"I'm so glad you're here," Valerie said, closing the door behind Rosa. "Come in."

Rosa was startled when Louper came running up, long tail wagging, to greet her.

The dog looked fine, perfectly healthy.

Rosa turned toward Valerie. "What—" she began, and stopped.

Valerie was aiming a gun at her.

"Let's go into the living room, shall we, Rosa?" It wasn't really a question. The expression on Valerie's face looked evil, menacing, as if she was waiting for Rosa to make a misstep so she'd have reason to shoot her.

What the heck? Rosa hadn't seen anything like this coming.

And Carleen's sister seemed so mentally unhinged at the moment that she didn't need an excuse to shoot.

Rosa felt certain she wouldn't get out of this alive.

But only for a moment. She had to figure this out, figure Valerie out—and definitely figure out a way to end this as safely as possible.

She proceeded to walk in the direction Valerie pointed with her free hand, through the entry area and into a room off to the side that was filled with matching dark wood furniture with taut bright red upholstery.

Bright red. Blood might not show up on it…

"Okay, Valerie," Rosa said, as she took a seat on the sofa Valerie pointed at, and Louper came over to get petted. "What is this about?"

"You'll find out soon enough." Valerie shooed Louper out of the room and closed the door. Good. At least the dog wouldn't actually get hurt. Then Valerie dragged one of the two chairs to face Rosa and sat on it, gun still pointed at her. She pulled her phone from her pocket with her left hand, glanced at it as she used her thumb to push a button, then, after a few seconds, said, "Hi, Liam."

Rosa gasped but said nothing.

Valerie continued. "I assume you're done working for the day, right? Back at your quarters?" She smiled and held the phone out.

She must have put it on speaker, since Rosa heard Liam say, "…eating here tonight, not at the restaurant. But I'll get there one of these days again, probably before the full moon."

"Full moon," Valerie continued. "Funny you should mention that. It's partly why I called. You see, I want you to bring me some of your super-duper elixir before then—like, right now—so I can keep my human mind and all, this time."

A pause, then Liam said, "I assumed you understood why that's not possible."

Rosa's mind was working—hard. If she said something to Liam, would Valerie shoot her? But why was she allowing Rosa to listen in?

"Oh, but it's got to be, even though I'm not a near enough relative and your damned experiment is on hold, anyway. You see, I've got Rosa with me, and unless you bring me a good supply of that elixir right now, at least a year's worth, and one of those lights, poor Rosa isn't going to be around much longer." She looked toward Rosa and said, "Are you, Ms. Veterinarian?"

What should she do? What should she say?

Calmly, she said, "Liam, I'm with Valerie at your brother's house, and she has a gun. I know there isn't much you—"

"Damn you, Valerie!" Liam shouted. "Don't you dare hurt Rosa. I'll go talk to the officers here and see what I can do. I'll call you back soon."

"Real soon," Valerie said with a huge grin. "You know, I've heard people talk about their trigger fingers getting itchy. Just assume mine is. I'll be eager to hear from you." And she pushed the button to hang up.

So would Valerie pull the trigger now? She could get rid of Rosa and just wait for Liam to come with the elixir—and Rosa had little doubt that Liam would come with something, at least, to try to convince Valerie to calm down, give up.

If Rosa wanted to stay alive, she needed to keep Valerie occupied in a way that still gave her power. And she did want to stay alive.

"I'm sure you know, Valerie," she began calmly, although she heard a waver in her voice, "Liam and I are friends. But though we see each other socially some that doesn't mean we're particularly close."

Which was fairly true and a damn shame, Rosa thought. Maybe, if she survived, she would try to move their relationship up a level, or several.

"But—well, I'd really like to understand why you're doing this." Maybe because she considered it unfair that her sister, who happened to be married to a man related to an Alpha Force member, had been allowed to sample the elixir, at least a bit. It had crossed Rosa's mind before that it might not be completely fair, but Valerie had seemed to accept it.

"Because I want some of that damn elixir," Valerie spat. She started shaking as she remained sitting there. "Do you know how long I tried to develop something like that myself? I'll tell you how long. Most of my life." Her glare seemed to stab Rosa as she continued. "You probably think I've spent my life as a restaurant server. Well, hell, though I like doing that and admire good servers, until I moved here temporarily I was a scientist. By design. I'm a shifter, and so's my family. I also like being a shifter—but it's got its drawbacks, like being all wolf when I've changed, and having no say about when I change."

Valerie proceeded to describe to Rosa her interactions with other shifters attempting to achieve the same kinds of results—more control. Scientific experiments. Not-so-scientific stabs at anything she heard about or thought of. She'd put together some pretty good formulas that she'd hoped would allow her to change when she wanted, keep at least a little of her human cognition when she did—but nothing really worked.

She was particularly excited when she learned that her brother-in-law's brother was being recruited into the military—especially when she heard the rumors that the group recruiting him was a very special unit of shapeshifters...with powers. She'd assumed that if all that was true, family would be included, too.

And was horrified to learn that wasn't the case.

She kept on trying to create something herself. Made it clear to Chuck and Carleen—without allowing herself to nag—that she'd be interested in what was already out there, too.

Interested? Hell, she craved it. Deserved it.

Would do anything for it. Planned to analyze the elixir and make a lot more for herself.

"And that's not all," she said, once again waving the gun.

Rosa shuddered again. Would Liam be able to help... somehow? She was sure he couldn't, wouldn't, surrender any of the elixir.

And maybe, to prevent this clearly mad shapeshifter from getting anything that could increase her powers, Rosa should figure out a way to attack her, stop her—even if the result was that she was stopped permanently, too.

Liam had contacted Drew first after hearing from Valerie.

Not, of course, to beg him to hand over a bunch of elixir to that insane indirect relative of his. But, oh yes, it did involve the elixir.

Could he be sure Valerie wouldn't harm Rosa? Of

course not. And he didn't think the best way to handle this would be to let Carleen and Chuck know. They wouldn't be able to convince Carleen's sister to become sane suddenly and back off. He knew they were working late at the restaurant tonight, a good thing—hosting some kind of party.

Hopefully, they wouldn't be around to get involved.

And his getting in touch with Drew was for a purpose that just might work to get Valerie under their control before she hurt anyone.

Before she hurt Rosa...

Now he sat in Drew's office. Fortunately, his commanding officer had still been at the base, and it hadn't been hard for Liam to get him to meet with him.

Not when he briefly explained what was going on.

"Damn. Well, I've got some ideas how to handle this." Drew leaned against his desk, watching Liam with his golden, intense eyes. "But I suspect you do, too."

"I do," Liam agreed. "I'm glad to hear yours, too, as long as we both do this quickly. But here's what I've got in mind."

He explained what had immediately rushed into his brain. He knew that every second they did nothing increased the danger to Rosa. But he still wanted as many shifters as were stationed at Ft. Lukman right now to participate.

And when he was finished describing what he had in mind, he was relieved to hear Drew say, "Good plan. I don't need to waste time telling you my idea. Let's do it."

Rosa realized it hadn't been very long since Valerie had contacted Liam. Even so, it felt as if hours had elapsed.

Hours in which that gun remained aimed at her.

At least Valerie kept talking, so maybe she had a shred of sanity left that was large enough for her to want to justify all that she had done.

Not that talking about it truly helped her achieve that. But it was keeping Rosa alive for now.

"So I tried in so many ways to be nice to those people Liam works with," Valerie was saying. "Making sure they were served their food quickly and nicely when they came into the restaurant and I was there. Smiling and chatting with them and even kidding around a bit, since they knew I was also a shifter. I hoped my niceness would convince them that I deserved to be in their experiment with their damned elixir, too, but it didn't work that way. And so I got mad."

Mad? She surely was psychologically mad, but Rosa knew she meant angry. "I understand," she told Valerie, to keep her talking.

"And of course I did something about it." She whisked her silvery hair away from one side of her face in a strangely proud gesture that once more made Rosa shake inside.

"What was that?" she had to ask, partly because she knew she was expected to, and partly because she wanted to know.

"Well, I told you I'd been experimenting with something on my own before I even heard of that damned Alpha Force elixir. And like I said, it never worked. In fact, it sometimes caused problems when I took it—not a drink like that elixir, but some powders I blended together that had some similarity, but not enough."

"I see," Rosa said. She could in some ways understand the woman's frustration, but—

"No, you don't see. But you will." This time the grin on the face of the woman who looked so much like her sister was broad and seemed evil, almost devilish. "You know that both that Drew guy and Liam happened to be at the restaurant early on evenings before the moon turned full, right?"

Oh, no. Rosa could guess where this was heading. "Yes," she said tentatively.

"Well, I just happened to add a little flavor—and more—to what they ate. And guess why they weren't able to shift back to human form?"

Chapter 23

The bad thing was that Chuck and Carleen lived in a planned development containing streets lined with houses.

The good thing was that their home was close to the only park in that development.

That was where Liam stood now, and he wasn't alone. No, two wolves and three regular humans were with him—members of Alpha Force who had drunk the elixir and were assisted in shifting, thanks to their aides who were with them.

Liam hadn't shifted yet, but he would do so soon. His own aide, Denny, had accompanied him, and held out a vial of the elixir that Carleen's sister had demanded he bring.

Well, he had brought some. Just not for her.

"Are we all ready?" Liam asked. He received confirming head bows and growls from his two shifted comrades, and a yes from all the aides. "Then let's go."

It was dark enough, fortunately, that they weren't obvious as they all walked in shadows of trees and houses toward the home that was their target. Then the two shifters and all the aides walked quietly onto the porch of that home and crouched down behind the partial wall at its outer end so they wouldn't be readily visible to neighbors.

Liam rang the doorbell. He heard Louper bark inside.

A minute later the door opened, and Rosa stood there. Her eyes lit up immediately, then grew frantic, although the tone of her voice didn't show it. "Well, hello, Liam. Thanks for coming."

He saw all sorts of questions in her expression, but neither of them could talk about anything that Valerie wouldn't overhear.

"Please come in," she finished, although he saw a slight shake of her head, as if she didn't want him to accept her invitation.

"Thanks." He immediately saw why she didn't want him to come in, but having Valerie right behind her, revolver barrel thrust against Rosa's back, wasn't a surprise.

"Yes, come in, Liam." Valerie's voice was much too sweet, and Liam had an urge to attack her with all the one-on-one combat skills he had learned in the military. But he wouldn't necessarily be fast enough to prevent her from shooting Rosa.

No, he would wait and get involved in a conversation with her—and find a way to open a door or window to let his comrades in.

First thing would be to put her off guard as much as possible, although he had no doubt she wouldn't trust him any more than he trusted her.

"So," he said, after the door was closed behind him, "I don't understand, Valerie. Why are you doing this?"

"You do understand," she contradicted. "Did you bring the elixir and light?"

He nodded. "What you asked for is in my car, right outside." Well, not far down the street, but he'd be able to point it out to her if she insisted.

He wished he could reassure Rosa that he was lying, because her scared look took on an angry glint for a moment. "Valerie was telling me before," she said, "that she'd been trying to come up with her own kind of shifting formula—and that she'd put some in your food and Drew's at different times before the recent full moons."

He felt a cold wave shoot up his back. "And that's what prevented us from changing back."

"Exactly." Valerie sounded so proud he wanted to throttle her. Heck, he wanted to throttle her for so many reasons. "Now go out and get that damn elixir of yours."

"In a minute," he said. "Could we go somewhere and sit down and talk? I'm really impressed by your skills and want to know more. How did you come up with that kind of formulation?"

He saw Valerie take a deep breath as she stared at him, and then another. "Okay," she said. "Let's go into the kitchen, but just for a minute. I'll tell you that and more. I'm damn proud of who I am and what I've done, and I'm mad that your stupid Alpha Force wasn't nicer to me. But I've gotten back at them…and you."

Keep her talking, his mind said. And he actually wanted to. Got back at Alpha Force? How?

They soon were seated at the familiar square plastic table in the kitchen—at least Rosa and he were.

Louper was in there, too, pacing around. Valerie remained standing, and she kept the .357 Magnum trained on Rosa, damn her. That made it harder for him to do anything at the moment.

But he would. Soon.

"You're going to go get that elixir and bring it in here," Valerie said as she leaned toward Rosa, sticking the gun into her side hard enough that it made her wince—another reason Liam had to prevent himself from acting. "But first, I want to tell you one more thing, since we won't be seeing each other again after this. I didn't only get back at Alpha Force by giving you and that Drew guy stuff to harm you. You know I'm aware somewhat of what you do for that stupid military unit, working with their online stuff to protect their reputation, such as it is, since you try to keep it secret. Well, I knew about it thanks to Carleen. And since they were so unkind to me, I figured I'd be unkind to them. You know of my background with computer technology as well as science, don't you?"

Vaguely, he recalled that Carleen had mentioned her sister's multiple skills, although she hadn't gone into detail. But he wished now that he had pressed Carleen to say more—since he suddenly knew where this part of the conversation was going.

This shifter was versatile. And clearly quite smart.

But so was he. Now, all he had to do was prove it—and make sure Rosa remained okay.

"Yes, I know," he said, biting the inside of his mouth. "And I'll bet you're the one I've been looking for—one of the people who've hidden their identities but blabbed about Alpha Force's shifters and lied about what they do during a full moon."

"Exactly," she crowed, fluffing her silvery hair away from her face with her free hand. "I'm Orion. Or at least I'm that Orion. I met the guy around here who calls himself that, liked his name and adopted it myself. And sometimes I'm Diana or others, although I don't take on too many female goddesses' names since I don't want it too obvious I'm a woman. But I've been really good at hiding my background, don't you think? No, don't answer. I know I'm great at this stuff, but figure you won't admit it."

Again Liam had to hold himself in check. Had the Alpha Force members with him moved around the house at all? Any of them? Could they hear this? Could Drew hear this?

"I see," he made himself say calmly. "I'll admit that you're definitely skilled in many things." *And I'm going to shut you down*, he promised himself—and Rosa. She was watching him and undoubtedly recognized the fury within him despite how cool he attempted to keep his expression.

Well, enough of this. It was time to act.

"Okay," he said. "I think we need to end this now. Let me go out to my car and get the elixir and light." And backup.

"Very good. But just remember I'll be in here with your sweetie, Rosa—or whatever she is to you."

He didn't like that Valerie watched him so closely. That she remained so near him just then.

He needed a good way to get his backup into the house. But he'd been unable to open any doors or windows.

Still, he'd had a chance to look around—and knew what he was going to do.

"I'll be right back," he told Valerie, aiming a wink at Rosa. Of course they followed him to the front door, so he couldn't leave it ajar.

He had an idea now how this should go, especially after he scanned the area while standing at the door. "Are you going to wait for me back in the kitchen?" he asked, hoping the answer was no. "It seems appropriate, and—"

"If you like it, then forget it. We'll wait for you in there." Valerie flipped the gun toward the living room beside them, then back toward Rosa again.

"Oh. Fine." Liam tried to sound just a touch perturbed, even though her response was what he'd hoped for. "I've got several bottles to remove from my car, as well as the light. I'll be as quick as I can."

He would definitely be as quick as he could, but not doing what he had told her.

He'd be doing something else—something that would allow him to shut her down, and in a way that might teach her a lesson, as well. Or not.

He had to stop this malicious shifter who could only harm her wonderful race, as well as the regular humans they lived among.

Stop her now.

He put his hand on the doorknob, looked at Valerie as if asking permission, then slipped past Louper, who was pacing again—probably aware that there were other beings nearby. Liam went out the door and down the walkway to the street, after trading glances with the shifted wolves who crouched there.

They'd be waiting.

Liam headed past his car—and went quickly into

the nearby woods, where Denny waited for him with elixir and a light.

And very quickly, behind trees so as not to be seen, Liam began to shift.

Rosa wondered what would come next.

She knew Liam wasn't going to obey Valerie's command and return with elixir for her. But a little time had passed, and—

Louper stood up, looking around, at attention. The sweet dog had barked just once before, when Liam had rung the bell. He'd seemed uneasy a lot, such as when Valerie had made Rosa accompany her out of the living room to greet Liam. He had acted interested in going outside then, but Valerie had ignored his unspoken request. Rosa half figured the dog would reach a point and then leave a puddle in the house, but that hadn't happened yet.

He'd been in the kitchen with them, then followed them once more to the front door. And when Liam walked out, Louper had seemed agitated once more.

"You may want to take poor Louper outside," Rosa told Valerie, as the woman shooed her back into the living room, the gun, of course, still pointed toward her. "I think he needs a potty break."

"I don't give a damn what he wants," Valerie shouted. "You're not using that as an excuse to get away. If he goes inside, so what? I won't be here much longer, anyway."

Her nasty gaze suggested Rosa wouldn't, either.

Rosa decided to shut up and wait. Sitting on the red-covered sofa again, she nevertheless scanned the room for any kind of shelter, any cover where she could duck if—when—Valerie decided to pull the trigger.

"Where is that damned soldier buddy of yours?" Valerie glanced down at the watch on her wrist. "He's taking too long."

"There's a lot of stuff he needs to bring in," Rosa said. "He may need to figure out the best way to carry it."

"But he got it in the car before. How hard can it be—"

Louper stood up just then and barked—even as the large front window, behind thick draperies, shattered.

Valerie screamed.

Within moments, three wolves resembling the dog who belonged there leaped in. The first one grabbed the heavy curtains in his mouth and yanked them down to cover the broken glass, as the others, following him, sped directly toward where the two women sat in the middle of the room.

Shifters. Rosa knew it. Alpha Force members who'd shifted outside the full moon.

She threw herself onto the floor, hoping Valerie, who hadn't stopped screaming, would be too distracted to shoot her.

Then she couldn't shoot. All three wolves leaped onto her, knocking her down, and one grabbed her wrist in his mouth. Valerie dropped the gun. Another wolf jumped onto her back, holding her in place. That one looked at Rosa, and she knew it was Liam. She had seen him shifted often enough to recognize the silver-and-black markings of his fur. She also recognized one of the others: Drew.

Louper stayed back, but barked.

Rosa assumed there were aides outside, so she called
out over Valerie's voice—swearing now—"They've got
Valerie under control. You can come in." Too bad Valerie had hidden Rosa's phone somewhere, or she'd use
it to call Liam's line, assuming Denny would answer.

"Great!" yelled a voice from outside. "Denny here.
Can you open the door?"

Rosa hurried to the front door and opened it. Denny
stood there with Captain Jonas Truro and Sergeant Kristine Parran. Jonas was Drew's aide, and although Kristine helped several shifters, Rosa figured that the other
shifter in wolf form was Captain Patrick Worley.

The aides hurried in, guns drawn, and immediately
aimed at Valerie once they'd called off the wolves—
which they didn't need to do, Rosa figured.

These particular wolves had human cognition.

"Okay," Jonas said, securing Valerie's arms behind
her back as he lifted her from the floor. "You're under
our control now, Ms. Corland."

And she was.

Rosa gave a huge sigh of relief, dropping to her knees
to hug the wolf who was Liam.

It was over.

Chapter 24

"This meal is on the house," Chuck said, as Carleen and he served burgers and sides including salads and fries. The group, mostly in camo uniforms, was seated around the large table once more created by pushing a lot of small tables together at the rear of Fastest Foods.

Which was a nice thing for his brother and sister-in-law to do on a night after the latest full moon, Liam thought, as he took a sip of some wine that had been brought in special for this occasion.

It was also nice of them to close the place early for this party, which included all members of Alpha Force currently stationed at Ft. Lukman. After all, they'd closed the restaurant early last night, too, since they'd shifted, as had about half the people there.

Though he understood why they did it tonight. This was definitely a celebration for them.

Despite what they had been told before, Chuck and

Carleen had been permitted to use the elixir. Drew had told them that morning, when shifting was over with no problems at all, that the experiment had gone well enough that they were going to get some elixir for every full moon for the foreseeable future—and the experiment would also expand at some point to allow them to use the elixir outside a full moon.

They were thrilled—even as they remained embarrassed and very sorry about all that Valerie had done. Carleen, tears flowing from her eyes, had apologized over and over for her sister's actions—and for her own failure to see even a hint of what had been going on.

"So," Drew said, standing at the head of the table. "Let's toast Alpha Force and all this wonderful military unit does."

"Hear, hear," called a lot of those who were there—and Liam heard a couple additional female voices behind him do the same.

One he'd anticipated hearing. Had been eager to hear—and to see the lovely, sexy, wonderful woman it belonged to.

He turned.

Sure enough, Rosa was there, just entering the place holding the hand of Drew's older child, Emily. Melanie was with her, carrying Andy.

Good. Liam had known Rosa would come. She had told him so.

She had told him a lot since he had helped to bring down Valerie—and prevent the insane shifter from doing further harm. A lot of what Rosa had said was "Thank you." But it included "I'm so glad she didn't hurt you, too," and "I'm also happy that you now have your answers about who posted all those nasty things online about Alpha Force."

They'd spent a lot of time together since then, too—although Valerie's attack had been only a few evenings ago. But those nights together... Liam felt his body move as he thought about them.

And after the shifts to wolf form during the full moon, Rosa had been there in her veterinarian role in case medical assistance had been needed. Which it hadn't, fortunately.

Without Valerie around to spike their food or whatever, all the shifters had changed back right on time.

Liam saw Rosa's gaze scan the table—and light on him. He grinned and motioned toward the empty chair beside him, which he had saved for her.

She walked to the other side of the table, where Drew was, first. The unit's commanding officer had saved seats there for his family, and Rosa turned Emily over to her daddy.

Then Rosa headed to Liam's side. He wanted to grab her in his arms and give her a huge kiss. But this wasn't the right time. Instead, he just took her hand and basked in the glow of the big smile she gave him as she sat down on that saved seat.

"Hi," she said.

"Hi back."

But before Liam could say anything else, Drew spoke. "Welcome to my family, and welcome to all of you. Tonight is special in many ways. All went well last night—and thanks to the capture of the person responsible for our prior problems, all should continue to go well."

"What's going on with Valerie?" prompted Denny, who sat at Liam's other side.

"She is awaiting trial, in federal custody at a covert maximum security prison," Drew responded. "One with special solitary confinement facilities—so she shifted all by herself last night."

"And back," Patrick added.

"Anyway," Drew said, "we've got a couple of surprises pending for later. But for now, let's eat. And drink. And be merry."

There was a buzz of conversation as everyone quizzed him and others on what he was talking about, but he wouldn't explain. Not yet, at least.

Although Liam hoped for one very special thing…

As everyone finally got settled and continued eating their meals, Liam turned to Rosa. "Everything okay at the vet clinic today?"

"Sure," she said, looking him deep in the eye as she smiled at him. "But I did happen to be a little tired. I stayed up late last night."

He laughed. "Me, too."

"And everything okay online about the world of shifters?" she asked him.

"Everything was fine—mostly because there was almost no mention online of shapeshifters over the past few days, including today, and none at all making accusations against some bizarre military unit of shifters hurting people."

"Good," Rosa said, giving a crisp nod.

"Yes, good," Liam said. Were regular humans finally accepting the existence of shifters? Maybe, and maybe not.

But he still hoped for that to be reality someday.

* * *

Rosa was so pleased to be here with Liam and with his whole local Alpha Force gang. She felt part of it despite not being a shifter.

But heck, she liked shifters.

One more than the rest, of course.

In fact, she knew now that she loved Liam.

Although it was premature to let him know that. But he was smart, sexy, techie yet tough, and he had saved her life.

And she wanted so much to crow about that to the world, even though this group already knew it.

She also wanted to melt into Liam's arms and stay there. Forever.

But for now, she just ate her burger and salad and drank her wine.

Liam and she talked about what it had been like on the night of the full moon for both of them—him as a shifter at the edge of Ft. Lukman, and her there, too, observing him and the other wolfen Alpha Forcers.

They weren't relating anything new to each other, but continued to have a good conversation, sometimes including Denny or Melanie or Drew or anyone else.

When they were done eating, Liam said, "There's something in the kitchen here I'd like to show you."

"Some new appliance Chuck bought?" Rosa was teasing. She figured Liam, like her, wanted to share a kiss, despite all the other people here, who didn't need to see it.

That was more than fine with her.

They both stood, and he held her hand as they slowly made their way past the others, some of whom turned to talk to them. But soon they were in the kitchen.

Then Liam led her out the back door and onto the parking lot driveway. "It's quieter here," he told her. "And maybe a little more romantic."

She laughed. "Oh, I like that last part. Romantic." She took a step toward him, wanting to throw her arms around him. But he stepped back.

"Wait a minute," he said, and she felt hurt.

But only for a moment, since he reached into his pocket…and pulled out a small box.

She gasped. It surely wasn't…

But it was. He opened it. It contained a ring. One with a lovely, nice-sized diamond.

Liam did the customary thing and got down on one knee. "Rosa, I love you. I've been fighting it because I figured you might like shifters, but forever with one? So… I'm not really sure you feel the same way, but just in case—"

"I do," she interrupted, and realized those words might have a different meaning someday in the future, assuming he was proposing.

For when he asked if she would marry him, she immediately said yes.

He rose, put the ring on her finger and gave her the deepest, sexiest, most loving kiss she had ever experienced.

Then another one.

And when they finished the third, Rosa said, "We'd probably better go back inside. Did Drew know about this? He mentioned something about some surprises tonight."

"I told him about the possibility," Liam said, grabbing her left hand where his diamond now sparkled as he began leading her back inside. "I told him not to hold his breath, since I wasn't… But boy, am I breathing well now."

Rosa laughed and followed Liam. She determined to ask Melanie about the shifting capabilities of her kids, since she might need to know that someday soon.

Back in the dining room, someone Rosa vaguely recognized was talking. "Isn't that—" she began in a whisper.

"That's General Greg Yarrow, the highest commanding officer of Alpha Force," Liam whispered back. "He must have come in from the Pentagon today."

Like many of the others, the general was clad in camo, although his uniform had a lot of stripes and medals on it. He appeared to be a senior, although his hair was dark black. His voice was strong.

"I'm here to thank all of you again for being members of Alpha Force," he said, "and also to greet Chuck and Carleen and congratulate them for participating in our experiment. There may be more changes looming for Alpha Force, though that's not certain yet. But you can be sure your group is considered very special to those of us in Washington who know about you—including some like me who wish at times I had your shifting skills."

The group laughed, then everyone raised their glasses as Greg did and toasted Alpha Force.

And when the general sat down, Rosa saw Drew look directly at Liam, who nodded.

Drew rose. "Let's again toast the future of Alpha Force," he said, and they all did. And when they had finished, he added, "Let's also toast some very special people around here, one of our own, and one who's my dear wife's wonderful assistant. I believe that Liam and Rosa just became engaged. Right, Liam?"

"Absolutely," said the wonderful man beside Rosa, who was now her fiancé. He also stood and drew Rosa to her feet. "I'll certainly drink to that." Which he did, looking her straight in the eye.

"So," said Drew, "let's all toast Liam and Rosa and the future. May they have a wonderful life together."

"Hear, hear," came the call, and everyone with wine took a drink.

Then Rosa, still standing, rose on her toes and gave Liam a brief but sexy kiss. She lifted her glass. "To Alpha Force, and to my Liam, and to all of you. Here's to a wonderful future for all of us."

She took a long sip, again gazing into Liam's eyes—and looked forward to later that night…and forever.

* * * * *

Linda Thomas-Sundstrom writes contemporary and paranormal romance novels for Harlequin. A teacher by day and a writer by night, Linda lives in the West, juggling teaching, writing, family and caring for a big stretch of land. She swears she has a resident muse who sings so loudly, she often wears earplugs in order to get anything else done. But she has big plans to eventually get to all those ideas. Visit Linda at lindathomas-sundstrom.com or on Facebook.

Books by Linda Thomas-Sundstrom

Harlequin Nocturne

Red Wolf
Wolf Trap
Golden Vampire
Guardian of the Night
Immortal Obsession
Wolf Born
Wolf Hunter
Seduced by the Moon
Immortal Redeemed
Half Wolf
Angel Unleashed
Desert Wolf
Wolf Slayer
The Black Wolf
Code Wolf

Harlequin Desire

The Boss's Mistletoe Maneuvers

Visit the Author Profile page
at Harlequin.com for more titles.

CODE WOLF

Linda Thomas-Sundstrom

To my family, those here and those gone,
who always believed I had a story to tell.

Chapter 1

Detective Derek Miller howled at the moon...

And that call was answered.

He sprinted down a side street, careful to avoid the stares he'd have received if any of Seattle's human population saw him all wolfed up. Humans weren't in on the secrets of his kind, and it was best to keep things that way.

His lethal claws made driving as impossible as ignoring the moon would have been. That big, bright, full moon over his head. Thing was, the claws came in handy on nights like this, when bullets and the usual paraphernalia tied to the justice system wouldn't take down a supernatural enemy. And there were plenty of enemies like that around.

The air he breathed was pressurized and heavy with the odor of trouble. The enhanced capacities that came with being a werewolf made it all the more intense, when his preference would have been to avoid that smell altogether.

No such luck, though.

Full moons brought out the worst in everyone, no matter what species they belonged to. Who the hell knew the actual reason for that?

The moonlight that ruled Were shapes always made his job tougher—the job he was doing in order to get a jump on bad stuff before it happened. He took to the streets most nights around the moon's full phases, when the crazies came out to play, even though big moons made keeping his werewolf identity to himself in a city Seattle's size damn near unmanageable.

When the moon called, Weres obeyed.

Besides the obvious risks of being outed as an *Other*, working the night shift had its perks. He wasn't the only Seattle Were in law enforcement, and the bonus of having packmates for backup was important when another species showed up.

Not many folks would have understood about the presence of monsters, the way he and some of his friends did. And though most werewolves didn't classify themselves as monsters, humans around the world would have if they knew they weren't the only species sharing the place.

Derek was all right with that, though. He was a good detective and also the alpha of a two-dozen-strong werewolf pack that was helping to clear this city of the morbid creatures stalking it.

Running suited him.

Chasing bad guys suited him.

Tonight, he had a larger body, more muscle and longer hair, which were giveaways of his species. A slightly longer face and more feral features rounded out the look. Still, he might have been recognizable if viewed up close by someone who knew him well enough. And it was a fact that any guy running around Seattle shirtless wasn't normal even if there was a badge pinned to his belt.

Got to love those perks, though...

He used his enhanced sense of smell to break down scent particles so that he could follow the foul odor blowing in from the eastern part of the city.

That odor was bad news.

Unreleased growls rumbled in his chest like a bad case of heartburn as he inhaled.

Streets in the east were crowded with apartment buildings and lofts in renovated warehouses, where people were piled on top of each other. Singling out the source of that odor there could have been tricky, even for a werewolf. But he had no problem. There was nothing like that particular smell anywhere else. The foulness in the wind had a name, and that name was *vampire*.

He hated vampires.

Upping his game, Derek ran on legs that seldom tired. Any indication of vamp presence was cause for immediate action, and the packmate that had responded to his call would also be heading this way.

Keeping near to the shadows and squeezing between them, he skirted the public places people frequented on Friday nights, careful to avoid being seen. Detective Derek Miller was a wolf on a mission that required his full attention.

Bloodsucking parasites had become the bane of his existence for two years straight. He must have killed a hundred of them already, but for every one vamp taken down, five more popped up in its place.

Nighttime hours meant snack time for vampires. Old brick exteriors in the eastern portion of Seattle made those buildings easy to climb, and picking off people had become easier for bloodsuckers on the prowl.

Growling again, Derek hopped a curb. His boots were heavy, making stealth difficult. His size didn't help, either. Still, there was nothing to be done about that at the moment. Because his job was to protect and serve, Derek was already working on a creative reason to explain any human deaths that could possibly occur. Lately, that kind of creativity was not only imperative, but it had also become a full-time job.

Tonight's moon was going to be the equivalent of a giant dinner bell for fanged parasites. Luckily for this city's inhabitants, that full moon also gave him a leg up in dealing with them. In werewolf form, Weres were twice as strong as any human and meaner than hell when it came to trespassers with evil intentions.

He didn't like this, but he was used to the routine.

Come on, bloodsuckers. I know you're here somewhere.

The odor he had detected became noticeably stronger as he rounded a corner. In case he changed back to a more human form, the gun strapped to his belt was loaded with silver bullets, one of which could take down a vampire if the shooter had good aim.

A small dose of silver to the head or chest would send those undead bastards back to the kind of afterlife they should have been experiencing.

Of course, a sharp wooden stake would also suffice…though a proper staking would require meeting a vampire face-to-face and up close and personal. Which he'd never advise.

Following the fetid trail, Derek slipped into the narrow space between two buildings, where the atmospheric pressure he had noticed earlier got worse. He ended up in an alley that appeared to be deserted, but wasn't.

The stench he sought had competition here. Overflowing garbage receptacles lined the walls. Beer cans and paper littered the ground. Although there were no artificial lights, broken shards of glass glittered like gems in the thin streams of moonlight shining down from overhead.

Other than his breathing, there was a marked absence of sound. Yet somewhere in all that darkness, among the discarded detritus that could have masked their presence, a couple of pale-faced lunatics hid.

Her pale-faced lunatics. Minions of Seattle's vampire queen. Two of them, at least, were using this alley for their hidey-hole and probably waiting to do their Master's bidding.

Got you...

Derek took another deep breath to process the danger. The air here was rife with Otherness that only supernatural beings were attuned to. From experience, he had a good idea these vamps would be fledglings. The degree of foulness saturating the air hinted at this being the case.

There was no mistaking the metallic scent that pointed to the blood meal these vamps had recently ingested. The pair had been sloppy at the dinner table and were coated in the evidence. It was unlikely that their victim, or victims, had survived.

His next growl echoed off the mildewed walls, sounding like thunder.

I met your queen once, he would have told these abominations if he had proper vocal cords in his Were state. *I saw your grand dame near here on the night my ex-lover was almost killed.*

The thought sickened him to this day.

I know your Master's name. I've seen her face.

He had heard that vampire's name whispered during a midnight battle with her kind, and afterward had caught a glimpse of the black-haired soulless diva whose talent for drawing every bloodsucker within this city's boundaries to her side was no joke.

The fanged bitch was like a black widow spider, thriving in her lair while her creepy hordes fed off the living and created an army. *Damaris* was her name. Most divas only had one.

He owed her a good fight for personal reasons as well as professional, so Derek scanned the darkness with his claws raised, ready to do some damage.

As he waited, Derek adopted a wide stance and slowed his breathing. Seconds passed. The fangers would have to eventually acknowledge his presence, if they dared.

Derek was counting on his formidable appearance to provide an edge. His normal height of six-two stretched upward when he shifted. All that new muscle rippled with anticipation over how this might go down.

He moved his jaw, clenched his teeth. His face might have been more human than wolf, but it wasn't enough like a human to confuse the two species. It was helpful in this instance that one of Seattle's most decorated detectives looked like everyone's worst nightmare.

Come out, you filthy bastards.

Nothing moved. The vampires would be sizing him up and preparing their response. Finding and dealing with them like this was vigilante justice, but justice nevertheless. They couldn't be allowed to kill more of Seattle's citizens or break the spell that hid Were existence. For humans, the supernatural world didn't exist.

His pack and other packs like it policed the shadows, exacting payback on misbehaving monsters that preyed on the humans in this jurisdiction. The goal was to keep the peace and maintain Were secrets, and Derek had taken this goal to a whole new level after the woman he had loved left Seattle because of the influx of monsters.

There was also the fact that his ex-lover hadn't known about his secret wolfish life and the moon that ruled his kind. But that was history.

His fault.

Long story.

The packmate he had been expecting silently slid into place behind him, barely ruffling the air. Derek didn't have to turn around to know who this was. Dale Duncan was a fearless cop and no stranger to things that went bump in the night. Officer Duncan was good to have around no matter what outline he presented to the world.

The two of them could have taken on a slew of vampires. These fledglings had to know it. Word traveled fast in underground circles.

Bathed in moonlight, he and Dale stood like sentries near the entrance to the alley. There was nowhere for these bloodsuckers to go. As newbies they'd be full of themselves and energized by their recent kill. Maybe they didn't yet know about all that ancient enemy shit between Weres and vampires, and that it continued today. Was it possible they believed vampires were the superior species?

When Derek's packmate growled menacingly, the ground shook. Near the opposite end of the alley, a tin can rolled.

"Monsters have to try to fit in now," Derek silently chastised. But the warning wouldn't have done much good if the vamps had heard it.

He added, *"Werewolves, for the most part, have evolved alongside our human counterparts and most of the time can fit in with the society surrounding us. You guys have obviously never gotten the memo."*

A slight, sudden wave of extra pressure in the darkness suggested movement. The back of Derek's neck tingled in acknowledgment of what that meant.

"Any minute now," Dale messaged.

What Derek failed to mention in all this was his anxiousness over finding himself less than half a block from the building his ex-lover had once occupied—the same building where real vamp trouble in Seattle had begun two years back. His pack had cleaned out this area after that event. Keeping the public from finding out about it had been a cleanup job worthy of the Nobel Prize.

So what the hell had happened?

Why were the vampires back?

Even the smallest twitch was a waste of energy, but Derek rolled his neck to ease some of the tension building there. Waiting made him angry. There were too many memories in and around this place.

When he heard the swish of a swipe of claws, he nodded. Dale had torn holes in his jeans, and the scent of blood filled the air. *"Smart move,"* Derek messaged.

That smell might draw vampires lacking the facts about how bad furred-up werewolves tasted.

However, a positive outcome was never completely assured when dealing with fanged hordes that were almost subliminally fast on their feet and ruled by an outrageous thirst that no one alive could possibly have understood.

Derek dared a quick sideways glance to calculate the exact distance to the building he had often visited in the past in order to court and bed McKenna Randall.

Too damn close.

His nerves buzzed. His skin burned white-hot. Hell, he still missed having a talented bed partner.

"The place is cursed," Dale messaged to him.

Derek grunted in agreement.

Both of them knew what to expect here. There weren't going to be any surprises in this alley tonight, hopefully.

To catch more moonlight, Derek took a step forward. Silvery moon particles settled on his bare shoulders like a hot lover's breath, setting off a series of internal sparks that in turn started a chain reaction. All of that centered on the word *anger*. And okay, maybe also a more personal need for revenge.

Behind him, Dale was experiencing something similar and waiting for the signal to get this over with.

Tired of playing hide-and-seek, Derek gave that signal.

Chapter 2

Riley Price blinked back an almost supernatural wave of fatigue and unlocked her car without getting in. She leaned briefly against the cool metal of her silver sedan and glanced up at the moon, wondering if she should howl at that big round disc the way werewolves did in the movies.

She sighed instead.

The hours at work this week had been long and tough to get through, leaving little energy for extras no matter how fun those extras could have been. After her first days on the job, she could have used a little jolt of excitement. Listening to other people's problems day in and day out was exhausting, especially when she had a few fantasies of her own.

Wasn't that the premier joke about psychologists—that people in this kind of field went into it because of their own need for answers?

The boulevard was crowded with people coming and going at 9:00 p.m. Shouts, laughter and revving car engines nearly drowned out the sound of the keys jangling in her hand.

And there was something else, wasn't there? Beyond those normal city noises, Riley could have sworn she heard another sound. Something that didn't quite fit in.

If she hadn't just thought about howling at the damn moon, she might have imagined that someone else had.

"It sure sounded like that," she muttered.

The back of her neck chilled. In spite of the common sense she had always been known for, she secretly wished for adventure. It was one of those personal issues she had to deal with. The desire for a little action was probably what was craved by every female who had done her schoolwork straight through and ended up in a job with no break whatsoever.

Riley Price, PhD. Helpful, empathetic, on her way to becoming successful and, these days, quite bland. Bland on the outside, at least. Deep inside her was where her more rebellious ways had always been corralled.

She turned back to the car, opened the door and slid carefully onto the seat, respecting the restriction of her black pencil skirt. But she didn't get both feet inside before that same eerie, slightly discomforting sound came again from somewhere in the distance.

A wolf's haunting howl?

"You know you have a vivid imagination," she reminded herself with a stern head shake. One strange belief too many and she, in spite of all her education in this area, would be in need of a psychiatrist's comfy couch.

How many times had she thought that she should have become a cop like her father and let out all of her pent-up energy? For cops, the world was viewed in black-and-white terms, without too many murky gray zones. As it was, her need for independence and a life of her own outside of law enforcement had dictated taking another route toward helping people. So here she was, several states away from her family in Arizona, and on her own.

One more head shake ought to do it.

"Wolves in downtown Seattle? Give me a break."

Feet in the car, key in the ignition, Riley released a slow breath and closed the door, then paused before starting the engine. Opening the door again might have been willful, but she did so anyway. She hoped to hear a repeat of that eerie sound and wished that things didn't actually have to be black and white in terms of reasonableness and reality.

She shivered at the incoming breeze of cool night air and was overtaken by a sudden onslaught of chills that weren't related to a change in the weather. Waves of ice dripped down the back of her neck to lay siege to sensitive skin beneath her baby blue sweater. She did hear that howl again, didn't she?

"I'm sure I did."

This third sound made it seem like there had been no mistake. Someone had howled. Not some*thing*, because everyone knew there were no wolves in the city and no such things as werewolves. So who, like her, was digging into the beauty and mythology of this full moon? Who, like her, had watched a few too many movies that had activated their imagination?

She could try to find out. Chase down those sounds. Meet that person. Though those ideas were intriguing, women weren't always completely safe on their own in a city the size of Seattle after dark. It wasn't that she was afraid of the statistics. Fear hadn't been part of her upbringing, and inquisitiveness was a trait that had been tightly wound into the strands of her DNA. But it wasn't wise to throw caution to the wind all at once for the sake of folly.

Somewhere out there a human being with a similar sense of fun and fantasy was having one on. Since moving to Seattle, she hadn't met anyone quite like that. Didn't that fact alone determine the need for a closer look?

Fatigue melted away. Riley was out of the car in seconds, listening hard, and issuing a whispered challenge. "Come on. Do it again. I dare you."

Cell phone in hand—she wasn't stupid, after all—she locked the car, turned toward the sidewalk and started out in three-inch heels that wouldn't let her win a race, but would get her far enough.

She hadn't experienced tingling nerves like this in some time. They drew her half a block to the east, where she'd still be within safety limits. Men and women strolled in both directions, oblivious to the finer art of adventure. None of them glanced up at the sky. Noise from the pubs and restaurants blurred her ability to hear much else.

When more chills arrived, along with a sudden awareness of being stared at, Riley slowed to glance at the man who leaned against the side of an open doorway. His face was half-hidden by the shadows of an overhead awning that spanned most of the sidewalk, and yet Riley knew he was looking at her in a predatory way. Not man-to-woman stuff. Something else. Something more.

With a tight grip on her cell phone, she passed by him, careful to avoid any kind of contact that might have been misconstrued as an invitation. She'd been fed those kinds of self-defense tips for breakfast in the Price household and knew them all by heart.

Show no weakness.

Be a predator, not someone else's prey.

Almost able to hear her dad say those words, Riley smiled, which would have been the wrong thing to do if she hadn't already put some distance between that creep by the bar and herself. Nevertheless, she took one more quick look over her shoulder...just before she felt the firm grip of a hand on her arm.

Derek silently counted to five, nodded and took another step forward, hoping to taunt the vampires that were hiding here into showing themselves. Possibly they were going over their options for getting away, as if they actually had some.

Another step took him closer to the cans lining the walls. The stench of rotting food was unbelievable. And this was taking too damn long.

He kicked the closest can with the tip of his boot, providing more incentive for the fanged abominations to make an appearance. Vampires had sensitive hearing and didn't like noise.

He kicked the can again and it rolled sideways, spilling what was left of its contents—unrecognizable stuff with an unbelievable odor.

The challenge worked.

One of the vamps dropped from above the trash cans as if it actually might have been half bat, as the old wives' tales suggested. Its partner followed. They were a pair of completely colorless creatures whose dirty and tattered clothing suggested they might have recently crawled up from the grave.

A ripple of disgust rolled over Derek.

Both of these guys were drenched in blood that was now darkening. Tiny red rivulets of what had been some human's life force ran in tracks down the sides of their white faces. Red-rimmed eyes peered back at him with dull, flat, lifeless gazes. Whatever kind of voodoo had animated this pair remained one of life's great mysteries.

Derek didn't waste any time in going after them. In this instance, their newness to the vamp bag of tricks was in Were favor. The dark-eyed pair had speed, but he and Dale far outweighed them. When their bodies collided, the two vamp fledglings shrieked with anger, yellow fangs snapping, but couldn't escape the claws that snagged their rotted clothing.

After spinning his bloodsucker around in a circle, Derek tossed his opponent against the brick. The bloodsucker quickly rallied and was on him again in a flash with arms and legs flailing. The creep was a hell of a lot stronger than he looked.

Derek's muscles corded as he fought to send this ghastly creature back to its natural state of death. Actually, he was doing these monsters a favor, because who would have wanted to end up in such a sorry state?

He felt the breeze of snapping canines that had gotten too close to his face and he roared with displeasure. The sheer menace in that preternaturally wolfish sound temporarily stunned the vampire in his grasp.

That's it. Those teeth of yours won't harm anyone else in this city. You won't accidentally make another

*bloodsucker in your image, and further contribute to
the pain in my ass.*

Dale had maneuvered his vampire to the back of the
alley, where there was an even slimmer chance for it to
escape. Derek danced his flailing abomination in the
same direction, whirling, ducking, lunging to the side
to avoid the sucker's uncanny ability to recover.

The only way to keep those pointed teeth from making contact with his flesh was by taking a firm hold on
the bastard's neck. But since vampires didn't actually
breathe, a good squeeze wasn't going to suffocate the
creature into submission.

The vampire's spine hit the wall with a thud that
shook the brick. The wily creature brought up its filthy
bare feet and straddled Derek's body with legs made
mostly of brittle bone and strings of sinew.

Fine little hairs on the back of his neck lifted as Derek
shoved off the creature. With a fresh round of strength
fueled by disgust, he finally got the vampire on the
ground, on its back, where it fought like it had five limbs
instead of four. When the sucker gurgled with anger,
black blood bubbled from its lips.

*"This is the end. I'm sure you'll thank me later. And
really, there is no pleasure in this, and only a necessary kind of justice."*

Dale, close by, tossed him a stake, which Derek
caught in one hand. With one final burst of energy, he
stuck that wooden stake deep into the vamp's chest, in
the spot where its heart had once beat.

Go in peace, vampire.

The creature exploded as if it hadn't been actually
composed of flesh and bone at all, but merely a bunch
of musty pieces that had been glued together. Seconds

later, a rain of nasty, odorous gray ash swirled through the area like a twister.

A second explosion rocked the area moments after that. Amid a flurry of ash that was temporarily blinding, Derek turned his head to see Dale smiling back at him.

"Mission accomplished," Derek messaged to his packmate. Or so he thought before the soft, muffled sound of a human in trouble reached him from the street beyond.

Across the filthy, ash-strewn alley's crackled asphalt, above the musty gray dust that had quickly settled to the ground, Dale's eyes again met his.

Chapter 3

Riley was no weakling, but the guy was extraordinarily strong and fast, using his other hand to spin her around. He now had her by the waist with a hand clamped over her mouth.

Despite her rocketing pulse, she got one good kick in before he pulled her into the shadows so fast, it happened between one blink of her eyes and the next. Still, she wasn't going to play dead or be reduced to a teary mess, and managed to connect with the guy's shin with a second kick. When his hand fell away from her mouth, Riley shouted for help.

The fight she put up had surprised her attacker. His hold on her waist loosened enough for her to pull back and spin sideways. They were near the entrance to an underground restaurant and yet no one had seen this happen because the asshole's timing had been impeccable.

She heard her phone hit the sidewalk and didn't have the opportunity to retrieve it. Hands came at her again as if the guy was half octopus, and as if he had more at stake here than she did. He clasped her throat to choke off a call for help.

"Bastard!" she shouted.

A filmy blur of movement danced around her, reminiscent of a storm system moving in. The whirlwind was so strong, she flew backward, stumbled and almost lost her footing. The jolt of hitting a wall knocked her senseless. Her head snapped back. Stars danced in her vision and her stomach turned over.

That's when things really got fuzzy.

Did the ass who had manhandled her have accomplices? There were now three moving blurs of speed in the area. Mere streaks of movement. Nothing defined. And she had a concussion. Either that or these new guys were larger than any humans she had ever seen. The sounds they made were fierce, threatening, and similar to sounds animals made in the wild. Each grunt and growl added to the pressure in her skull.

It occurred to her that she had been dropped into the middle of one of those horror movies she had been thinking about. Strange sounds under a full moon reinforced the thought.

Looking up made her dizziness worse. Her knees started to buckle. Her vision narrowed as a hovering net of blackness slowly descended. Riley dug deep for more courage. She could get away while no one was looking, find the phone she had dropped and call for help.

Another arm closed around her before she had completed the plan. Although she struggled to get free, she could hardly breathe past the pain in her head, let alone rally for another attack.

Uttering a string of curses, she tried to focus her eyes and found nothing in front of her but a wide expanse of someone's bare chest.

"Damn it."

She whispered more curses as she was lifted up and swept off her feet. The only way to stop the unusual sensation of having the ground ripped from beneath her was to close her eyes.

Another sound ricocheted inside her head, seeming to echo noises she had heard before. Though she couldn't have been colder, a new round of chills arrived when she recognized what that sound was.

With her heart rate nearing critical mass, Riley slowly opened her eyes and took a breath before having to face whatever her fate was to be.

Nothing happened immediately. Cool wind on her face soothed the icy shame of having put herself in harm's way. But she was in somebody's arms, and moving away from the street. For some reason, she didn't sense harm here, though.

Her inner defiance sparked and anger burned like a beacon.

"Put me down. Let me catch my breath."

The arms holding her loosened considerably. Riley again felt the hard support of a wall behind her as the man did as she asked and set her down.

In her vision, this guy's body continued to move as if he had the ability to fluidly alter his shape. Yet she knew that couldn't be right, and after a tense moment of silence, he spoke.

"Can you stand?"

The husky, overtly masculine voice cut through the pain behind her eyes.

"You'll be all right in a minute. We've called this in and someone will come to get you," he said.

Hell, had she just been rescued? Was that what all the commotion was about?

Shaking off the last vestiges of dizziness, Riley focused all her attention on the person who had spoken to her, grateful that someone had heard her shout for help. Her attacker had been thwarted and she was going to live, after all.

Her rescuer leaned closer to her, his bare chest wide and bronzed. Her gaze traveled slowly over that broad expanse of flesh before she worked her way upward. The thanks she had meant to offer was delayed by a question that took precedence over anything else she might have said.

"Why are you half-naked?"

"You're welcome," the shirtless man returned after a beat.

He hadn't stepped back to leave her. Instead, her rescuer seemed to be waiting to make sure she actually could stand up.

His physique was rock-solid. Since he towered over her, there was no way to see his face without again banging her head against the wall behind her. One concussion per night was all she could manage.

"I'm sorry." Riley's voice wasn't as steady as she would have liked. "Thank you for helping me."

The guy didn't respond verbally. His hard, muscled body pinned her in place for a few more seconds, as if body language had its own form of communication. Riley hadn't noticed how much she had been shivering until she felt the warmth of the man's closeness. Through the loose weave of her sweater, her rescuer's heat was welcome.

She sighed.

He leaned closer.

"Not an invitation," Riley warned, turning her head to the side.

"Didn't think it was," he replied.

His voice was gruff, as if he hadn't spoken in a while. At any other time, she probably would have been intrigued by that. Now she just wanted to go home.

He spoke again. "Will you be okay? I'm sorry, but I have to go. I'll have to leave you here."

The wail of a siren in the distance reminded Riley that this guy had mentioned something about calling in the incident. But as she contemplated that, wondering again why this Good Samaritan was roaming the city without his shirt, he disappeared.

His heat was gone and the night's coolness returned. She had no one to lean against now. It was a miracle she was still standing.

The first thing that popped into her mind as she waited for the police to arrive was a ludicrous reaction to what had happened, and meant nothing, really. Nevertheless, she pursed her lips, took a deep breath and howled softly, almost to herself.

"Ar-rrooo-ooo…"

The heat returned, quick as a flash. The man who had rescued her was there to pin her to the wall again. With a mouth that was as feverish as the rest of his body, he brushed his lips across her forehead and down her right cheek. The featherlight touch, there and gone in a few fleeting seconds, left Riley breathless.

Had she made a mistake in thinking this was a good guy?

Inching backward far enough to put a finger under her chin, he carefully tilted her head so that he could look into her eyes with a studied observation. His eyes were light, maybe blue, and surrounded by dark lashes.

Riley couldn't look away or break eye contact. The intensity in those eyes would have held her captive if his body hadn't. In his gaze she found something weirdly beautiful and at the same time troubling. She detected a flicker of real wildness there.

Had she made this guy up in some head-injury-induced coma? Could she have banged her head that hard?

Because…

She was sure…

No. She wasn't sure at all, actually. How stupid would that have been?

Riley listened to the absurdity of the words that came out of her mouth next, and winced when she was done.

"There are no such things as werewolves. You do know that?"

The smile this stranger offered her made her feel like she was being bathed in white light. She saw pearly teeth in a tanned face. The area around his eyes crinkled slightly at the corners, above chiseled features partially darkened by a five-o'clock shadow.

That's all she got, all she was allowed, before she found herself alone again with the lost cell phone he had somehow placed in her hand…and a splitting headache.

Chapter 4

Derek had to leave the woman or risk being caught by the people he took such pains to his hide true identity from on a daily basis. Dale was already sprinting in the opposite direction in human form, racing from shadow to shadow. But though Derek had also downsized to a human shape, he hated to leave before further help arrived for the woman they had rescued from harm. That part of being a werewolf sucked.

The woman had howled. Sort of. And she had mentioned werewolves. That alone would have intrigued him, even if she hadn't been so damn beautiful.

What did she know about his kind? Anything? Could it be that she was just having him on with the werewolf remark, with no real idea how close to his reality she had come? Or was she fully equipped with knowledge about his kind?

She was a fierce little thing. No wallflower when

it came to protecting herself. He'd witnessed that kick she had given to the imbecile he and Dale had left unconscious and handcuffed to a drainpipe.

She'd handled herself the best way she could without succumbing to shock. That took courage and also meant that her girl-next-door, wholesome looks were somewhat deceiving.

Small and *feisty* would have been a turn-on for a big bad wolf if he had time for such things…and if she hadn't been human. Add to that her pale oval face, big eyes and mass of shiny blond hair, and she became a real curiosity.

With so many battles to fight these days, it was best for him to ignore distractions. He hadn't indulged in anything that could have been considered a relationship since his heart had been broken, and he was still picking up the pieces of that breakup. It was also possible he had been wallowing a bit too long in its aftermath.

The only reason he had risked a shift back to human form in this woman's presence was because she hadn't been in any kind of state to have recognized what was going on at the time. Only by shifting could he have offered assurance that she was going to be okay. Her eyes had barely focused. She had been confused.

Still, and again, she had howled and mentioned werewolves.

Dale was waiting for him around the next corner, at the edge of a dimly lit parking lot. He stood in the shadows of a large sign, just any old half-dressed human to an observer's eye. Dale also was a big guy, and formidable. No one in their right mind would have moved closer for a better look, or questioned his shirtless state. Dale's posture alone would have prevented that.

"Do you know her?" Dale asked as Derek pulled up beside him.

"Never saw her before," Derek replied.

"You got sort of cozy back there."

"I just had to make sure she was all right."

Dale grinned. "Yeah. Well, you took a while to do that. And you shifted in the presence of a human."

"She was half-unconscious at the time," Derek pointed out. "And she's unusual."

"She's no Were," Dale said. "I'd have thought you had learned a lesson about human women."

Derek nodded. "Learned it loud and clear, my friend. Have no fear about that."

Dale's gaze swept over the parking lot. "It's quiet now."

Derek didn't want to jinx things by agreeing or mentioning unnecessarily that there usually were a few moments of calm before a storm. The moon had only been up for a few hours. There was more night ahead. He figured that when word got back to the vamp queen about two of her young fledglings being dusted, vamp activity would pick up. He had a special sense for that kind of thing.

"We'd better get back to it," he said.

"Right," Dale agreed with a big breath as he stepped into the moonlight and, to get Derek to laugh, pounded on his chest the way male apes did in the wild. Then he pinned another grin to his rapidly morphing features. Unlike Derek, Dale was a more frightening rendition of their werewolf species—wolfish body, wolfish face, fur follicles and all.

When the light hit Derek, he closed his eyes. With an internal rumble, the changes began. The expansion of his chest came first, followed by an icy burn in his hips and legs as the mysterious chemical reaction coded into him gave his system a bump.

In a quick lightning strike of pain, his arms and torso muscled up, stretching his skin and the bones beneath. Light brown hair, usually only a little too long for a detective in Seattle, lengthened, as if a year had gone by with no trim. Last to alter were the parts of his face that took on another look with a brief, sharp, short-lived sting.

Weres, early in their lifetimes, had to either learn to adapt to these physical changes or die. The first shape-shift often weeded out the weak. There was no escaping or hiding from the inner explosions that set off a shape-shift. Everyone supposed this was a survival-of-the-fittest sort of biological trick. But getting used to the art of a body's physical rearrangement was a Were's mission. Being Were was a serious game of species-imposed destiny.

Dale was waiting for him to acknowledge the job of alley sweeping ahead, and Derek nodded. More vampires would come out sooner or later, and he and Dale had to be ready.

"I suppose you'd like to drop by that place and make sure the woman and her assailant were picked up?" Dale messaged wryly.

"Do you think you can read minds now?" Derek returned.

"Not all minds. Just yours."

Derek barked a laugh. It was true that he wanted to go back there. He wanted nothing more, in fact.

"Just to check on the perp," he sent to Dale.

"*You go right ahead and tell yourself that,*" Dale messaged back.

Hell, maybe Dale really could read minds…

"*It's dangerous to retrace our steps,*" Dale warned.

Derek shrugged his massive shoulders. "*Dangerous for whom? The idiot that tried to attack a woman on a busy street, or us?*"

"*Well, you've got me there.*"

Dale matched Derek's confident stride across the parking lot as they turned to the east again with renewed purpose.

At the very least, Derek decided, he had to find out who that woman was, and what her remarks about werewolves meant. She would have been questioned by the officers who picked her up, so there would be paperwork filed. Her personal information would be on that paperwork.

Even better, with the attacker in custody, she'd have to be questioned further. And he knew just the right detective to help with that, even if doing so might mean treading on another detective's casework.

"*Smell that?*" Dale asked.

"*Hell yeah,*" Derek returned.

They exchanged glances, growled in unison and took off in the direction of the latest ill wind.

Four cops arrived in Riley's rescuer's wake. She marshalled her strength, since she needed to make sure they took the guy who had caused all this chaos into custody.

The jerk was still unconscious and was handcuffed to a pipe near the entrance to the nearby alley. Cops were looking from her to him with unspoken questions on their faces.

"A couple of big guys came to my rescue," she said. "Looks like this was my lucky night."

"They did that? Cuffed him?" one of the officers asked, checking out the standard-issue cuffs she had seen a thousand times hanging from her father's belt loops.

"Cops?" the officer continued.

"Possibly," Riley replied. "Though they weren't in uniform."

The officer nodded. "Plainclothes guys, most likely. Are you hurt, ma'am? Are you in need of medical assistance?"

Riley thought about that. Actually, she was okay, except for the headache and the thought of having had a near brush with death.

"A ride would be nice," she said. "To my car."

"We'll have to take a statement," another officer pointed out.

Riley nodded. "I can give you that."

She knew the drill about that, too. She could talk about the attempted abduction, but she couldn't even begin to describe her rescuer in any way that wouldn't make her sound crazy. Shirtless male? Rippling muscle that didn't seem to be able to settle on his big frame? Volcanic heat? Eyes like laser beams?

Maybe since these guys assumed she'd been helped by plainclothes officers, they wouldn't ask too many questions or press her for descriptions.

Should she mention those howls she had heard?

No way. Absolutely not. In doing so, she'd be putting her reputation on the line before she even had a reputation. Besides, the strange noises she'd heard had nothing to do with what had happened here. She had merely been in the wrong place, at the wrong time.

No longer dizzy or wobbly in the knees, Riley glanced up at the sky. Though clouds were moving in, the moon was on full display. After what had happened tonight, that moon suddenly seemed kind of sinister.

A young officer—the badge on his shirt said his name was Marshall—helped her to the cruiser parked at the curb with a steadying hand on her elbow. Silent and subdued, he waited until she sat down inside before making eye contact. Then he smiled knowingly, as if they were co-conspirators and shared a secret. Riley recognized the look.

"You know who my rescuers might have been?" she asked.

The officer shrugged.

"Will you thank them again for me?"

He nodded as two more cops walked up, and then Officer Marshall backed away without looking at her again. Whether or not he knew anything, she'd have liked a way to speak with that young cop again and get a line on finding out about the men who had quite possibly saved her life.

She owed them so much more than a beer.

Tucked into the cruiser, Riley answered each question she was asked to the best of her ability and with as much detail as she thought prudent under the circumstances.

Adrenaline still pumped through her body from the fight she had put up. In spite of regaining some strength, her shivering had doubled, leaving her longing for the kind of warmth she had been temporarily offered by the nameless, shirtless man who'd come to her rescue on a cold night.

A guardian angel was the way she'd think of her rescuer from now on…except maybe for the few seconds when his lips had traveled over her face. She wasn't sure what to make of that.

Had he wanted a special kind of thank-you for helping her? Should that have left her feeling further abused and icky?

Used to looking inside events in search of deeper meaning, Riley wondered what the guy might have been searching for in such an intimate touch. It seemed to her at the time that he had been seeking a way under her skin to get a look at the real Riley Price, not the professional cover-up artist she had become. She didn't need another shrink to try to analyze that idea because the absurdity wasn't lost on her.

If she were to perform self-analysis, her interest in this rescuer had been caused by a latent sense of loneliness, of being alone in a big city, and so far from home. That, along with a healthy suspicion that she might actually have met a real live superhero tonight.

Unfortunately, as a mental health professional, she realized there was more to it than either of those things.

That man's touch had left her feeling exposed and excited, and sorry there hadn't been more excitement, all at the same time. She had wished for adventure and it had smacked her on the head a bit too hard.

One little kiss that wasn't actually a real kiss at all, from an anonymous man, and the memory of how that had felt, was keeping her pulse on warp speed.

Nope. There was no way she could mention much about her rescuer to these cops and come out unscathed.

Something in her voice would give away her interest if she mentioned him out loud. The creep who had attacked her was now in custody, she was okay, and that was that.

Statement, check.

Witness form, check.

Perhaps an interview at the police station would follow in the next day or two, and life would go on.

Crowds had gathered on the sidewalk and in the street, lured by the presence of cops like insects to a bright light. Riley tried to find the officer who'd seemed to know her rescuer as the cruiser pulled away from the curb, but had lost him in the throng of spectators. She told herself it didn't really matter, anyway. Things were what they were, and all that mattered was that she was going back to her small, rented house in one piece.

Nevertheless, she peered out the back window of the cruiser and hoped for a glimpse of the broad shoulders that would now be the highlight of her dreams. And as the car wove expertly into traffic, Riley clutched the edge of the seat and gasped, thinking she just might have caught that glimpse.

Chapter 5

"*They're back, and we need to go,*" Dale messaged, vying for Derek's attention, which was riveted to the cruiser getting ready to pull away from the curb.

He and Dale were on the rooftop of the pub, peering at the scene below after taking this slight detour from their agenda, though it could be a costly detour if they didn't get moving toward any new vamp problem that turned up.

He just had to be sure *she* was safe.

Derek turned around, nodded to Dale and walked to the opposite edge of the roof, where the shadows were deeper and there was no hint of human presence. It was a shame, he decided, that the owners of these buildings didn't upgrade their lighting systems. Bloodsuckers hated lights almost as much as they hated noise, and would have been much easier to spot without all that pooling darkness.

"Marshall will take care of her. You know that," Dale added, following along in Derek's wake.

"Yes."

"She's not your type anyway, Derek."

"Most assuredly not," Derek half-heartedly agreed.

But the woman had some kind of hold on him that he could not shake. Or didn't want to.

She had smelled so damn good. Her skin was like velvet. Yes, she wasn't a Were. They had nothing in common. Yada yada.

His head came up. There was a scuffling sound to his right and an unnatural wave in the shadows below where he stood. The sudden distraction broke into Derek's inner discourse on the pitfalls of human-Were relations. It seemed that Dale had been right. Bloodsuckers were gathering here.

Hell...

Derek knew there'd be no way to slow down these numbers unless they could find and deal with their queen. Without a Prime or Master, most vampires couldn't survive on their own for long. The undead didn't possess the brains and the skills to keep up their attacks. A Master was just that—the mastermind behind the nest. The core that kept a nest growing.

There might have been one sure way to find this one, but he wouldn't go that route, since it would entail bringing back the immortal Blood Knight, who had faced this queen down years before. The same f-ing immortal that had driven a Harley away from Seattle with McKenna Randall on the seat behind him.

Immortality aside, some women seemed to prefer bad boys in black leather.

"Five," he sent to Dale as he peered into the dark. *"Five more parasites down there."*

"Is that all?" Dale messaged back.

Derek looked at his partner. *"Piece of cake?"*

Dale nodded and leaped onto the brick ledge next to Derek. *"Right behind you."*

"I wonder," Derek sent back, *"why it is that I always have to go first."*

"Shinier badge," Dale said as they jumped.

They landed in the alley side by side and on their feet. Derek's announcement of their presence was a deep, guttural growl that served to halt the moving trail of shadows now hugging the building beside them. He really was tired of fighting vampires without ever seeming to stem the tide, but if he and his pack were to give up, who would take over?

Beyond the alley, several police and fire sirens wailed in earsplitting decibels that might have caused these vampires to think twice about emerging from behind the pub, if in fact they maintained thoughts about self-preservation. As it was, the swirl of moving darkness pressed on.

Derek caught one of them with his claws and dragged the bloodsucker backward. The sucker didn't have much time to protest or put up a good fight, and was reduced to a cloud of flying dust seconds later.

The vamp in front of that one paused, whirled and hissed like an angry cat through chipped fangs that no longer could have punctured human flesh. Derek tossed that one back to Dale and held his breath as the filthy, foul-smelling ash rained down.

That little deletion left three remaining vampires. If he and Dale took care of them quickly, he could get a last look at that woman before the officers took her away. One final glimpse was all he needed to settle his nerves and maybe even the question of why he wanted that last look so damn badly.

He barreled through the vamp lineup like a football lineman and turned to head them off before they reached the street. With Dale bringing up the rear, the three vamps were squeezed between them. It wasn't much of a party, and the fighting, which didn't last long, wasn't pretty. Black blood dripped from Derek's claws. Ash swirled everywhere like dark, discolored snow.

Wasting no time, Derek stepped onto the street, careful to keep to the shadows that no longer stank of vampire presence. He leaned forward to view the cruiser that was making its way into traffic. His heart was beating faster than normal and his boots were already starting to move him in that direction…until a claw snagged his belt.

Dale's message came through loud and clear. *"I wouldn't recommend taking that next step, boss. And I think you know why."*

Well…maybe he did know why.

And maybe he didn't have to like it.

Riley stared out the window of the police cruiser until her chills had subsided, but hadn't gotten anywhere in terms of finding her rescuers. When she thought she saw something, it turned out to be nothing more than a passing flash of tanned flesh seen against a dark backdrop, and could have been anyone.

She didn't speak to the two cops in the front seat. It angered her to think that she had nearly been a victim of a violent crime, and that she might have placed herself in danger by following a whim.

"Turn right, here," she finally said as the cruiser approached the parking spot where she had left her car. "This is it."

No longer feeling quite so weak or frightened, Riley opened the door and got out on steady legs. Her hands didn't shake when she brushed her hair back from her face.

"You'll be okay?" one of the officers asked.

"Yes. Thanks for your help." She fished in the pocket of her skirt for her car key. "I'll be fine."

"We'll follow you home, all the same," the cop said.

She hated to turn down an offer like that. The only problem was that she had to. The car key wasn't in her pocket. The damn thing was missing. Short of heading back to the site of the incident to look for it, the only way she was going to get home would be to either take a bus, or have these nice officers drive her. Then she'd have to break into her house because she had left her purse, which contained the rest of her keys, locked inside the car.

Riley blinked slowly to absorb all of that.

The alternative was to go to her office, where she kept spare keys. The building's night watchman would let her in to get them. Although she didn't particularly like the idea of going into that building alone after what had happened tonight, it would be all right. Plenty of people worked late, and the building was well lit and secure.

"Thanks for the offer. I need to go back to work first to pick up a few things. My office is just down the street," Riley said.

The cop that had helped her out of the patrol car nodded as he peered into her car. "No key?"

"I seem to have lost it," she admitted.

"I can help with that lock."

He had it open in less than thirty seconds with a slim-jim device, and it was difficult for Riley to hide her relief. But it still didn't help in the long run, since she couldn't start the car without that blasted key.

After retrieving her purse, Riley glanced at the cop and shrugged. "I'll be fine now." She waved a hand at the street. "There are lots of people around."

"You sure?" the cop asked.

"Positive."

He nodded again. "Please come to the precinct tomorrow for a more formal statement. And take care."

"I'll do both of those things," Riley said.

She searched the street in all directions when the patrol car drove away, knowing she had to get going, but unable to shake the feeling of being watched. *More imagination?*

Instead of wondering who had made those howling sounds that had kicked the night into high gear, she now wanted to punch that person for his or her part in nearly getting her killed.

Derek couldn't help taking a closer look at the woman whose rapid steps gave away little of what she had been through tonight. His packmate's expression was filled with sympathy, but there was only so far a Were could go in a disagreement with his alpha. And Derek had never been mistaken for stupid.

Both he and Dale were in human form again. Derek's nerves were charged from changing back and forth so many times in a single night. Shape-shifting came with a cost, and he was experiencing that cost now. Prolonged time spent as a wolfed-up version of himself not only heightened his senses for a long time afterward, but actually also left him feeling kind of beastly.

His animal instincts were working overtime at the moment and directing him to go after the woman who had looked into his eyes not more than an hour ago. He had questions about her that needed answers. For instance...how had she seemed to have gotten past the incident so quickly? She was carrying on as if nothing had happened.

She was tough, at least on the outside.

He liked that.

Who are you? I wonder.

Dale leaned against an ivy-covered wall, content for the time being to have dealt the vampires a warning blow. But in terms of the antics brought about by a full moon, the night was still young. Hell, the hunting hadn't even really begun.

"Happy now?" Dale asked, stripping most of the wryness from his tone.

"I wonder where she's going," Derek said.

"Maybe she has a hot date."

Though Derek gave Dale a long glance, Dale persisted. "A hot *human* date."

Jealousy was an ugly emotion that Derek understood all too well, having had a tough time watching his ex and her new lover together. Still, he experienced a brief pang of jealousy now for whatever lucky bastard had this woman's attention.

"We'd better check in with the pack," he said, ready to put his muscles to more good use. He couldn't just follow the woman to wherever she was going because of a wayward bit of electricity that had flared between them earlier, or because of the fact that he still felt that electrical buzz when they weren't anywhere close.

He had lost sight of her, and shrugged off the desire to follow. There were more important things to take care of in the city's shadows. Other Weres would be out and about now, and as the alpha of a Seattle pack, he was needed for his directions.

Coming from his human throat, the growl he issued sounded downright rude. Even as his boots thudded on the asphalt and he moved in the direction of the last skirmish with the vampires, he felt the tug to turn around. It had been a long time since his allegiance had wavered between duty and a woman, and he had solemnly vowed never to let that happen again.

From several steps behind him, Derek heard Dale say, "Good choice."

Chapter 6

After Riley reached her office, the thought of going outside again wasn't appealing. She had made it this far without collapsing, but wasn't sure she could keep up the farce for much longer. Although her dad had long ago taught her about the art of the good cop face, no one was around now for her to have to pretend with.

She wasn't all right. The shaking had started up again, so hard that Riley had to sit down. All the moments leading up to this one merged into a single thread of riotous emotion.

She had not made up any of this. Just because tonight's events were over didn't necessarily mean she could move forward without recriminations. She had paid dearly for her stupidity, sure, but why did she have to feel so stupid now? Why did she want to march back out there as soon as her legs were capable of carrying her and find the men who had rescued her from harm?

Hero envy was an emotion she was familiar with. In her job, she had dealt with a few cases of people who had come close to death. And though it was true that she could empathize, and invest in years of clinical-training work in order to try to help others, being affected by such a thing herself was a different ball game.

Cops had always been her heroes. Had those two guys been undercover? Maybe she'd see them tomorrow at the precinct and get a better look at them.

She rubbed her temples with cool fingers and sat back, aware of a growing ache in the spot on the back of her head where it had struck the brick. Her fingers drifted to the cheek her rescuer had touched. She remembered it all as if it had been etched on her brain.

What she couldn't do was break through the fog that blurred out several minutes of the ordeal. The moments when she had actually started to believe that the man whose lips had rested on her cheek might actually have possessed some sort of superhuman powers.

All that warm, rippling muscle…

The long hair…

His incredibly handsome face…

Riley clapped a hand over her mouth. What had she said to him in place of a proper thank-you? Had she actually mentioned werewolves? Maybe it was insanity he'd searched for in her eyes.

Well, it was over, and here she was, snug in her office, where street noise was blocked by dual-paned windows and howling wolves had no place among the credentials and diplomas framed on her wall.

She would not go back out there, that was for sure. Possibly she'd spend the night here on the couch and go home in the morning for a shower and clean clothes.

Relieved to have made up her mind, Riley stood up and walked to the window that offered her a good view of the street for half a block or more in two directions. Traffic was light at the moment. Signals on the corners flashed red, yellow and green. All of this was normal. The problem here was that she wasn't.

After shaking her head to clear her mind of the notion that if she looked hard enough and long enough she'd find her rather wolfish rescuer or others like him out there, Riley continued to search. When she closed her eyes, she could see him. She could again find the light-colored eyes that had seemed to see deep into her soul. She felt him beside her, leaning in.

With her eyes open, the only thing she experienced was the sense of her own mortality and a reminder of how closely she had managed to escape.

The glass was cool when she rested her forehead against the window. "Thank you," she said aloud to the nameless man whose face she would always remember. "And if it turns out that there are such things as were-wolves, you'd be a perfect specimen. Just so you know."

She headed for the bookcase and the decanter of amber liquid she had hoped to reserve for special occasions in the future, but was necessary now.

She poured some in a glass and swirled the contents. Never having been a fan of alcohol, she held her breath as the glass touched her lips, and then felt the burn of the whiskey as it trickled down her throat.

Carrying the glass with her, she moved back to the window feeling slightly better, thinking she'd be able to handle the rest of the night like a pro. After all, she was a pro. Those framed credentials said so. And besides, everyone she had treated so far in her short time in this office had seemed comfortable on her couch. She'd make do with it tonight in lieu of going back out to the street.

Just in case things weren't as safe out there as they seemed.

His pack was a formidable bunch. Most of them were around his own ripe old age of thirty-two in human years. A few were slightly younger. The older Weres tended to hang out in areas beyond the city proper, and patrolled no less vigorously than their younger counterparts.

Having seen plenty of action already, they all helped to foster the kind of enthusiasm every Were needed for handling the things that hid in the shadows. Every good-guy Were had a place and a job. The pack was a second family to most of them. For some, it was their only home. For Derek, who had lost his family to a vampire attack in Europe fifteen years ago, the pack was a real comfort.

They met for the meeting two streets over from the precinct, in a private room in the back of a restaurant whose owners liked having cops around. Four Weres were in uniform, the rest weren't. The rule was to behave in public, get their orders and dish out their own version of justice to fanged troublemakers.

Because there had been vamp activity tonight already, the plan was to comb the streets and alleys within a quarter-mile perimeter of the incidents. Energy levels were particularly high tonight as the Weres dispersed. Even Weres under a full moon had to remain alert to the danger those vamps presented.

Dale led the charge so that Derek could stop by the precinct for a look at the interesting woman's attacker. In honor of that visit, he had put on a T-shirt and leather jacket, and thought he looked almost completely human.

Alone again, he stood on the sidewalk, beneath the overhang, silently contemplating where his senses were urging him to go...though he could have predicted where that was. In his estimation, another little detour was warranted. A quick in-and-out, and then he'd get on with the plan.

That's what Derek told himself, anyway, as he tilted his head back and called up the fragrance that seemed to have coated his lungs. Her fragrance. That woman's.

He sent his senses outward to locate the trail of that one unforgettable scent among so many others, and walked west, then east, keeping well away from the moonlight until he found what he sought. Then, grinning like he had won the lottery, Derek whispered, "Got you," and smiled.

The building he'd found was a nice one just steps off the main drag. Four stories' worth of large windows over-looked the street. There was a revolving front door. Inside, his boots echoed loudly on the black-and-white marble tiles. The only hang-up was the security guard manning a reception desk not quite twenty feet in.

Derek showed him his badge. "I'm looking for a woman."

The security guard smiled, his expression saying, *Isn't every guy in Seattle?*

Derek continued. "I believe she would have come in not more than an hour ago. Tall, slender, blonde, in a black skirt."

"May I ask what you might want with a woman of that description?" the guard asked.

"We're missing a few things on the statement she gave us tonight about an incident. I'd like to clear that up."

"And you didn't get her name?"

Derek strengthened his tone. "I'd appreciate it if you

could help me with that, silence being a possible obstruction of justice, and everything."

Derek's inner wolf was bristling over being repressed when there was a full moon. He could easily have yanked the guard over the desk and spoken to him nose-to-nose, but he refrained. The Seattle PD was trying to upgrade their image with the masses, and this guard was only doing his job.

"Name's Price," the guard finally said. "Third floor, three-ten."

Derek nodded. "Miss Price is here now?"

"The after-hours policy is that she would have had to sign in and out. She hasn't signed out."

Derek nodded again. Though his insides were throbbing and his pack was out there doing the dirty work, he told himself that he just needed one little peek at the woman in 310 in order to put his overactive imagination to rest.

"Okay to use the elevator?" he asked.

"The middle one is in operation," the guard replied, pushing a notebook and a pen toward Derek.

Derek signed in and headed for the elevator. As a rule, he didn't like small spaces and the feeling of being confined. He especially didn't like those things tonight.

So, he asked himself as the doors closed, what did he really want from this unauthorized visit? He had already memorized every detail about the woman. A second look at her wasn't going to change any of those things.

It was that remark... But he wouldn't tell her that. Bringing up the word *werewolf* would only cause her to focus on it more.

Another reason for showing up on her doorstep unannounced was to find out if she would recognize him. There was danger in such a move, and a lot at stake if

she put two and two together and came up with a connection between him and the shirtless werewolf vigilante that had helped her out of a jam.

Nevertheless, Derek didn't even consider turning
around. He blamed this brazen act on the wolf that
tugged on his insides in need of freedom.

When the elevator doors slid open, Derek looked
around and then turned to the left. Number 310 was
halfway down the hallway. Double doors. Brass plaque.

He read: Dr. Riley Price, PhD.

Price...

The name had a familiar ring to it. Then again, there
were probably hundreds of people in the city with that
name. *Riley* was unusual, though. He decided it suited her.

Riley Price had walked away from the attack as if it had
been a minor thing when he knew better than to believe
that. He had felt the quakes that rocked her and could still
see the expression of fear, hurt and confusion in her eyes.

His hand stopped in midair before his knuckles actually stuck wood. He closed his eyes, able to *feel* her in
there, knowing such a connection with a human was also
unusual.

He knocked three times. So that he wouldn't frighten
her more, he called out, "Seattle PD, Miss Price. I just
need one more thing to help with this case. The security guard told me you were here. Can I have a minute?
I know it's late."

Stepping closer to the door, Derek willed her to respond. To grant his request.

The strange thing was that she did.

Chapter 7

Riley hesitated before turning toward the door, annoyed by the interruption. The glass was still in her hand, though she had only managed one more sip.

There was a cop in the hallway. The front-desk guard wouldn't have let him in without showing proper identification, which meant she didn't have to worry about that. She could either respond and let him in or ignore him. He wasn't going to break down the door if she stayed where she was. Eventually, he'd go away.

Riley found herself heading to the door, hoping that this would all be over with sooner, rather than later, and then she could get on with her life.

She paused with her hand on the knob. "What's your name, Officer?"

The same deep voice that had requested a minute of her time said, "Miller. Detective Miller."

"I'm quite busy, Detective."

"I won't take up much of your time, Dr. Price."

Riley took a deep breath to settle down and opened the door. The man in the hallway appeared to be as surprised as she was when their eyes briefly met. There was something familiar about him.

"Do I know you, Detective Miller?" she asked, breaking the silence that had stretched for several seconds. "You seem familiar."

"I'm sure we've probably passed on the street. I get around on the job, as you can imagine."

That could have been true, Riley supposed. But besides the eyes, there was also something distinctive about his voice that caused her to tighten her grip on the glass in her hand.

His gaze drifted to the glass.

"For my nerves," Riley explained.

The hunk in the hallway nodded. "You've had quite a night."

Detective Miller truly was a hunk. He was tall, dark-haired, and obviously more badass than desk jockey in his worn leather jacket and fitted white T-shirt. He said, "Can I come in, or would you prefer answering questions like this?"

Her sudden interest in guys who looked as good as this detective surprised her.

This guy, at first glance, hit most of her attraction buttons. She liked the shaggy hair, his height and the shape of his face. *Action* and *adventure* were probably his middle names. But he was a cop, and she had vowed never to put herself through what her mother had suffered, never really knowing whether her husband would come home at night or be killed on the job.

With that thought firmly in mind, Riley stepped

back, opened the door wider and gestured for him to come in with a wave of the glass.

The room was dim, lit only by a lamp on her desk, and yet she easily saw every move this detective made. She was glad the dimness wouldn't allow him a closer look at the paleness of her face. Putting the desk between herself and the detective, she said, "What do you need from me?"

He hesitated for a few beats too long for her not to notice. "You're a psychiatrist?" he asked.

"Psychologist. And very new to the business."

"That's good."

"Why?"

"Maybe you can better manage what happened tonight and put it in perspective."

He again glanced at the glass she was clutching.

Detective Miller's voice was deep enough that its vibration quietly filled the room. His eyes, however, told another story, and made Riley imagine he was on good behavior and playing nice at the moment.

"What is it you need?" Riley repeated.

She set down the glass.

The detective had only walked far enough into the room to get a distant view of the window, but he looked there. "Will you be able to identify your attacker?"

"I'll never forget his face," she said. "I have a knack for remembering faces."

More beats of silence passed and the detective still hadn't said anything to warrant this visit. She had already told this same thing to the officers at the scene.

"I just needed to corroborate your place of employment, Dr. Price, and to make sure you're credible," he said.

"Credible how? What's my job got to do with anything?"

"It makes things easier for us all if you are believable in your statements."

Riley pointed to her throat. "Want to see the bruises that guy inflicted?"

She flushed when his gaze landed on her neck, and began to think this detective might have had another reason for coming here. However, since she had already allowed her imagination to run amok once tonight and had landed in trouble because of it, Riley waited for whatever he'd say next.

"I'm sorry to have brought this up so soon and to have disturbed you," he said. "Tonight's attack must have been terrible for you. So how about if I apologize for the intrusion and let you get on with whatever you were doing? You can answer more questions tomorrow."

Riley nodded. "Thanks for showing some concern."

She wasn't going to vocalize how Detective Miller's presence lent an air of safety to a truly awful night, or how knowing that guys like this were on the streets doing their job made her feel slightly better.

There was no way in hell she was going to submit to fanciful thoughts about this guy, or let herself believe he was strikingly similar in size and looks to the man that had come to her rescue on the street…because that would have been pathetic.

"Well, I'm glad to see that you're going to be okay," he said.

"Yes, thanks to two of your guys out there."

The detective's inquiring gaze returned. "Did you mention anything concrete about them to the officers who took your initial statement? Descriptions? Conversations?"

"It happened so fast, I'm afraid I wasn't in good

enough shape to speak or to note many details about who those guys were. One of the officers later suggested some ideas about who my rescuers might have been, though."

"So you wouldn't be able to identify them?"

Riley eyed her glass on the desk, wishing she actually liked whiskey and that she'd taken another sip if there was going to be much more of an interrogation.

"I was just glad they showed up in time to save my ass," she said.

Detective Miller's gaze was like being caught in a tractor beam. Never one to shy away from a challenge, Riley met that gaze with an equally studious one.

"Nothing?" Detective Miller asked. "You can't describe them in any way?"

"Other than the fact that neither of them wore shirts, not much was clear…which is strange, when I think about it. So I'd prefer not to think about it and just be grateful."

When the detective smiled, a further ripple of familiarity returned to her in a flash of repressed memory of the night's events. Her rescuer had dark hair and light eyes that were a lot like this guy's. They both had the same kind of unshaven face that highlighted handsome, angular features. She had sensed wildness in the man on the street as well, and both of these men possessed the same kind of male vibration that affected her after only a glance in her direction.

She ran a fingertip down her cheek—the same cheek her rescuer's lips had illicitly touched. That touch left her feeling breathless.

Detective Miller's expression was again one of concern, though he didn't close the distance.

"Are you all right, Dr. Price?"

"Yes. I... I just need time to process this."

"Did you remember something just then?" he asked.

Rile shook her head. "Nothing that would help."

The detective nodded, turned and walked to the door. Riley tracked his movement without calling him back, though every cell in her body urged her to ask him to stay. At the door, he paused as if he might have been reluctant to leave her.

"I don't see myself as a victim," Riley said.

He looked at her over a broad shoulder. "I can see that you don't."

As he crossed the threshold, she added, "Actually, the man who came to my rescue looked a little bit like you."

He paused again, then said, "I get that a lot. I'm thinking it must be the jacket. Good night, Dr. Price. Maybe we'll meet again tomorrow."

As he closed the door, Riley took her first deep breath and headed after him. Changing her mind at the last minute, she leaned against the door and strained to hear the sound of the elevator, but felt as if she were listening for something else. Like the howl of a wolf. Or the velvety growl of a light-eyed, dark-haired, chisel-faced, half-dressed werewolf with the kind of voice that resonated, even now, in her soul.

Just like Detective Miller's had.

Derek leaned a shoulder against the wall of the elevator and looked up, as if he could see through the ceiling to a couple floors up.

"Good night, Riley Price," he muttered. "He looked like me, did he?"

He had taken a chance by coming here to speak with

her, but at least he now knew the things she did and didn't remember, and could take comfort in the fact that she hadn't been able to identify him outright while standing several feet apart.

"I'm no less interested, just so you know," he added.

She was safe up there in her office with the guard manning the front desk. At the very least, he didn't have to worry about that. Her memory was another issue altogether. Psychologists were familiar with all sorts of tricks to spark repressed memories. Meeting her again would not be wise.

And yet he wanted to see her again. He wanted to see her again right now and get to the heart of the werewolf remark she'd made on the street. But that would probably serve no purpose whatsoever other than to place his pack in jeopardy.

He signed out and exited the building with a curt wave to the guard. From the sidewalk in front of the building, Derek glanced up at the moon and said, "Fine. Let's get on with it." He walked toward the car he had parked near here earlier in the evening, before the night's antics had begun.

He removed his jacket, tossed it on the seat and took one more look at the street corner from the shadows of the two buildings that hid Riley Price's building from sight. Then he ducked into the alley, where the subtle scent of werewolves filled the night air like its own brand of dangerous perfume.

From her window, Riley watched the detective turn the corner. He did look a little bit like the man who had rescued her. At least, she thought he did.

Grabbing her jacket and her purse, she locked the

door and went down to the street, determined to find the truth of what she now had come to suspect—that Detective Miller and the man who had helped to save her life could, in fact, be one and the same. If not, maybe Miller had a brother on the force. A twin.

He had headed east with purpose, as though he knew exactly where he was going and what he'd find there. His stride had been graceful when viewed from above, and radiated confidence. Miller was a dangerous man in his own right.

Riley gripped her cell phone tightly in her hand as she exited the elevator, signed out and started out after the detective, hoping she'd catch his trail before both sanity and the need to think about her own safety returned. The fact that she wasn't alone helped somewhat. There were plenty of cars moving in both directions. Couples laughing and holding hands breezed by her, and she had a momentary pang of desire to be like them.

She couldn't really recall the last time she had shared a light, loving moment with anyone. The flicker of wildness in her nature made her want to find her soul mate instead of settling for anything less, and she had never found that certain someone.

At the intersection, she paused, knowing Miller was long gone and that she was a fool for thinking she could have found him.

But then…

She heard a sound that made her hands quake. Was it an engine turning over, or could it have been a growl?

You know better, Price.

Go back to the office or go home.

She ignored both of those options. As if tonight's events had never happened, Riley crossed the street.

She headed for an area where shadows pooled and
moonlight failed to reach the sidewalk, drawn there
for reasons that felt insane. If Detective Miller had been
looking for trouble, the shadows were where he was
going to find it.

Chapter 8

Derek again scented a problem.

Two of his packmates had already come this way, and he could almost picture them in his mind. They were riled up and anxious because they had found something nearby. He knew what that something had to be.

The alley he had entered was a dead end. He searched the dark before climbing over a short brick wall, and jumped down on the opposite side with both of his hands raised and ready for whatever showed up. But he didn't step into the moonlight. He wanted to see what kind of creature would come out for a look at the man who had just possibly walked into a trap without realizing it.

His packmates had beaten him here and were hidden from sight. One of them was on the rooftop, all wolfed up and as motionless as a Gothic ornament. The other wolf was behind a partially boarded-up window.

If these vampires didn't feel the danger in their midst and were inept as to how the supernatural world worked, they would soon show themselves, the way their cousins had earlier. If they were seasoned blood-suckers, they would avoid three werewolves like the plague and ply their trade elsewhere.

Derek kind of hoped for the latter on this occasion. He would have preferred more time to think about Riley Price, but just couldn't allow personal issues to take precedence over his job. Nor could he afford to let a perfectly good full moon go to waste.

"Anyone here?" he finally called out, lowering his hands and feeling his claws spring as he turned in place, very near to the light.

His two packmates were silent, intent on what might happen next. Derek took in a breath that was tainted with a new and potent scent of Otherness before a figure appeared in the distance. Derek squinted to make it out. The damn thing seemed to be wrapped in its own fog, and that left its outline unclear. The creature also appeared to float several inches off the ground.

The whole image was murky at best, and decidedly different from anything in Derek's experience in dealing with vampires.

He inched closer to the stream of moonlight next to him, ready to meet this thing head-on, and said, "Who are you?"

The voice that came from the fog might have been either male or female. Derek couldn't be sure as he heard it say, "You trespass here, wolf."

This was a seasoned vampire that knew a wolf when it saw one. And that could potentially make the task of taking this creature down a hell of a lot messier.

"I could say the same thing about you," Derek returned.

"Werewolves belong in the forests," the newcomer said.

"And vampires belong underground. Which makes me wonder why you're walking around."

"It's a very long story."

"I'm all ears," Derek said.

"The thing is, I'm not sure I owe you anything, certainly not an explanation for my existence. I just am. Nothing more. Nothing less."

"And you're here now, in this alley, for what purpose?" Derek asked.

"I came to warn you."

"About?"

"Where to find your next fight."

"You mean the next fight after dealing with you?" Derek said.

As he watched, the fog began to dissipate slightly. Not enough to actually see the thing hidden inside it, but Derek did see a tall, thin figure of unknown gender.

"You can't fight me, wolf," the creature warned. "I think you already know that."

"I'm not sure I do. Why don't you enlighten me?"

The creature's reply was as cryptic as the rest of this conversation. "I believe you have better things to do at the moment than to deal with the likes of me."

"Such as?" Derek said.

The fog floated to the left, which gave Derek a decent view of what was beyond it. He saw the street, and cars going by. Then he saw someone stop to peer into the shadows in the break between the buildings.

He felt a chill on the back of his neck. His heart gave a thunderous roar and a few treacherous beats.

"It helps to find out that wolves have not only soft underbellies, but other vulnerable spots as well," the creature remarked.

Damn it...

The wolf on the roof began a quick descent. In seconds, one of Derek's packmates was standing beside him looking big, dangerous and lethal, with his sharp canines exposed. The fog remained on the sidelines, like a dark cloud that had swallowed whatever the thing was that used it for camouflage.

"I don't know what you're talking about," Derek said.

But he did know, of course. And for the first time, Derek also understood that he had exposed himself to the vampires tonight in another way. A new way. Because it was Riley Price who stood there on the street, looking on.

And there was probably a vampire to keep him from reaching her if this vamp had brought friends.

Riley hit the wall with a shoulder that was already sore, and winced. The protests she wanted to utter got stuck in her throat. Either the shadows were playing tricks with her eyesight and she actually did have a concussion from hitting her head earlier, or there was a werewolf in this alley.

A real, live werewolf.

No joke.

She stumbled back and toward the street, numb with shock. The fact that she had wanted to find a werewolf melted away behind the actual sighting of one. The phrase that kept repeating over and over now in her mind was that she wasn't insane after all, and might never have been.

Still, she refused to believe that seeing a werewolf in Seattle was anything other than the very definition of insanity. So she turned around and walked away, heading back toward her office with her skull humming and her pulse hammering away at warp speed.

She'd call Detective Miller and tell him about what she had seen. Would he think she was crazy? Could he possibly understand that no governing body would issue a license to a therapist whose own sanity they doubted? As for proof of what she had seen...by the time she got to the precinct or found another way to reach the detective, that werewolf would probably be long gone.

As Riley consciously willed her legs to carry her forward, she knew there was no way she could win this, prove this, or convince anyone about what had been in that alley. She also knew that she had to try.

Derek glided into the moonlight to join his packmate in a standoff with a vampire that was far too enlightened for anyone's good. He wondered what the wolf beside him thought of this discussion.

There was a chance the abomination hadn't meant its remark the way Derek had taken it after seeing Riley there. Yet it had sure felt that way. The comment had seemed pointed and personal.

He knew that Riley had to have seen his packmate in full moonlight, and that for her the werewolf comment she had made earlier had now taken on new weight.

What would she do next?

Where would she go to feel safe?

Who will you tell, Riley?

His shape-shift took seconds. Derek roared in the moonlight, daring the creature in the alley to challenge two Weres in spite of what it had said. But the creature, which had to be some special kind of vampire, didn't rally. It hovered near the street for some time before Derek decided to break the face-off.

He rushed forward, wanting to get to Riley, knowing that in order to reach her, he'd tear this bloodsucker apart if he had to.

Intending to ram the vampire's body, Derek barreled forward with his backup on his heels. The foggy bastard he lunged for wasn't solid, so he passed right through it and pulled up a few feet from the street, snapping his not-quite-human teeth.

His packmate had no better luck.

Angry, Derek whirled around to try again. But the vampire remained elusive, shifting in time to avoid any direct confrontation as it drifted over the Weres. It was as if the spooky sucker had the ability to fly.

Again and again, Derek and his mate challenged, spun and went for the abomination. Time after time, their teeth and claws came away empty. Finally, the bloodsucker floated to the street and spoke. "You see, wolf, that I was right to warn you, and to call to your attention the vulnerability attached to your new weaknesses."

The next remark the vampire made came in the form of a touch on his mind.

"She is not for you, wolf. Stay away from her or our next meeting will not go nearly as well as this one."

Derek clutched his chest—he was suddenly short of breath. He hadn't been wrong. The warning had been pointed and had pertained to Riley Price. Who else could this sucker have been talking about?

Madder than ever and refusing to give up, Derek and his packmate sprinted toward the creep like rabid animals, biting, clawing and punching at nothing even remotely physical enough to maim or injure. They kept this up until the vampire simply disappeared, as if it had never really been there at all.

Derek stared at the empty alley with his heart racing. When his packmate turned to him in an equal state of confusion, Derek sent a message. *"I hope to God there aren't more of those things around."*

It was at that moment that Dale arrived, alone and calm. After a quick look at the two Weres, Dale asked, "Did I miss something?"

"I think it must have been a ghoul," Derek's current fighting partner, still wolfed up and wild-eyed, messaged back. *"That thing was seriously demented."*

Though Dale looked to Derek for an explanation, Derek was already miles beyond thinking about the fight. There were new questions to be answered—carefully, cautiously and with as much diplomacy as possible. The thing they had faced had shown off new tricks, and also knew about Riley. It didn't seem to want him hanging around her, and had issued that warning.

It was possible the creature had purposefully allowed Riley to see the werewolf in this alley, so that she'd be frightened enough to stay away from the streets. Why, though? What did that creature have to do with her, and more to the point, what did it want?

"Derek?"

Derek glanced at Dale.

"Maybe you can explain what happened after you've

changed back, boss. Tonight was quiet everywhere else we patrolled. The pack is reconvening at the park for your summary and for further instructions."

Derek didn't feel like downshifting. He felt like running. Like howling. Like tearing apart that damn fog in any way he could so that he'd be able to sleep.

But who was he kidding? There'd be no way to sleep when he had to find Riley Price and convince her that she hadn't seen what she had seen.

There'd be no way to rest until he made her understand there was no such thing as a werewolf, and that she must have been mistaken due to the darkness of the alley if she thought there was.

Those urges had to be tamped down for the moment, however, because his pack was waiting for their alpha.

Was the weakness the vampire had mentioned about Riley?

Did he believe that?

There was no way to skip over this encounter with the vampire, or ignore what it meant. Either the vamps had evolved somehow and learned new crafts, or he had just come face-to-face, more or less, with their damn queen.

Damaris.

If that was true, he had, for the first time, experienced the power of a centuries-old vampire that had been around as long as there had been history. A powerful female bloodsucker that had gone after his ex-lover two years before and had caused McKenna Randall to accept the so-called *blood gift* that only a pair of fangs could offer in order to fight back. McKenna had accepted immortality by way of a Blood Knight's kiss. Her new lover's kiss.

McKenna had been given the gift of an everlasting life span from an immortal warrior who had walked the earth for as long as Damaris had, and who once had gone by the name of Galahad. The same motorcycle riding superpower that had stolen McKenna's heart, and then had taken her away.

A goddamn immortal who rode a Harley instead of a steed.

"Derek?" Dale called out.

Derek backed into the shadows and absorbed the flash of pain that came with downsizing again. He headed for the street, already planning what he had to do to warn his pack about the future, before he'd try to find Riley Price and get to the heart of the problems piling up.

In his mind, like a lingering echo, he heard that vampire's message. *She is not for you, wolf.*

It was no longer to be an average fight with a vampire. Whether or not anyone liked it, the stakes had just gone up.

Chapter 9

Riley made it to her car and got in wishing she had avoided coming out in the full moon altogether. With a shaky hand, she finally got the key inserted and started the engine, not sure which direction to go, but needing to get away from where she was.

There had been a werewolf in that alley, and though the beast had looked dangerous, it hadn't come after her. Two close calls in one night made this the worst night in her life as far as stumbling into danger went. It also made her the luckiest woman in Seattle to have emerged relatively unscathed.

She pulled away from the curb, nearly scraping the car parked in front of her. Though she drove too fast, she couldn't help it. Adrenaline pumped through her body in a fight-or-flight reaction to what she'd seen in that alley, and there hadn't been time to tame it.

She had to tell someone.

She couldn't call her dad after what they had been through. There was no way she could mention the word *werewolf* to her father.

The western headquarters of the Seattle PD was housed in an old building north of the city's hot spots. She found it easily, parked and turned off the engine. Above the roar of her pulse, Riley tried to remember the name of the officer who had spoken to her after the earlier incident, hoping that if she found him, he'd help her find Detective Miller.

And then what?

Was there any way to explain about what she had seen?

She didn't get out of the car. Instead, Riley sat there, watching cruisers and cops come and go, comforted by the uniforms and the badges that were reminders of her family and of her home. The truth was that she was afraid to actually find Miller. She was now afraid to mention any of this to anyone at all.

After fifteen minutes had passed, she reached for the key, still in the ignition, ready to back out of what she had been about to do. Startled by a knock on her window, she glanced sideways to find one of the police she had been looking for. Officer Marshall, the cop who had hinted at knowing the men that had come to her aid during her attack.

Riley opened the car door. On legs that were astonishingly solid after the night she'd had, she got out and faced the young officer.

"Do you need help, Miss Price?" he asked politely.

"I'm wondering if you might help me find Detective Miller."

"Is there anything *I* can help you with?" he asked.

"He came by my office to ask me some questions and I wasn't in the mood to answer. I thought I'd make up for that now if he's around."

"On a night like this one, Miller seldom comes in."

Riley met the officer's dark-eyed gaze.

"When a full moon comes, all sorts of crazy things happen in this city," he explained. "Most of the guys that work here have to put in some overtime to help curb all that. Miller and his crew are on the night shift tonight. They'll be driving around, waiting for a call."

Though Riley tried to smile, her lips wouldn't comply. While she should have felt relieved about not having to face Miller with her story, there was no relief at all, just an inexplicable, deep-down feeling of being at a complete loss as to how to even begin to explain what she'd seen.

"Can you please tell him I came by? He knows where to find me," she said.

Officer Marshall nodded. "Sure." Then he waited, probably in case she had something else to say.

"Is Miller a good detective?" Riley asked.

"One of the best," Marshall replied.

Riley glanced up at the officer and said the stupid thing that had been on the tip of her tongue for the last five minutes, then immediately regretted it.

"Does he always wear a shirt? On the job, I mean?"

The young officer smiled to placate her. "I would assume that he does. Is there a reason you asked? Maybe you're thinking about the men who helped you tonight? You said they didn't wear shirts, I believe?"

"Yes, well, the detective sort of looks like one of those guys, and I was just—"

"I doubt very much if our detectives who aren't undercover run around half-naked," the officer said. "I can't account for all of them, of course, you understand. But it's highly doubtful that your guy and Miller are one and the same. I will tell the detective you stopped by, though."

"Yes. Thank you."

She got back into the car feeling a little foolish about bringing up the shirt detail, yet not nearly foolish enough to let it go. So she spoke again to Office Marshall in parting. "He'd probably look good without a shirt. But you don't have to tell him I said that."

Officer Marshall closed her car door. Though he remained sober-faced and professional, Riley was sure he was trying not to laugh.

Derek didn't mean to ignore his inner chastisements, and didn't actually realize his mind was elsewhere until Dale punched him in the shoulder hard enough to wake him up.

"It's not a good sign," Dale said. "If that thing in the alley actually is what you think it is, why would a vampire Prime show up now, after all this time? Why would she suddenly come out to confront us?"

Derek had no idea how to answer that.

"It could be the reason for the strange scent in the east," Dale suggested. "The vamp queen brought it with her."

"Right now I imagine it is," Derek agreed, though he was having a hard time wrapping his mind around this new predicament. No one had seen or heard anything about that vampire queen for two years, so what had they done now to receive the honor of such a direct form of contact with the central villain of Seattle's vampire hive?

"Her appearance might be connected to the woman we helped tonight," he said to Dale, thinking out loud, rehashing everything that had happened and hoping something would eventually make sense.

What if was a game all cops played to try to reason things out. Events had to be studied from all angles, no matter how absurd they might seem. There was no way he was going to mention anything about a weakness for pretty psychologists, though, or the vampire's remark about her, when Dale already knew about his interest in Riley Price.

Dale said, "You think our little victim might have caught the vampire's eye, and that out of all the people in and around Seattle, a vamp queen could be interested in the one person we helped out of a jam? Why would that even occur to you?"

"The two things happened on the same night. And Riley showed up at the head of that alley where the monster confronted us, as if she had been summoned there."

Dale appeared to mull that over. "Such a scenario could mean this heartless vampire bitch might be interested in our Miss Price because we helped her. But we help people all the time, so what's so special about tonight?"

He added with a meaningful sideways glance at Derek, "Maybe the vampire is interested in Price because of who helped her. Her sudden interest could be in retaliation for us dusting some of her newbies tonight."

"Then why didn't she just go after us in the alley?" Derek said.

Dale shrugged. "I don't know."

Derek would never forget the problems they confronted the last time Damaris came out of hiding. If it hadn't been for that renegade Blood Knight heading off the vamp queen, none of his pack would be around today.

"Our Miss Price showing up again near that alley could be a coincidence," Dale suggested. "We have to consider that."

"One hell of a coincidence," Derek said.

Dale went on, "You've shown interest in Riley. Could that vampire actually be interested in you, Derek, rather than Riley Price?"

Derek had gone over those same questions fifty times since meeting with his pack an hour ago, and hadn't yet gone to find Riley because of his fear of involving her further.

He could feel Riley out there, and couldn't trust that sensation. They had no real connection. She wasn't a Were, so they couldn't have imprinted by gazing so intently into each other's eyes.

The only serious relationships for his kind were Were-to-Were. A special look, a lingering kiss, or a roll in the grass without their clothes, and two Weres were as good as engaged if they were meant to be mated.

Imprinting was serious business. Some Weres used the word *fate* to describe the immediacy of such attractions. And though imprinting rarely happened between a Were and a human, Derek supposed it didn't have to be impossible if the circumstances were right and the stars lined up. He just hadn't heard of any such cases. Still, he couldn't shake the thoughts that kept him tied to Riley.

Dale picked up on this unspoken thread, probably by reading Derek's face. "If your sudden interest in Riley is the reason for the vamp's interest, then you can't go near her until we know for sure."

Dale leaned against a pillar in the parking garage. "I can't help wondering why this happened tonight, out of all the other nights."

"I guess finding that out will be our new priority," Derek said.

"Will Price be safe in the meantime, if we're the ones who brought this shit down on her?"

"We'll have to make sure she is," Derek replied. "I thought I'd hand that job to you."

Dale didn't even blink at being nominated for the task, though it was a dangerous one. "Should I start now? Do we know where she might be without going in to see her file?"

"I can find her," Derek said without stopping to hear how that might sound. Thing was, he knew he could find her wherever she might have gone. That acknowledgment alone should have made him wonder.

Dale waved a hand. "Lead on, wolf. The sooner we find out what's going on, the better. Isn't that right? We won't have the moon to help us forever."

"Exactly right," Derek agreed, already sorry that he had handed over Riley to Dale, who would watch her from afar without getting any of the answers to the questions Derek had.

They didn't really know anything at this point, and weren't any closer to figuring things out. By contrast, the vamp queen would know that werewolves were the strongest under a full moon, and that tomorrow might be another story if she decided to play this game.

It truly was best for him to keep his distance from the woman while he scoped out the shadows and pieced this puzzle together. He wasn't a decorated detective for nothing. When he put his mind to a task, he got things done. In a supernatural playing field, he usually came out on top.

What about Riley, though? Without an intimate knowledge of the shadows and what they hid, how would she get along? Beneath a talented vampire queen's studied scrutiny, how long would a human last, whether or not she was the real focus?

Riley's sweetness sat on the tip of his tongue, behind the lips that had touched her soft skin. Derek fisted the hands that had held her in place when quakes of fear rocked her.

Nevertheless, as he had previously acknowledged, Riley Price was no weakling. Tonight, she had taken what the world had dished out, and then walked away proudly with her head held high. In his book, that made Riley special. And he hadn't experienced *special* in a very long time. The fact that he might have found such a woman again was what had to spur him on now.

"Get on it," he said to Dale. "I'll go back out there and snoop around."

He added silently, *"Make sure she's safe. Riley Price might turn out to be the key to finally ending this war with the vamps if we're lucky."*

As he turned to go, Derek said, "Wouldn't that be something? The hand of fate just falls in our laps with the help of a small blonde?"

But if that was true, and Riley was to be the key to finding Damaris, the beautiful psychologist's chances of survival were slim at best.

And that just wouldn't do.

Chapter 10

Finding some solace in movement, Riley drove around until her gas tank was empty before she parked in front of her office building again. Engine off, she sat back in her seat, reluctant to get out and in need of a few more seconds of thought.

Moonlight bounced off her dashboard, reflecting in the small crystal pendant hanging from her rearview mirror. Usually, she would have considered this a sign of good luck, but now thought seriously about using that pendant to hypnotize herself to make sure she had seen that damn werewolf.

After meaning to go home, she had ended up here instead, and Detective Miller had been at the center of that decision. He might return to her office if the other cop told him she had stopped by the precinct to see him.

Riley hoped he would return, and also hoped he

wouldn't, for reasons that were clear in some ways, not so clear in others.

Why should I trust you, Miller?

Have you done anything to deserve it?

She had only spoken to him once. So why did she want to see him so urgently right now?

It took her another ten minutes to get out of the car. Riley carefully searched the street for areas engulfed in shadow. Satisfied there weren't many, she rushed into the building, nodded to the guard, said, "Please sign me in," and lodged herself in the elevator before taking the time for a deep breath.

She unlocked her office door, moved inside and then locked it after her. She muttered, "So far, so good," and almost believed that until a tingle at the base of her neck suggested there was another presence in the room with her. Something silent. The sudden pressure of something hidden in the dark.

"What do you want?" She waited with her back to the door, feeling around for the light switch and getting ready to bolt back to the elevator.

She heard a hissing sound that reminded her of steam escaping from a kettle, and tried to concentrate on getting her eyes adjusted to the dark. Where was the damn light switch?

The blinds were closed and she hadn't left them that way. There was no moonlight to help her see what kind of danger she faced, though the guard wouldn't have let just anyone in. So, who the hell was this?

"I'm going to turn on the light," Riley said without making a move toward the wall switch she now remembered was located on the opposite side of the doorway from where she stood. "You might as well tell me who you are."

"I can see you well enough without it," a voice returned.

The low timbre of that voice made the words seem sinister. The only way this person could have gotten here, past the guard downstairs and through a locked door, was by way of the window.

She looked there.

"Maybe you have the eyes of an owl. Unfortunately, I don't," Riley said.

The warning tingle turned into chilling waves of sensation that slid down her back. She labored for each breath. The palms of her hands felt moist. She'd barely gotten over the last two scares tonight...*and now this?*

"It would be easier to have whatever kind of conversation you're expecting face-to-face," she suggested. "Are you in need of my help?"

She wanted to shout "Did you break the window?" but thought better of it. The thing to do was to get this person to speak again, so that she could figure out where he, or she, was, and detect their state of mind.

"Maybe you prefer the dark?" Riley asked with her fingers on the door's lock, hoping whoever this was didn't have great hearing.

"Don't you?" the hidden guest returned.

"Don't I prefer the dark? No. Actually, I don't like the dark much at all these days."

"I find that strange," her visitor said.

Riley controlled the quake in her tone. "Why is that strange?"

She could open the door and flee. She might be okay if the person in the room with her wasn't fast enough to catch her at the elevator, if there was a nefarious reason for this visit.

"I suppose they never taught you to honor the night," her invisible visitor said softly, though the danger behind that softness came across loud and clear. "I'm here to fix that omission, and see that you learn."

"Thanks, but I'd rather not deal with this tonight," Riley said. "I have office hours most of the day on Monday if you'd like to come back. We can continue this chat then. I'm afraid I've had a rather long day."

There was a swish of fabric that told Riley the visitor had moved. From very near to her, the strange, uninvited guest spoke. "If you don't learn about your heritage, it might be too late to help you."

What the hell?

Riley inched the door open, praying that the hinges wouldn't squeak.

"What are you talking about?" she demanded loudly enough to cover any sound her exit might make.

She didn't get to hear the response to that question, if there had been one coming. The door burst open. A dark figure rushed past her into the room growling like a big cat. Like a lion or a...

Riley suddenly felt light-headed. Not willing to wait, or to find out what was going on, she ran into the hallway. Avoiding the closed door of the elevator, she sprinted toward the green exit sign and flung open the heavy fire door.

The echo of her shoes on the concrete stairs seemed outrageously loud. When she reached the ground floor, Riley shoved open the door and sprinted across the marble tiles, barely noticing that the guard wasn't at his post.

"Damn you," she said angrily as she reached the sidewalk. "Damn you all," she shouted just before she rammed into something hard and unrelenting.

Two arms wrapped around her. Breathless from a combination of fright and exertion, and afraid this was the final straw, Riley looked up to meet the concerned stare of a man's familiar eyes.

"You!" the woman in Derek's arms whispered, hardly able to get that one word out.

Her face was bloodless. Quakes rocked her so harshly, he feared she might crumble to the ground.

"Riley," he said to focus her attention. "We have to get you out of here. Can you walk?"

She nodded, seemingly treading the line between panic and disbelief that a night like this must have caused her.

"Okay. Good," Derek said, looking up at her building.

Dale had gone to her office after finding the guard was missing, and had messaged Derek. Dale would do what he had to do to take care of the problem.

Derek stepped back to ease his hold on Riley. He had shown up despite what he had said to Dale about the possible danger of seeing her again.

"Time to go, if you're able," he said.

The defiant look he'd seen earlier tonight reappeared in her eyes. Though she shook fiercely, inner strength was going to get Riley Price past this moment. If nothing else, Derek liked her even more for that.

They backed away from the building's front door, careful to keep out of the moonlight. What Riley might do if confronted with a werewolf close up was something he didn't want to find out. He would take her to the precinct and keep her there. She'd be safer off the streets. He'd see to it that she'd be watched over until the night was over, so that nothing with fangs could come calling.

After he'd taken one more step, a crashing sound from above spun him around. Seconds later, a shower of broken glass rained down.

Derek's reflexes kicked in with a white-hot surge. Flexing his arm, he reeled in Riley, spun her around and pressed her to the wall to protect her body with his, as something much larger than the shattered glass of the window also hit the ground.

Derek didn't have to see what it was. His body rippled with tension that had only one cause.

Tearing himself away from Riley, he swung himself toward the vampire, who had landed on both feet without breaking a bone. The thing was dressed in black. Its face was a white death mask. Dark, red-rimmed eyes found Derek's, and the creature's spectacularly fanged mouth turned up in a sneer.

"Just the beginning, wolf," the bloodsucker hissed as it turned on its heel.

"Not if I can help it," Derek said.

Ready to send this abomination to a new afterlife, he reached for the wooden stake tucked into his boot. The vampire was quick, but Derek was angry, and that made him faster. He caught the vampire by its coat-tail and dragged the creature sideways until it struck the wall.

Without giving a thought as to why the vampire didn't put up much of a struggle to free itself or sink its fangs into his arm, Derek raised the stake and was about to finish off the bloodsucker when he remembered why he was there, and who was watching.

He turned his head to look at Riley. Their eyes met and held. His knew his eyes were wild, but hers were worse. She had mentioned werewolves and now it was too late to keep her from finding out what other kinds of creatures existed.

When he turned back to the vampire, it was with a sudden acknowledgment that this sucker had known he wouldn't strike in this situation, with Riley looking on. But that was a gross error, since every vampire taken off the streets was a point in human favor.

Derek brought down the stake.

The vampire's pasty face registered surprise. It hissed again menacingly, and then exploded as if it had swallowed a bomb. The only sound that remained was Riley's gasp of horror.

Chapter 11

It felt to Riley as though she had left her body. The real world had simply melted away and nightmares were the new norm. What she had witnessed was so bizarre, there was no logical way to accept it.

Yet here she was, standing under a rain of dark gray, awful-smelling ash. And there he was, Detective Miller, holding a wooden stake in his hand that he had used to explode a…

To kill a…

"Vampire," he said, turning to face her. "You can choose to believe it, or not. Maybe you'll wake up tomorrow and call this a dream, but that wouldn't be wise. Ignoring what happened here might put you in more danger."

Riley didn't know how she was able to speak. She didn't understand why she was still standing. "It's too much."

The detective nodded. "I get that. You're now one of the few people who know about these things, and that kind of knowledge isn't pretty. But it is what it is. You haven't made this up."

She found that there wasn't anything else to say at the moment, and wouldn't be until she processed all of this information.

"The immediate danger might be over, though that doesn't mean this guy didn't have an accomplice," Miller warned. "Will you come with me to the precinct, where you and I can sort this out?"

"Do the cops know about these…things?"

"Not all of them, no. It's not a secret those of us who do know are willing to share."

"Wouldn't everyone be safer if they were on the lookout for creatures like that?"

"There would be panic, and that's worse. The world as a whole isn't ready to acknowledge the shadows. We just have to try to manage them. And we really should go now."

"I'd rather go home," she said breathlessly. But she realized she wouldn't be able to drive in this state and didn't want Miller to take her there. She was afraid she'd want him to stay.

Her heart was beating so fast and so loudly, Riley had to work to hear her thoughts. Believing Miller, and her own eyes, meant that the world was a different place than the one she thought she knew, and not in a good way. How was she supposed to come to terms with that?

"Vampire." Above her heartbeats, Riley's ears rang with that word.

"Yes," Miller confirmed. "One of many."

Riley mustered her courage, hoping it would carry

her through the next few minutes. She had seen how fast Miller moved. Running away from him on foot wouldn't get her very far. Besides, you couldn't outrun budding feelings for someone, even if you didn't know that person very well. There was no explaining attraction, and how feeling safe with him stopped her insides from churning in the aftermath of the terror she had just encountered.

Riley wasn't ready to let any of this go without further explanation.

"They're real?" She pressed herself to the brick wall, glad to find something truly solid in a dreamlike world.

The detective waved at the remains of the falling ash. "This is what's left of the one that came after you."

What he said caused her synapses to fire. "Why would a vampire come after me?"

"I don't know. I wish I did," he replied. "Until I find that out, you'll be safer if you're not on your own after sundown."

This was so absurd, Riley almost smiled. "Because vampires sleep during the day?" Her tone was cynical.

The detective's eyes darkened. "The precinct will be the safest place for you, for now."

"Maybe so." Taking her eyes from this detective was tough. Other than the wall behind her, he was the most solid thing in sight. He had helped her and was willing to do more. She would be safe with him, except for the undeniable attraction she felt. Was this a case of hero worship?

"What about the man that attacked me earlier tonight?" she asked. "Was he one of them?"

"Not one of them, no. Merely your average drunken pervert on a bender."

She got no relief from that. And after what she had just witnessed, how could she fail to believe that vampires were real?

"I'd like to go home," she said.

A flicker of disappointment flashed in the detective's eyes. His handsome face creased slightly. "All right. If you insist on that, I can post an officer at your door."

"Is that necessary? I have a good dead bolt."

He pointed to her office. "Don't you wonder how that sucker got in?"

Miller was right, of course. The office door had been locked.

"Climbing suits them," he explained. "If you saw how they do that, you'd never leave your windows open again."

Riley's thoughts spiraled back to the reason she had been in such a hurry to get back to the safety of her office. All of a sudden she wasn't so sure how to bring that up. She remembered the howls that had started all this, and what she had seen in the alley around the corner.

She looked Miller straight in the face, and recalled how she had seen the same flicker of wildness that darkened Miller's eyes in the eyes of the gorgeous shirtless man who had dealt with her earlier attacker. *She* again shivered when she thought about how there had been two attempts on her life tonight. And the two men that had come to her aid were indeed similar in subtle ways.

Her shaking stopped when Riley remembered that facing trouble was in her DNA. She had to stay strong now—advice her father would have given her if he had been here.

"And werewolves?" she said to the detective, who

observed her with concern etched on his handsome features. "What about them?"

He'd been caught between an explanation and a hard place without a viable way to extricate himself, Derek realized. He had started Riley down this path and wondered how far he could take her.

Should he tell her the truth, which would place his pack and others in a tough spot? Or maybe keep her in the dark about this one important thing?

She had briefly seen the vampire, and she had also seen his packmate in the alley. By taking the reality of that werewolf sighting away from her, would Riley ignore his warnings and talk herself into believing she had made the whole thing up, vampire and all? He knew for a fact that human minds were capable of twisting things when they were overloaded.

Her eyes were on him. Riley was waiting for him to answer her question about werewolves. The decision he had to make was either to pull the rug out from under her with excuses, or to share a few more secrets with the hope that she would keep them to herself.

It might be tough to stop her from passing on secrets. He'd have to be prepared to tackle that problem. As the alpha here, he had to protect his pack above all else.

She was waiting expectantly. And since psychologists were probably experts at detecting mind games, Derek decided to try the truth, unable to see any other viable way to go at this point.

"Werewolves do exist," he said.

Riley's reaction turned out to be nothing like he had expected. She exhaled a long stream of the breath she'd been holding as her eyes again met his. Blinking slowly, she wet her lips with the tip of her tongue.

"I knew it," she said in a soft voice that lacked any hint of skepticism.

What Derek wanted to do to her, with her, that very moment and on a public street, could have landed him in jail. He had desired her from the first moment he laid eyed on her, and was aware of how long it had been since he had allowed himself to feel anything at all.

Two steps forward brought him close enough to Riley to follow where those impulses led. She didn't back up or retreat, probably because she had no idea he was one of the creatures she was asking about...and also since she was already pressed to the brick wall behind her.

"Well, now you know," he said.

This was exactly why humans and Weres didn't mix. There were too many secrets to protect.

"I wonder what you'll do with that information, Riley Price."

"What do you do with it?" she responded.

"I patrol the street, keep those secrets to myself and try to maintain peace."

"With a wooden stake in your boot."

Derek shrugged.

"And for the werewolves?" She looked up at the moon. "How do you go after them?"

"We don't have much trouble from the Weres," Derek confessed.

She had looked away but her gaze now returned to him. "Why not?"

"Weres are reasonable most of the time and blend well with humans when there's no full moon."

"Blend well with humans?" she echoed, picking up on his slip in word choice.

"With people," he corrected.

She bit her lip before continuing. "Have you met some of them? Werewolves, I mean?"

"Yes." There was no need for him to expand on the answer at the moment. "Now it's time to get you off the street."

Instead of turning, Riley moved closer to him. The heat of her focused curiosity made the wolf inside him anxious to be set free. His claws pressed against his fingertips as if ready to spring. Shoulders that had borne the burden of all these shape-shifts tonight twitched in anticipation of what he might do next.

Kiss her...the wolf urged.

Take her home.

He didn't have the chance to do either of those things. Riley Price reached up to place her hands on both sides of his face and gently pulled him closer. Her breath was warm and fragrant when she spoke with her mouth inches from his.

"Thank you," she said. "Thank you for letting me know I haven't gone mad."

When she touched her mouth to his, Derek's wolf, tucked deep inside, silently howled.

Chapter 12

A shudder of shock ran through Riley as her lips met Miller's. The suspended moment was no less intense than being chased by a vampire.

Warmth flooded her body. One little touch of skin to skin, and her chills were history.

So was her mind, it seemed.

Neither of them moved right after that. Possibly, Miller was as surprised as she was by this brazen act that had turned out to be so much more than a simple thank-you.

The fact was that her body betrayed her. Rumbles of longing and need heated her from the inside out. More closeness was what she wanted. More of Miller. Because along with his confirmation of the existence of werewolves, and without knowing anything about her or her past, he had set free another part of her.

His hands slid around her waist. With her body tight

up against his, Riley again felt immersed in the dream that had allowed all of this to happen. There was even a fleeting thought that her dad would approve of her dating a cop.

But she and the detective hadn't been dating. Not only had they just met, they had also bypassed everything else by going along with the new urgency that sprang into place between them.

When Miller's instincts began to take over the direction of this closeness, Riley let him have that role, lost in the wonder of a heat that was like no other. Her reaction to the hardness of Miller's body produced a raw physicality she hadn't previously experienced with any man, or even known existed.

What had been a light, exploratory kiss quickly became a drowning act composed of mutual greed. And it wasn't enough for her. Not by far. Though they had spoken about werewolves, she felt like the animal here.

I've gone insane...

She breathed a soft groan into Miller's mouth. If he was really good at detective work, he had to know what might come next, and what she was willing to do.

Strangely enough, he didn't act on their obvious mutual desires. Miller paused, then eased back. Cool air rushed in to replace his heat as his light eyes searched her face.

What was he looking for? Something deeper than skin and the telling thunder of her pulse?

Riley recognized that look, just as she had been familiar with the flash in his eyes. She recognized the shape of the face in front of her, as well as the wide shoulders and the way Miller's shaggy hair fell across his forehead. The most significant thing about that was the way her body responded to his. Just like before. Like the previous meeting tonight that Miller had failed to mention.

Detective Miller and her earlier rescuer truly were one and the same. This was the shirtless man she couldn't get out of her mind—the man who had responded to her earlier remark about werewolves as if he had known all about them.

She was an idiot for not pressing the point when she'd thought of it, and for failing to ask Miller outright about what he might know from the start. It had taken a certain level of closeness to see this. See him.

Same eyes.

Same immediate and inexplicable physical attraction.

Same man.

The expression Derek saw cross Riley's face was one he had hoped to postpone. She had put two and two together, and he had to avoid the conversation that might follow.

"It's okay," he said. "I'll drive you home."

He couldn't do that, of course, without stepping into the moonlight. The best he could manage tonight, under that full moon, would be to take Riley through the back alleys on foot while trying to avoid any vampires that showed up on the way to the precinct. Either that, or he could call someone who could drive her wherever she wanted to go.

Tonight, the moon ruled even Weres with special skill sets like his. This wouldn't have been the case any other night. Still, the back alleys weren't really an option at the moment. One little beam of moonlight on his face, and Riley would see the result.

He pulled out his cell phone. "Marshall? Miller. I have someone who needs a ride. Check the coordinates to find us, and hurry."

Riley hadn't yet said a word, though her breathing had slowed and she had opened her eyes. *What did you make of that damn vampire, and the way I took care of the problem?* he wanted to ask her. Were enough worlds colliding in her mind to muddle up proper reasoning, even with all her psychology training?

"It was you. You helped me out earlier when the guy attacked me," she accused.

"Why are you so sure about that?"

He saw how she struggled to come up with an answer for something that was as inexplicable to her as the existence of vampires and werewolves. Riley was seeking explanations for reactions that couldn't really be tied to a physical description. She didn't know Weres could fast-track emotions and get to the heart of male-female closeness with the simplest eye contact...if that connection was meant to be.

He knew this was meant to be. He felt the connection acutely, and was going to have a tough time letting Riley Price out of sight when Marshall showed up.

All this pent-up emotion meant that he could no longer avoid the word he hadn't been willing to consider: imprinting. Even though it wasn't supposed to take place between their species. Either that's what had happened here, and he and Riley had forged a type of special bond, or he was an idiot for thinking it possible.

Imprinting meant that they were connected on a level that had to do with the soul. Fate and the soul. Possibly there'd be no way out of that kind of connection for either of them if she harbored the same feelings, while for him, now, here, the chain was already being forged.

Dale appeared beside him. Derek acknowledged his packmate with a nod, glad of the distraction. Dale would fill him in about that vampire in Riley's office later. Although the thought of leaving Riley in order to give her time to think, and to get on with his job, was an unwelcome one, some common sense, at least, kicked in. Riley had to get off the damn street, no matter who took her.

As for the imprinting phenomenon...

Well, if that's what had happened here, he'd want to tear up the world to get to her when they were apart. He would never be satisfied until he and Riley had joined in every way possible. That's the way imprinting worked. It was a particularly feral type of hunger.

Did he dare tell Riley all of this, or wait and see how this played out? Maybe that hunger was different for a human, and she'd be able to ignore it and get on with her life. But even his love for his ex hadn't been the same. Not like this. He had, after all, let McKenna Randall go.

Marshall's cruiser pulled up. He rolled down the window and leaned across the seat with a simple question.

"Where to?"

Derek couldn't walk Riley to the car without being exposed to moonlight. Neither could Dale. So he released her hand and gestured for her to get into the cruiser.

"Tomorrow," he said. "We can talk tomorrow, when you're ready."

Riley stepped off the curb and turned back. She spoke to Dale. "If you helped me out up there—" She pointed to her office. "You have my heartfelt thanks."

She got into the police unit and closed the door.

Derek watched the cruiser drive off.

Dale was unnaturally silent for a Were used to stating his opinion more often than not.

"I know," Derek said, reading the signs, if not Dale's thoughts. "Damn thing, timing."

"I see you found Detective Miller," Officer Marshall said, then fell silent.

Silence was okay with Riley. She was afraid to tell him that she knew Miller was the shirtless man who had helped her earlier. Someone might have been listening in.

They pulled up in front of her house. Officer Marshall walked her to her door and waited while she went in before speaking again.

"I'll be right out here for the rest of the night, Miss Price."

She faced him. "Did Miller ask you to babysit?"

"Call it an unspoken request. A healthy precaution."

"Will you be comfortable out here?"

"I'm used to the gig," Marshall replied. "First, though, I'd like to walk through your place to make sure everything is in order. Is that okay?"

"Not only okay, welcomed."

Riley stepped aside so the officer could precede her into the small house she had been lucky to find after arriving in Seattle. There wasn't much to see, and few hiding places in the five rooms.

The officer searched the closets, checked the windows and looked under the bed before returning to the front door. "Shout if you feel scared, or if you hear anything," he advised with a touch of his fingers to the holstered weapon on his belt.

Riley thanked him and got the door closed before her legs gave out and she sank, loose-limbed, to the floor. She sat there for a while as her heart continued to spike dramatically and her mind whirled with thoughts that would seem unreasonable to anyone else.

But fact was fact. She had seen things tonight that didn't fit into neat files she could categorize and label, and was shocked to have discovered that the world had more secrets than anyone knew.

There were important questions to consider now that couldn't be ignored. The main one, the surface problem, was the question of why she had become such a monster magnet and what she might have done to deserve that. Wrong time, wrong place? Twice?

And that, of course, tied in to her ability to deal with the fact that vampires and werewolves actually existed.

More important, however, was how she was going to deal with the hurt that had to do with her past; with what had happened to her mother so long ago that tied her together with the word *werewolf.*

There was no way in hell she could call her father and discuss any of this. She couldn't put him through echoes of the things he had tried so hard to put behind him.

After hiking her skirt up so that she could get off the floor, Riley stood up. After she took a quick look out of the peephole to make sure Officer Marshall was indeed there and visible to anyone who might try to bother her again, Riley dragged herself to the bathroom.

Dropping her clothes on the floor, she took a good look at herself in the mirror before heading into a hot shower that would hopefully wash away the silliness of kissing Miller. It was either that, or she might start screaming.

* * *

Though the night seemed terribly long, it had been mostly uneventful after Riley went off with Marshall. His friend and coworker was one of the few humans who knew about what went on behind the scenes, and was good at keeping those things to himself. Marshall would take good care of Riley.

Back in his apartment by dawn, Derek paced from room to room as he went over the night's events and came up empty on reasons why Riley would have been involved in the antics. What was so special about her that he and Dale hadn't been able to reason out?

No other vampires had appeared to make the rest of his shift more miserable. The bastard he had staked by Riley's office building hadn't brought cohorts. There had been no throng of spectators. Worst of all, though, in the aftermath of tonight's trials, was the thought that he'd have to exact a promise from Riley not to reveal to anyone what she had witnessed. He'd have to make sure she kept that promise, or his remark about most of Seattle's Weres not causing trouble would be a lie.

Derek leaned a shoulder against the wall by his front window, feeling antsy, though his mind was fatigued. In a few hours, and if he chose to participate, he would see Riley at the precinct when she came in to go over her statement. He wasn't sure that would be such a wise move after the connection that had snapped into place between them.

Are you thinking of me, Riley?

Will you have fitful dreams?

More important, would what she had witnessed free her tongue in front of others in the department?

If he was there, he could warn her about that. At the

very least, he could change the direction of the conversation if she looked to be headed that way. How could he win? She'd be better off if he didn't show up, and his pack would be better off if he did.

You are a wild card, Riley Price.

It was never wise to involve a human in supernatural affairs. He and a whole host of others worked hard to keep things out of the public eye, and had done so for years. Why let anyone spoil that now? was the question his pack would be asking.

With his eyes closed, Riley's face appeared before him like an image he could reach out and touch. Her scent still filled his lungs. Her observant stare continued to haunt him. He was stuck in a loop centered on her.

Will your humanness allow you to choose a partner more wisely, Riley?

He knew the answer to that question already and without having to reach for it, because Riley had kissed him first.

Like it or not, they were going to become lovers, and that was thanks to some strange hand of fate that had once upon a time twisted werewolf DNA far enough to create beings who could fit in with Homo sapiens… And one of those Homo sapiens had howled at a full moon.

Derek smiled in spite of the obstacles ahead, and removed his hand from the doorknob without knowing how it had gotten there. It was way too soon to visit Riley again. He had to wait to see what she would do tomorrow.

"Good night," he whispered to her. "This might begin to make sense someday, when you know it all. If you're to know it all."

As he headed to his bedroom, Derek had to wonder what a young psychologist would make of the events that had already occurred, and if she had the tools to deal with such a radical shift in reality.

Hell, maybe she could hypnotize him out of a relationship that really had nowhere to go. Possibly he could even afford to pay for a session like that.

The problem was that he didn't want an end to what had only just begun. He was just too damn interested in another tryst with those lush pink lips for his own good.

Chapter 13

The day dawned cloudy and gray. Riley believed it
was a miracle she'd been able to sleep for part of the
night, and that she hadn't dreamed about fangs, wooden
stakes or full moons.

Thoughts of the handsome detective returned soon
after she woke, and plagued her as she made some coffee.

In the daylight, the events of last night seemed dimmer, more distant, almost as if they had happened to
someone else. If more people knew that vampires and
werewolves actually existed, would there be a mass ex-
odus from Seattle? Would the National Guard be called
in to exterminate?

Yes. Miller had been right about people panicking.

Miller's watchdog was missing from her porch this
morning, and that was okay. Vampires slept in the daylight, right? At least according to works of fiction and

Miller's unspoken implication. No vampires would be coming after her until dark, if at all. And the full moon had passed, which took care of worrying about were-wolves.

All that was left to worry about today were good, old-fashioned people, and she was making a career out of dealing with them.

Since she seldom saw clients on weekends, she dressed casually for her interview at the precinct in a good pair of jeans, soft ankle boots and a blue turtleneck sweater worn in honor of the ring of bruises encircling her neck, where the bastard by the pub had choked her.

The interview with the cops today wasn't a bad thing, but she didn't need to make this into a pity-party by showing off the damages she had incurred in that in-cident. She was here. She had survived. End of story.

Except that it wasn't the end of anything really, and was in fact the beginning of something else that felt a lot like having entered another dimension.

A quick brush of her hair and a swipe of mascara finished the look she had been going for. Nothing about her appearance suggested that she might have wanted to impress Detective Miller. All she had to do now was to put one foot in front of the other and get into the taxi she had already called, having left her car downtown.

The air outside was bracing and fresh. Careful to lock her door, Riley hiked down the pathway toward the curb to wait for the cab that was due at any minute. She hadn't meant to bring the nightmares back so quickly, but thinking back to how that vampire had exploded into foul-smelling ash made her head hurt.

One damn howl had been her downfall. Chasing dreams. Her overactive imagination.

And okay, she had to admit that maybe loneliness was in there somewhere, too, which was why she'd had nowhere to go after work and time to roll along with her imagination.

Sometimes moving so far from her home and family seemed like it might have been a bad idea. On the other hand, when every cop on the force knew her at home, due to her father being one of them, there wasn't much room for adventure. And then there had been the looks she'd gotten, early on, because of what had happened to her mother.

"Suck it up, Price."

Everyone would be better off if she played this interview straight with no mention of fangs, broken windows and furry types in dark alleys. *You know...straight.*

In other words, she'd have to lie.

Omit was a better word choice, Riley decided as the cab arrived and she got in. As she saw it, two interviews were necessary today. After the cops grilled her about her attacker, she'd need a one-on-one Q-and-A session with Miller about everything else.

They could pretend that kiss didn't happen. She sure as hell wouldn't bring it up. He might have been her white knight, but she wasn't the kind of girl to kiss and tell. Nor would she hold him to the rich promises in that kiss, even though she'd like to.

"It was a damn fine kiss, Miller," she muttered.

In point of fact, it was the best kiss she'd had in quite a while. In months. Maybe even years.

This whole thing, it seemed to her, was centered not only on herself, but also on the detective that had shown up at every turn of her little supernatural wheel of fortune. Big, outlandishly handsome Miller, who looked almost as good in a shirt as he had without one. Whose chiseled face suggested a hardness that was the exact opposite of the compassion he'd displayed and the concern he had shown for her.

And who just happened to carry a wooden stake with him around Seattle...and knew how to use it.

Even better...

Knew whom to use it on.

"She's here," Dale warned as Derek strolled into the room. "Interview room two. How do you suppose this is going down?"

"I'm here to find out," Derek said.

"I left her place early this morning, right after Marshall's departure. Nothing out of the ordinary happened, so she's okay. I can go in there for her statement if you'd prefer."

"I'll handle it. Thanks all the same."

Derek repeated to himself that he shouldn't go into that room with Riley. He told himself that same thing over and over all the way down the corridor until he stopped at the door. If she was going to mention supernatural activity, he needed to be the one to hear it.

Swear to God, though, he felt her behind that door without having to open it. Her perfume lingered in the hallway—earthy, fragrant, feminine and like a trail leading him to her.

After rolling his shoulders, Derek opened the damn door, ready to find out what Riley Price was going to say about last night.

He stopped on the threshold as her eyes met his. There was no coy lash-lowering on her part when she saw him. She showed no outward signs of discomfort, even though he sensed the shudder she quickly suppressed.

"Dr. Price," he said in greeting, carefully monitoring his tone. She was even more beautiful in the light, if that was possible. "Thank you for coming in this morning, after a night like the one you endured."

"Not a problem, Detective," she said. "I'd like to make sure the guy that attacked me gets what he deserves."

He hadn't forgotten the deepness of her voice and how it affected him. But he couldn't let that be a distraction. He needed to listen to her without veering from his duties or giving away the concerns he had over the swiftness of the connection they had made and why there had been a vampire in her office. Neither of those things could be mentioned here.

Though Riley was the first human to be in a situation like this in a very long time, having survived a meeting with a vampire, she wasn't the least bit hysterical. He approved of her self-restraint, but had to wonder about his.

"Just some quick paperwork and you'll be free to go." Derek sat down and handed over some forms for her to sign. "It would be a good idea for you to read through it first and make sure everything in your statement is correct."

He looked at her intently. "Or if there's anything you would like to add."

She stared back. Her lips moved with unspoken questions. "How there could be such things as vampires?" was what she'd want to know. She might also address the way he had so easily dealt with the bloodsucker that showed up last night, and how he knew about werewolves.

Did she expect him to mention that kiss and apologize for his part in it?

Derek slid the papers closer to her, over the top of the table. "Your attacker is in custody, so you won't have to worry about him going after anyone else."

She glanced at the papers, then back up at him. The fluorescent lights highlighted her porcelain skin, which was unlined and ivory-smooth. Behind her bland expression, however, Derek perceived a hint of her desire to bring up her second attacker.

To her credit, she didn't mention it.

It occurred to him then that the camera in this interview room hadn't been turned on, and no taping was necessary for this session. No one would be observing them from outside because it was nothing more than dealing with paperwork.

The second thing that crossed Derek's mind was that the room wouldn't be able to contain the heightened degree of interest they had in each other for long. His reaction to her was visceral, and physical enough to bring him out of the chair.

Riley stood up seconds after he did. Backing toward the wall behind her, she said, "I don't fully understand what's going on."

"Maybe I should get someone else to come in for that paperwork," Derek suggested.

"Maybe you should," she agreed.

She didn't mean that. Her eyes were wide and her lips were parted. His Were senses picked up on how fast her heart was beating—not out of fear, but something else. Something neither of them wanted to discuss out loud.

Riley probably didn't have any idea what was going on between them. How could she? The word *imprint*

wasn't in everyone's everyday vocabulary. If this kind
of drama and tension persisted every time they met, he
was going to have to explain things to her sooner rather
than later, and that would take some finesse.

He wanted her. The wolf inside him wanted her. He
hungered for her in a way that was almost obscene.

Derek rounded the desk in three strides, but didn't
touch her. "You can file a complaint," he said.

"For what?"

The slight tremble in her voice should have warned
him to keep his distance. He wasn't known for allowing his wolfish hormones to get the better of him, and
liked to believe he was in control of his baser needs. Yet
he said, "For this," as he closed the distance. "And for
the record, this would be worth the trouble that complaint would cause."

Chapter 14

In that moment, as Miller invaded her space, it didn't matter to Riley what she had intended to say, or how many times she had vowed to keep things on a professional basis with this guy. As soon as he was close enough for her to look up and see his face, she knew she would go along with whatever he had in mind.

He didn't hesitate or pretend to ask for her permission to pin her to the wall. Inside her, sparks ignited. His mouth hovered over hers, almost touched down and then hovered again as he slid his hands up the wall and leaned closer to her. All she could think was *To hell with vampires—he's the dangerous one.*

She closed her eyes. Her heart pounded. When his mouth met with hers, all bets for self-control were off.

Okay. So I'm an idiot, she thought.

There was nothing light or tentative about the kiss.

Fierceness dominated it. Strange and unlikely passions reigned.

Miller's skin was warm and his mouth was hot. She couldn't have described his taste, and knew she'd never get enough of it to satisfy whatever they had going on.

He took her mouth in the same way he would have taken her body if he'd had the chance. At that particular moment, she would have let him have it all and helped him to take it. The power and strength he possessed were turn-ons, as was the aggressive, intuitive way he seemed to know she wouldn't argue or protest this level of closeness.

She kissed him back with equal fervor and allowed him the leeway to explore her mouth—taking, yes, but also giving back in kind. When her hands slipped to his back, he caught them and held both over her head, against the wall he'd trapped her with. He held her captive with his mouth and his hard, exquisite body.

Riley felt every inch of him from his chest to his thighs. She melted into his warmth as if she was starved for affection. The kiss deepened, demanded more, required her to tap into an emotion she had never experienced in order to find something she'd never known existed.

The rumbling sensations that started up deep inside her were like an oncoming storm system, and were painfully similar to the sensations of an impending orgasm. That internal storm moved through her, rolling, rising, beating against her insides with a demand to be acknowledged.

She groaned and let go of the last remaining vestiges of resistance to the sensory overload. If he had touched her anywhere else, any other part of her body, she would have exploded like that damn vampire they'd encountered last night.

She waited for that touch, equally wanting and wishing to repel it. Wanting to stay right where she was, and also desiring to get away before this went any further. She was already losing sight of her objectives and knew she was a goner, when in the periphery, an unfamiliar voice called out.

"Derek."

Then, "Detective Miller."

The mouth-to-mouth assault stopped. Her sexy detective drew back, tugging on her lower lip with his lips as his mouth separated from hers completely. There was no way Riley could open her eyes. The thunder inside her hadn't stopped when the kiss did, and was still rolling toward one specific spot that hadn't yet been discovered by the man before her.

Reality intervened when her detective released her hands and stepped back to turn toward the speaker, taking his heat with him.

"Emergency call," the other man announced.

Only then did Riley open her eyes to face what she had done here, in a room of Seattle's police precinct, with a man who was one of them.

Derek nodded to Dale, who stood in the doorway, and took a deep, settling breath. "On it," he said hoarsely. "Give us a minute."

When the door closed, he again faced Riley. "Can we continue this conversation later?"

He watched her big eyes blink several times, and noted how the pink tint in her cheeks had spread. Although he was the only wolf in the room, his senses now told him that Riley was no ordinary human being, either. She had the look of something much wilder. Something as hungry as he was. There were flashes of gold in her baby-blue eyes. A defiant expression returned to tighten her beautifully symmetrical features.

"Over dinner?" he said.

She shook her head, but he didn't let that deter him.

"There are some things I need to explain. I'm sure you have questions, and so do I," Derek continued. "If that conversation needs to be in a public place, it's your call. You choose the location and I'll either pick you up or meet you there."

He raised his hands as if to press home the point that he wouldn't touch her again, at least over dinner.

"I don't think that would be a good idea," she said soberly. "You're much too..."

"Pushy?" Derek finished for her when her voice trailed off.

She looked him right in the eye. "Yes."

"Just dinner," he said. "And talk."

"I don't think so, but thanks for the invitation."

Riley Price sidestepped him, took the papers from the table fairly calmly and headed for the door. She ignored Dale, who was standing in the hallway, as she left.

Derek blew out a low whistle and shook his head.

Dale said, "It might have been better if you'd have let me get those papers signed."

"According to what line of reasoning?" Derek returned.

"In honor of the decorum and sanctity of being inside our place of business...or some such shit like that."

Derek looked at Dale. "I blew it, didn't I?"

"Some people might think so, but hey, you're the boss."

"There's this thing between us that I can't explain," Derek said as he headed down the hallway.

"Yes, well, finding you speechless would be a first," Dale remarked.

"So, what about this emergency call?" Derek asked.

"A strange break-in last night at a therapist's office downtown needs looking into. Sound familiar?"

"I'm on my way," Derek said. "Before anyone else gets there."

"And, boss?" Dale called after him.

Derek paused to look back.

"I'm free for dinner, if she isn't."

The pleasures of partnering with a smart aleck just never waned. Derek gathered up his jacket from the back of his desk chair, barked an order to the guys nearby and exited through an exterior door, trailed by enough of Riley Price's lingering scent to make his muscles twitch.

Riley didn't want to go home or to her office, where she'd have to face the damage to her windows. There were already three calls from the office management company on her phone, which she hadn't answered. How would she explain the inexplicable, even if she had no other excuse for all that shattered glass? Who in their right mind wanted to hear the words *a vampire went through the window*?

The thought of what had actually happened last night made her stomach queasy and also upped her fear level. Thoughts of what she had just done in the police precinct with Miller almost made her feel worse.

What part of *fiction* didn't those monsters get?

Detective Miller had some of the answers. The problem was that he had been all heat, and no explanations. He had managed to sideline her agenda, and that might have been on purpose. The only way she could possibly have asked the questions she'd held back was to have accepted his offer of dinner. *And then what?*

She couldn't assume anything more would come of another meeting when it was obvious the lust they felt for each other would continue to get in the way. All that heat, plus the fierceness of the way Miller kissed, haunted her.

She didn't like the vulnerability of being disturbed like that, and hated the loss of self-control she had exhibited. Due to their getting carried away, she still didn't know squat about the monsters roaming the streets of Seattle.

Riley stopped on the street to look behind her, knowing she would have to see the detective again, and that the handsome bastard might be expecting her change of heart any minute.

She stared up at her office from the corner of the block. There was a police cruiser at the curb. A cop stood next to the front door of the building...and there *he* was, appearing as suddenly as if he had simply materialized out of thin air. Miller.

Of course he'd be the one to lead this investigation, since he had something to do with what had happened last night. At least, he had been there.

Riley eyed him warily from her position on the corner. The good detective would have to either lie about what he had seen or cover it up. In any other case, that would render this investigation tainted. But this wasn't like any other case. Not even close.

As though he had some kind of special sense, Miller glanced her way. He didn't address her or make his way over to where she stood. Derek Miller had a job to do here. And since it was her office they were investigating, there would be another interview.

Riley watched the detective and another cop enter the building. She waited a few more minutes before leaving the scene, needing time to come to grips with what was going on and wondering if she'd be able to go back into that office without imagining a vampire there to confront her.

She was afraid, and had to admit it. Nothing in her background was going to help her, because nothing actually made sense no matter what angle it was viewed from.

Someone called her name when she reached her car. "Riley?"

Deep baritone. Velvety syllables that made the base of her spine ruffle.

Riley reluctantly turned around.

Chapter 15

"**I**'m sorry if I made you uncomfortable back there," Derek said, keeping a few feet of distance between them.

She nodded. Changing the subject, and in spite of the people passing by on the sidewalk, she said, "How many of them are there?" without mentioning vampires by name.

He looked at her for a few seconds before speaking. "If you're asking about the office intruder, the answer is that there are too many of them for anyone's good."

She went on, hitting hard and to the point. "Who, besides you, knows about them?"

Gone now was the pretty pink tint in her cheeks. One of her hands rested on the roof of her car. Her other hand tugged at the collar of the sweater that matched her blue eyes.

"Very few people know," Derek said.

"Why not? Why doesn't everyone have that information when it's so important? Why haven't you told them?"

"I've already mentioned to you about the panic that would ensue. You can imagine it, can't you?"

"There was a vampire in my office," she said in a hushed voice when there was a break in pedestrian traffic, and as though she needed to say those words out loud in order to grasp the ramifications.

Derek nodded. "Yes. There was."

"What about the other ones? The monsters that aren't vampires? You said most werewolves don't cause problems, so you do know about them."

Before he could reply, she went on. "I heard them howl and thought it was a prank. That sound was the thing that kept me on the street."

The remark she'd made last night began to make sense to Derek now, and it also left him feeling guilty. If Riley had followed the sound of a Were's howl for some reason, and that howl had been his, then he had put Riley in danger.

Still, he was curious about why she had been lured onto the streets by a wolf's howl when no one else had paid any attention. And why she had tried to howl at him.

She hadn't actually seen anything when he and Dale arrived to help her with that attacker by the pub. She hadn't been in any kind of shape to see them in their alternate shapes, and yet Riley first had chased a wolf-ish sound and then had mentioned werewolves to him after her attack. In retrospect, there had to be something more to her story than a whimsical love for adventure.

"I do know a few things," he said.

Derek had no idea how he was going to get out of this

conversation gracefully. Riley wouldn't have been owed any explanations if that damn vampire hadn't followed her. She might never have seen him again.

Had that bloodsucker in her office been his fault, as well, as he and Dale suspected? Derek supposed it was possible the vamps had been observing him and that they might have picked up on his interest in Riley.

If any of that was true, he did owe her something for the trouble he might have caused.

"I have to get back to the current investigation," he said. "But I'm not going to keep those answers from you. Meet me tonight and I'll explain. It will take a little time, and I don't have that right now."

"All right," she said, surprising him yet again. "Tonight at Orson's. Eight o'clock. But first, one more question."

"Ask it," Derek said.

"Why would a vampire single me out, if, in fact, that one did?"

"Maybe it didn't. How are we to know that unless we make an attempt to find out?"

She opened her car door and turned to face him again before getting in. "You won't stand me up tonight, Detective?"

"I wouldn't dream of it," he said.

That much at least, Derek thought to himself as Riley drove away in her silver sedan, was true.

She had chosen one of the most popular eateries in Seattle for this dinner because the place would be packed on a Saturday night. It would also, Riley knew, be noisy enough to cover the strange conversation she and Miller were going to have.

At home, her anxiousness over everything that had happened manifested not only in the way she checked every nook and corner in her house for intruders, but also in the way she dressed for this next important meeting.

Her black dress, which was smart, and not too short or too sexy, would work as camouflage in a hip restaurant full of other black dresses. Her strappy high heels would be easy to slip off if the need came to run...

She drove fast to reach the restaurant and scored a good parking space. When she walked up to Orson's, Miller was there, waiting for her in front. He hadn't changed his clothes, probably because he had taken time off from the job to see her.

Miller's tight T-shirt hugged his torso. His loose, worn black leather jacket almost covered his jeans-clad hips. She had prepared herself for the sight of him, but seeing him standing beneath the restaurant's overhead lights gave Riley a jolt of pleasure. He truly was gorgeous, and he radiated a confidence only slightly magnified by the power of his badge.

As she walked toward him, Riley couldn't help noticing the interest he got from other women. Miller's sexual vibe affected females on a primal level, and she felt it as she approached him.

He was observing every step she took as though she was a suspect in an investigation. Maybe he was sizing her up to see whether he could trust her with the information she'd asked for.

He didn't smile. Of course he wouldn't, since this was not a date, and for perhaps the first time in a while, he was the one in the hot seat. She might have grinned over that idea if the situation hadn't been so serious.

"Detective Miller," she said in greeting.

"Dr. Price," he returned.

All business, he avoided commenting about how she looked, though Riley was sure there was appreciation in his eyes.

"Are you finished up at my office?" she asked.

"For now."

"Will there be more interviews tomorrow?"

"Yes, if you'll oblige."

Riley already sensed an undercurrent of electricity passing between them and had to ignore it just to get through this. If she had met Derek Miller at any other time, and in any other circumstances, she would have enjoyed whatever was making her skin tingle each time she looked at him. Now, however, she needed a lot more than male-female warm-and-fuzzy feelings.

"I believe your father is also in law enforcement? A captain?" he said as they headed toward the entrance.

"You've done your homework, I see, Detective."

"All in the name of piecing together a puzzle."

"That puzzle being?"

"Your two brushes with the dark side, Dr. Price."

It was a cold night, and his reply made Riley feel exposed. She tugged at her jacket and gestured to the door with her clutch purse. "Shall we go inside?"

"It's crowded," he noted.

"Exactly."

He nodded. Locks of shiny brown hair fell lazily over his forehead when his eyes returned to her. "After you."

The decibel level of the noise inside the restaurant was deafening, though the night was still young. People were two-deep at the bar, but Riley passed it by. This meeting might have required alcohol, and yet she was again going to play it straight and see how far she got.

Miller had fans inside the trendy restaurant, too. He and Riley were shown to a coveted corner table, near the back wall. Riley shook her head when Miller moved to help with her jacket, and sat down. Ignoring the menu she was handed, she carefully rested her hands and her purse on the table. There was a small tape recorder inside that purse.

"You're sure about this?" Miller asked, giving her an option to back out of this conversation.

"It's safe here," Riley said. "At least, I think so. Maybe you can tell me if I'm wrong about that."

"They wouldn't come here, or to any place where people gather in numbers."

The way he said the word *they* gave Riley a healthy round of chills even though she'd left her coat on.

"Vampires?" she asked.

"Yes."

"How many of them are we talking about, exactly, Detective?"

"Enough."

"Which is?" she pressed.

"People are good food, and there are plenty of people around."

Her hands slipped from the table. "That's obscene."

"It's what you wanted, isn't it? The truth?"

Riley blinked slowly to take in what he'd said. "Besides you, who else knows about this problem?"

"Maybe a hundred of us, give or take."

"Do you all carry wooden stakes?"

"It's highly recommended when we're poking our noses into dark alleys and backstreets. Since you've seen one example of the species, I'm sure you can imagine the trouble vampires can cause."

Riley shifted in her seat, thinking *only a hundred people know?*

"It jumped from my window, three floors up," she said.

"Through the window," Miller corrected.

To keep from trembling over that memory, Riley bit her lip and took a moment before speaking again. "Doing so didn't seem to hurt it."

"Not much would when they're already dead."

The trembling spread to her hands, which she kept folded in her lap. *It's better to know*, Riley told herself. *Danger rides in the wake of ignorance.*

"Have you come up with a theory as to why that thing was in my office?" she asked.

"One you probably won't like, and yet it's only a theory," he replied.

"I'd like to hear it."

"What if I ask you to listen to it with an open mind and stay where you are, in that chair, for a while longer, no matter what I say?"

"Open minds are my business, Detective. And I'm familiar with the concept of a theory."

His nod was pensive. Did he think she would run away now, when she didn't like anything about this conversation so far, and had been ready to run from the moment she sat down?

"That vampire might have been sniffing you out because I had been there, in your office. It could very well have been trying to find out the reason for my visit, though the fact that this particular bloodsucker could have been researching and planning would be highly unusual."

She needed a minute to make sense of that, and took even longer to respond. "You know their habits that well?"

"I have to if I'm to keep this city safe."

"You've encountered them before," she noted.

He nodded. "On too many occasions."

Miller's gaze was boring into her, she knew without having to look. He was again gauging her reaction to what he'd said.

"So, that one could have been in my office because you go after them, and it might have wanted to retaliate? It might have been after you, not me?"

The fact that Miller had to think over his answer to her question made her quake.

"That could very well be the case," he conceded. "If so, then you were in danger because of me, and helping you out of that situation was the least I could do."

"Is that the only theory you have?" Riley asked.

"At the moment, yes. But we're working on others."

She had been studying psychology long enough to know when someone was holding something back. Nevertheless, Miller was under no obligation to tell her everything, and Riley knew it.

She said, "Is there a theory about how those creatures can exist? How they came about? Why they're here?"

"Only the things fiction writers point to, and that's not necessarily reliable," he replied.

"So, you take them down when you come across them and hope to keep their numbers from increasing? You do this in secret, with others?"

"Yes."

"And the public won't ever know about vampires?"

"Not possible," he said. "Not any time in the fore-seeable future, anyway."

She eyed him without caring if he noticed how much she was shaking. "Maybe a little panic would be a good thing."

Miller shook his head. "You'll have to trust me on that."

When their eyes met, heat flooded her cheeks. Un-comfortable with that reaction, Riley broke eye contact.

"It's my turn to ask something," he said. "Why don't you tell me about what you thought you were chasing on the street last night after you heard a noise like a howl?"

Riley suddenly found herself mute. Seconds ticked by, and maybe even minutes, before she took a breath, settled her shoulders and confessed, "I have a thing for werewolves."

That was the truth, just not all of it.

Miller's gaze was disconcertingly focused. But after hearing herself say those words, Riley stood up, picked up her purse and left him at the table to stare at her re-treating backside.

She hadn't meant to run. But she was more afraid of hearing what Miller might have said about that little confession than what he'd said about vampires.

He'd had the strangest look in his eyes. And she had just given him a hint of the secret she had protected for most of her life.

Chapter 16

Derek went after his fleeing date—the woman who was now privy to one of Seattle's greatest secrets. Better than that, he now knew the *thing* she had for werewolves was what had brought them together.

What were the odds of that happening, even if she had just meant the creatures in the movies?

He didn't actually believe in fate. He had never stopped to consider why he was a Were, and different from everyone else in Seattle.

Riley Price just happened to have an appreciation for the species he belonged to without having known that werewolves actually existed. Now that she did know, what would she do?

He caught her outside the restaurant with a hand on her arm and said, "We can't possibly be finished with this conversation. You don't get to leave me with an exit line like that and hope to get away without an explanation."

When she turned around, he saw how flushed her cheeks were. Instead of avoiding him, she took a step closer to meet his studied gaze.

"I now know there are more things going on in this city than you're willing to talk about, and I also understand how strange my remark might seem to someone like you, who knows about most of them."

Derek couldn't tell if Riley was afraid or testing him in some way, hoping he would tell her more than he already had. But he wasn't quite ready to go there.

Her scent was delicious, and her body was close enough for him to want a replay of the kisses they had shared. Willpower was the key for getting him through the next few seconds without pulling her in for more.

"Spill," he said. "Tell me why you don't want to talk to me now, and why you ran."

"I don't know," she confessed. "We're speaking about nonsensical issues that are no longer nonsensical. The world has changed. My world has changed. How am I supposed to get used to that in the five minutes since I've known about it?"

"You deal with the truth," Derek said. "Better than most, you should understand the reasons for facing whatever comes up."

Her eyes were bright. She was shivering in the night air. "Do you want to go back inside?" he asked.

"No. I was wrong to choose this place. I'm sorry."

"Someplace else, then?" he suggested.

She shook her head. "Will vampires come after me again?"

Derek wanted to say no, but couldn't. He just didn't

know what to expect. Even now, they were together again, and vampires could easily have been observing them from nearby rooftops.

"Just in case the one theory I have turns out to be right, it's probably a good idea if we don't meet so visibly after dark until I understand what's really going on," he warned.

Derek could have sworn Riley looked disappointed at that suggestion. It was possible, however, that he was mistaken, and what he actually saw in her expression was relief.

She glanced around before bringing her attention back to him. "It's creepy. This whole vampire thing is creepy."

"It is."

"How long have you known about them?" she asked.

"About three years, though their numbers have increased dramatically in the past two."

Her eyes widened. "What should I do if one of them comes after me again? I don't have any wooden stakes. Not even a good steak knife."

Derek smiled. He couldn't help it. She was trying to put a light spin on a dark situation, and not too successfully. It was possible that levity made her feel better, though her face was extremely pale.

"I'm going to ask you to trust me," he said. "Can you do that?"

"Because of your badge?"

"Because I happen to know more about this problem than most people, and out of necessity have made an art of studying vampire habits."

"You won't always be around to watch over me. I need to know how to protect myself."

He remained silent, waiting for her to answer his question about trusting him.

"Yes," she finally conceded. "I suppose I can trust you."

"Then come with me."

"Where to?"

He waited again for her to come around. She finally did with a curt nod and a whispered "Okay."

What Riley Price didn't say, but probably wanted to, was *"Will going with you, trusting you, hurt me, or be any crazier than the last two days?"*

That just happened to be the question he couldn't have answered truthfully.

Riley felt the strength in Miller's hand when he laced his fingers through hers. She wanted to absorb some of that strength as he led her down the sidewalk and away from the restaurant. She didn't question him again about where he was taking her, and remained watchful of her surroundings.

He stopped beside the entrance to an alley two blocks down and turned to face her. "Showtime," he said. "Are you ready?"

Hell, no. Ready for what? her mind warned, though Riley didn't say that out loud.

Miller bent down to remove the wooden stake from his boot, as she had seen him do the night before. When he handed it to her, Riley felt like throwing up.

"Take it," he advised, closing her fingers around the unusual weapon.

The stake was smooth in her hand, with a pointed tip. *Well-used* was the word that came to her as she clutched the stake. Did he expect her to use this? She prayed there wouldn't be an opportunity to do so as Miller headed into the dim alley assuming she would follow him.

Riley had a hard time moving her feet. The street, with its lights and traffic, had become scary enough without leaving it for the city's darker places. She had already seen a vampire and a werewolf, and that was more than enough.

She could head in the opposite direction and say to hell with Derek Miller, and yet the little spark of inner defiance wasn't going to allow her to do that.

"Please tell me you're kidding," she called out when he paused to wait for her to catch up.

"We should be quiet now," he warned.

Since she didn't want to be left behind and on her own, Riley took a few steps with the wooden stake raised. Her heart rate spiked into the red zone, the way it had last night, when she thought she'd heard a werewolf's howl and chased the sound. Adrenaline surged through her with hefty electrical jolts that fired up her nerves and obliterated her chills. She had wanted adventure and truth, and it didn't get any bigger than this.

Her restless mind kicked up all kinds of scenarios as she moved forward. Was Miller going to show her another vampire? Was this going to be a lesson on how to protect herself and what to look out for...with her dressed in heels and a little black dress inappropriate for the occasion?

Swallowing back her fear over what they'd find in the alley, Riley remembered that so far in their short acquaintance, Miller had come through when the going got tough.

She could do this.

Like a shadow, Riley kept as close to Miller as she could without tripping over him. She reminded herself to breathe, and kept a death grip on the wooden stake.

Miller stopped again just past the edge of the building beside them and gestured for her to wait. He took several more steps that made him blend into the shadows that were lit only by a single overhead lamp hanging from the back of the building, high up.

A sound in the periphery numbed her with fear.

"Come out." Miller spoke to the dark space beyond the reach of the light.

Riley's ears picked up static, like the kind radios make between stations.

"It's just me," Miller said to whoever or whatever was out there. "Me, and a friend."

Every separate system in Riley's overstrung body sent up a red flag for her to get out of there as quickly as possible. She had experienced this same warning twice before in the span of twenty-four hours.

"Some of you wanted to see her, and here she is," Miller called out. "The last vamp who wanted the same thing didn't fare so well."

Riley's throat constricted. Her breathing grew shallow enough to leave her light-headed.

"Last chance," Miller said to the darkness. "Take it or leave it."

Leave it. Please leave it... Riley silently pleaded.

But that was wishful thinking, since they had invaded a vampire's space, and the man beside her was calling out the monster.

Miller kicked up some alley detritus with his boot, an action meant as a further challenge for any creature that was here to show itself. Riley couldn't have moved if she had to.

With her eyes riveted to the darkness ahead of them, she waited without knowing exactly what she would see, whether some kind of supernatural creature accepted Miller's taunt. The vampire in her office had been little more than a blur. Miller hadn't given it much time before he had taken care of the problem.

She didn't want to see this, but had to.

There was a movement in the darkness. With a slick sideways glide of dark overlapping black on black, something emerged. Feelings of impending doom engulfed her as a light face appeared, a ghostly pale face that stood out from their surroundings and seemed to hover too far off the ground.

"Vampire," Riley said.

Miller nodded. "A fresh inductee that didn't bother to hide its scent."

Riley didn't want to know what that scent might be. The odors in the alley were enough to cause a gag reflex.

When the white face floated closer, Miller offered encouragement. "That's right. Come on. You can smell her, can't you?"

The creature was close enough now for Riley to see that its body was swathed in a black robe that had rendered the vampire invisible in the dark. This was a vampire. No mistake. Nothing else could have looked or moved like this. Nothing alive, anyway.

"Riley," Miller said to her without taking his eyes off the vampire. "Meet your nightmare. Not the worst one, but a decent example of what happens when a person has risen from the grave into an unintended afterlife."

The vampire's hiss was almost as frightening as its appearance. Riley fought the urge to back up and run. She held Miller's stake so tightly in her hand her knuckles were as white as the creature's face. If she left, Miller would have nothing to protect himself with.

She clenched her teeth and waited for what would happen next, telling herself that Miller was a pro and able to handle this vampire. He had done it before, right in front of her, with relative ease.

"This alley is in my jurisdiction," Miller said to the creature. "There are a lot of people nearby, and I'll bet you're hungry."

The vampire didn't advance or make another sound. Dark eyes studied her and Miller both, as if they were prey.

"Do you have to kill it?" Riley whispered to Miller. "I mean, I get that it's already dead. Is there no way to reason with them?"

"They are animated corpses driven by a thirst for blood. They prefer human blood and are indiscriminate about where they get it. This guy would drain you dry in about twenty seconds. Don't think he isn't considering how to do that right now," Miller said.

"So you have to…"

"Yep. I've seen far too much of the carnage these bloodsuckers leave behind. It's either us or them."

The vampire opened its mouth to show off the tips of two ungodly long and pointed teeth. Riley raised the stake and held it aloft, as though it was a magical talisman that would keep the creature away…

Just before the vampire attacked.

Chapter 17

Derek blocked the vampire before it could reach Riley, grabbed the stake from her frozen fingers and spun it around for a better grip. He caught the creature by its robe and hauled it backward so that he could take aim at its chest.

The thing hissed again loudly, but Derek had heard this before on so many occasions it had no the effect on him. Some new vampires were wily and some weren't. Like most of the vamps he'd met in the past few weeks, this one believed itself to be invincible and the bigger threat.

That would be its first and last mistake.

The creature kicked out and fought back as though it had ten limbs instead of four. The newly made blood-sucker was fast, but not thinking too clearly. The blood-lust was upon it, and Riley was a delicacy it wanted to reach with those nasty fangs.

Behind him, Riley hadn't moved. She was all eyes,

and tense, but he could tell a good portion of her fear was for him. In that moment, as he again hauled the vampire back from reaching her, Derek realized that Riley would help him if she found a way to do so. She wasn't actually frozen in place, but was waiting for the opportunity to present itself.

He heard that thought run through her mind as if he had the ability to read it.

Surprised by the intimacy of that connection, Derek let the vampire slip from his grasp. It lunged for Riley, fangs snapping, before Derek caught hold of the creep again. But it had gotten close to her—close enough for Riley to smell its fetid breath.

She recoiled in time to avoid a bite to her left shoulder. With reflexes Derek silently praised, Riley slapped the bloodsucker in the face and jumped aside. The vampire turned to catch her, angry, hissing like a startled cat.

"Enough," Derek said.

As Riley moved to stand behind him again, he kicked the vampire, knocking it to the ground. He placed his boot on the vamp's chest, raised the stake in the air and then it was over. *One more down. Case closed.*

Standing upright, he turned and looked at Riley, who was still behind him, and breathing hard. Her face had lost half of its color. Gray vamp dust littered her head and shoulders, but she hadn't run away this time. She had stayed.

They stood there looking at each other for some time without speaking. The air was loaded with tension that hadn't fully been used up. Derek's muscles rippled beneath his shirt and jacket. Riley's hands shook. Neither of them broke eye contact this time because they both understood that the only way to get rid of the adrenaline rush was to use it up. Wear it out. Short of finding another vampire to fight, there was only one way to do that.

Like the hunger the vampire had possessed, Derek's desire for Riley and for what might occur in the next few seconds burned him up inside. Somehow he sensed the same thing happening to her.

"You're a surprise, Riley Price," he said. "And also much more than you seem."

"I could have told you that," she returned. "I am a cop's daughter, after all."

But that wasn't it. That wasn't what Derek had meant. She also kept something hidden from the world. He saw this in her face, and in her eyes. Riley Price had secrets, and he had just witnessed one of them in the way she had behaved here, by his side.

"You weren't very afraid," he noted.

"I nearly lost my lunch," she said.

Her eyes dared him to delve deeper. "No. That's not it. That's not everything," he suggested.

"I have no idea what you're talking about, and you're the one with the answers here."

Maybe that was true, but Riley was being equally as unreasonable. He was painfully aware of her body, her eyes, and the way she was looking at him. Sexual tension surrounded them like a fog. Invisible lightning crackled in the air. His next move was in response to all of that.

Derek took her by the shoulders and drew her in until their bodies were molded together. As with the night before, she didn't protest when his mouth found hers. Her lips were already parted and ready for the kiss that was to come. But a kiss wasn't going to do it for either of them. Not tonight.

He took her mouth like the wolf he was. It was a fierce

action, a teasing lead-up to the next inevitable step in their crazy, short-term relationship.

It crossed Derek's mind that he was becoming involved with a victim in two open police cases, and also that it didn't matter, since he would help her out no matter what took place. Riley was now privy to what went on in this city, and his part in that.

Her mouth was feverish, tender and greedy. She kissed him back the way a she-wolf would have in similar circumstances. For Weres, there was a grand finale to fighting and vanquishing a foe, and that finale was sexual.

What did it mean for her?

Derek drew back far enough to take her hand. "Not the place," he said. "Too many eyes. Too much filth."

She let him lead her to the street. They walked fast and said nothing. His need for her didn't ease once his muscles were in motion. If anything, heading toward a safe place where they could go at each other like animals served to intensify those cravings.

He would find out what her secrets were.

He couldn't wait to peel back the mask.

His apartment wasn't far and there was no need to take Riley's silver sedan. They just had to get there before anything else came up that could get in the way of what he had in mind.

Derek glanced at Riley as they turned the corner of his street, looking for her go-ahead. The green light.

She smiled.

She'd seen her second vampire and was still standing. Walking, actually. Riley didn't know how that could be, other than the fact that her trust in the man beside her had become a tangible thing she wanted to touch with both hands, and there was only one way to do that.

Just now she wanted to be the one to bite the man beside her—run her teeth over his neck and his bare shoulders to see what kind of control the big, bad detective had then.

Most cops were wild at heart and Derek Miller was no exception. Riley supposed she had her father to thank for passing that wildness to her, though it had taken years of hard work for her to tame it.

Miller lived on the second floor of a newer apartment building, not far from one of the main boulevards. They passed up the elevator in favor of a steep flight of stairs, barely slowing down until they reached his door. One turn of the key and they were inside. Without taking the time to look around, Riley found herself on her back, on top of his unmade bed.

Miller leaned over her and kissed her again. She tasted his passion, heat and desire. There were, however, too many clothes getting in the way of satisfying their mutual needs.

Miller had to have been thinking the same thing. He stood up, tossed his jacket to the floor and then pulled off his shirt. He stood still long enough for her to take stock of everything she suddenly wanted so badly.

An image flashed through her mind of her first encounter with her rescuer as she stared at Miller's gloriously bronzed muscle. Long hair, a taut body and eyes like diamonds in the night were things she would never forget.

He pulled her to a sitting position and removed her coat. Then he tugged her to her feet and wrapped his arms around her so that he could reach and find her zipper.

The sound it made in its downward slide was erotic.

In the otherwise quiet room, that little piece of metal moving along its track was a heady signal that two adults were agreeing to have sex.

Cool air brushed across Riley's naked back, and she sighed softly. The handsome detective wasn't kissing her now. Her head was pressed to his bare chest, where his heat was fierce. The guy was on fire, and she needed heat.

She had worn black lacy lingerie to match the dress and didn't stop to wonder if Miller would like what he found. He was one-hundred-percent involved in undressing her, and he was savoring every minute, just as she was.

His fingers slipped seductively over her spine and began an agonizingly slow journey upward, taking time to explore the feel of each vertebra until he reached the nape of her neck. By then, Riley was ready to jump him and cling. But his breath in her hair and the way he was taking his time with the foreplay were turn-ons.

With her ear against his chest, Riley heard Miller's heart beating with a slow, rhythmical cadence that was the exact opposite of hers. She kept her eyes closed as his warm hand slid upward and into her hair. He took hold of a few strands and drew her head back so that she had to look up at him. When his eyes flashed, Riley felt as if she was falling, and as though she was about to drown in the blue blaze of those eyes.

He pressed the soft black fabric of her dress over her shoulders. They were too close together for the dress to fall, and close enough for her to feel how aroused Miller was. The pleasure he was already giving her was extreme. She felt it all, each move, each flare of warmth. She heard him whisper but couldn't catch the words.

The seduction was like a song, in that it built up

slowly in tempo. Miller was priming her for the moment when they could no longer stand being apart, but she was already shouting inwardly for him to hurry up.

He lifted her to let the dress fall to the floor, where it puddled next to his jacket. Riley kicked off her shoes. Her legs were bare.

Miller didn't even back up to look at and appreciate the body she had worked hard on in the gym, or the lacy lingerie she wasn't going to wear for long. Hunger overtook them both at that moment, uncontrolled and primal in its intensity.

She was against his bedroom wall and he was kissing her senseless. A minute later she was back on the bed with Miller perched above her. There was no way to put off what they both wanted any longer. Their breathing was shallow. The hardness behind his jeans, against her thighs, proved Miller was as expectant as she was.

She dug into his back with her nails as he reached down to free her from the fragile black-lace barrier that was keeping him from taking what he wanted. And then he freed himself.

He entered her gently at first. Riley writhed beneath him, encouraged him to get on with this. It wasn't supposed to be making love. This was nothing more than an attack of mutual lust and a few moments of unparalleled passion between people who were barely more than strangers.

Her lover gave her what she wanted as he moved into her with an agonizing slowness, then withdrew again so that they could both take a breath. His eyes never left hers.

Then he came back, moved slightly faster with a plunge into her depths that took her breath away. Gripping his arms, Riley kept him close as he again withdrew. But after that, they couldn't take their time any longer.

She made appreciative sounds as he began to move with a gradual buildup of depth and speed. She couldn't stop herself. Every new thrust, each withdrawal, infused her with a blistering heat and the desire for more.

It didn't take her body long to flood with the sensations he was providing. A thunderstorm began deep inside her and grew steadily, quickly gaining in strength. The thunder rolled toward her lover, rushing to meet at the point of their merging bodies.

He again whispered something to her that she didn't hear—words that got lost in the storm system she was experiencing. But something about the way he said those words, and the velvety tone of his voice, brought her to the vortex of that internal storm, and made her peak.

The climax hit hard, and with real fury. Riley bit back a cry of pleasure as her body seized, caught in the throes of a new and exotic kind of sensory overload.

She didn't open her eyes now. Couldn't. Her lover pinned her to the bed as the waves of her orgasm crashed over her and kept coming.

He found her mouth, and kissed her, absorbing her cries as he let out his own sound—part sigh and part groan of pleasure. His body finally slowed its wicked rhythm with a satisfied gasp of release.

Only the sound he made wasn't a gasp.

It was a growl.

Chapter 18

Riley held her breath until her lungs were ready to burst before she exhaled slowly, hoping she'd be able to breathe normally sometime in the near future.

Echoes of the bliss she had experienced still tickled her insides. Her legs were tangled with the legs of the man who had given her so much pleasure.

Miller was looking down at her with his bright blue eyes, but instead of reflecting the satisfaction of the past few minutes, his expression was one of trepidation. Maybe he thought he had gone too far. That they had gone too far.

The sound of satisfaction he had made hung in the air. Had he growled because of her earlier confession about liking werewolves? Did he expect her to smile and appreciate that he had listened to what she'd said when it had been silly for her to admit to such a thing?

She didn't really know this man at all.

But she had to say something. It was what people always did after sleeping with a stranger.

"You're good at that," she said.

Miller raised an eyebrow. As incredible as the sex had been, it had, in the afterglow, become awkward.

"Thanks," he said without easing up on his keen stare, or moving aside.

"I'll have to go," Riley said, avoiding his eyes, afraid that if they found that same connection again, she'd be up for round two. The truth was that she was already up for it.

"So soon?" he asked, though he couldn't have missed her breathless, slightly anxious state.

"What is it, Riley?" he added in a tender tone that brought her more ripples of heat. "Please say you don't feel regret."

"No. It's…"

"It's what?"

"You're much more than you seem," she said.

"Was that a compliment?"

It actually was a compliment in a roundabout way, Riley decided. And this wasn't the time to ask the questions that returned now to plague her, though she felt she had to say something else. That growl had brought back a dozen thoughts and memories from last night.

"I saw a werewolf in an alley," she said, moving from pleasure to the nightmare of the night before as quickly as those thoughts arrived.

Miller's expression registered his surprise. He clearly hadn't expected her to return to the supernatural subjects still on the table. But he didn't avoid addressing her remark.

"I told you Weres exist, Riley. I believe you saw what you saw."

"Not a guy in a costume. A real live werewolf," she said. "Please don't bother trying to evade the subject. Don't lie to me about vampires being the only immediate threat. That wolf was fierce and like nothing I've ever seen. I heard one of them howl when I was first attacked."

The room was quiet for a few seconds before he nodded. "That's highly likely."

Riley actually had nowhere to go from here and couldn't think of anything else to say. The other items on her list floated away as the warmth of Derek Miller's next exhaled breath touched her cheek.

He backed to his knees and stood up. He offered her his hand, which Riley took, feeling far too exposed now in the few scraps of lace still covering her. She put on her coat, skipping the dress. Miller watched with interest as she leaned over to slip on her shoes.

Wearing just enough to make a quick getaway, she looked at Miller, figuring that she could think of him as Derek now, after this, though cops almost never went by their given names.

"Talk to me," he said. "You can, you know."

Riley hesitated, not sure how to begin. "I can't go home, can I, in case a vampire might be waiting for me?"

"You'll be protected, I promise," he replied. "Nothing with evil intentions will get to you there or anywhere else."

They were avoiding the elephant in the room. Dancing around what had just happened on his bed. Withholding things made the transition from the rawness of their passion to normality uncomfortable.

He wasn't going to pressure her or argue, though. "I'll take you home if you want to go," he said, then, after a few beats, added, "But why don't you stay here? I'm due back at work, so you'll have the place to yourself. More protection will arrive as soon as I make a call. You can make yourself at home."

Riley looked around. The bedroom was small and tidy, except for the unmade bed, and was sparsely furnished. There was a large rug, a dresser and one shuttered window.

She recalled passing through a living room to reach the bedroom, and catching a glimpse of a kitchen. But she wouldn't have felt at ease in Derek Miller's house when his scent was everywhere, especially after what they had just done. Being among his things felt too private. She wasn't ready for that, so she had to go home.

As if he had read her mind, Miller nodded. "Fine. Wait a minute while I make that call. Then I'll take you home. Grab a drink from the refrigerator if you'd like. There's a bathroom down the hall."

As he left the room, he glanced at her over his shoulder. "I'm truly sorry if something I've done has put you in danger. The only way I can make up for that is to see that you stay safe. Will you let me do that? Will you stay off the streets until I find some answers?"

"Yes," Riley said, because what other option did she have? Having this detective watch over her meant that she would see him again, though she promised herself she wouldn't return to his bedroom until they knew each other a lot better. Until she felt sure about any feelings she might have for him beyond the kind of lust that had gotten her here in the first place.

She did have feelings for him. Damn it, she did.

He had stopped in the doorway and was waiting for her to look at him.

"I can do that," Riley said as she turned to find the bathroom, in need of a few minutes of alone time in a space Derek Miller didn't occupy. "I can give you time to sort this out."

Due to the strangest circumstances possible, she was going to be a prisoner of sorts for a while. Derek was offering protection every time the sun went down. She wondered how many times he might take a shift.

In the bathroom, she dabbed cold water on her face and sat on the edge of the tub. Several minutes and a thousand heartbeats later, she emerged to find Derek in the living room, standing beside the front door. He held up her dress. "There's time for you to put this on."

"Thanks, but I'd better get going."

She took the dress from him. Their hands brushed. Riley felt another flush of heat in her throat, caused by the man who could mesmerize her without trying.

Being near to Derek Miller was a threat to her sense of reason, and looking at him made things worse...because he was the epitome of every woman's wet dream, in the flesh.

When he opened the door for her, Riley realized that besides her thing for werewolves, she was going to have to add Detective Derek Miller to the list of her interests.

They drove in silence. There wasn't much more to say that hadn't already been covered, except to acknowledge how their bodies had fit so well together and how their passion had merged perfectly in his apartment, on his bed.

He hadn't lied to Riley about trying to keep her safe.

The wolves in his pack would help with that without asking questions when they heard about the vampires' sudden interest in her. Now all he had to do was worry about why Riley had been targeted.

Derek didn't like what one of the bloodsuckers had said, and the words kept repeating in his mind, adding to the puzzles needing to be solved.

She is not for you, wolf.

He was fairly sure she was for him, and that what had taken place in his apartment confirmed it. His next step would be to have Riley realize, and admit to, the same thing.

He pulled the car into her driveway and cut the engine. "Please wait," he said, and got out to greet Marshall and the member of his pack who had answered his call for assistance.

Although no explanation was required, Derek said, "Vampires have tagged her." That was all they needed to nod and get on with the job of watching over Riley while he went to investigate the issue.

Derek wished he could watch her himself. Stay with her. He didn't want to let Riley go, or allow her to think that all he'd wanted from her was sex, though he still wanted that. Beyond the urges tugging at him, however, there were bigger issues to be dealt with. Riley Price was only one piece on a moving chessboard…even if she was such a lovely one.

Derek walked her to her door, went in with her and checked the rooms. Back at the door, he finally spoke up.

"It was better than good, and only the beginning."

She hadn't looked at him on the short drive, but did so now. Her blue eyes gleamed with the same kind of longing for a rematch that he had, and her struggle to hide it from him didn't work.

Her voice was breathy. "I might hold you to that."

Turning from Riley, leaving her there, was a necessity, and also one of the most difficult things Derek had ever done. With his inner wolf whining and his hands fisted, he smiled, nodded to her and went outside, where the foul stink of vampires drifted to him on a cold, incoming breeze.

Chapter 19

"Damn it," Derek growled.

His ginger-haired packmate moved to back him up. "Not the usual neighborhood for bloodsuckers," Jared noted, and that was true. Riley lived on a quiet street lined with trees and small cottage-style houses. Families lived here. Children would play in manicured yards during the day.

Derek had never seen a vampire this far west of downtown, but he realized what the draw had to be. "Marshall, are you ready?" he asked.

The off-duty officer was wearing jeans. He pulled out his specialized gun.

"Rounds?" Derek asked, keeping his focus on the street.

"Silver, just as you requested," Marshall replied, two-fisting the weapon in front of him. "I wonder what the other guys would think of this."

The unpleasant odor was growing stronger though there was no vampire in sight. Derek backed his way up the driveway to search the roof. Zeroing in on the rooftop of the house next to Riley's, he muttered, "There you are."

He realized right away that the thing on the roof wasn't a new vampire. Brand-new vamps wouldn't have been able to peg two of the three beings standing there as werewolves without a full moon to prove it.

This bloodsucker traversed the rooftop with the agility of a cat. Instead of backing away, it moved silently toward the front of the roof and paused there to peer down at Derek's keyed-up threesome.

"Guess we're not scary enough for this guy," Jared said.

"On the other hand," Marshall remarked, "I'm totally creeped out just looking at him. It. Or whatever the hell that thing is."

"Sorry you have to see this in person," Derek said to Marshall without taking his eyes off the vampire. "Hearing about such things and actually facing them are experiences that are worlds apart."

Though vampires, like werewolves, had exceptional hearing, the one on the roof didn't react to the conversation going on beneath where it crouched. If it hadn't been cloudy, there would have been enough brightness the night after a full moon for Derek to have seen its face. As it was, even with his Were abilities, Derek couldn't view the monster as clearly as he would have liked. Its smell, however, was that of rotting debris.

"We've got all night," Derek called out after minutes of inactivity had passed. "But I don't think you do."

The taunt was a half-hearted threat, since it was

probably closer to midnight than to daybreak, so there were plenty of dark hours left before the sun came up.

The vampire stood up, providing a better target for the silver bullets in Marshall's weapon. Marshall took aim. But the bloodsucker became a moving target when it leaped from the roof to land in the yard. With speed that was truly exceptional, and almost a blur, it hopped onto the fence next to Riley's cottage, and from there jumped to her roof.

"Oh, no you don't," Derek warned, heading for Riley's front door. Over his shoulder he shouted to his packmate, "Go around to the back. Find that sucker."

Riley had locked the door. Derek pounded on it with a fist and called her name loudly enough for anyone nearby to have heard.

The door opened. Riley stood there, dressed exactly as she had been when he'd left her minutes before. Derek took hold of her arm and hustled her outside, wondering if that was the safest move, but he had to do something to keep her in his sight. She didn't say a word or ask what was going on. The wideness in her eyes suggested she already knew.

He led her to Marshall's car and put her inside before he nodded to Marshall and then sprinted back to the house, muttering every obscenity he had ever picked up.

He raced into the house, remembering how vampires had gone after his ex two years before. Back then the reason had been to lure her new lover into the open. The guy she had fallen for. It turned out that the vamp queen also had the hots for that new guy, and had kidnapped McKenna to get rid of the competition.

But this was happening in the present, to him and to Riley. So he had to again consider the possibility that Damaris had set a plan in motion for reasons only she knew about. Could it be to lure Derek into taking a misstep that would leave Seattle without a diligent alpha and open to a full-on vampire invasion? Were his pack and others like it the only barrier to a possible future bloodbath?

How did Riley fit in with that plan?

No. That line of reasoning couldn't be right because the warning he had been given was that Riley wasn't for him, and that he was to leave her alone. Him. Personally.

He blew through Riley's house like a tornado, and the search turned up nothing. Exiting through the back door, Derek met Jared in the yard.

"No sign of it," Jared said.

A chill at the base of Derek's neck provided the impetus for his next sprint, which was in the direction of Marshall's car.

Riley pressed her face to the glass, anxious about what was going on. She recognized Officer Marshall out of uniform. He stood by the hood of the car with his gun raised.

She sat back when she heard shots that sent her anxiety level skyrocketing. This incident could be a break-in or a random trespass, but Riley doubted it could be anything so simple after the events that had preceded it. Due to Officer Marshall's presence and the warnings Derek had given, this had to be another vampire sighting…which meant the monsters had found out where she lived.

Why, though? What made her a target?

Officer Marshall fired two rounds. The noise was shocking, but she couldn't see what he was shooting at outside the car window. It wasn't hard for her to remember the vampire she'd met tonight in the alley Derek had taken her to, and the way it had blended with the shadows.

Riley sat up straighter to see what would happen next, and found Derek looking back at her through the window. She withheld a sigh of relief. This was the man who had promised to protect her from monsters, and he was adhering to that promise.

Another shot rang out. She heard Officer Marshall shout. A face appeared on the opposite side of the car, pressed to the window on her right. It was a terrible face—deathly pale and wicked, with dark, red-rimmed eyes and a gaze that pinned her to the seat.

She sat between Derek at one window and a vampire in the other. Derek's eyes were on the vampire. The vampire only had eyes for her.

"Fuck you," Riley said to the monster.

A fourth shot ricocheted off the door, creating sparks on the metal. Derek vanished. So did the vampire.

Riley reached for the door handle and stumbled out of the car, thinking that in the old days, a weapon like Officer Marshall's would only have had six bullets in the chambers and that only two would have remained. But there were other options now, and she hoped to God this gun was more up-to-date.

She saw Derek running across the lawn of the house next door with another man on his heels. Officer Marshall barked a curt "Get back in the car" without turning to face her.

Riley put a hand to her chest, as if that could possibly have slowed her hammering heart. She didn't want to get back in the car. Somehow she felt safer in the open.

"Did you see it?" she asked Officer Marshall, who kept his gun raised. "You know what that was?"

"I know that thing shouldn't exist, and that we'd all be better off if it didn't," he replied.

"Was there only one of them?" Riley figured that had to be right, since Derek had given chase.

"One is enough." Officer Marshall held his weapon steadily, without any hint of shaking or visible surprise.

He added, "They're coming back," careful to keep anything moving toward them in his sights.

"Not—" she began, her query cut off by Derek's familiar voice.

"Did you get it?" Marshall called out.

"The bastard got away." Derek crossed the lawn accompanied by the man who had followed him in the chase.

"What now?" Marshall asked, lowering his gun.

"Now Miss Price will have to relocate, at least for a while," Derek replied as he approached. To her, he added, "Are you up for that?"

Riley leaned against the side of the car. The lingering echo of the sound of gunfire underscored her lover's words. "Is there actually a place that would be out of their reach?" she asked.

"Yes, though you might not like it much, either."

He glanced at the tall, muscled young man who had backed him up, as if seeking that man's confirmation of the place he had in mind, and received a nod in return.

"Where is that?" Riley asked as Derek again took her arm.

He leaned toward her and lowered his voice so there would be no opportunity for it to carry. With his blue eyes on hers and a gentle grip on her arm, he said, "You know that species you have a thing for?"

Riley wasn't sure why her pulse spiked so dramatically when her heart shouldn't have been able to beat any faster than it already was. She met Derek's steady, direct gaze. "Please tell me you're kidding."

But he wasn't kidding. "No one can reach you or even dare to try if you're surrounded by my pack," he said.

Riley gave his words time to settle in, but they didn't. They couldn't have, because two words dominated all the rest, and those were *my pack*.

Pack. As in a group of people with similar goals...

Or a group of wild animals that lived and hunted together. Like wolves.

But Derek had said *my pack*.

For the first time in her life, Riley thought she might faint. The problem was that she didn't like playing the part of a victim and had always passed on the concept of females being the weaker sex.

So she looked into Derek's eyes. "You were that shirtless guy. Only you're not actually a *guy* after all, right? You're a—"

"Werewolf," he said.

Chapter 20

There it was. Cat out of the bag. A confession of sorts
to a human who otherwise wouldn't have guessed his
secret. They had been heading in a good direction before this. What would Riley do now?

She had gone pale. Her beautiful face was slack with
disbelief. Again, though, if he had put her in danger, he
was responsible for her safety. Beyond that commitment
to her, there was now another kind. Riley had gotten
under his skin. She was all he could think about. Her
image accompanied every thought he had.

He waited for her to let his news sink in, wondering
if she would start shouting, and if her legs would give
out. He had just confirmed her suspicions about the existence of werewolves, and she couldn't possibly have
expected him to be one of them.

They had shared the most intimate connection there
was. Whatever came next was in some part out of their

hands if she felt the tug on her soul in the same way he did. For him, sex had sealed him to Riley as if his soul had been chained to hers.

Not many humans would have wanted to be a werewolf's mate. Not many of them could have handled what that entailed.

But Riley was different.

There was so much more that he needed to say to her, and he couldn't take the time. The damn vampire had gotten away. Once a vamp had targeted its prey, it seldom gave up on that target. Like a bloodhound on a scent, this one would return for a second pass at Riley. Derek was sure of that.

This sucker had been unusually strong, and fast on its feet. It had stolen a good look at Riley. Derek pictured the bloodsucker licking its lips in anticipation of getting even closer to her. The Lash, a term to describe the extremes of the unholy vampire beast's raging hunger, had shone in its eyes.

Since Riley didn't speak, he had to. "Those fangs got too damn close."

There was no real way to read into her silence as she continued to stare at him. He heard her heart beating frantically inside her chest. The vampire wouldn't have missed that, either.

"Gather a few things," he said. "Enough to get you through the night. You can return tomorrow if you want to, and you can continue to work. But before sundown, from now on and until we get to the bottom of this, I'll take you to stay with my friends."

"Pack," she said without meeting his gaze. "That's the term you used."

Derek nodded, glad to hear her speak. "Yes. Pack."

"Because you really are a werewolf."

"Yes."

"And I'll be safer with a bunch of wolves than any-where else."

"Infinitely safer."

She turned to Marshall with an accusation. "Are you one, too? A werewolf?"

"No, ma'am," Marshall replied. "I'm just a regular old human being who has some supernatural friends."

She looked to Jared. "Yep," he said before she could ask him the same question.

Everyone gathered here had to be wondering the same thing about why she didn't question this further, and how she could seem so calm in light of being hit with such news. Without calling them all crazy, and without any outward display of what she had to be feeling, Riley turned toward the house, as he had directed.

Derek turned with her, loathe to leave her alone in case she had a delayed reaction to what was going on. In the doorway, she paused. He anticipated that move, waited for it.

"Nothing is as it seems on the surface, Riley. I think you already knew that."

"If I didn't know it before, I do now," she said.

Derek perceived the slightest tremble in her voice. Weres were highly attuned to fluctuations in emotions, and his emotions were now connected to hers.

He stayed by the door and listened to Riley rummage through drawers in another room. She returned minutes later with an overnight bag in one hand, looking tired, her energy spent. Derek took the bag and followed her to the car. He tossed the bag inside and kept Riley from getting into the back seat.

He brought her around to face him with a gentle tug on her arm. "I'm glad you know about me," he said.

She didn't look up.

An overwhelming desire to kiss her tensed his insides. Although Riley needed to wake up from the shock she'd had, the fact that there were others present kept him from acting on that desire.

He wasn't going to lose her over this, Derek vowed. Riley would come through. She was intelligent and streetsmart. She had been trained to listen and to analyze what she heard from others without rushing to a judgment. Her profession was one of tolerance and secrecy, while his was partly the opposite. In law enforcement, he faced violence and intolerance on a daily basis.

It was, however, a strange turn of circumstances that with so many she-wolves lusting after him, he had chosen to go so far out of bounds by finding a human partner. This human. *You, Riley.* And it seemed even odder to him that vampires also wanted Riley Price for reasons of their own.

"One sign," he messaged to Riley on the Were channel she couldn't hear. *"Give me a sign that you're still on board."*

A tingle at the base of his spine warned Derek that she was going to respond to his message as if she had indeed heard it.

She stood straighter, rose onto her tiptoes and placed her hands on the sides of his face. Her gaze traveled upward slowly. After looking at him closely, she touched her lips to his briefly enough for Derek to believe he could have imagined it.

Although long lashes partially covered her eyes when she backed up, Derek had seen those eyes flash with a warning of her own. It told him that Riley Price was more than a mere human woman. She was more than anger, defiance, sex, strength and courage. And she was going to prove that to everyone, including him.

Starting now.

She got into the car without an argument, without being told exactly where she was going. Which meant Riley still trusted him in spite of everything she had learned. He couldn't accompany her. He had to let her go and remain at her house in case the vampire made a quick return visit.

Jared would see to it that Riley arrived in one piece at the special location outside the city, where some of his pack had set up a community. It was a place where no one had to hide their identity. Only there could Weres feel almost totally free all the time.

"You'll be surrounded by some of the fiercest Weres around," he said to her. "As my guest, you'll be welcome."

That was true, though the members of his pack would be as wary about having a human in their midst as she would be about being around them. Still, minus a full moon, she'd fit right in.

He tapped the roof of the car, giving the signal for Marshall to drive on. In the front seat, Jared gave him a thumbs-up gesture that confirmed his acceptance of the responsibility that now rested on his shoulders.

Riley was leaving, and Derek hated the thought of a separation.

"Turn around," he whispered to her as the car pulled away from the curb. "Look at me, and I'll know where your thoughts lie."

He waited for that to happen. Willed it to happen.

It almost didn't.

The car was at the end of the block when she glanced back at him through the rear window. And for that one small favor, Derek's heart felt a tremendous surge of appreciation and hope.

They drove for a long time, eventually heading out past the city limits. The purr of the engine lulled Riley into a temporary peaceful state, which was a respite from both internal and external chaos. Away from the city, it was easier to believe none of this had happened.

She rested her head against the back of the seat and closed her eyes. Despite her knee-length wool coat, she felt chilled. But that wasn't surprising. She had been face-to-face with two werewolves and shared a bed with one of them. Dreams had indeed melted into a strange new reality. Parts of her past had come forward to bite her, proving that she did live in a world where werewolves exited.

Werewolves and other things.

Who would have guessed that about Detective Derek Miller? While he had rugged good looks and was formidable, he also walked and talked like the people around him and held an important job that made a difference on Seattle's streets. Wasn't that what being an alpha meant? That he was a protector and a leader?

How did someone go about becoming one of them? How had werewolves come to be?

After she'd gone to bed with Derek, would that wolfishness spread to her?

She tended to doubt that last part. Derek wouldn't have put her in that position. Sex couldn't be the way to spread werewolfism from one being to another. Or so she hoped.

Derek. You bastard. How could you keep that from me?

She was sick of all the dead-end questions, and thought about pumping the Were in the front seat for details. But this guy didn't owe her anything, other than seeing to her safety in Derek's absence. Derek had implied that she wouldn't need protection from the werewolves they would be joining, so did that mean most of the Weres Derek knew were intrinsically good, and that horror stories had gotten that wrong?

At this point she was still in the dark, and anyone else might have been happy to stay there. Too bad she wasn't like everyone else.

The car slowed once they'd left most of the city lights behind. Riley ran a hand over the seat next to her, wishing Derek was there and that she could form a clear picture of what she'd be facing.

There was no way to tell what time it was. Her wristwatch was missing; she had removed it in Derek's bathroom. Leftover adrenaline hadn't completely dissipated. Thinking back to the vampire's appearance at her home, heat flashed like a bad sunburn across the back of her neck, clashing with her chills.

As the car turned off the main road a few miles past a low-lit strip mall, Riley emerged from her stupor enough to pay closer attention to her surroundings. Moments later, they turned onto a street marked as private. Soon after that, they encountered a gate.

"Are we here?" she asked.

"I believe we are," Officer Marshall confirmed.

Without turning around, Derek's packmate grunted a low reply. "They know we're coming, so it's okay."

His response caused Riley to wonder what would have happened if Derek's friends hadn't known that a human was coming to meet them.

"It's late," she pointed out.

"We like the night."

So, okay. This was it, and scary as hell. She was about to enter an area populated by werewolves. Right? Real, live werewolves.

Riley pressed a fingertip to her lips to keep from speaking, and swiveled on the seat to avoid the ache centered low in her body that was proof of what she and Derek had done in his apartment.

What she had done with a werewolf.

When the gate opened and they drove through, she saw additional lights in the distance. Riley rolled down the window to let the cold air reach her face, anxiously awaiting what lay ahead. This was Derek's pack. Maybe some of them were his family. She didn't even want to think about what it must have been like for a werewolf being raised in a human world.

Derek had been right to assume that vampires wouldn't trespass here. Hell, she was beyond being scared already as the lights kept getting closer, and she was supposed to be a welcome guest.

She hated to think what might happen if any Were enemies passed that gate, if Derek and the red-haired wolf in the front seat of the car were any indication of the breed.

Gathering her courage, Riley slowly counted to ten.

Chapter 21

Derek sat on Riley's front step with Marshall's gun in his hand. He could have held the silver bullets this gun contained in his bare hands with no problem at all, contrary to what some people believed.

Most of the whole werewolves-are-vulnerable-to-metals rumor was just that, rumor. Myth. Hollywood fantasy. The only way silver could harm him or any other Were was if he were shot by one of those silver babies in a vulnerable spot, with no doctor around to remove the bullet in a hurry. It was called evolution—and vampires hadn't fully kept up.

He was good with a gun, and more than just a decent shot. If the bloodsucker returned before dawn, it was going to be one sorry dead guy.

Odds were better than good that it would come back.

"Make it quick," Derek muttered, frustrated that he

couldn't take Riley to the pack himself, and angry he'd had to delegate that task.

"You know you want to return," he said out loud, thinking of the vampire that had caused this round of trouble. "Her fragrance is a heady draw for me, too."

Sitting on her step brought him all kinds of Riley-related scents, and he liked them all. But he couldn't afford to overlook the other odors he sensed in the night.

He stared at the street, the neighboring houses and their lawns, with a need for action, and clapped a hand to the back of his neck to acknowledge a sudden nudge of awareness. He stood up slowly with the gun at his side and started toward the street with his muscles tensing.

"So damn predictable," he said to the newcomer whose presence caused his body temperature to rise.

The lights Riley had seen turned out to be street-lights in a neighborhood of houses that could have existed anywhere, except for one thing. There were no people in them, according to Derek. Just werewolves.

Officer Marshall drove slowly. Guided by the other guy in the front seat with him, Marshall finally turned into a driveway and let the car idle.

Riley took in the ranch-style house with its long covered porch. There was a green front lawn, a brick walkway and more brick on the stairs. All of that seemed so normal she felt like laughing, as if the joke was on her and there were no werewolves here or anywhere else.

The front door opened and a man came out. Like Derek—and the guy he'd mentioned was named Jared, the only other example of Derek's packmates she'd met—this guy was tall, broad in the chest and shoulders, and handsome. An aura of energy surrounded him that Riley could have sworn passed right through the car window.

Marshall spoke to the Were beside him. "Christ. Are you all that big?" It was possible that Marshall had never been here before, either.

"Not all," Jared replied as he got out of the car. "Just most."

As Riley strained for a decent breath, she became aware of a low-pitched humming sound. Her body reacted to it by producing another swiftly moving wave of heat that radiated outward from her chest.

Startled by her reaction, she took a better look at the man who had emerged from the house to stand by the car. An odd flicker of recognition came to her when he asked, "Is everything okay?"

Suddenly, she was thrown back in memory to the city, to the street where she had first been attacked last night. She again felt the roughness of the pub's exterior wall, where she'd been held fast by a pair of strong hands.

"You'll be all right in a minute. We've called this in and someone will come to get you," her rescuer had said.

Beyond that smooth, mesmerizing voice she hadn't been able to forget, she now remembered hearing someone else give a warning about having to get out of there before anyone saw them. There had been two rescuers. She had known that. But she hadn't recalled that the second guy had spoken until now, after hearing the same voice say to Marshall, "Thanks for bringing her. I'll take over from here."

She slid toward the door to get a better look at the speaker, but didn't recognize him. Only his voice was familiar, and yet she had the impression that this guy was tightly connected to Derek in some way, and thus to her.

Wait a minute, her mind nagged. She had seen him before, hadn't she? She now recognized the dark hair and lean body. Wasn't he Derek's partner? The guy who had arrived after Derek had staked the vampire near her office? It was hard to tell, since she'd been in shock at the time and Derek was the only thing she had paid attention to.

In case anyone hadn't noticed, she was still in shock now.

When the car door opened, Riley didn't balk or hesitate. She got out and stood tall with her coat closed tightly around her. "Is Derek alone back there, left on his own to fight my battles?"

The big Were smiled. "One thing you will soon learn is that Derek does whatever he wants to do. Case in point—bringing you here."

Riley dialed back her assertiveness a little. "He might get hurt."

Her new host's smile remained fixed. "Just so you know, he rarely is. Besides, we're blessed with exceptional healing powers that enable us to spring back almost miraculously. And we taste bad to vampires."

Riley looked from the Were to Marshall, then back to the Were she was speaking to. "Will Derek come here later?"

His reply was earnest, and also slightly cynical. "I'd be willing to bet that nothing short of meeting up with Seattle's vamp queen herself could keep him away from here for long."

Some of Riley's tension settled. Derek would come here. He would be all right, and so would she.

"Would you like to come in?" her new host asked. "There's a room ready for you."

Riley shook her head. "If you don't mind, I'd like a minute to myself. If that's allowed."

"You're not a prisoner, Dr. Price, though I wouldn't go off on your own, and I'd advise you to stay in this yard."

"I just need a minute," she said.

Jared got her bag from the car and tossed it to the Were she'd been speaking with. After that, Jared wandered off with a promise to return in an hour.

That left her in the yard with only Officer Marshall for company. When he turned back to the car, Riley stopped him with a hand on his arm. "You're not one of them, so maybe you should have someone look at that wound on your neck."

Wearing a solemn expression, the young off-duty officer shook his head. "Maybe we shouldn't bother anyone here with that just now."

"You're bleeding."

He ran his fingers over the wound and wiped off some of the blood pooling there, giving Riley a first-hand view of two tiny puncture marks beneath his left ear.

The skin around those punctures was raw, red and swollen. The holes themselves looked like they had to be painful. Riley knew what they had to be. The subliminally fast vampire at her place had gotten to Marshall. And she was to blame.

Marshall's face had paled somewhat, but he shrugged. "It might be too late for anyone to help. I can't be sure.

But I'm not dead yet. That monster didn't have time to finish me off, so I guess I was lucky."

"I'm...sorry," Riley stuttered, feeling sick again, and helpless.

She watched Marshall climb back into the car, and stayed where she was long after it had disappeared from sight. That's when she made a vow, a promise to herself and to that officer to join in the hunt for the monsters that had put the Seattle PD on high alert, and had ruined what could otherwise have been a perfectly good night.

The vampire approached Derek with a gait that reminded him of someone on roller skates. Derek wasn't impressed.

"Back for more?" he asked.

The abomination stared back, so white-faced it looked like a moon had descended to street level.

"She's not here," Derek said. "You can tell that to whoever sent you. I doubt if you'll find her again, so you might as well target someone else. I'd recommend that you take Riley off your fetish list, or you'll have a pack of Weres to deal with each time you resurface."

The damn thing finally spoke, though its fangs made the words difficult to understand. "You know nothing, wolf."

"No? Then why don't you enlighten me?"

"She is wanted."

"By whom?" Derek asked.

"Someone far more powerful than you."

"I can think of only one someone that would fit that description. Could that vampire be your Prime?"

"You know nothing," the vamp repeated.

"Let's not go backward, okay? I'm trying to understand why Riley is so special."

"Why is she special to you?" the pasty-faced bloodsucker countered.

"Part of what makes her special to me is the fact that all of you want her so badly. I'm trying to figure out the reason for that."

"I can smell her on you, wolf, which means that she is special to you for other reasons as well."

"Maybe you're right," Derek admitted. "But is your interest centered on any feelings I might have for her? Because that would make this whole stalking nonsense about me."

"You merely make things more difficult."

It was evident that this was a well-spoken vampire he faced. In his experience, only the ancients of the species possessed the ability to make real conversation of any kind…and Christ, how many of them could there be?

"You can go now," Derek said. "Trot back to whomever you report to and tell them you failed to reach your prey."

"Humans are vulnerable," the vampire said. "Choose your friends wisely, wolf, or some of them won't survive for much longer."

Derek didn't like the sound of that threat. He raised the gun, aimed and fired…but there was only empty space where the vampire had stood.

He lowered the gun and swore loudly, wishing he had a car.

Chapter 22

"Riley?" her Were host called out.

She had been out here too long, Riley supposed, and had lost track of time waiting to see the telltale headlights. Derek's. About to give up, she finally saw a car heading toward the house.

"He's coming," she said to the Were that had walked up to stand beside her.

"And driving too fast," he remarked.

Was Derek equally as anxious to get to her, or was there another reason for his speed? Either way, Riley knew she wouldn't feel so alone among strangers when he arrived, though he was actually little more than one of those strangers.

This was Derek's pack. He was in charge. She wondered if, in addition to his apartment in the city, Derek also had a home here. She also pondered how much her life had changed in just two days. Tonight she had become the consort of a werewolf and might live to regret it. At the moment, however, she was really glad to see him.

Tires squealed on the road as a black SUV stopped in front of her. Riley thought about running to Derek for the warmth and familiarity he'd provide, but waited for him to get out of the car.

His eyes found hers immediately. The air crackled with the same kind of electricity that had driven them to the brink a couple of hours ago. Some people would have labeled the buzz passing through her body as a form of sexual chemistry, the internal acknowledgment of a mutual attraction. But looking at Derek now, without being close enough to feel or smell him, was torture. And that was yet another surprise.

"Vamps gone?" the other Were asked Derek.

"Gone, but not forgotten," Derek replied as he walked toward her.

"The sucker got away again?" the Were asked with an incredulous tone.

"Faster than it should have, and not without issuing a threat." Derek glanced around. "Where's Marshall?"

"He left a while ago."

Derek's gaze came back to Riley. "Are you all right? That thing by your house didn't touch you?"

"I'm fine," she said, and silently added, *Now that you're here.*

"Was Marshall okay?" he asked. "Did he seem to be all right on the way out here?"

She couldn't recall if the officer had asked her not to tell the Weres about the marks on his neck. Maybe he just hadn't wanted to worry these guys with the fact that he had been wounded by the monster they had faced.

Marshall was human. He wasn't fueled by wolfish superpowers and didn't belong to this pack.

"He seemed all right," Riley said, when that wasn't necessarily true. Though Marshall had tried not to show it, he had looked alarmed.

Deep in her gut was the awareness that those puncture marks on Marshall's neck could mean he would become like the monster that had bitten him. Still, she had no real notion of what it took for a human being to turn into a vampire, so she didn't want to worry Derek about his friend unnecessarily.

"Good." Derek's relief was obvious. "Glad to hear he's okay. Marshall is a necessary member of this team."

He came closer to her, reached out to her. "How are you holding up?"

"I'll manage as long as I don't think about tonight too closely."

"You handled the situation bravely, and better than most people would have," he said, darting a glance to the Were that stood next to her. "You don't have to meet all of the Weres here. Only a couple at a time."

"And only the best of us," the other Were said with a smile.

"Riley, meet Dale Duncan, a personal friend of mine and my first choice for backup in the city."

"Cop?" she asked her handsome, dark-haired host.

"Yes, ma'am," Dale Duncan said. "But don't hold that against me."

Riley looked around. "Vampires don't come here?"

"Would you, if you were them?" Dale said. "There are over a hundred of us here, give or take."

"Two packs call this valley home," Derek explained. "It's private land. Being here is by invitation only."

She eyed both Weres. "Werewolves don't fight among themselves?"

"Not since we became civilized, which was several decades ago," Derek replied.

The relief flooding Riley's system felt like a wave of warm water. Vampires weren't coming here, and that was good news. They couldn't get in or out of a place teaming with werewolves like the two next to her. If all one hundred of Derek's friends, or even a good percentage of them, were as formidable as the examples she knew, no monster in the world could afford to take that kind of a risk.

For the first time in a while, Riley found it easier to breathe. She was actually accepting everything, and that these two guys were what they said they were.

A larger flash of heat returned as Derek took her hand. He led her up the steps and across his friend's front porch. Dale preceded them into the house. When Derek stopped her from entering, Riley braced herself for what might come next. More kissing and further closeness were what she desired, but those cravings didn't involve a human male and couldn't possibly lead to any kind of acceptable future.

Derek brought his face close to hers. In a tone that wasn't so much like velvet as gravel, he said, "Now tell me the truth about Marshall."

Derek observed the change in Riley's expression that told him she was debating how to answer his question. He had pondered his own take on Marshall soon after the police cruiser had driven off from Riley's house. Marshall had been uncharacteristically reserved and a little white around the edges.

"Riley, it's important that I have all information about what happened tonight," he explained. "It's possible you sense this, even if you might feel an obligation to withhold certain pertinent facts."

His eyes delved deeper into hers. "If, in fact, there are more details."

Riley faced him bravely, for all that had gone on in the short time he'd known her. Once again, he silently applauded her ability to cope and bounce back from events that would have driven other people out of their minds. She had met vampires and werewolves, and she was here because of some internal switch that allowed her to dial up the ability to confront issues like this without panicking.

He figured she was compartmentalizing. Locking up her fear in an iron box. If that was the case, it might not be long before signs of distress showed up.

"There were marks on Marshall's neck," she said.

He had been afraid of something like that and took a minute to consider what it meant.

"Scratches?" he asked.

"Punctures. Two of them."

Her reply served to confirm Derek's worst fears. Seattle needed cops like Marshall; cops who had seen a few things that were out of the norm, and kept on ticking. Marshall was extremely valuable to the Weres both on and off the force. He was even more valuable to the people he served.

"Did he talk about them, Riley? Those marks?"

"He said he'd be okay because the vampire hadn't finished him off."

Derek hoped to God that was true.

"What could potentially happen to him, Derek?

Since this was my fault, I need to understand the ramifications."

She had called him by his first name. He looked into her clear, wide-set eyes.

"Those wounds alone won't necessarily affect him more than being painful for a while. Vampires can drink from a vein and leave their victim standing if that victim doesn't die of shock over the ordeal. This vampire didn't have time to binge."

He didn't like scaring Riley. After taking a deep breath, Derek cautiously continued. "It's the venom that's dangerous. Vamps are like rattlesnakes in a way. Their saliva contains toxins that can both paralyze and hypnotize their prey. If they use that venom and leave their prey alive, the unlucky victim might fall sway to vamp demands without having a say in the matter."

Riley uttered a groan and closed her eyes. Derek tightened his grip on her hand.

"Let me stress that you're not responsible for any of us, Riley. We hunt vampires. This is what we do. What we've done for centuries. The only thing special about the past few days is your involvement."

The way she looked at him made Derek's pulse jump. Riley was a damn good actor. However, in that moment the bond they shared exposed her true feelings. He saw confusion and dread in her expression, where there had formerly been only anger and defiance. Her emotions were so strong he was almost able to feel them.

"It will be okay," he said. "Trust me, Riley. We take care of our own. We'll get help for Marshall and we will take care of you."

He again perceived the faint tremble in her lower lip.

That quiver was the only way she was going to let her fear visibly manifest.

He needed to convince her that he was telling the truth and put Riley's mind at ease. She was intelligent enough to comprehend that the danger was only postponed. Tonight's confrontation had been managed, but tomorrow was another night. And there'd be another one after that.

She had become a target, and Riley felt the bull's-eye painted on her back.

"The best thing you can do at the moment is to put your trust in us and get some long-overdue rest," Derek said.

"Promise me Marshall will be all right." Her voice was little more than a whisper.

"I made a call on the way here as a precaution. Someone will be waiting for him, and will check him out."

Her eyes searched his.

"Let's go inside," he said.

"You'll stay here? Stay with me?"

"I'll be here when you wake up," he promised.

"You expect me to sleep?"

"I'd recommend it."

"I won't be able to close my eyes."

He smiled. "I think you'll find that you can, if you try."

In spite of being needed in the city, he was going to put aside his responsibility in order to be closer to this woman—something he would never have done in the past.

Damn it, he couldn't help himself. The Weres in the city would have to take this shift in his stead. Riley was more precious than anyone realized, and not just to him.

Other eyes were on her, and as long as she remained alive and well, there was a chance he could find out what was going on, and why a vamp queen like Damaris was so interested in her.

There had to be a reason Riley was a target. He'd dig out that reason if it took facing fifty more bloodsucking bastards to do so.

Riley tried to hide the drawn expression that sent bolts of white-hot anger up his spine. Pulling her in, Derek whispered in her ear, "Let's make the most of the hours until sunrise. You and me. What do you say? We can sort the rest tomorrow."

Acquiescing, she turned to the doorway, but not before he saw the terror that had darkened her eyes.

Chapter 23

All night, Derek held her cradled in his arms. No kisses, no sex, just a comforting offer of warmth and some semblance of safety. Now and then, he whispered assurances to her. In a crooning voice, he told her things about werewolves that slid in and out of her mind and finally lulled her to sleep.

Riley slept soundly. There were no dreams because she was already living them. When she awoke fully, the sun was up and she found herself alone on a single bed in a light-filled room with a decidedly masculine touch. Blue-painted walls. Narrow blinds on two large windows. Wooden floors. Modern furniture. Her overnight bag sat on a seat by the window. There was no sign of Derek.

She sat up.

Though she was still dressed in her coat, Riley remembered kicking off her shoes before Derek had scooped her into his arms. The bedspread beneath her was rumpled. She was covered in a blanket.

Her body still ached, and it was easy for her to guess why. Their session the other night on Derek's mattress had been wildly fulfilling. Since she hadn't slept with anyone else for over a year, physical stamina had been lost in the interim. Derek was a good lover. The best.

Getting out of bed took effort. Beyond the bedroom door was the great unknown. Derek might be there. Dale, the Were she had met last night, might be there as well, along with any number of Derek's packmates. The thought of facing them made her anxious.

What she needed to bolster her courage was a shower and a toothbrush. Riley padded to the bathroom connected to the bedroom by a door. It would be her private sanctuary for a few minutes. She'd emerge more presentable in both body and spirit.

The water in the shower was hot. She stood beneath the spray, waiting to regain her composure and the ability to think ahead, and struggled to remember the things Derek had said as she lay curled up in his arms.

Werewolves have existed since the beginning of time, he had told her. *No one knows how wolf and human DNA got mixed, or if werewolves appeared as their own species from the start.*

There are good Weres and bad ones, as with any other species, including the human race. Weres learned to police our own kind early on so that our secrets could be kept, and to prevent the spread of what some called a werewolf virus.

She remembered something else. Derek had mentioned that a bite or a deep scratch from a werewolf's tooth or claw could transmit enough wolf blood to a human to make the human into a werewolf. He'd said that this kind of activity also had to be closely monitored, since wolf gangs had increased in size in some cities by creating their own underground armies.

Riley braced herself against the shower wall, despising the thought of criminal werewolf gangs roaming city streets along with vampires and who knew what else.

She was forced now to openly think about what might have happened to her mother in a past that was never forgotten.

The shower was steamy and felt good enough for her to want to stay in it all day. But that would have meant she was hiding, and if her father had been around, he would have scolded her for that. Her dad knew a lot about life, but as she had recently found out, he had also missed a few important details.

Still, he would have said that the Prices were tough, and no one in the family had ever let weakness get in the way of setting things straight. Her father was usually a good example of that credo.

When the door opened, Riley turned her head.

"We've rustled up some clothes for you."

Derek's voice made her heart race, the way it did each time she heard it. But she didn't ask him to join her.

When he said, "Can I come in?" Riley held her breath. But it turned out he only entered the bathroom far enough to leave the clothes and a pile of fresh towels on the sink.

"I have to go, Riley. Dale will take you home. I'll come for you again before sundown."

She didn't reply. Any response she might have had

to Derek's announcement would have gotten stuck in her throat.

Hearing the door close again, Riley peered out from behind the shower curtain. Part of her was thankful Derek had gone. Other parts weren't so keen on the idea.

Dale handed her a cup of coffee when she arrived in the kitchen with wet hair, dressed in borrowed jeans and somebody else's gray sweatshirt. The only shoes she had to top off the outfit were her high heels, so this morning she didn't exactly exemplify the term *chic*.

"Breakfast?" Dale asked. In the manner of a paid television ad, he said, "You know it's the way to start your day."

"Thanks. Just coffee for me."

Today, Riley could afford to smile. She sipped the aromatic coffee gratefully, ignoring the soft rumble of hunger in her stomach. With this Were watching her every move, she was too nervous to eat.

As Dale moved around the kitchen, Riley revisited the question of whether or not all of Derek's friends might be equally as large and handsome. And why weren't there female here? She wanted to know everything about this breed. Had to. What would female Weres look like, anyway?

With the issues nagging in the back of her mind, it wasn't long before she lost the smile and set down the cup.

"I'll pull the car around," Dale said. "Take your time and come out when you're ready. There's a whole pot of coffee on the counter."

After nodding to her, he left the room. Riley leaned against the counter, more than ready to go home. It was Sunday. She needed to think things over and begin to regroup. She toyed with the idea of calling her father, and dismissed it. It would give away her current state of mind. If he got worried, he would hop a plane to Seattle and discover something that wouldn't jibe with his reality. He might stay. Her father's presence might keep Derek away.

Riley retrieved her overnight bag and brought the coffee cup with her onto the porch. A tan, standard-issue unmarked police sedan was parked at the curb this morning and Dale stood beside it in a lazy, relaxed stance. As Riley went to meet him, she decided that werewolves had to be at the top of the food chain, and therefore didn't have to fear much of anything.

Dale opened the car door for her, and closed it after she got in. He climbed into the driver's seat and started the engine before speaking to her again.

"Can you be ready for pickup before sunset, Dr. Price?"

"My name is Riley. And yes, I'll be ready. What will you and Derek do today?"

"Snoop around. Sniff things out. Make some calls. Finish up paperwork. It's easier to find vampire hidey-holes in the daylight, when they're sleeping."

"And when you do find some?" Riley asked.

"We take care of them one by one, unless there are too many in one place. Then we have to burn them out."

Riley kept her focus on her coffee cup so that the Were sitting next to her wouldn't see the disgust she felt over picturing the things he had said. If that's what it took to keep Seattle safe, and Weres could do things like that, she would have to rethink how she might be able to help. The wooden stake Derek had placed in her hand last night had felt foreign, and yet what other kinds of defense did she have against a fanged enemy that was supernaturally strong and dangerous…and coming after her?

Derek had searched four city alleys by the time Dale showed up. He looked to his friend for word about Riley.

"Home, and fine," Dale said. "I have to admit she's tougher than I would have imagined. Are you sure there's none of our species in her background somewhere?"

"I'm not sure of anything, other than how exceptionally well she is taking all of this."

"Any new theories we haven't explored as to why the vamps are interested in her?" Dale asked as he scanned the back of the alley.

"None at the moment. I can't piece this together yet. On the surface, Riley is simply a newly credentialed psychologist."

"Maybe our vamp queen is in need of a shrink," Dale suggested.

Derek knew his partner was joking but wasn't ready to ignore the idea altogether. His mind raced, trying out other ideas, and finally landing on one.

What if the vamps that had approached Riley hadn't come to kill her, and instead had been sent to fetch her?

After two visitations from Damaris's bloodsucking minions, Riley hadn't been hurt, when it had only taken three seconds for one of them to take a bite out of Marshall under everyone's noses.

Dale said, "I know that look on your face, so you might as well cough up what you're thinking."

"Riley is alive," Derek said.

Dale was quick to follow where he was going with this. "And that's unusual for a target."

Derek nodded. "Even with Weres guarding her."

"So they will wait until she isn't guarded, which will never happen again after sundown. And they can't move around during the day, so...?"

"So," Derek said thoughtfully, "either they're completely clueless, and will try again to reach Riley when the sun goes down, or else they will have to adapt to a new time schedule and find her in full daylight."

"That's impossible," Dale remarked.

"Yes," Derek agreed. "Impossible."

But he wasn't going to rule anything out. He was already heading back to his car parked on the main street so he could get to Riley...just in case any of those theories weren't as absurd as they sounded, and losing sight of Riley in the daytime wasn't a good idea.

Chapter 24

Riley stood frozen on her front step for so long, she felt like she'd become one of the pillars holding up the roof. The sun was up this morning, so no vampires would be hiding in her house. No one else would be waiting inside, either, and yet she couldn't make herself use the key.

Cars drove past. Down the block, kids were playing in the street. Everything seemed like a typical Sunday morning, except for the fact that things weren't normal. She had slept with a werewolf in his human disguise. She'd seen bite marks on Marshall's neck. For real. She was absurdly okay with knowing about all of those things because she had to be. What other option was there for processing the truth?

After a little reminder to herself about bravery being a virtue, Riley went inside the house that would never feel the same. Vampires had tainted both her home and her office, and they knew exactly where to find her, so she was screwed.

She changed out of the borrowed outfit and folding everything, then packed more clothes for when Derek came to take her back to the wolves. She placed her bag in the entryway, unable to remember where she had left her car. And, anyway, it didn't really matter, since she didn't feel up to a drive and wasn't able to focus properly. The damn vehicle could have been sitting right in the driveway and she wouldn't have noticed.

Her cell phone, resting on the kitchen table, was dead. She plugged it in to recharge before heading outside again. Walking downtown would burn off excess energy that had nowhere to go. On foot, it wouldn't take her much more than half an hour to get there.

With a backward glance at the house, Riley set out, happier than usual to feel the sun on her face when her insides were so damn icy.

Dale hopped in to ride shotgun as Derek cranked the engine of the black SUV. "We need more information," he said. "Riley can't be our prisoner forever."

"She's not a prisoner," Derek reminded him.

"She's going to think so if she's under surveillance twenty-four-seven."

"Yes," Derek agreed. "She will."

"And we don't actually believe that vamps can walk around in the daylight, do we?"

"I don't see how they could."

"Then you can probably rest easy, Derek, and it might be a good idea to give her some space."

It sounded simple when someone else said the words Derek had been thinking ever since he'd left Riley earlier that morning. However, he couldn't give her space after the imprinting phase had been sealed on his bed the other night. In the initial stages, Weres were faced with unrelenting desire, like being on a honeymoon, times ten.

He glanced at Dale, and found his friend grinning.

"Making the connection wasn't wise, boss," Dale said. "But I guess it is what it is. Right?"

Derek blew out a breath, expecting Dale to say "I told you so." When that didn't come, Derek echoed, "For whatever reason, it is what it is."

"Does Riley know what's happened, as far as you two are concerned?" Dale asked.

"No way she could, if she's not one of us."

"Are you going to tell her?"

"Yes. Today," Derek said. "Though I'm afraid that kind of information might push her over the edge. How many days has it been since we helped her out?"

"Try three, including today," Dale replied, though the question had been rhetorical. Dale dropped the grin and added, "Good luck with that. I'll get out of your way if you'll pull over."

"Check her office for me, will you?" Derek said.

"On my way."

Dale got out at the next stoplight. Derek drove on, considering how a Were could explain the bonding process to someone who didn't understand the first thing about Weres. He hoped the right words would come.

And if you want out, Riley Price?

What then?

Hell, if she wanted out of what had only just begun, he was going to need a shaman to remove the chains binding him to her.

As he was leaving the main downtown district, Derek saw Riley on a street corner, and he took the next right turn to circle back. She had paused when she recognized the SUV and was still there when he pulled around the corner.

Parking was easy Sunday mornings, and Derek found a spot not far from her. As he got out of the car, he was able to feel the buzz of Riley's interest from eight feet away. The earthy vibration increased as the distance closed to three feet. Two feet. Then one. After that, it was all over, and her body was up against his as if they were magnetic, and the only two people around.

"It's not time yet for you to get me," she said breathlessly.

"I couldn't wait for sundown. How's that for a confession?"

"I was feeling lost," she said. "I want to go to my office, and I'm afraid of what I might find."

"I'll take you there. It'll be okay. The window was fixed late last night and the guard is back at his station."

"How do you know that?"

"It's my job to check on things."

She nodded. "Okay. I have files to go over for tomorrow's appointments."

"Do you feel up to going back to work?"

"It will keep me sane when everything else is—"

"Crazy?" Derek said, finishing for her. "Unbelievable?"

She nodded again.

Neither of them moved toward her office building.

"You're going to tell me why I feel this way, right? About why it feels like I've known you in another lifetime?" Riley asked.

"I can do that," Derek said.

"Does it have to do with you being a Were?"

"Yes, though maybe not entirely."

Words like *fate* and *serendipity* ran through Derek's mind, though he again rejected those possibilities as the basis for his feelings for Riley. This was something else. What?

"Do you possess some kind of magic that attracts females?" she asked as a woman passing by eyed him in the same way others had in front of the restaurant the night before.

"Were males have potent pheromones that some females might pick up on. Were females have it, too, as well as some human women."

"Do I have it?"

"Lots of it," he said.

"Are you making me feel this way about you?" she asked.

"What way would that be?"

"Like I want to…" She lowered her gaze without completing her sentence, and then started over. "I have to know everything about what I've gotten myself into. That's only fair."

"Your office, then," Derek said.

They still didn't move or try to separate. With Riley's body against his, Derek was feeling a level of arousal that was new to him. Riley felt so small and delicate when compared to his larger, more muscular bulk. He liked that, even though there was nothing small or delicate about her. Intelligent women were sexy, and Riley was smarter than most, which helped to make her so very appealing and damnably hard to resist.

"I don't want to be a vampire's plaything," she said.

"You won't be."

Riley looked at him even more soberly. "I don't want to be afraid each time darkness falls."

"We just have to find out what's going on," Derek repeated. "We can do that with a little more time, and then things will be all right."

Though he didn't want to lose the closeness of their bodies touching, Derek slid his hands down her arms and backed up slightly. When he took her hands in his, her fingers relaxed.

The way her lips parted and moved let him understand that Riley wanted to speak, and couldn't. That mouth alone could have driven him mad with desire if they had been in a safer, less conspicuous spot.

Riley wasn't so very pale today. Her skin was an iridescent ivory, and free of makeup. Each time she moved her head, he smelled the rosy scent of the shampoo Dale had left for her in the shower.

The collar of her purple sweater showed off enough bare neck to make his inner wolf restless, and didn't completely hide the marks he had put there while in a fit of passion. In the olden days, those marks would have branded Riley as his mate, proven she was his, and announced to the world that Riley Price wasn't to be touched by anyone else, ever again.

If she had been a Were, they wouldn't be standing here now. They wouldn't be talking, they'd be doing. But Riley wasn't like him, and he couldn't ask her to become like him, even when that path might be open to them in the future. If seeing that werewolves and vampires existed was frightening for her, he couldn't imagine asking Riley to join his species.

She was eyeing him back as if she was trying to follow his thoughts. He refocused on the present problem.

Yes, he had to tell her the things she needed to know. She would then decide what to do. He would let her make that choice and abide by whatever decision she made.

But he would stay by her side until the mystery of all this vampire activity was solved, no matter what the outcome was.

Derek led her from the corner with a protective arm around her shoulders, not caring if Seattle's vampire queen had spies. He was off-duty, and was going to make the most of his time with Riley.

"Feel free to ask whatever you'd like," he said as they walked. "You're right, and fair is fair."

Keeping his hands and his mouth off Riley until they reached her office, and after they got there, was going to be a momentous task. Right now he was going to have to prepare reasonable answers to whatever questions she had, and hope she'd be as receptive to the truth as she had been so far.

Chapter 25

There was a new guard at the front desk when they signed in. When they got in the elevator, Riley found that being cooped up with Derek in the tight space was tough. It was hard to breathe properly when he was around. Although Riley couldn't smell the wolf pheromones Derek had mentioned, her body gravitated to him on both conscious and unconscious levels. Unwilling to give in at the moment, she leaned against the wall opposite from where he stood.

She felt relieved when the door opened onto the third-floor hallway and he let her go past him without pulling her back. She walked quickly to her office and used the key to get in.

Derek had been right. Riley saw no evidence of an intruder having been there. There was no broken glass. Nothing was out of place. The window looked the same, as did the frame. Derek must have had a window company on speed dial.

She circled the desk to create distance between them, reminding herself that she'd need to keep a clear head to ask all of the questions she had. Thankfully, Derek honored that distance as if he understood.

"We can start at the beginning, I guess," she suggested. "You told me a few things last night that sank in. So can we start on the street where I was attacked, and go from there?"

Derek didn't sit down on the chair or the couch. He, too, was restless His energy careened off the walls.

"Why me?" she began. "Why were you interested in me after we'd met out there?"

"I don't really know," he replied. "Does there have to be a reason for one person being attracted to another?"

"There does when things happen this fast."

"I wanted to know you after just one glance. Then you mentioned werewolves before knowing anything about their real existence, and later admitted to liking them."

Not liking, exactly... Riley thought. *More like being interested.*

"And you found that promising?" she asked. "After a first glance?"

"I found it curious. I looked into your eyes, saw the fear and the defiance in them, and liked what I saw."

She couldn't argue with that, since it was a reasonable assessment.

"Next question?" he said.

"Can I go with you tonight if you go hunting?"

That surprised him. He obviously had anticipated her asking him something more personal about werewolves.

"It would be too dangerous, Riley."

"I don't care. Maybe I'd get the opportunity to ask one of them what I have to do with any of this. Cut to the chase. Get things in the open."

"I don't want anything to happen to you. They aren't what you think. Trust me, in numbers, they're far worse than anything you've experienced so far."

Riley rounded the desk without thinking about it, eager to press the issue. Before she could speak again, Derek did. "Most of them are minions. Mindless monsters ruled by thirst. Half of them can't remember how to speak, or why they're here.

"Other vampires are ancient and way too smart. They gather in nests and are truly dangerous. And all vampires breed like rabbits, only not in any natural way."

"By sinking their fangs into innocent necks," Riley said.

Derek nodded. "Unlike with a bite or scratch from a rogue werewolf, vampires pass death on to their victims most of the time. They feed until the hearts of their victims stop beating, draining their victims dry, then accidentally or on purpose give a small amount of their own black blood back into the open wounds."

It made Riley sick to think of it, but she also felt a ray of hope. "Then Marshall will be okay. He didn't die, and he didn't run off to do their bidding."

"It's likely he will be all right," he agreed.

"If being around them is so dangerous, how do you plan on finding the answers we need?" Riley asked. "I can't remain in the dark as to why they're chasing me, and what they want."

She moved closer to Derek. "I don't relish the thought of hiding forever. Do you?"

He was studying her again, probably looking for cracks in her armor. Riley didn't give him any reason to find them.

"There's a long history here that doesn't involve you in any way," he said. "A vampire Prime, which is the equivalent of a Were alpha, has only so much control over its family when vamp numbers get out of hand. But Seattle doesn't just have a Prime in residence, it has a female that has set herself up as queen bee."

"A woman?" Riley was surprised how much that news bothered her.

"She's no woman, Riley, and hasn't been for centuries."

"You've seen her?"

"I have. I helped someone chase her underground once, where she refuses to stay."

Specially attuned to emotion because of her profession, Riley perceived how Derek was blocking his. She said, "There's no way to get rid of this vampire queen?" and sensed how disturbed Derek was over how he was going to answer.

"I don't see how that could be managed," he admitted. "The most we've been able to do is to try to keep her pool of bloodsuckers from increasing in number exponentially. Most of the time that seems like an uphill battle."

So, she had the truth now, and it was disconcerting.

"Is the Prime angry with you for staking her vampires?" Riley asked. "Could that be why she might want to harm me? For getting close to you? For revenge? An eye-for-an-eye type of payback?"

Derek walked to the window and turned his back to her, which made Riley sure he was hiding something.

"The truth," she said. "Remember?"

He turned to her slowly and spoke as though he was divulging a secret. "I believe there might be a chance that Damaris doesn't want to harm you at all."

"It doesn't look that way to me. What else could she—Damaris, is it?—get out of scaring the life out of me over and over?"

Damn it, even the vampire queen's name was frightening. Riley replayed it a few times in her mind.

Derek raised his hands in surrender. "It's a theory I'm exploring. I don't know what else to think at the moment."

Riley's voice was steadier than she thought it would be. "All the more reason for us to find out what the truth is. Tonight, where you go, I go. The only way to stop me, Detective, will be to chain me to a post."

That won her a smile, sad as it might have been.

"I can find a post," he said. "And a chain."

"Over my dead body."

"That is exactly what I'm attempting to avoid, Riley."

She couldn't have stayed away from him for much longer no matter what he said. It wasn't even noon, but her body was already shaking with the thought of tonight, and what she was willing to do to put an end to the craziness.

Did Derek get that?

Derek stayed very still. Their frank discussion, the airing out of all the fear in the room, served to accelerate the onset of something that closely resembled trust. But he had to be careful.

Riley came toward him as if he had called her name, and he stepped forward to meet her. If he wanted to be fair, he'd have to suppress the urge to take her in his arms, when he wanted that so badly. A kiss would hold him over. One kiss that might distract them both long enough to keep Riley from going out to meet the vampires.

"Don't," she said as if she understood what he had in mind. "That would be too easy."

A sound at the door broke the next little moment of silence. Derek knew who was knocking. He had set the plan in place with Dale, hoping to avoid a moment like this one, and Dale had almost been too late.

Without waiting for an invitation, Dale entered the office, stopped when he saw them and was silent for once until Derek eventually glanced in his direction.

"I've got news," Dale said. "And I'm not sure if either of you is going to like it."

Riley backed up and turned to face Dale. Derek did the same.

"News for me, or for Riley?" Derek asked.

"Both, actually."

"Shoot."

"Dr. Price might want to sit down first," Dale suggested.

"It's Riley, remember?" she corrected. "And I'd prefer to stand."

Dale nodded to her and then looked at Derek. "I've been checking records. Did you know Riley's dad is a cop?"

"Yes," Derek said. "That makes sense, doesn't it? I now see where she gets her courage and fortitude. Growing up with a cop in the house isn't always easy."

"There's more," Dale said soberly.

"Go on."

"This news is about Riley's mother," Dale warned.

Derek glanced at Riley again. Her serious expression was still in place, though she might have paled slightly. He wondered what kind of news Dale possessed that might have made her lose color.

Before Dale could continue, Riley spoke up. "My mother was sent away when I was young. She was institutionalized for a while, and then she died."

She looked at Dale. "Is that what you're referring to? You've done a background check because of the incidents I've been involved with?"

Derek looked to his friend, then back at Riley. "We have a database for law enforcement. Chances were that your father's name would come up when we ran it. But I don't need to know anything about your personal issues unless you're willing to confide the details—"

Dale interrupted. "I think there are a couple of things that should be brought up in light of how you two are behaving and what else is going on."

Derek waited for Riley to address that statement. Reconsidering her refusal to sit down, she folded herself into the chair and reluctantly nodded for Dale to go on.

"It seems that Riley's mother was sent away because she thought she was a…"

"Werewolf," Riley said. "My mother believed she was one of you."

Chapter 26

Silence followed her statement. Inside that moment of quiet, Riley's ears rang with an echo of the confidence she had shared.

You might think Derek's question about her *thing* for werewolves had just been answered, at least in part, though Riley didn't see any sudden enlightenment reflected in Derek's expression. However, it didn't take a trained psychologist to figure out that she again had succeeded in surprising the alpha.

"What?" he said, as if he hadn't heard properly.

He was staring at her. Everyone was wondering what she'd say next, including Riley.

"People tend to hide things like that," she explained. "Those of us who were left after she was taken away never talked openly about it. Young people wouldn't go around chatting about being the daughter of a madwoman, would they?"

She waved a hand at Dale. "Now look. Both of you are living proof that my mother might not have made it up."

Riley let her hand fall. "Imagine my surprise when I found that out. Then again, my mother never proved she was like you, so I suppose no one would have really ever known the truth."

She stopped Derek from taking a step by shaking her head. "You can't possibly understand how glad I am to have discovered this weekend, and after all that time, that my mother might not have been so crazy after all. I've spent most of my life hoping I wouldn't turn out like her."

She watched Derek stiffen as the full extent of what she'd said began to dawn on him. But his expression gave away nothing as to what he might have been thinking.

He took some time before speaking again in a soft, uncertain tone, as if he still didn't believe what she was telling him. "You do realize that if she wasn't lying, and your mother was a Were, she had to have passed along that Were blood to you?"

From the sidelines, Dale muttered, "And that, my friends, explains a lot."

Riley had grown tired of the racing-heart routine long before this and ignored the pounding in her chest and the throb in her neck, not willing to give in to the chaos going on inside her.

"Until now, I was more concerned about the madness part being hereditary," she said.

"Riley…"

"I'm nothing like you," she said to Derek. "So there's all the more reason to doubt what you've just proposed."

Derek was sure to see the fear on her face. Riley recalled how he had been trying to find a hint of something he couldn't quite see ever since their first meeting. Had he been searching for a reason for their instant connection, as she had?

Did that connection have anything to do with her mother's beliefs and the possible concoction in her own bloodstream that he might have detected without actually recognizing it? The concoction she hadn't known existed? The one no one had believed existed?

No...

That line of reasoning was absurd and didn't warrant any more time spent on it, because that would mean her mother had been telling the truth, and might have been locked away unjustly by those who either didn't know about the existence of werewolves, or did know, and had to keep that secret locked away.

"Absurd," she muttered, thinking back, desperate to see what they all might have missed. "My mother was nothing like you, either."

Yet if it had been true, a heinous crime had been committed and Riley might have saved herself years of studying in order to deal with her mother's condition.

Riley didn't like the room's new atmosphere that made breathing a chore. She didn't particularly like the quiet, either, or the direction in which her thoughts had turned.

"You can stop looking at me like that. My mother could have made it up. There are plenty of cases like that on file. The syndrome is called Lycanism. She didn't have to be a Were."

With both Weres staring at her, Riley felt compelled to go on.

"I don't howl at the moon," she said.

Okay, that was a lie, Riley had to admit. She always

howled when a full moon rolled around, and she had done so the night all this trouble began.

"I've never sprouted claws, and if I had ever turned furry, I would have committed myself."

She looked to Derek for support, willing him to smile, laugh, or tell her he didn't believe it, either. But he didn't do any of those things.

Her office suddenly felt crowded, and as though a lightning storm was gathering between four walls. It was possible that was always the result when two powerful Weres occupied a small space, and when all that subdued power was concentrated and contained.

"It was likely just a story," Riley said. "My father thought so. They all thought so."

"It was a just story until now," Derek said.

He turned to Dale. "We need to reevaluate events to include the possibility of Riley's latent inheritance."

"I'm not—" Riley began.

Derek cut her off. "Actually, Dale is right. It would explain a lot."

Riley's memory kicked up something then. It was what the vampire had said to her. *If you don't learn about your heritage, it might be too late to help you.*

Heritage.

Learn about her heritage.

Had the vampires recognized she could be part werewolf before anyone else had figured it out? The idea was unsettling and absurd, and still failed to explain why they'd want to bother her.

She got to her feet. "Don't be ridiculous. How could I have missed something like that? With all the work I've done, don't you think I've gone deep into my own psyche? Believe me, Derek, I found no wolf there."

The problem was that a seed of doubt had been planted in her mind, and that seed was going to take over unless someone put a stop to it.

She thought of her father. For him, her mother's commitment had been the source of years of loneliness and pain. He had loved his wife greatly. He didn't remarry after she died, and Riley doubted her father was over all of that even now.

"I'm not…" Riley again protested weakly. "I can't do this. I refuse to go through it all again. You have no idea what…"

She couldn't finish a damn sentence. Nightmares from her past had welled up again. The vampire's remarks continued to ring in her ears.

Derek was beside her. "Close your eyes, Riley."

"There's no sense in trying to hypnotize me, Derek. I have all the tricks down pat."

"Close them, Riley. For a few seconds. No more than that. Please."

She shut them to avoid the flash of new interest in Derek's eyes. With him, she had experienced what hunger was like and also how it drove two beings together. She had also, however, been privy to his moments of tenderness, and the way he had held her in the dark.

If her mother had been like him… If it turned out that her mother had been a werewolf…

God. What was she supposed to make of that?

"Breathe," Derek directed.

She squeezed her eyes tight.

"Open your senses, Riley," he said. "Listen. Smell. Feel. Believe."

She tried to follow his instructions, though she wasn't really sure what he was asking.

"Listen," he whispered to her.

In the distance, Riley heard cars on the street even though the windows were double-paned. She heard the clock on her desk ticking and the faint rustle of Derek's jeans as he came closer. She heard the irregular beat of her pulse, due in part to the fantastical ideas floating around the room.

And she heard Derek's heart beating.

"Smell," he urged. "Take a breath and process it. Break what's in the air into manageable layers."

Derek's voice had a mesmerizing quality that she had noticed before. Her mind willingly went along with his suggestion, but the only thing she could pinpoint was Derek's familiar scent—the overpowering maleness he exuded.

Wait. There was something else in the air. She definitely caught the fragrance of well-worn fabric and a trace of a muskier scent. Was that how werewolves smelled?

Derek's expression had changed when she opened her eyes to give him a challenging stare. Riley saw that he wanted to believe she had wolf blood hidden somewhere—locked away, without a key. But if her body contained hints of wolf, no matter how small or inert, her life as a human being had been fraudulent, and her mother had been unfairly cheated of a normal life. Riley didn't think she could bear the thought of either of those things.

"Was there anything out of the ordinary, having to do with your senses?" Derek asked, his blue eyes riveted to her face.

Riley didn't know how to answer. The situation she found herself in was moving too fast. She couldn't just become what Derek wanted her to be by breathing deeply and listening to her racing heart. And yet she hesitantly said, "That means they killed her for no good reason."

As a shudder passed through her, she met Derek's gaze and added, "Is there a better way to be sure?"

"Yes," Derek said, stifling his excitement. "There is a way to find out the truth."

"Like we don't know already by now?" Dale interjected.

Derek ignored the remark. This new revelation explained a lot, including the immediacy of his interest in Riley. In hindsight, his wolf must have picked up on the wolf in her from the start, though hers had been deeply buried by a psychologist who knew how to bury bad things.

"How do we do that?" Riley asked tentatively, and as though she didn't really want to hear the answer.

"Wolf calls to wolf," he explained. "By your being around Weres, any wolf traits you possess will eventually show up as if drawn to the surface."

"Like cream rising to the top," Dale added.

"No," Riley argued. "Animal attraction is just a figure of speech. What I feel for you, Derek, has nothing to do with the fact that you're a werewolf."

"Doesn't it?" he countered. "Can you be sure?"

He had known Riley felt the same way he did about this budding relationship, but was glad to hear her confirmation of those feelings. Proving she was a Were would be even better, and would solve issues they would have had to confront in the future. It also would help to eventually keep the vampires away from her.

"I didn't find out about your secret until you told me,"

she reasoned. "There was no big wolf reveal. I didn't get any sense of you being anything other than human."

"Maybe," he conceded. "And maybe some part of you related to what I am."

From behind him, Dale chimed in with a reminder of the bigger picture. "That might explain your attraction to each other. What it doesn't do is tell us why vampires are so interested."

Riley was at the window now, with her back to the room. The way she held herself, the straightness of her spine, told Derek its own kind of story. He had touched that spine with his fingertips and had explored each delicate bone and curve. But she was so rigid now. Her fear had grown to momentous proportions.

Memories of her mother had to have haunted her, and rightly so. The little girl who had braved her mother's traumatic incarceration was back now in full force because he had pushed her memory there.

Did Riley think she would suffer a similar fate as her mother if it turned out that she was a werewolf? Was she grieving all over again for her mother's plight and imagining what her mother must have gone through?

Caging a werewolf was tantamount to torture. His skin crawled with the thought of Riley's mother's ordeal.

When Dale plucked the next question from Derek's mind, Derek realized he must have beamed the thought over Were channels.

"Even if the vamp queen had figured out about Riley's latent talents before we did, Weres aren't exactly good dinner fare," Dale said. "We aren't scarce around here, either. So why would the vamp Prime seek out someone who is half wolf, at best, and who, up until now, didn't even realize it?"

Riley turned slowly. After tossing her hair over her shoulder, she eyed Dale almost fiercely. "Why don't we ask her?"

The question might have made sense in some other universe. In this one, it was absurdly unrealistic.

"No. Absolutely not," Derek said. "Damaris is unreachable. Treacherous."

"So I'm to run and hide forever, or until the vampire queen catches up with me? I'm to make even worse the danger you and your pack already face in this city after dark by hiding? How is that fair to me or to your friends? How does that get us closer to an answer for this riddle?"

"We'll deal," he said.

"The question here is how to deal with *her*. With this queen of the vampires."

He could have told Riley about the last time he'd met Damaris, but that would have been cruel. *I could tell you how I felt about losing a woman I once loved because we were different species. How Damaris had abducted that woman and then had nearly taken her life away, drop by drop, in a dank, dark and unimaginable place. But what good would that do? How would it help us, Riley?*

"I'll go with you tonight," she said. "Tell me more of what I can expect to face."

The sound of Derek's cell phone buzzing added an unspoken punctuation mark to Riley's demand. He read the message on the screen and then glanced to Dale.

"Go on. Take the call. I'll get her some food and stick around," Dale said.

"I'm not hungry, and I don't need a keeper," Riley argued.

"Maybe you're not hungry," Derek said, "but you'll need all the energy you can muster for tonight, no matter what you decide to do. They're not all so easy to take down, you know. It isn't all about wooden stakes, young, inexperienced vampires and closed alleys."

Riley's eyes widened. Her body grew stiffer.

"You shouldn't be alone right now," he advised. "Please don't think you can fix this or face what's out there on your own. I don't want to lose you, too, before…"

Derek let the rest of what he wanted to say lie there a minute. "We'll meet up later. Okay?"

Riley placed a steadying hand on the windowsill. The energy she radiated was wild and scrambled. She had a stronger scent when fear gripped her. There was no way to convince her of the level of danger these vampires presented, or make her begin to comprehend how powerful their queen was. No one could possibly have conceived of those things unless they had encountered them in person.

Yet he had no claim on Riley Price and couldn't prevent her from facing the future, whatever that future might bring. Her life was her life. She was missing some important details about what she was and how strong the enemy they faced was, but in her place, he would have wanted to confront his problems, too.

He willed Riley to meet his gaze. "This is a lot for you to take in at once. Promise me you'll let me have the lead and that you'll trust me to handle things in the best way I can."

"Okay," she replied after a short pause.

But hell…

That *okay* didn't satisfy him much.

Chapter 27

Darkness fell over Seattle faster than Riley had anticipated. From her place by the office window, where she
had stayed for some time, she watched Derek head back
into the building, marveling at how normal he looked
when her nerves were lit up like bonfires.

Dale had brought her food from a nearby restaurant,
but she hadn't been able to eat.

She regretted insisting that she go with Derek after
nightfall. For him, hunting for vampires was a normal
pursuit. For her, just waking, breathing and thinking
had taken on the aura of a bad dream. But running away
didn't really suit her, so she had to step up.

Derek didn't knock when he arrived at the office door.
She wasn't to be left alone, so Derek, Dale and Jared
were tag-teaming on the watch schedule. That should
have made her feel safe. Instead, Riley again felt cooped
up, restless and in need of fresh air.

She had to figure things out and believe that Derek knew what he was talking about with regard to her welfare, when it was difficult for her to turn her life over to anyone. She loved her father, but had come to Seattle to live her own life and be on her own.

Derek came into the room like warm wind. The first sight of Derek was always the same—thunder inside her chest, a pulse-pounding rise in blood pressure—as though in half a day she could have forgotten how gorgeous and commanding he was in person.

Was this their inner wolves talking?

Steps past the doorway, he paused to wait for her to acknowledge him before he spoke. "You'll need to lose the loose clothes and anything else a vampire might latch on to if you still insist on accompanying us."

"I have a running shirt in my bag," Riley said.

"Hair?"

"I'll pin it up."

"The pack is out in force. Without a full moon overhead, we're strong, but not anywhere near as scary as when wolfed up. Tonight, there's safety in numbers."

"Won't anyone notice extra muscle on the streets?" Riley asked.

"Four will be in uniform on foot patrol, and two more in cruisers. Five of my friends will be out there in plainclothes. Jared and Dale will shadow us closely."

Riley hid her shaky hands by stuffing them into the pockets of her jeans. "Will she show up?"

"Damaris rarely shows herself. When she does, the situation rapidly goes from bad to worse. We'd prefer not to have that happen."

"Then who will we be looking for?"

"Any of the old ones she sends to get a bead on things, and on you," Derek replied.

"Will they tell us what she wants?"

"Not voluntarily."

"I'm scared," Riley confessed.

"We don't have to go out there. You don't have to go."

"You're wrong about that if it's me they're after," she argued. "I'd like to remain free, and not have to move from place to place, constantly looking over my shoulder."

Derek leaned against the wall. "I'll wait for you to change the shirt," he said.

"And then?"

"Then we'll take a little stroll to the bad part of town and see what comes our way."

Her office had a small bathroom. Riley took her overnight bag there. Without bothering to close the door, she tore off her sweatshirt and slipped on the snug long-sleeved dark navy blue shirt she often ran in on cold days. She wound her hair into a knot and secured it with a rubber band.

The woman who stared back at her in the mirror didn't resemble her much. The face was too thin, too pale. Dark circles under her eyes looked like crescent moons. The top edge of the circle of bruises on her neck showed above the shirt's mock turtleneck.

If she was a Were, as Derek and Dale had suggested, wouldn't she know it? Wouldn't she also possess the powers of miraculous healing that went along with the werewolf mythology?

She could see Derek in the mirror as well. He hadn't moved from his post by the door. It was a testament to the one strength she had developed over time—her willpower—that she didn't call the whole thing off. If anything, her mother deserved this the most.

Derek's concern for her was mutual. Half of her— was it the half he said could be like him?—wanted to settle for another hour or two in bed, in lieu of hunting vampires. She would have chosen to close her eyes and wish this all away, if that had been an option.

What does that make me, Derek?

Does it prove that I'm as crazy as my mother for believing you?

"I can read you at times, you know," Derek said when she emerged. "Your thoughts are like wind in my ears. I get the emotion behind them, if not the wording."

"I do a similar thing with my clients. Read their emotions."

Silence made the next few seconds seem longer as Riley wondered if that was a sign of possessing a Were trait.

"Ready?" he asked.

"No."

His reply was patient and understanding. "I can wait."

"No," Riley said again. "It's time to face the music. Isn't that how the old saying goes?"

She walked past him and out the door, able to feel him right behind her. She was glad he was so close, but worried he would turn out to be right, and that she wasn't one-hundred-percent human after all.

But really…in spite of everything she knew about herself, she did want to run.

Derek signed out at the desk. When they exited the building, Riley matched his long strides. He stopped on the sidewalk to give Riley time to catch her breath. The shirt she wore was tight enough for him to see each rise and fall of her chest.

He hoped for a quiet night, just this once, and for the bloodsuckers to stay off his radar. He was off duty, as far as the department was concerned, and still there was plenty to do.

As they stood on the sidewalk assessing the situation and deciding which direction to go, a light rain started to fall. Derek's only thought right that minute was that Riley would be cold.

And then another thought struck.

Due to the fact that all he could think about was the female standing next to him, he wondered if Riley had somehow been sent to him as a distraction. A way to sideline him and temporarily dull his senses where vampires were concerned.

Nope. They had already covered that scenario, so his mind continued to whirl. Planting a distraction to way-lay vampire hunters would have meant that vampires could plan strategically. Not many of them had that ability. But there was one that did. *Guess who?*

Taking this one step further was part of his job. He couldn't quite let go of the idea.

"Hell," Derek muttered, because if there was a plan like that, Damaris would have set him up. The black-hearted diva would have had a hand in placing Riley directly in his path for exactly that purpose. Distraction.

Derek's fingers ached the way they did when his claws were about to spring. His shoulders bunched from the tension gripping them. The wolf inside wanted to run back to that alley where he had last seen Damaris and bite, scratch and claw his way to the truth. Even if it took more strength than he had to deal with her. Even if it required the attention of a creature as old as she was, and equally as strong.

"What's wrong?" Riley asked, worried and as tense as he was.

"Mental jumble." It was the excuse he used to keep those ideas from reaching Riley. "Let's head toward the restaurant."

She fell in with him when he started out. Now that such an idea had solidified in his mind, though, it was starting to eat him up. Chief among his questions was what Damaris might want to get out of distracting him when her monsters were already multiplying faster than he could keep up, and he was barely making a dent in their population?

A Prime couldn't possibly keep track of her nest when there were so many vampires in it, so what difference would one more wolf in Seattle make? A half wolf, at that?

Riley stopped walking, which made him stop.

"Something's not right," she announced.

"The whole thing stinks," Derek agreed.

"You took me to find them last night and weren't worried about it then," she pointed out. "You put the stake in my hand."

"Would you have used it?" he asked, attuned enough to their surroundings to sense that Riley was onto something, and that trouble was heading their way.

"Would you be able to take down a vampire if one appeared right here?" he asked her. "If it was going to be you, or them?"

"Yes," she said, though Derek heard the uncertainty in her voice.

"They are already dead," he reminded her. "They don't breathe. They're not the people they were before they died. Some crawled up from the grave. Some of them were bitten and drained dry on streets not unlike this one and didn't know what hit them. They are animated corpses bent on destruction. Ghouls. Ghosts. Parasites feeding off the life force of the living."

Riley's beautiful face couldn't have been whiter. She was shivering in the damn shirt, mostly because she was afraid, not because she wasn't wearing a coat.

"You're trying to prepare me for the fact that one of them is coming," she said.

Derek turned around when he heard footsteps. Since vampires didn't make any sounds when they traveled, he expected to see people strolling down the boulevard.

It was a couple. A woman and a man were walking arm in arm, talking among themselves and enjoying a Sunday night. But Derek wasn't relieved by the sight. His pulse had revved. His inner wolf whined and struggled to get out, as if it would make an appearance whether or not there was a full moon to lure it into existence.

He didn't—couldn't—let out the wolf in front of Riley.

In what felt like slow motion, a shadow spread across the sidewalk half a block down from where he and Riley stood. That's all the warning those two humans would have gotten, had they known about the monsters in their midst. But they didn't know. No one had warned them.

One second the young couple was visible, and the next second they were gone…and Derek was running toward the spot where they had last been seen with Riley's hand in his.

Chapter 28

Riley didn't have time to swear. She had seen the couple vanish and realized what it meant, as well as who had to have orchestrated their abduction. Derek wasn't merely going to show her a vampire this time, he was going to try to save that couple from becoming like them.

They ran down the block, located a small space between buildings that she hadn't noticed before and went through in single file with Derek in the lead. His tension, transferred to her through his hand, made her nerves spark with the fight-or-flight instinct that had first started with cavemen. She and Derek weren't fleeing the monsters in this case. They were going to fight them.

She followed Derek into an area she never would have guessed existed. Leaving the modern brick building facades behind, they stumbled across pieces of a much older foundation. Beyond the low concrete barriers stood one remaining wall of an ancient two-story building that had long since fallen to ruin.

Part of one wall leaned against the side of the building behind it, with enough space between the two for a nice, dark hidey-hole.

Her stomach churned at the sight of that hole.

The alley carried an odor of death. Piles of small bones littered the ground like bleached ivory confetti. Dead dogs and cats maybe, Riley thought. Dead mice, rats and God only knew what other kind of vermin had been caught here. The foulness of the odor was so strong she covered her nose to keep from choking.

Her mind told her to stop the madness and to get out of there as quickly as possible, but Derek's grip on her hand and her own sense of mystery wouldn't have allowed that. And besides, there was no way she'd abandon Derek in a place that reeked of danger, no matter how strong and experienced he was in situations like this one, or how useless she might turn out to be.

Beyond his desire to help the people of Seattle, Derek was also doing this for her.

There was a shoe among the detritus on the ground. A light blue high-heel shoe. Only one of them, and out of place in the filth. The sight of that discarded shoe threatened to make Riley throw up.

Where was its owner? Were Riley and Derek in time to help those poor people? Could they actually help? The space appeared to be deserted. She saw no one at all.

Derek flew to the opening and she stumbled after him, now seeing the need for all the hours Derek and his pack put in hunting down evil in this city.

There was a war going on in Seattle, a secret war that pitted a few good werewolves against hordes of vampires. Werewolves were the good guys here, so how did that happen? What kind of evolution had taken place to produce justice-minded males like Derek and his friends, who looked like everyone else most of the time and fought to protect humans?

"Here," Derek said, letting go of her hand. "Wait."

"No way. I'm not staying here alone," Riley argued. "I'd rather face a pair of fangs than watch you disappear."

It was too damn dark inside the opening in the wall. On closer inspection, the hole was actually the entrance to a long corridor that was unforgivingly dark, where the severity of the foul odors increased by a factor of ten.

Riley wished she had that damn stake now. If anything jumped out at her, she was going to scream.

She moved along by trailing one hand along the interior wall, thankful it wasn't slimy. The brief flashes of moonlight from behind the rain clouds outside were gone. The floor in the corridor was dry, and she didn't dare think about the small mushy things that now and then tripped her up.

Derek was silent. Could he hear how loudly and frantically her heart was beating? It boomed in her ears like cannons going off.

When Derek suddenly stopped, she ran into him and let out a surprised squeak.

"Listen," he whispered to her.

She thought she heard a woman moaning.

Derek's arm around her waist kept Riley from backing up. He placed something in her hand and closed her fingers around it. It was the wooden stake. The weapon that for whatever reason killed vampires.

"Use it if you have to," he said. "Don't think. Don't

delay. You've seen how fast they move and how they operate."

After that warning he released her and was on the move again, walking so fast she had to trot to keep up. The crude weapon she clutched seemed like such an insignificant thing in the dark when human lives were in limbo.

There were sounds behind her now, too. More footsteps. Somebody was moving equally as quickly. It couldn't be a vampire. Hadn't Derek mentioned that vampires made no sound...or had she invented that fact out of sheer desperation?

Derek had to have heard those footsteps, though he didn't slow down. Afraid to speak again in case doing so might alert the vampires in this corridor, Riley walked on with the wooden stake held in front of her with both hands, thinking that actually meeting a vampire would be better than waiting for the unknown to jump out at her from the dark.

A scream echoed through the corridor. As if it had been the gunshot that started a race, Derek was suddenly all legs and speed. And it was a speed Riley couldn't hope to match.

Something solid pushed past her as she ran forward, also moving fast, and scared her even more. But there was no option for giving up, and there was no going back. She had asked for this. Her request had brought them here.

There were more footsteps behind her, then next to her as another body pushed past. This one had a scent she recognized, and her heart leaped. Derek's packmates were here. Dale had come. Jared was here.

Although the situation remained desperate, Riley wanted to cheer.

* * *

Derek pulled out the small flashlight holstered on his belt with one hand and his revolver with the other, glad he had reloaded with silver bullets. With Dale and Jared on board, finding whatever lay ahead of them would be easier. He wouldn't have to worry about Riley quite so much.

In the tight space of the corridor, and with darkness all around, he read Riley's emotional upheaval as if she was telling him about it. With her lineage in question, that unspoken link of communication was a point in favor of Riley being a werewolf.

Another scream, originating from somewhere ahead of him, ripped through the darkness, which would have been absolute if it wasn't for his flashlight beam. That scream might have been a good thing and mean that the woman the vamps had snatched wasn't dead yet. It also meant that she had the use of a throat that hadn't yet been rendered silent by razor-sharp fangs.

"Right behind you," Dale said. "How many are involved?"

"Two people were taken," Derek replied.

He considered whether the vampires could be making her watch the death of her partner as an added form of torture. Maybe they were taunting that poor soul, like cats playing with a mouse for a while before they went in for the kill.

"Damn leeches," he growled.

The corridor they raced along grew narrower for several feet and then opened up to a larger space. Derek barreled into a cavernlike room with Dale on his heels, following the beam of his flashlight. But there was light here. Two lanterns illuminated a twenty-by-twenty-foot area occupied by five shadowy figures. Three were vampires.

Sliding to a stop on a slick floor without caring to think about what might have caused that slickness, Derek took aim at the pasty-faced bloodsucker that was leaning over the body of a man on the ground. Though blood dappled the vamp's white face, Derek sensed the downed man's heartbeat. They had made it here in time to save a life. Hopefully two of them.

He fired the gun without speaking. The woman, pressed to a wall by one of the ugliest suckers Derek had ever seen, screamed again. The vampire trying to drink from the prone man's veins flew backward as the silver bullet struck its chest. Derek fired again, anyway. As the vampire exploded into ash, the other two came at him with their fangs exposed.

"I'll take the cute one," Dale quipped as the vamps came on. He got his gun out in time to take care of one of them right away.

The third vampire didn't attack. It stopped in its tracks and stared at Derek with flat black unreadable eyes. Derek experienced a moment of complete stillness as their gazes connected. With that stare, Derek suddenly understood why the sucker had stopped, and what was going on.

The rail-thin vampire lifted its arms and spread them wide, offering itself to the future impact of Derek's silver bullets, providing the way for a direct shot to its defunct, functionless heart.

"Why?" Derek asked.

Speaking in a deep voice that showed no emotion, the vampire answered. "Would you want to be me? Be this? Become like them?"

514   Code Wolf

"No," Derek said. "Most assuredly not."

"Neither do I," the vampire confessed.

"You could tell us a lot before I pull this trigger."

"I'd tell you nothing you don't already know."

"Where to find *her* would be a good start."

"She is everywhere and nowhere, wolf. Only the old ones have the privilege of meeting the Prime face-to-face, and they would rather not."

"She wants something from us," Derek said.

"I have no knowledge of that."

"You're different, though."

"Which explains my desire to end this dreary existence."

Derek waved the gun. "Can you change? Be trusted? Is that possible?"

"Not possible for me. The thirst is all-consuming. If you don't kill me, I will kill this woman before you can change your mind."

"Even when you don't want to?"

"Even then," the vampire replied.

"Then I'm sorry," Derek said.

"And I'll go back to being at peace."

Sensing Derek's hesitancy, the vampire advanced, showing fang and producing strange guttural sounds in its throat. Derek didn't have to turn around to figure out that Riley had entered the room, and that the vampire had seen her.

The creature moved toward her with the fluidity of running water. Jared shoved Riley aside the second the vampire reached her and looked the creature in the face.

Pale hands went for Jared's throat as Derek rallied. Dale was there, too. The vampire lunged, spun and caught Riley by the arm. Derek watched her wrench it away.

The fabric of her shirt tore, stuck in the vamp's long fingernails, and exposed one of her shoulders and part of her bruised neck.

The vampire could have slid its fangs into her right then, before Derek got enough of a hold to yank the bloodsucker back. But it didn't take that bite. As the creature glanced to Derek with a look that said, "You have to kill me. You know you do," Riley slammed the stake into its back, high enough to have punctured its chest if she had been strong enough to get it through. Derek finished the fight by helping that blow find its mark.

Gray ash swirled in the air and then rained down like the weather outside. Riley stood there as it fell and shivered, staring at her empty hand that was now missing the wooden stake.

Dale, having taken down the vampire he'd been fighting, rushed to help the woman who had been captured and who, though untouched, had sunk to the floor. They were going to have to find a way to convince the woman that she had not seen who had abducted her and what had taken place in this cavern. It was going to be a tricky business. Maybe Riley, with her training in psychology, could help with that. Forgetting was essential, so they would have to try.

Jared went to help the man on the floor, who was still alive and very lucky. Derek observed the end result of a fight that was like so many others in his experience, other than the fact that a vampire had purposefully choreographed its own final death.

That creature might not have harmed Riley, but who was to say? It appeared to have wanted to push Derek and his packmates into sending its soulless body back to wherever it belonged. This was something Derek had never encountered before. Something he had to consider in the days ahead, if there were to be more vampires like that one.

For now, two people were alive to see another day. Riley was safe and she was in his arms...though he couldn't remember how she had gotten there.

Chapter 29

Shock had the power to change a person's chemistry at the cellular level. Riley actually felt it change hers.

As she stood with her back against Derek's chest, stress hormones weaved through her system. Though the chaos and danger she had faced were over, the effects were going to last for some time.

She had helped to destroy a vampire. She had wielded the weapon that had dealt him the blow. They weren't considered living things, Derek had explained, since they were dead already and existed according to somebody else's plan. Therefore, she hadn't actually killed anyone at all.

Yet she had felt the jarring sensation of piercing something solid as the stake went into the vampire's back. She had felt the pointed stake veer off the bones of the creature's spine with an impact that shuddered through her arm and shoulder.

Riley was both horrified and elated to have helped to save herself from such a cruel fate as the one that had twisted the vampire species into being. Yet she had stepped up. Lucky for her, she had also been surrounded by a few good Weres each time a vampire came around.

The scene in front of her was like another aspect of the nightmare that clung to the outer recesses of her mind. Dale was attending to the woman who had nearly met her death. He had lifted her up in his capable arms. The fact that she still wore one blue shoe was a heart-breaking detail.

Jared had hoisted the woman's male companion over his shoulder, and walked with an unburdened pace toward the corridor they had all used to gain entry to this terrible place. *Two lives* was the phrase Riley kept silently repeating. *Two lives saved out of how many others that might have needed help tonight?*

These people had also been extremely lucky to have Weres watching their backs.

Speech remained an impossibility as Riley watched the Weres clear out with their human treasures. When only she and Derek remained, he broke the silence. "Are you okay?" Before she could reply he asked, "Can you use those long legs to carry yourself out of here?"

Riley nodded twice—one nod for each of question. She was thankful that Derek was encouraging her to move on her own volition.

"It will wear off," he explained as he turned her toward the dark opening in the wall. "The shock will be assimilated once you view what happened here in perspective. You're probably already aware of that, I suppose."

Riley found herself back in the tunnel-like corridor, in the dark. The vampire gymnastics were over for now. She and the Weres were headed for fresh air and a cloudy night sky. Like a benediction of sorts, she would welcome the rain on her face.

Preceding Derek in the dark hallway, she heard Dale and Jared conversing in the distance. Some of the shock she had suffered was already easing, and it felt good to move on legs that didn't falter.

Jared and Dale were waiting in the narrow space outside. Although the rain had stopped, the ground was wet.

"Boss?" Dale asked.

"Hospital," Derek said, reaching for his cell phone. Into it, he barked two words. "Code wolf."

Riley wasn't the only one looking at him now and trying to imagine what the hospital staff was going to say when these two victims showed up. Or when they spoke up.

"There's no time to correct this," Derek explained. "The guy will need a transfusion. And she…" He glanced to the woman in Dale's arms who seemed to be in a catatonic state. "She won't dare to repeat what happened here, will she, Riley? For fear of reprisals."

"No," Riley agreed. "She won't tell."

If the woman with the one blue shoe so much as mentioned the word *vampire*, she, too, might be locked away in an institution. *Like my mother was. And like I might be someday if I believe I'm a werewolf.*

Derek was getting all that. He was reading her again, picking up on her thoughts with his special Were antennae. If he was expecting her to speak, he was going to be disappointed. Really, what else was there to say? *Good job, boys? Bravo on the rescue of two innocent people, and now make me one of the pack?*

No amount of accolades could put a dent in what

these three Weres were due for their bravery and their
sense of justice. Derek had championed a series of good
deeds tonight. And damn it, in spite of her sickness over
what she had done with that wooden stake, Riley was
in awe of Derek and his friends, as well as how tonight
had played out.

"Dinner, Riley?"

She wasn't sure she had heard Derek correctly. She'd
been concentrating on the sound of the cruiser now
idling at the curb beyond the narrow passage to hell between her and the street. Jared and Dale were already
squeezing through that passageway with their human
bundles. More cops had arrived to help.

Derek caught hold of her arm when she moved to follow the others. "Dinner," he repeated a bit louder, as if
she'd been deaf the first time.

"You and me," he added. "Some small place nearby
where we can unwind and talk."

The thought of sitting down in a restaurant was alien
at the moment. Unsuspecting people would be dining.
Glasses would clink. Food would be served. No one would
be aware of what was happening in the dark spaces all
over the city and how close some of them might come to
a gruesome death if they crossed paths with a monster.

There was no way she could face Derek across a dinner table. Her pulse still thundered. After she'd seen so
much blood, it would be a miracle if she'd ever be able
to eat again.

"You will," Derek said way too astutely, since she
hadn't voiced those thoughts. "You will be able to eat
and sleep, and now is a good time to start the process
of getting back to normal."

"Normal?" Her voice was pitched dangerously low.

"We might as well enjoy the downtime while we can," he said.

Downtime... He probably meant they'd take advantage of a brief lull before having to fight off more vampires in the near future. It was going to be an endless cycle of vampires on the rampage.

"I have just the place," Derek went on, ignoring the signs of her uncontrollable tenseness, and acting as if nothing out of the ordinary had occurred here.

He again took her hand in his...

The pleasure Riley got from the warmth of his skin and the support of that hand was a complete surprise compared to the grit and grime of a supernatural crime scene.

She closed her eyes to absorb the sensation of connecting to Derek. Little licks of flame flowed up her arm and into her shoulder, leading her to believe she might be crazy—insane, even—for reacting this way, at this time.

Because what she wanted right this minute—more than food, more than facing a werewolf in a crowded little restaurant without announcing to the world that everyone in it was in real trouble—was the sudden, unquenchable, totally flammable desire to have Derek inside her. To wrap her arms and legs around him and never let go until she became like him. Until she became one of *them*.

A werewolf.

A synonym for strong and fierce...

And just like my mother.

In honor of a moment that was both rich and terrible, Riley looked up at Derek's exquisitely chiseled face, and frowned.

Derek's wolfishness surged beneath the surface of his skin. His chest constricted. Phantom claws that were mere ghosts of the real things made him tighten his grip on Riley's hand.

How he felt about Riley was the impetus for his wolf struggling to get free from where it sat curled up until he called upon it to appear. Though his wolf wasn't actually a separate entity and was as much a part of him as his heart and his breath, Derek felt his inner beast stir as if it actually was distinct.

Riley now knew some of his secrets, but not all of them. Very few people knew the reality of what he kept inside, and what actually made him the alpha of this pack. *Lycan* wasn't a word most Weres understood properly or fully, and yet that was the word that best defined him and the talents he possessed but didn't often show off.

Being near to Riley was like being flooded in moonlight.

He wanted to devour her. Save her. Be with her.

"You're right. A restaurant is a bad idea," he agreed, voice tight, body tighter.

The eyes staring back at him were dilated, so that most of the blue was gone. Riley's body gave off the kind of seductive female pheromones that his body readily translated. She didn't move or try to explain what was happening to her. She didn't have to. He knew what this moment was and how it had to end.

Riley was caught up in the hype that followed a fight, and that hype registered as being sexual. She had staked a vampire, nearly been scared to death, and had survived. Her nerves were hot-wired. She was high on a cocktail of fear, thrills and adrenaline, and her body needed to release all that energy and emotion somehow. Like his did. Like every other Were in a similar situation did.

Riley Price, with her fair hair, big eyes and trembling

lips, was exhibiting telltale signs. She was proving to him and to herself that she was no longer the human being she thought she was, and never had been.

"Wolf to wolf," he whispered to her as he backed her toward the street. "This is what it is. This is what we do."

Her eyes darted away and then came back.

"Go ahead, Riley. Try to ignore what we both want."

Her left shoulder grazed the brick in the narrow space. She winced but kept backing up. They were ten steps from the street. The cruiser was gone. Dale and Jared were gone. And like the damn vampires he fought on a weekly basis, Derek wanted to take Riley's soft ivory skin between his teeth tenderly enough to hear her shout his name.

They reached the street far too soon and found the sidewalk mostly empty. When Derek stopped, Riley did, too. He wasn't touching her now, and again felt the ghostly claws she seemed to be luring from him by eyeing him so fiercely.

Riley's face whitened further as he felt his own emotions modify the expression on his face. It was too late for her to bypass the charges running through her. The charges he felt as if they were his own. Her eyes flashed with need. Her body swayed slightly.

Instead of stepping back, Riley stepped forward to meet him.

Chapter 30

Riley couldn't slow the reaction that drove her toward Derek. Activity on the street around her faded into the background as soon as her chest bumped against his. They were in the middle of nowhere, on a public street, and she wanted him right then as badly as she had ever wanted anything.

"Riley." His tone was low, his voice hoarse. "I can explain this, and about what you're feeling."

"Don't you dare try," she said.

Derek's acutely handsome face lost some of its seriousness as her rebuttal sank in. Right then she wanted to find a safe, private place where they could go at each other like the animals they were supposed to be. Like the animal *she* was supposed to be. The animal she felt like right then.

Her quick remark was all it took to get them moving.

Although they couldn't actually sprint down the street, the pace they kept up was invigorating.

A light rain fell as they rounded the corner where Derek had left his car. Raindrops clung to her hair and eyelashes. The updo she had pinned to the top of her head was long gone, and her shirt was plastered to her torso.

As they approached the SUV, Derek swung her around, his arm gripping her waist. Pressing her damp hair back from her face, he leaned into her. Their bodies couldn't have been closer. There was hardly room to take a breath, and yet Riley knew this was only a teasing taste of what would take place once she got into the vehicle.

Her stomach was on fire. So was her throat. Derek's heat was similar to being up against a wall furnace, and left her even more breathless.

His mouth hovered above hers, taunting, teasing. Accepting the challenge, Riley closed the distance and bit his lower lip...but not too hard. Enough to tell this wolf she was game.

Crazy...her mind warned with really poor timing. *This is so freaking crazy.*

Derek got the door open somehow and backed her inside. His mouth returned for a kiss that was deep, molten, obsessive and much too short. Then he slammed her door, circled the SUV and got in. After starting the engine, he stopped long enough to look at her, his demeanor revealing the preternatural predator that he was.

Excitement flared inside her. "Turn it off," Riley whispered. "Turn off the damn engine."

Although Derek had to know exactly what she was suggesting, he said, "Not here. Not like this." He shook his head and added, "I can't believe I just said that."

They stared at each other for a long time, each daring the other to cave on the idea of fulfilling their fantasies in the back seat of Derek's SUV. That might have been someone else's dream date, Riley supposed. It remained hers for about ten more seconds before she nodded and sat back.

Derek was right, maybe not for the reason he intended, but because there wasn't enough room to contain their sudden need for each other.

He drove like a madman, but didn't resort to using the police light he could have tossed onto the roof of the car. His apartment was closer than her house by several minutes of driving time, so he headed there.

Riley anticipated the moment when she'd come to her senses and remember what they had done tonight in the cavern behind those buildings, and what she had seen that had made her so sick. But both the tingle centered between her thighs and the buzz of electricity that spanned the length of the seat separating her from Derek, refused to dissipate.

He parked on the street. Riley didn't wait for him to open her door. They didn't touch when they raced up the stairs, when he unlocked his front door and while they both tore off their wet shirts inside his place.

They didn't make it to the bedroom or the bed.

Derek, with his bare, bronzed arms and strong hands, simply pulled her to the floor.

The hours passed by in a blur. Finally spent, though he was quickly regaining his strength and up for another round of mind-blowing sex and seduction, Derek listened to the rain hitting the window and the sound of Riley's breath as she was lying in his arms.

She was awake. Patches of her bare skin glowed with

a light shimmer of perspiration. Their lovemaking had been feral in intensity. It had taken them to a place he'd never really known could exist for a male and a female.

"I will never get enough of that, and you." He didn't look at Riley when he spoke, sure he'd start all over again if they made eye contact. But he needed to give her respite. Her entire backside had to be aching already from the hardwood floor.

They had made love several times and on varied surfaces, from the floor to the sofa and the dining table, and had ended up right back where they'd started, which gave them more room to spread out. Riley had to understand at this point that no mere woman could have kept up or walked away from the past couple of hours on her own two feet.

He toyed with the idea of bringing the subject up.

"What can I expect?" Riley asked, beating him to it. It was the first time she had spoken since he'd brought her here tonight.

"How will the wolf part of me show up?" was her second question.

"Your wolf has already made an appearance," Derek replied.

She took some time to think about that. "Am I supposed to feel different?"

"It will take a while for you to mesh with your new senses, and then we'll find out how things are to go. I'm guessing you're already using some of those special senses without realizing it."

"Like my ability to read people fairly easily at work?" she asked, having remembered that from their conversation in her office.

"Yes. Like that."

"Will I be able to shape-shift?"

"I honestly don't know. Some half-breeds can. Others never do."

"Half-breed." She repeated the word.

"She-wolf," Derek said.

Another minute passed before she asked, "How many people do you think I meet, either at work or in my personal life, who are werewolves?"

"Probably more than you might think. Weres don't outnumber the people in Seattle. We're just a small sect trying to blend in."

She had more questions. "What will happen to me now?"

"Nothing, unless you want it to. But you'll have to wait for the next time a full moon comes around to be sure."

He quickly added, "Some people who share their DNA with humans remain human, as you have for most of your life."

"So I can choose for things to stay the same?"

"Possibly."

Rolling onto her side, Riley looked at him now. She said, "And possibly not?"

"What has developed between us has a name. It's called *imprinting*. When that happens and when both Were parties feel the bond that forms, latent Were abilities are often exposed as if they've been tugged out of hiding."

"I can choose not to accept that part of me," Riley repeated.

"The best you can do after this—" Derek gestured to the floor "—is to learn to control whatever shows up. I can help with that. So can the rest of the pack. Everyone will be willing."

"Imprinting is the driving force behind what we just did?"

"Yes."

"It's a real thing?"

"It has ruled Were behavior since the beginning of time and has kept our kind from extinction," Derek explained.

She sat up, whispered, "Our kind," and said louder, "This now makes us inseparable? You and me?"

Derek nodded and wondered what she thought about that. He couldn't read her face at the moment. Riley's father, also a cop, would have been the poster boy for teaching his daughter the art of the good cop face.

"I can't tell him," Riley said, as if she had heard his thoughts. "I can never tell my father about this. Never let on about Weres or vampires. He wouldn't understand."

Her eyes, Derek noticed, were again a bright sky-blue in the sliver of light coming through the open window shutters.

"We keep our secrets," Derek said. "We keep them for reasons like the way your mother was treated, and for so much more."

Now that Riley's wolf had retreated, content to have sampled what a Were male could do to activate and satisfy that part of her, Riley would have time to think. Without the pressure of her wolf battering at her insides, she was again free to be the psychologist who dissected the problems and issues in front of her.

She was almost painfully beautiful. With her blond hair in tangles and her soft lips daring him to kiss them again, Riley was the epitome of a bona fide she-wolf. Naked, wild-eyed and willful. Intelligent, streamlined and strong. He had never seen anything quite like her.

"I'm sorry if this isn't what you want," Derek lied. He was excited about the prospect of keeping Riley with him and getting to introduce her to his world.

"I'm sorry this complicates things with your family," he added earnestly, wondering if Riley had siblings, or if she was an only child. "There will be more time to talk. This, I hope, is only the beginning of a new trust between us."

He watched Riley get to her knees, then to her feet. She stood up, showing no sign of being self-conscious about her current state of undress. Tall and sleek, with her ivory skin gleaming, she faced the window for a while before walking away from him.

She'd want a shower, time in the bathroom, a drink or some food, Derek thought. So he stayed on the floor, hoping she wouldn't be long.

The sound of a door closing jerked him to attention. Heartbeats bounced off his ribs as he sat up with the sudden realization that it was the front door.

Riley walked down the stairs and onto the sidewalk in front of Derek's apartment house while pulling on her damp shirt and zipping up her jeans. Her shoes dangled from her hand. Chills cooled her flushed skin.

She had to get away, needed time to think about things without Derek gumming up the process. How could anyone just accept the fact that they were part werewolf when it could be a toss-up between truth and hearsay, and with a mother who had fought against the system and died believing she was one?

Justice for all? Innocent until proven guilty? Didn't those same things apply to everyone, in any circumstance? Didn't doctors have a way of knowing truth from falsehood?

She had toyed with the idea of werewolf existence early on, half-heartedly wanting to believe. Her father had never known about that. After his wife had been committed, her dad's time away, on the job, had increased exponentially.

When Jessica Price died in that institution, most of the communication between father and daughter had died with her. But Riley loved her dad, and he loved her. He was proud of how she had turned out. Or had been…though now, when the werewolf theme had returned to bite them all in the backside, she wasn't sure how he'd feel. She'd never know, because she couldn't tell him her secret.

You have no idea what it's like to finally find out the truth, she wanted to shout to Derek. Life was painful sometimes. It could be bleak and heartless. But the fact remained that no one had helped her mother prove she was right, and that was the pain that made Riley grimace as she strode away from Derek in her bare feet.

Werewolves existed. They were real, and here. Not just that, but they said she was one of them.

"Damn it. I am one of them," Riley whispered.

Derek would come after her. He'd be worried and would want to help with the dilemma she now faced about her future. Her lover was perfect and everything she could want in a mate. Yet his presence was too powerful and too overwhelming for her to be around at the moment. With him, she had let out the wildness she had kept buried inside. Being near him at a time like this might influence the decisions she'd have to make.

Had that inner wildness always been a sign of her real heritage?

Riley said over her shoulder, with a brief glance at the apartment house, "Don't follow me. Please let me go."

Derek stood on his front step in all his shirtless splendor, looking every bit the sexy wolf detective. How could she not love him for the brilliant combination of all those things?

Love...

"Don't," she repeated, loud enough for him to hear her warning.

She began to walk faster, listening for the sound of footsteps without hearing any. Half of her wanted to turn back, but that was the part of her that had fallen hard for Derek. The part that made her howl at the moon and fantasize after-hours about a supernatural world. That, and the blood her mother had given her.

The other part of Riley Price had been trained to analyze those things unfavorably. Unfortunately, that part of her was shrinking. She felt it beginning to go.

Don't turn back...

At the corner, she paused to look behind her. Derek was still there, watching her, observing her departure and giving her some space. He was worried, though. Something glittered in his hand. His cell phone. He would probably call for help.

It was dangerous for her to be alone. She had seen what could happen. Though vampires were after her, Riley could not make herself turn back. "Not yet. I need time," she muttered. "Give me that time. A minute to breathe."

She walked past more apartment buildings, determined to reach her office, reasoning that after one vampire had died trying to reach her there, no others would try, at least for a while.

She might even have been right about that, but wasn't, her senses told her. Half a block from the warmth and safety of Derek's apartment, one of those monsters was waiting for her.

Perched on the rim of a bench on somebody's front lawn, crouched there like a bird or a goddamn bat, a white-faced apparition in a long black coat blinked its ghastly red-rimmed eyes and smiled.

Chapter 31

Danger rode the breeze.

If anyone assumed he'd let Riley walk off into the night alone after everything that had happened in the past few days, Derek would have called them mad.

He knew exactly what to expect. Letting Riley learn her lesson the hard way, over and over, would eventually change her mind about alone time for the foreseeable future. For now, she was too vulnerable to see that, and was thinking with the human side of her brain.

He didn't place a call for backup. Sensing what was waiting for Riley, he was already moving, following her at a discreet distance.

With some luck, chasing off the one vampire he sensed without wolfing up would be a piece of cake for him. Fists clenched, lungs filled with the odor that threatened to overpower Riley's sweeter fragrance, he sent a message to her over Were channels, hoping enough of her wolf had risen tonight for her to hear him.

"Don't engage or do anything stupid. I'm on my way."

The back of his neck iced over when he caught up to her. Recognition struck when he saw that the creature that was nose-to-nose with Riley was the same blood-sucker he had chased off her property. Pasty face. Long black coat. The damn thing really wasn't going to give up.

It didn't turn to look at him when Derek approached. It was searching Riley's face the way he once had, as if the fanged bastard also wanted to see for itself what might have been hidden behind all that beauty. If the abomination had discovered her secret that she was half wolf, why would it and so many other vampires be interested in her?

That question remained on the table.

Derek needed to focus on those fangs, and how close they were to Riley's skin. The question of why it hadn't already tried to bite her in the seconds preceding his approach nagged at Derek's mind, but he shoved it into the background for now, out of necessity.

"Back away," Derek directed as he came up behind Riley. "Do it now."

The creature ignored him. Its dark eyes were locked on Riley.

"She's one of us," Derek said. "One of my kind, and not very tasty."

"She is more than you think," the vampire remarked.

"If you're trying to get at me, I'm right here. Harming Riley will do nothing," Derek said.

"This pretty morsel is like you, you say?"

"You can sense her wolf if you're any good at sensing anything other than how to find your next meal."

"I wonder," the vamp said slowly, with great precision and without looking at Derek, "if you've looked very deeply into the thing you also covet."

"I'm right here, and I'm not deaf," Riley said with a shaky voice. "What is it you want?"

"I want to find out why my Prime wants you so much," the vampire replied.

"I don't know anything about that, nor can I conceive of a reason for being harassed by her or by you," Riley said bravely.

The vampire cocked its head. "Her? You know about the Prime?"

"I do," Derek said in Riley's place. "We've met, or nearly did."

The creature turned dark eyes to him. "Then you'll understand why I must take your new pet to her, wolf or no wolf."

Derek said, "If that's the case, I'm wondering why you haven't taken her already, and why you're standing here speaking to us."

He also couldn't figure out why the damn vampire was again showing off the fact that its wits were intact.

"I have learned to bide my time, since I have an endless supply of it," the vampire said.

"What do you want?" Riley repeated.

She hadn't moved. Derek sensed the quaking Riley was trying to hide. There was the slightest flutter in the tousled strands of golden hair that draped over her shoulders, and her hands were fisted.

"Back off," Derek warned. "Riley is not going anywhere with you. Not tonight. Not ever. You can tell Damaris I said so."

His remark immediately captured the vampire's attention. Again, the dark eyes found Derek's. "Damaris?"

Derek took in the way the creature repeated its Prime's name.

"I'm guessing I've just provided you with information you didn't have," Derek said. "Perhaps we can call it a trade."

With an incredible show of speed, the vampire had Riley by the throat with both of its hands. With nearly equal speed, fueled by his anticipation of the creature's next move, Derek had his own hands on the vampire's bony arms, restraining it.

The curious thing was that Riley didn't struggle. She didn't duck, strike out, scream or try to fight the monster in front of her. She continued to stand there quietly. Now that he was by her side, Derek witnessed the fiery flash of anger in her eyes.

The vampire put its face closer to hers, but Derek had a firm grip that would have stopped those sharp fangs from reaching Riley's artery if that's what the vamp had in mind.

"Damaris," it repeated, studying her.

"Go to hell," Riley said.

"Hell is my middle name," the vampire replied. But it backed off, dropped its hands, stepped away from Riley and turned to Derek. "She will never stop coming for this one. She knows, you see."

With a flip of its coattails, the vampire turned away with a last word. "And now, unfortunately, I also see."

The dark-eyed beast was gone before Derek could yank the vampire back to ask for clarification. What had it gotten from this little meeting? Names had power, sure, but wouldn't a vampire as old as this one have found out Damaris's by now?

Riley was motionless. Now that the immediate threat had been removed, the shaking overtook her. Her shirt and her pants were still damp from the earlier rain. She stood on bare feet and was as white as the vampire she had just faced.

"I think that thing found what it was searching for," she said, her teeth starting to chatter.

For the life of him, though, Derek had no real idea what that discovery could have been. Between keeping his wolf from making an unscheduled appearance in front of Riley and prying those fangs away from Riley's throat, he was sure he had to have missed something crucial.

Fear and shock kept Riley motionless. The vampire had gotten too close. She had been foolish again to have so blatantly ignored Derek's warnings, and he had come to her aid when she already owed him more than she could ever have repaid.

So much for taking time for herself to think things through. She was tired of being the center of attention for both sides of this ongoing war. The only way to get out of this stranglehold on her freedom was to dig deeper and try harder to figure things out. Get down and dirty. Think outside the box.

"What did it feel like when that creature got close?" Derek asked, gently rubbing her chilled arms with his warm hands.

"It was like being sheathed in ice."

"You had no sense of what it was thinking?"

"When that freak looked at me, I guessed that it saw something, but not until you mentioned the name of its Prime," Riley said. "After that, every breath I took seemed to be tied to that vampire somehow. I can't explain it, Derek, other than to tell you that some part of me responded to that creature's hands on my throat as though I had experienced a moment like that before."

"You have been close to them before," Derek pointed out.

"It was like that one touch produced a memory I couldn't quite reach—information hidden so deep inside me, there'd be no way to access it without cutting me open."

That brief explanation seemed to worry Derek even more, Riley noted. Damn it, it also worried her. Derek had said she was half wolf. She had tasted that kind of wildness when they made love, and was now ready to believe it. She wanted to believe it. On the other hand, being close to that vampire had left her with a strangely similar feeling.

The urge to be sick returned with a flourish. Riley covered her stomach with both hands in a futile attempt to settle it. It was the incredible warmth of Derek's body that she melted into now, grateful to have his support, sorry she had left him without a word about what she was feeling.

If she had just told him she loved him, despite the short duration of their unusual relationship and the fact that they weren't actually human, things might have gone better.

The mix of feelings stirring her insides was causing a riot. Thoughts about digging into what had happened here with that vampire were starting to fade, the way extraneous thoughts usually did when Derek was around. The alpha wolf's presence was dominant. The suddenness of her need to be like him, and with him, took precedence over everything else each time he looked her way.

Wolf to wolf, he had said. That was the way things happened for the Were breed. How else was such an intense relationship to be explained?

Her burning desire to be with him was her animal side coming to the forefront: her wolf making its first appearance. Nevertheless, in order to get a grip on what faced her, she had to find a way to put aside those feelings. She had to delay her wolf's arrival and allow her intellect and psychological training to take the lead.

"Could I have something else inside me?" she asked without expecting Derek to understand the question, let alone answer it.

His handsome face creased. Fine lines edged his eyes as Derek struggled to comprehend what she meant.

"Not just a wolf I never knew about. Would there be room for anything else? Anything more?" she asked.

His tone was serious enough to make her wince. "Like what, Riley? What are you suggesting?"

"Is there any way I could also be a vampire?"

Derek shook his head. "No way in hell."

When she fell silent, he said, "Had you ever met a vampire before?"

She shook her head. "Before a few days ago? No. Who could forget something like that?"

"Do you have a craving for blood?"

Her stomach reacted to his ludicrous question with a whirl. Riley closed her eyes to ride the feeling out.

"You aren't a vampire, Riley. No one can be half

vampire, or even part vampire. They are the walking dead. Every one of them has died sometime in the past and been reanimated by an ingestion of the blood of their maker. That's the only way it happens."

She didn't miss how the last few words of his argument had been offered in a different tone, as though something Derek had said keyed a thought that hadn't previously occurred to him. She opened her eyes when he stopped rubbing her arms. His eyes met hers, and Riley saw pain in them. She watched him catch and hold a breath. The bronzed features of the face she loved lost some color.

Fright was already making a comeback when he said, "Oh, hell no. Christ, Riley…it can't be happening again."

Chapter 32

"It can't be happening again."

The realization sat heavily on Derek's heart. He blinked, and then blinked again so that Riley wouldn't see his anger rising.

He wasn't sure about the idea that had hit him like a runaway train, and yet it made sense in a perverted sort of way. That vampire's temperament had changed when it heard Damaris's name spoken, though anyone would have imagined the creep had to have already heard it in the long years spent in her service. No, this new insight had more to do with connecting that name to Riley.

There was only one reason for that. One reason that, if proved true, would seem like a curse had been laid on him, and that curse had found a way to include Riley.

"You're scaring me, Derek."

He was leaving her in the dark, yes, but there was no way to explain the horror of what he was thinking.

How could he tell Riley there was a chance, a possibility, that she could be housing the stray soul of a monster? That the essence of what had once been Seattle's vampire queen when she was still a human being resided in Riley's body?

Out of all the people in Seattle, a city with a huge population of humans, a stray soul might have landed inside Riley as an unwelcome guest? A freeloading parasite? That same floating soul had also chosen to reside within his former lover, McKenna, and because of that, had kicked off the last big battle with Damaris's vampire hordes.

Because Damaris, now a soulless vampire queen, could no longer possess a soul, the black-hearted diva had somehow managed to set her old soul free at the time of her death. The story he'd heard from the immortal who had taken McKenna away from Seattle was that Damaris followed that stray soul around from human host to human host as though she hoped to get it back someday.

The odds of this kind of soul transference happening to two women Derek had fallen for had to be astronomical. And yet it seemed to be a very real possibility here, with Riley. What other reason would make vampires single her out?

Agitated, Derek turned around in a circle to check for the sound of vampires laughing, as if the joke was on him. He avoided Riley's beseeching stare, not willing to face the fear he'd seen in her face, or let her see his.

"Tell me what this means," Riley demanded. "I have a right to hear what you're thinking."

"Inside," he replied. "Let's go inside. You're shivering again."

"And you're procrastinating."

"Inside, please," Derek repeated, adding silently, *And I hope I'm wrong about this.*

Riley went with him without further argument. Back in his apartment, he handed her dry clothes that were four times too big for her and made her look even younger and more vulnerable.

She curled up on his bed with her back to the headboard and peered at him from beneath lowered lashes. "Talk," she said.

Derek paced back and forth beside the bed, needing to burn up his excess agitation. "We're talking about the past," he began, finding this hard to verbalize.

"Her name was McKenna. We were an item for a couple of years while she was a cop on the force. McKenna was shot on the job. She became a nurse after the department put her out to pasture, due to that injury."

Riley interrupted him with a question. "An item? You loved her?"

Derek reluctantly nodded. "Just not enough for it to go anywhere."

Riley was watching him. "Was she human?"

"She was human, yes. But it turned out that she also housed a soul that didn't belong to her. A secret soul that had no right to be hiding inside her."

He paused there to decide how much of the story Riley needed to hear to understand the reason for his new round of fear. His mind buzzed with thoughts that merged the past with the present.

What if this was a replay of those times with McKenna Randall? What if Riley did host a second soul that didn't belong to her?

He had no idea how soul transference could actually happen.

He swallowed and went on. "Someone new came to town and fell for McKenna, and that's when the real trouble began. The soul that had been hidden inside her was tied to that new guy without anyone realizing it."

"What soul?" Riley asked in frustration.

He stopped pacing again to look at Riley, wondering if he might see the truth of this new theory if he looked real hard…and if there could be evidence of what he now suspected in Riley's expression, or her eyes.

Would talking about it bring that hidden soul to attention? He didn't dare wake something that was so dangerous before Riley had a chance to protect herself from it.

"Go on," she encouraged, unaware of the degree of danger they'd face if his idea turned out to be true.

"After that stranger arrived, McKenna was hunted," he continued. "Things got messy real fast."

"She was hunted by vampires?"

Derek nodded. "They were after her because hers was the body a vampire's former soul had chosen to be housed in, and it just so happened that the stranger McKenna had hooked up with was both the best and the worst thing that could have happened to her because that stranger was also an immortal, and had, in a century long past, been that vampire's lover."

"What vampire?" Riley demanded, her voice rough, almost raw.

"The other soul inside McKenna once belonged to Damaris," Derek said.

Riley skipped ahead. "Did McKenna die?"

"No. And yes," Derek replied.

"Explain."

"She became an immortal in the end, like that stranger who helped her to survive the ordeal with…"

After a brief hesitation, Derek again spoke the name that had been elevated to the forefront of so many minds tonight. "Damaris."

Riley had slid to the edge of the bed after hearing that name. Her shaking rustled the edge of the blanket she sat on. She had to recognize the wariness in his tone each time he mentioned the vampire queen.

Derek fought the urge to take Riley in his arms, afraid that if he did, he would never get the rest of this story out.

"Damaris had given up her soul in exchange for the gift of immortality, but stayed close to the humans it found a home in through the centuries. The only thing you need to know is that the soul couldn't be returned to Damaris. That wasn't possible. Vampires have no souls. The souls of the people they were before being reanimated leave when they die."

He took another break for a breath. "Damaris couldn't have hers back but for some reason wanted to be near to it. However, the soul could no longer continue to attach itself to my ex, McKenna, after she became immortal. So it must have fled again, and…"

"It found me?" Riley's voice wavered. "You believe that soul might have migrated to me, over everyone else around here? You're serious about considering the possibility?"

She had more to say before he could answer her question. "I haven't been in Seattle for very long. Where would it have been before I came along?"

"I don't know. Maybe it's been through a couple of others before finding you."

He saw her disgust over that idea.

"If what you say is true, what would make me so special, so worthy of housing such a thing?" she asked.

"That's where I get tripped up, Riley. You're part wolf, and as such you're an enemy of the vamp nest Damaris lords over. It seems impossible that two of the women I've known could have been in line for such a thing, or that anyone with an ounce of wolf blood in their veins could be involved."

Derek waved at the air with a gesture of hopelessness and went on. "Nevertheless, I can't help thinking this might be the case, since you haven't been injured in any of these vampire sightings and that vampire tonight seemed to get a kick out of something he saw in you."

He paused to think that over. "It's inconceivable to think that souls have minds or powers that direct them, and that this one could be tired of Damaris chasing after it. Who would believe such a thing? But if any of this is true, having that soul end up inside a werewolf would be a final joke on Damaris."

Riley stood up. She didn't sway. Her voice wasn't panicky. "I'm not sure there even is such a thing as a soul. And this is getting more absurd by the minute. First, I find out I'm part wolf. Now you're proposing that I'm a wolf housing the soul of a vampire?"

Derek ran a hand through his hair. "Not the soul of a vampire. The soul of the human that vampire once was."

"You're serious?"

"I saw the vampire's reaction when it touched you. I heard the way it repeated its queen's name. Then what happened, Riley? It left. No argument. No fight. I can't tell you how rare that is."

Riley moved to the shuttered window as if she could

see past the shades. Her long hair was tangled enough for him to see evidence of chills rising near the graceful curve at the base of her neck—the spot male Weres loved second best in their mates. Derek longed to place his lips there and ask Riley to forget all the rest.

But he couldn't forget any of this.

"How do we find out if this is true? If it is, how would I get that extra soul out of me?" she asked.

Riley was again showing her trust in him by asking that question. She was considering his theory and weighing her options in case it actually was the truth.

Derek hated to say what else he was thinking. If he were proved right and Damaris didn't like having her old soul harbored in the body of a Were, their future would be bleak in the hours and days ahead. It meant Damaris might want to cut that soul out of Riley, or cause Riley enough damage for that soul to flee elsewhere.

The only being on the planet that was strong enough to take on Damaris was the immortal that had faced her the last time such a thing happened. Unfortunately, that immortal was long gone, and McKenna with him.

There was no way Derek was going to allow that same thing to happen a second time, not to Riley Price, the first female he had ever loved enough to kick off the imprint sequence. The female with whom he already wanted to spend the rest of his life. The woman who was wolf enough to carry Were secrets and become part of the pack.

Riley said, "It's just a theory."

He nodded. "Only that." Nevertheless, Derek believed it was the only explanation for Riley being hunted by Damaris so specifically, while not being harmed by the vamp queen's minions.

Riley was thoughtful. "That could explain the feeling I had of being like that creature, couldn't it? Something inside me recognized what a vampire is?"

Derek didn't respond to the question. He couldn't utter a damn word.

"Is your ex, McKenna, here in Seattle?" she asked.

"No."

"Then we're on our own with this theory?"

"We are."

"I'm half wolf?" Riley said.

He nodded. "According to what we know of your history, that's what we believe."

"If Damaris can't have the soul back, why would she bother with me or anyone else who had it? Why send her vampires after me?"

When Riley turned around, she again met Derek's eyes. "Maybe you're right, and she doesn't like the idea of her soul being housed in the body of someone associated with werewolves and surrounded by a werewolf pack. She can't get close to Weres, can she?"

Riley's words meant she'd been listening to him with an open mind. She'd started to believe—or already knew—that down deep she was a Were.

"So," she said carefully, "it was a mistake? Since I didn't realize I had wolf in me, and neither did you when we first met, could Damaris's floating soul have accidentally gotten lost in the body of an enemy it didn't recognize as such? Could that be right, Derek? Would she try to take my life in order to rectify the matter?"

Derek was out of ideas. They were going to need help in sorting this out, and he could only think of two places to get it. The first would mean finding McKenna Randall and her immortal lover, and asking them for backup, which would take time they might not have.

The second path would be to find the vampire that had been nosing around Riley and try to get some answers out of it…which was a dicey idea, at best, because what would it have to gain by giving information to the enemy?

"It's only a theory," Riley repeated half-heartedly.

"Only that," Derek again agreed.

Riley was silent for a long time. Finally, she spoke. "If all this is true, I might be in need of a wolf to get out of this in one piece."

"I'm here, and going nowhere," Derek promised.

She shook her head. "I meant that I might need mine," she said in a low, tight voice.

Chapter 33

Riley was right about the necessity of getting her wolf on, Derek thought. Even as a half-breed, she'd be stronger and more aware of her surroundings once she accepted the surprise coded into her bloodline. Her senses would be fine-tuned. She'd be better able to see trouble coming.

The wolf nestled inside her was ready to spring. They had succeeded in rousing it from dormancy during both of their sexual encounters, only to have Riley's refusal to believe in such things send it back.

He would protect her with his life if it came to that, but Riley wasn't helpless. She was tough when necessary and had proven that with a wooden stake. When she became one with her wolf, she'd see the world in new ways. He could see her weighing thoughts about that now.

He just didn't understand how Riley could have housed that runaway soul before he had met her. Had the transplant been more recent? Without figuring it out, he didn't see a way to help Riley in any meaningful way.

She was looking at him expectantly, so he nodded for her to say what she was thinking.

"You told me that being near other Weres would tug my wolf free from its bonds. Was that right?"

"Yes," Derek replied.

"Would finding my wolf rid me of that stray soul, if I had one?"

"Maybe. So we'll go to the pack and give that wolf of yours a little push," he said.

"We can do it now?"

"Now would be a good time if you're ready."

Derek wanted there to be a better way to initiate Riley into the clan. To get her in tune with her wolf nature. Another lovemaking session might have done that if they'd had more time, and if vampires weren't a continued threat.

Unlike humans and Weres, those damn vampires had too much time on their side. "An endless supply of it" was how the one they'd met tonight had put it. They could keep coming.

Together, he and Riley started for the door. But then they stopped outside, on the front steps, surprised to find a car already idling at the curb with the passenger door open.

Seeing Dale in the driver's seat of the dark SUV comforted Riley as she climbed into the car. Derek jumped in after her.

"Got the message loud and clear," Dale said as he stepped on the gas.

Riley didn't recall Derek making a phone call.

"Were channels allow us to communicate telepathically," Derek explained, as if she had voiced that concern aloud.

Of course, Riley thought. *That's why Derek can read my mind.*

"We need to get to the pack," Derek said to Dale. "We'll have to gather whoever is around."

Riley was sure she saw sympathy in Dale's eyes when he glanced at her, though she wasn't going to ask questions. She didn't want to find out what was in store, and what "giving a little push" to her wolf meant.

Dale drove expertly through the city, careful to keep an eye out for potential problems. Derek split his attention between watching what was going on outside the window and looking at her. Sandwiched between both big males, being entrenched in the heat their bodies exuded, made Riley feel truly safe for the first time since her encounter with the vampire that had stalked her.

"Do they like being vampires?" she asked.

Neither Were tackled that question. Riley couldn't imagine how anyone would want to end up like one of those creatures that lived off the life force of other living beings and couldn't set foot in the daylight.

The city lights eventually dimmed and Riley recognized the route Dale was taking to the Were community. They reached the gates and passed through.

Dale didn't take them to his house this time and instead parked near a small building that stood in the center of a neighborhood park. It was late, though who the hell actually knew the exact time? There were no children playing. No one milled round.

The absence of activity was in itself scary. Riley didn't ask any more questions, though, preferring to trust Derek with her welfare, counting on him to help her out of the jam she found herself in and hoping no blood-sucking vampires would decide to try their luck here tonight.

Derek opened the door. He led her toward the building, where flickering candlelight shone from behind the windows.

She hesitated on the walkway, unsure.

"It's okay," Derek said. "This will help. You'll see."

Riley took a firmer grip on Derek's arm as they entered the building, where there had to be forty people—make that forty werewolves—waiting to meet her.

It was called The Ceremony, an event that had been cultivated so far back in the past that only a few Weres understood its origins.

The original purpose of such a gathering was to save the Were species that had been hunted nearly out of existence. By breeding Weres with humans and accepting those half-breeds into the community, Weres could perpetuate the species as a whole in one form or another.

It was believed that this was how some werewolves had evolved to appear more like men than wolves when the moon was full. It was extremely rare these days for Weres to become real wolves, though it wasn't unheard of. Those special Weres were revered as throwbacks to the old days. Their bloodlines were coveted. They, like Derek, were known as Lycans.

Derek's secret nature fell within that definition. Although he didn't take on full wolf form, his unique coding allowed him to shape-shift with or without a full moon overhead, and anytime he wanted to.

The Seattle Were community included no other Lycans of his caliber and bloodline. Though human-Were bonds were no longer necessary or frequent, there was no prejudice here regarding the human race and the part they had played in werewolf evolution…except where Lycan bloodlines were concerned. In order to protect Lycan skills and traits and keep the lines undiluted, Lycans only mated with other Lycans.

He had fallen hard for Riley Price, though, and wasn't sorry.

Tonight, if all went well, Riley would begin to feel the wolf essence nestled up inside her. Nothing more than that. It would be enough for her to deal with and would show Riley that she was one of many.

"Will it hurt?" Riley asked as the faces of his friends appeared, accentuated by the light of a room full of candles.

"No one will touch you," Derek explained. "You just have to be here, among us."

Her eyes were again wide. "What if I'm not what you think I am?"

"I don't think there's a chance of that, but shouldn't we find out? Walk with me. Keep hold of my hand."

She did as he asked with her head held high and her blue eyes curious. *"I'm proud of you,"* he messaged to her. *"You just need to be able to hear me."*

"All you have to do," he said to her aloud, "is breathe and look around. Look at the faces of the Weres who have come to welcome you. Inhale their scent and internalize it. See if your body recognizes what that scent represents. Can you do that?"

She squared her shoulders and briefly closed her eyes. When he stopped walking, she stood silently beside him—a worthy she-wolf if she accepted that part of herself.

Derek waited for her to reach inside and find the part he had seen glimpses of. Through her hand, he felt every thunderous beat of her pulse as she looked around and took it all in—the faces of the pack that had supported him since he inherited the title of alpha.

This was where he had been raised. Where his family had lived for a while when they were alive, and before they had been taken down by vampires overseas. He knew every one of the Weres gathered here. They were his family now, as well as his friends.

"These are our allies, Riley. Can you feel their welcome, my brave and lovely wolf?"

She was quiet. Still. Maybe she was in shock. Derek perceived a trace of doubt in her expression as Riley did as he asked. He wondered if she was hearing him already on Were channels.

After several minutes of inactivity had passed, he began to sense something stirring inside her. It wasn't panic. He would have recognized those signs. There was a subtle change in the way she stood, a new straightness and a stiffness in her limbs. The fingers that slid from his curled into a fist.

Her shoulders quaked. She slowly turned her head. The circle of Weres around her began to close in. Everyone here expected her to speak, but she didn't. Instead, Riley groaned like she was in pain and doubled over.

When her legs buckled, Derek swore out loud. He had promised her there would be no pain, so what was this?

He reached for her as she sank toward the floor,

catching her under her arms. She was breathing heavily and was unable to regain control of her legs.

Murmurings rustled through the crowd, sounding like wind in the trees. He had to ignore that. He had to help Riley.

He swore again as he lifted her into his arms. The stiffness left her as soon as he held her close. She rested with her head against his chest and her eyes closed.

For about twenty seconds.

And then she began to change.

Shape.

The sound of her bones cracking pierced the silence. Her muscles began to dance. She shuddered, moaned, convulsed as if an alien entity had taken her over. As if something was twisting her body from the inside out.

Her head snapped back. Her chest rose and fell laboriously. She acted as if she was being squeezed, crushed… Why, when this meeting should have been so simple?

She began to tear at her clothes as if the confinement they provided was an added source of agony. The supernatural striptease left her without her shirt. Still in his arms, she wriggled out of the jeans, and he moved with her, struggling to keep her close.

Half-naked now, she opened her eyes. He saw their color had moved closer to gold on the spectrum. Riley looked him in the face, pleading with him to help her. He didn't know what to do in circumstances so far from the norm.

Dale was there beside him, and Jared. The other Weres backed away slowly to give Riley some space. In the end, though, there was nothing Derek or anyone else could do to help her. With an ear-shattering sound that contained all of Riley's fear and pain and uncertainly, she twisted so violently Derek lost his hold on her, and she dropped to the floor.

He stood back in utter disbelief as Riley's golden eyes again met his seconds before she turned and headed for the door.

On all fours.

In the form of a wolf.

A real one.

Chapter 34

A collective gasp went up from the room. From behind him, Dale loudly echoed Derek's curses. Everyone was as stunned as Derek was, and that was an understatement, since no one knew for sure what had just happened.

Riley was supposed to be half wolf only, and up to now that half had never been acknowledged. There was no full moon in the sky and hardly any light inside the room, and yet she had shape-shifted into the real deal.

The truth hit Derek like a battering ram. Riley's mother had to have been more than just a misdiagnosed Were. Hell, that woman had to have been a full-blown Lycan in order to produce a Lycan. Even then, Riley couldn't have managed a shape-shift like this one unless... Unless her father also was a Lycan.

And if that was true, her family had kept that incredible secret from everyone, including Riley.

Seconds after that thought, Derek was on the move with Dale and Jared on his heels, his mind moving as swiftly as his legs did.

Not only did the Prices have to be Lycans, they also had to be the rarest form of the breed—the rarest of the rare. They became wolves. Maybe, like Riley, they could shape-shift with or without the moon's influence. And they would have to have been so in control of what they were that they had been able to hide their true identities from everyone, including other Weres.

So, how had Riley's mother been caught?

That question rang like a bell in Derek's mind as he raced across the park at full speed. He had to find her. Christ, this rude awakening to the truth of her family tree was his fault, in spite of the fact that he was elated. Riley was a Lycan, like him, and also so much more. That's why the bond between them had formed so quickly. That's why he couldn't help loving her.

"Riley, stop!" he shouted. "Wait. Pease wait."

She wasn't fast. Not yet. And that was in his favor. Shape-shifting took time to get used to. She'd have to learn to coordinate all four legs and breathe with a new set of lungs. Her surroundings would be pressing in, one scent after another, to bombard her with information. He remembered his first shape-shift and had hoped to guide Riley through hers.

"Riley!"

He saw her on the street, where she had stopped to look back at him.

"Good," he said as he stopped several feet away from where she stood. "It's going to be okay, I swear. How could anyone have predicted this?"

Riley had paused near a streetlight, which gave him

a full view of what she had become. Derek didn't have time to process anything more.

"You're light-years beyond merely being special," he continued. "I'm sorry we didn't see it. You might be in shock. Anyone would be. If you'll come with me now, I'll help. This shift probably won't last long and is only a hint of what lies in our future."

He'd said *our* future, when it was possible she'd never trust him again after tonight.

"I can explain. Try to, at least," he said. "This new shape is a gift from your parents. Both of them, it would seem, and not just from your mother. That's one of the puzzles solved. We'll work on the rest."

Riley looked to have been carved in stone. The only thing to counter that impression was the way her soft brown fur, as shiny and silky as Riley's blond hair, rippled in the light.

"Riley?" he said as softly as he could, to get his point across. "Please let me help. Don't run away. You'll change back any minute. I'm here and will always be here. You can count on that. I'm swearing it to you now."

There was no way he could even think to utter the word *trust*.

"Come this way slowly. Do it, Riley. Let me help you."

When she turned her head, Riley's golden eyes caught the light.

"We can call your father and ask him to explain," Derek said as a last resort to get her to move. "In the meantime, you have all of us here to lean on." He gestured to the darkness beyond the lights, in the direction of the city. "Out of everyone out there, we're the ones who understand."

She took one step, paused and then took another.

Riley was still unsure how to maneuver her new body. Derek had to go to her. He willed her to allow his approach, as he also silently asked Dale and Jared to remain on the curb.

"It's okay," Derek repeated. "In either shape, you are beautiful, and you can handle this."

She let him get closer. As he reached out to touch her, he saw that the strength of Riley's wolf was already starting to fade.

Her reverse shift was fast and accompanied by snapping sounds similar to those of her initial transformation. Bones, ligaments and muscles all moved like liquid in a process that was ageless. Shoulders, hips, legs and arms morphed in rapid succession. The fur disappeared last, and the process left her panting.

What stood in the wolf's place was the pale, naked female he had grown to love and had vowed to protect. Derek loved her so much in this moment he was sure his heart would break if Riley rejected his help.

He caught her when she swayed, and again lifted her into his arms. He had carted several new Weres home in his time as alpha, but none like this. *"None like you, Riley."*

She was too weak to wrap her arm around his neck, and seismic shakes rocked her. He cradled her in his arms, inhaled her sweet scent, stared at the long blond hair that hung like golden streamers across her face.

"This might be the last time you allow me to be the strong one," he said to her. As a full-blooded Lycan, Riley would eventually be stronger than any of the Weres in Seattle because Lycans were genetically coded that way.

"Amid all the chaos, we've managed to find each

other," he said to her. "All the events have lined up, it now seems. Hell, Riley, maybe there is such a thing as fate."

Riley's insides continued to churn as though her body hadn't finished sorting out the multitude of shocks to her system. She still couldn't speak, but was thankful to have regained her shape. Like this, she could breathe. She didn't have to be so afraid or at a loss as to what to do or where to go.

She was a wolf, and nothing remotely like a half-breed. She had fur, a long face, all of it, and wasn't sure how that had occurred.

A new kind of sickness clenched her stomach. Her hands and feet still felt strange. She wanted to touch her face, make sure it was her face, but couldn't lift her arms. It was as if the wolf had sucked the life out of her, the way vampires would have if they had caught up with her.

She gave little thought to the fact that she didn't have any clothes on, and couldn't recall taking them off. It didn't matter to her who might have been looking on. The only thing she sought was the warmth she found within the circle of this man's arms, as she remembered the promises he had made. As independent as she was, Riley didn't relish the thought of facing the future on her own...like this.

She thanked Derek with her eyes, the only part of her that wasn't aching, and silently pleaded with him to take her home.

"All right," he said with relief. "Let's get you warm."

He began to walk, and his packmates followed. Riley found it odd how she heard every sound so clearly after her body had betrayed her and her pulse continued to pound in her ears. Footsteps, wind in the trees, cars in the distance and doors opening and closing were abnormally loud. The heartbeat inside Derek's wide chest drummed in her ears, alongside hers.

She thought she heard Derek's voice, though he hadn't spoken to her again. Like with his previous midnight assurances, he was urging her to be okay. If it wasn't for the way Derek's face had set and the tautness of his body, Riley might have gone so far as to wonder if she had made this whole thing up, too.

"Only the beginning," Derek said.

There were others in the periphery, hugging the darker areas of her vision. Derek's friends had seen what happened to her and were curious. Surely they had seen a naked woman before? And a wolf?

"*Woman* is no longer the correct term for you, my lovely she-wolf," Derek said, having again read her mind.

The term *she-wolf* sounded as strange as everything else. Did it actually suit her? Define her?

Was she going to shape-shift again?

Her mother had done this to her, Derek had said. Her mother had been special, too. Not mad or crazy. Truly special. So was her dad, for her to be able to shapeshift like that.

As they took the walkway leading to the house where she'd spent the previous night, Riley directed what was left of her flagging energy toward speech.

"No room," she said to her sober-faced lover.

He glanced down at her.

"No room inside me for both things, wolf and an extra soul. The wolf takes up all the space."

A look of surprise rearranged his features, which led Riley to believe Derek had forgotten all about that part of the puzzle they had been attempting to solve—the part about Damaris's traveling soul. For Derek, seeing her shape-shift tonight had been the revelation of the century.

And hell, that's what it had been for her.

Derek set Riley down in the bedroom, on the bed, and leaned forward with his face inches from hers. "This is a game changer, Riley."

She continued to stare back. He saw that her eyes were again a bright, summer blue, though the golden hints he'd seen in her wolf eyes remained as small flecks of light.

Derek pulled the blanket around her shoulders. The shock of what he had witnessed hadn't worn off yet, so he could only imagine what she must be feeling.

"You might be right about your wolf taking up space," he concurred. "In the meantime, and until we find out, Damaris doesn't know anything about what took place here tonight. Chances are good that she's still looking for you and the rest of us."

Her voice was rocky. "I was a wolf."

Derek nodded. "You certainly were."

"That's not normal?"

"Not in this community, though they all have heard the stories, like I have," he said.

"The wolf takes over everything, but leaves our minds? I was me, and not me. I had thoughts and recognition, except that my body wasn't my body." Her eyes keyed him to the alarm running through her.

"We don't go mad when we shift," he explained. "We

stay us, with a different outline. Only rogue Weres, who were bad to begin with, get worse when a big moon comes around and like to use their moon-induced strengths for no good."

"Will it happen to me again?"

Derek tucked the blanket tighter around Riley, hoping to stop the shakes that made her teeth chatter. "It's highly possible."

"Could my wolf combat the soul you believe is inside me?" she asked. "Force it out?"

"I don't know. I doubt if anyone does."

"Then I need to test it out. I need to change again and kick that vampire's old soul out of me if it's there. Maybe the monsters will leave us alone if it's gone. Maybe Damaris will go elsewhere to look for it."

Derek wrapped a strand of Riley's hair around his finger and let it slide off before tackling what she had said. His muscles were nearly as jumpy as hers were. Beneath his skin, his nerves felt like strings of fire.

"That doesn't sound like a healthy prospect for anyone, especially if the soul finds an unsuspecting human next," he pointed out.

"How many others has she chased down?" Riley asked. "Is Damaris content if her soul is inside a more normal human being? Does she merely keep an eye on it from afar, or does she interfere with everyone who houses what's left of her humanity?"

Riley didn't give him time to respond. Her words rushed out of bloodless lips. "The unknowns will continue to plague us. You and your pack might look at every death in this city as being something she had a hand in."

Derek said, "You're right about that, too."

"Then there's only one way to find out if that soul is what she's after," Riley asserted. "How can I ever be free of the curse until that soul is gone? How can we move forward if we believe it's there?"

Derek didn't care to hear the proposal that had to be coming. He was already building up to a hearty "No!" when Riley overruled his as yet silent protest.

"We can bait that vampire into coming into the open," Riley said. "Let Damaris come to us, on our terms, and we can deal with her once and for all. I'll shape-shift, if I can, and if you teach me how to do it. If I don't pass out with the effort, I can shove that soul out of me in front of Damaris."

Derek held up a hand to protest all of what Riley was proposing. But she had more to say.

"Will you teach me, Derek? I will try again despite how scared I am if it only means one soul stays with me. Mine."

"I can try to teach you," Derek replied.

She was waiting for him to go on.

"Maybe not until the next full moon. Maybe sooner. I told you you're rare. I can't predict what kind of instincts rule your system. To be honest, I've never seen anything like what you did tonight."

She continued to wait for more of an explanation, so he gave it to her.

"Only a few Weres can shape-shift without a full moon present," Derek said. "No one here becomes a full-on wolf, like you just did."

"Is my ability a good thing?" she asked.

"Yes. And highly unusual."

"Then you will teach me about it and help me adjust to a new identity? Will you do that?"

"And then what?" Derek said. "We dangle you like a carrot and hope Damaris takes the bait without cutting you down? You don't imagine that she's been around for centuries for a reason, and can probably handle herself better than any creature on the planet?"

Derek shook his head. "What you're suggesting is too damn dangerous and comes close to being suicidal."

"Yet it's the only option for getting what we all want, isn't it?" Riley insisted. "What I want and what you want. A little bit of peace."

Derek closed his eyes. His plan for Riley had worked too well. She had become aware of her wolf, all right. But he hated it when the most dangerous path forward from here was the only one with the slightest hint of promise.

Chapter 35

Derek had been reluctant about climbing into bed with her after her recent ordeal, but Riley needed him there on a nightly basis now, ever since her first shape-shift.

He satisfied every craving she had in the most delicious ways, and the rapidly growing strength of Riley's wolf learned from his, though she hadn't shifted again after that first time.

She was saving the next shape-shift for later.

They both went to work each day, and at night returned to Dale's house, where they were safely tucked away in the community of werewolves Riley had quickly become part of.

There had been no vampire sightings near her home or office in the past ten days. Riley spent no time in the city after dark to give them access to her whereabouts. She returned to her house only for fresh clothes in the morning, accompanied by Dale, Jared or Marshall, who, thank goodness, was okay after that bite he'd taken.

If Damaris had spies, they either hadn't been able to track her to the Weres behind their closed valley gate, or were afraid to test their skills against a whole community of werewolves.

Riley was one of the pack now, and held two honors as the alpha's mate and a full-blooded Lycan. Her strength increased day by day once she had accepted those things, and her mind had followed suit. Her energy had returned, as Derek had predicted. She was no longer so afraid of being something other than human.

The discolored bruises on her neck miraculously disappeared after that first shape-shift. Now that she knew what she was, she healed superfast. She was leaner, fitter, and worked to have better control of her muscles in preparation for the fight that lay ahead.

Together, she and Derek ran, talked, researched and explored her new status. They made wild, passionate love, and never stopped thinking about each other. And though she had not placed that call to her father about the secrets he'd kept from her, Riley finally adapted to what she had been destined to become.

It was all right. Being even remotely like Derek was what she desired most. Who wouldn't have considered added strength and finding a mate like Derek anything less than a dream come true, despite the discovery of her weirdly wired DNA? Then again, she supposedly housed someone else's soul, and that remained a burden.

It was on the eleventh day after her indoctrination into the Were clan that events took a turn. It was then, and for the second time, that Riley felt something other than her wolf stir inside her.

An inexplicable fluttering sensation came, centered way down deep. She thought about mentioning this to the others, but waited to see what those unusual stirrings might mean as she sat between Dale and Jared on the front seat of the black SUV that was idling at a red light.

There was a sudden and unexpected thud on the roof that was loud enough to make Dale jerk the wheel to the right. The SUV swerved toward the curb, where other cars were parked, narrowly missing one of them. Slamming on the brakes, Dale reached for the door handle, intending to find out what had happened, but Riley put a warning hand on his arm to stop Dale from opening the door.

"They're here," she said. "They've found us."

Dale muttered an expletive that Jared echoed. The two Weres looked at each other for a split second before both of them leaped from the car.

Riley whispered a curse of her own. They had been expecting this to happen eventually, but she had hoped it wouldn't be this soon.

The time for a showdown with the vampires had arrived.

Derek lifted his head and turned. With a glance to the window above his desk at the precinct, he growled low in his throat and tossed the file he'd been holding to the detective stationed next to him. "Emergency. Have to go."

"Backup?" the detective called after him, and Derek nodded to the Were.

He ran faster than he had ever run before, and without a thought for the pedestrians on the sidewalk. His car was too far away to reach when his deep connection to Riley told him she was in trouble.

The route Dale took to get Riley out of the city was planned in advance and changed daily. Vampires and their spies must have staked out each street that led out of town, waiting for the chance to score points with their Prime. Their damnably elusive queen.

It wasn't yet dark. The sky was a dusky shade of navy blue mixed with the purple haze of a cloudy sunset, so if vampires were out already, something had changed. *What?*

A cruiser turned the corner at 5th Street. The cop driving it must have seen him running. Derek waved as if to say "I've got this, thanks anyway," and hustled to the next light, where a second police unit trailed the path he was taking. This cop was okay, and knew what to expect as much as any of the Weres on the force did.

Calling Dale would have taken up time he didn't have. Streets here were in the open and in full view of anyone and everyone that might have been out at this hour. The plan had been to purposely avoid the darker places and potentially troublesome alleys that had become vamp dens and playgrounds, hoping to avoid this kind of attack.

When Derek saw the SUV, his heart skidded. Two vamps, wearing hoods and clothing that fully covered them up so they wouldn't burn to a crisp in what was left of the lingering daylight, were jumping on and off the hood of the car. Dale and Jared were fist-fighting with the bastards each time they hit the ground.

He couldn't see Riley, but she had to be in the car.

Derek's pulse amped up in seconds. He had made it here in time to help. His pack mates were fighting maniacally, as fiercely as if they had some devil in them. That same devilishness overtook Derek as he joined the fray.

Without a full moon overhead, and minus the claws and extra bulk these guys would otherwise have had, Dale and Jared were holding their own. Derek channeled his inner wolf without shape-shifting on the street, and fed off its extra strength. Fueled by adrenaline, his muscles geared up to do some damage to the suckers that would dare to confront either his friends or his mate in the open like this.

He hurled himself at one of the attackers, swinging his right fist while drawing his gun from his belt with his other hand. The chambers held two silver rounds, one for each of these monsters if there was a clear shot.

Luckily for everybody, the street was relatively quiet at the moment, though it wouldn't be for long. He didn't dare shape-shift here, though, where he might be seen. To any onlookers, this fight would look more like a tussle between the police and a street gang than a species war.

He yanked a bloodsucker off Jared and tossed the bag of bones sideways. The vampire hit the side of the SUV and bounded back as if its body was made of rubber. Dale had swung the other vampire away from the car so it wouldn't get a glimpse or a whiff of Riley.

Derek moved in to help without pausing to look through the window at the female he'd come to love more than life itself, hoping Riley would stay in the car.

He managed to get the hood off one vampire as Jared gave it a shove. Though there wasn't much light to speak of, the creature whined and scratched at its face with long, yellow-tipped fingernails. Then it slipped from

Derek's hold and faded away from the scene like a ghostly specter.

Dale wasn't faring quite so well. Since chasing after the other vampire wasn't in the cards at the moment, Derek and Jared rushed in to provide him with backup.

Derek managed to get the stake from his boot as his packmates bent the vampire over the warm hood of the SUV. Red-rimmed eyes stared blankly at all three Weres. The creature was surrounded by beings hyped up with adrenaline-pumped testosterone. Werewolves with a grudge.

Unable to extricate itself from their grip, the vampire snarled, writhed and kicked out with booted feet. But it was going nowhere, and had realized that. In an attempt to take one last bite, the vampire snapped its sharp fangs and hissed like a cornered snake.

"She's not yours to mess with," Derek snarled as Jared took the stake from his hand, looked to make sure the sidewalk was clear of pedestrians and drove the sharp end into the bloodsucker's chest.

Dark eyes looked directly at Derek in surprise before the vampire's body exploded. But by then, Derek had sensed a new problem. His neck chilled up as he pressed his face to the glass of the SUV's window. His heart, which had beat so strongly and so surely seconds before, seemed to stop when he saw that sometime during the fight with the two vampires, Riley had escaped from the car.

Riley had long since realized that the monsters would never stop attacking and never stop trying to harm the Weres she owed so much to for making her see the light. She owed them for giving her mother back to her, not as a madwoman, but as a caged Lycan with no hope of escape from the cell that had held her prisoner. And she owed them for helping to explain why her father had never remarried or spent much time at home. It was all about secrets, she now understood.

She felt her mother's spirit with her now, as well as that other, more parasitic thing that might be clinging to her like a black internal fog. There was only one way to solve this problem, one way to end this ongoing struggle for the dominance of Seattle's supernatural underworld. She was the key and had to be brave now, no matter what came next.

She walked swiftly down the street without bothering to use the sidewalk. People were coming out of their businesses to see what was going on, and that was okay, since the Were cops would take care of the mess before anyone got close enough to see what was really taking place.

Where there was one vampire, there were always more, Derek had warned, and the dusky sky was rapidly disappearing. Minutes from now, darkness would fall. If waylaying the SUV had been meant as a trap, she could expect to see more bloodsuckers anytime now.

Riley didn't feel so brave after she had left the Weres behind. She slowed her pace to look back. The SUV was parked at the curb and there were no longer any Weres in sight.

She sent her senses outward to locate the place she sought and the vampires that would be occupying it, chanting to herself over and over, *There's no stopping now, and no room for tripping up.*

Mistakes meant death. And yet Derek had also told her that no werewolf could share the kind of afterlife vampires inflicted on human beings, so there was a possibility she would survive this ordeal.

Too many nasty fang bites could eventually kill a werewolf, Derek had also told her, but since no Were could return as one of the opposing side, that much was in her favor, Riley supposed.

She reached the first block, where narrow alleyways were tucked between buildings. Her pulse sped. Her throat went dry. Two blocks from here was where she had been attacked by that drunken creep. Derek and his pack knew about this area and had been avoiding it when she rode along with them to and from the city proper.

This is where I met you, Derek...

And this is where I was kissed by fate.

An awareness of an Other slowed her pace. The air was tainted by a new scent that was more than smelly garbage cans and discarded detritus. She felt a squeezing sensation in her chest that wasn't a sign of a heart attack, but was her new detection system at work. Newly developed senses were warning her of danger, and that's exactly what Riley had been waiting for.

She stopped to allow people to pass her by, remembering what had happened the last time she visited the area. Vampires had been waiting to snatch unsuspecting souls, and she had made her first and only kill, with Derek's carved wooden stake. Tonight, all she had were her wits, her inner wolf and a parasitic soul that had once belonged to someone else.

Exterior lights were coming on to illuminate the sidewalk beside her. Riley fine-tuned her sight by staring into the darker spaces and allowing her eyes to adjust. But it was the smell, the directness of the odor that hit her, that brought the first wave of chills. Trussed up in that odor was a hint of vampire. Besides that awareness, there was another surprising addition. Wolf.

The blackness in the alley across from Riley started to fill with supernatural beings. She sucked in a breath in an attempt to sense the shape and the species of the creatures, processing the input her body was giving her with a shudder.

There couldn't be Weres here. She had left them behind. So why did the place smell as if there were more of them? The area reeked with the scent of over-the-top wolf pheromones that she was now used to, only this odor was stronger. It was an angry scent. An animal scent.

Something moved in the shadows.

Riley stayed motionless. When nothing emerged from that alley after a minute had passed, she called out, "Come out and face me. Isn't that what you wanted?"

She heard the sound of moving feet and something sharp scraping the brick. Her heart twisted as she waited to see what would answer her taunt.

When that creature showed up, Riley leaned a shoulder against the wall to keep from falling down.

Chapter 36

Derek was hot on Riley's trail five heartbeats after discovering her missing. He had an idea where she might be headed, and the dread that filled him was gut-wrenching.

His packmates fell in behind him, leaving the cop in the cruiser to placate the neighbors and pick up the slack from the street fight. Derek had a notion that Dale and Jared might have felt as sick as he did if they'd known what Riley was up to. If Damaris actually was to show up when Riley was alone, the situation would become dire.

He didn't want to face that vampire. This was the one thing he had tried to dissuade Riley from doing, obviously with no success. More time was needed to acquaint Riley with her wolf side.

They sprinted after Riley, able to smell the darkness gathering ahead. No one spoke. Their energy was con-

centrated, focused. Derek didn't want to believe the two
vamps that had attacked the SUV had been a setup, and
yet he couldn't rule that out. He had to consider that if
the vamp queen was so damn good at predicting out-
comes, she might have fostered this one by luring Riley
to her with a game of bait and switch.

He wanted to kill Damaris with his bare hands,
though that couldn't happen. She had died so long ago
Damaris might not recall her real death, only what had
happened afterward. The sad part, if there was one,
was how she still sought that old, abandoned soul of
hers to this day.

As he turned the corner, Derek saw Riley push off
the alley wall. He watched her take a step forward with
both of her arms and hands outstretched, as if to keep
whatever she was looking at from reaching the street.

"Don't," he shouted to her. "Do not go in there."

But it was too late to stop her, so the best he could
do was to fly into that darkness with her, with his eyes
wide open and both his gun and the wooden stake
clenched in his fists.

Shock rippled through Riley as she entered a darkness that siphoned the rest of the air from her lungs.
Her senses hadn't played tricks. There were werewolves
here, the likes of which she hadn't yet seen in Derek's
pack. One step toward the big Were that had come to
greet her was all it took for her courage to flounder.

He was the biggest Were she had seen: well over six
foot five. Long brown hair draped over his bare shoulders. His pants were tight enough for her to view his
outrageous musculature. He wore a black T-shirt and
short black gloves with metal spikes attached to each

fingertip that mimicked the claws he couldn't possess without the moon. Riley thanked her lucky stars there was no full moon tonight to make this Were even more terrifying.

When Derek and his packmates slid in behind her, she felt the surprise that rippled through them as well. *"Rogue,"* Riley thought she heard Derek say, so this had to be an example of one of the bad guys Derek had mentioned—a rogue werewolf with a mean streak who had chosen the wrong side to champion and ignored the laws governing his kind. However, his scent didn't quite mask the other, far more potent odor that pervaded the space.

"Vampire," she muttered.

That wasn't the worst part, Riley soon discovered as two more unsavory Weres like the one in front of her strode into view.

Derek pulled Riley back and addressed the three giants coming toward them. "You'd help an enemy? A vampire?"

Their closeness brought a new revelation that shut him up after that. None of these rogues could have answered him. Their lips had been sewn shut with black leather laces that left them looking like wolfish versions of Frankenstein's monster.

Menacing growls rumbled in their throats, unable to escape. Their metal-tipped gloves clacked lethally as they opened and closed their hands. Derek didn't see any way to get out of this, and inwardly vowed to fight to the death any of these guys that laid a hand on Riley.

He widened his stance, stuffed the stake in his belt and waved the gun. Dale was already aiming his weapon at the rogue wolves that had crossed over to the dark side. Jared growled, but carried no loaded weapon. Jared wasn't a cop, though he should have been one.

It was going to be three males against three in another minute. The air was already charged with anxiety and trepidation, but a sudden shift in the atmosphere made the rogues hesitant to move.

Derek felt this new presence before he saw what it was. The sensation that flooded his system was icy. Wave after wave of chills cascaded over him as he kept the gun aimed at one of the rogues.

Shadows parted as if this new presence controlled them. And perhaps she did. Seattle's vampire queen had arrived, gliding into the meager pools of light from the street like a phantom.

Black-haired, black-eyed and terrifyingly beautiful in her agelessness, with skin like white velvet and a rail-thin body draped in black silk, Damaris at last showed her face.

Her intelligent, curious, treacherous, dark-eyed gaze landed on Riley. She had a voice that was like listening to someone speak from the bottom of a well. "I believe you have something that belongs to me, wolf."

That voice alone could have scared off half of Seattle's population. Derek remembered hearing it before, many days ago, in an alley like this one.

Damaris's image wavered in and out of focus as if she also controlled how corporeal she could become. The harder Derek looked, the filmier she appeared, until he had to watch this abomination only through the corner of his left eye to be able to see her.

In Riley's place, he said, "That soul is no longer yours to command."

Riley also had found her voice. "I'll give it up gladly if you can tell me how to do that."

Damaris's gaze intensified. Derek couldn't take his attention off her in order to look at Riley. He didn't dare lose track of a vampire that had mastered the art of speed well enough to have evaded them all for so long, and for whom one move of her little finger could bring a horde of vampires to her side.

Damaris shook her head when her Were henchmen took a few steps toward Riley, and they stopped advancing, as if she had hit them with a spell.

"There is only one way I know of to take that soul from you, little wolf," Damaris said to Riley.

"Would that be to kill me?" Riley asked with steel in her tone.

"How else can a soul take flight?" Damaris replied.

"Yes, well, the problem with that is that I'm not ready to die," Riley said.

"I suppose we can't all get our way," Damaris returned.

"Exactly. So unless you have an alternative, I guess that soul you lost and now want back so badly will have to remain in the body of a werewolf."

Damaris's eyes flashed a demonic shade of red, but she modulated her verbal response to sound as calm as the exterior she presented. Her form was more solid now. Her black silk dress rustled as if the wind had given her a caressing stroke. But there was no breeze in the alley.

Derek didn't know much about Damaris's background or history. He hadn't been told how she became a vampire, and what she could possibly get out of remaining near the soul she had lost in the days that could well have been when knights lived in castles.

That's how he imagined her now—climbing the stone staircase of a castle in her black silk dress, with her ebony hair trailing behind her and fanged monsters bowing at her feet.

Hell...

Derek shook his head to dislodge that image. He was sure Damaris had slipped it into his mind as a further distraction. It might even have been her version of a way to solicit sympathy.

He refocused.

"Why do you want it so badly?" Riley asked the vamp queen.

Derek took Damaris's silence as a warning sign that the calm was about to end. He slowly moved the aim of his gun from the big Were's chest to Damaris's.

Riley went on. "If you can't have that soul back, why bother chasing after it? What good does it do you?"

She was asking the questions they all wanted answers to. But the rustling sound was back, though Damaris hadn't moved.

The odd thing about this meeting was that Derek sensed no other vampires in the area. Maybe their black-hearted queen didn't trust her nestlings to let her take her time toying with the enemy. It also could have been possible that Damaris didn't need help of any kind to get what she wanted, and was confident about the power she possessed.

That thought, out of all the others, made Derek's blood run cold. He could easily sense the power Damaris projected, and didn't like it one bit.

"I should keep the soul until you can give me a better option for passing it along to someone else," Riley said, as the rustling sounds grew louder. "Humans are so easy to kill, though, if you don't care for the person who gets it."

"Perhaps I'll take it from you now," Damaris returned with mounting venom in her tone.

"You can try," Riley said. "But I'm warning you, vampire, that I've been told I'm no ordinary werewolf so often that I'm starting to believe it."

Derek hadn't seen Damaris move and yet she now stood close enough to Riley to breathe in Riley's face. He inched toward them, proud that Riley was standing her ground instead of retreating from the seriousness of the threat in front of her...though he wanted her to run. He wanted her to survive this meeting and to be free of the burden she carried. He had to see to that outcome in spite of the odds.

So he fired at the black mass, guessing the bullet would miss its mark and daring Damaris to turn her attention his way.

Suddenly, she was in front of him with her hand on the barrel of his weapon and an expression of anger on her thin face. Derek wrenched the gun away, but by then, Damaris, living up to her reputation, had moved again.

The rogue Weres crowded in to protect a creature that needed no protection, expressing their displeasure with grunts and groans. Dale lunged forward and fired a shot that struck one of the rogue Weres in the chest. He backpedaled and hit the wall. No one took the time to see how much damage had been done, because all eyes were on Riley.

Damaris was floating through the shadows like a nasty dark cloud to hover in front of Riley in a second confrontation that again brought them nearly nose-to-nose. Wolf and vampire. The new Lycan versus a centuries-old queen of the undead.

Derek couldn't see any good outcome in this. Leaving the remaining rogues to his partners, he rushed forward, slowing only when Riley raised a hand.

"I don't want your leftovers," Riley said to Damaris. "Neither do I want any other innocent person to die by your hand for harboring something they don't even know about."

"You think I kill them?" Damaris countered. "And that I'd have reason to do that?"

Derek felt Riley's new strength begin to waver, and tried to bolster her by slipping closer.

"The rumors aren't true?" Riley asked. "You think I'd believe that lie?"

"So many of them aren't true," Damaris replied. "Including that one."

"And yet you're willing to kill me," Riley said.

"No part of me can belong to my old enemies. My soul cannot exist in the body of a wolf."

Derek supposed she could just as easily have been lying as telling the truth. Still, he began to have more insight into the problem.

He had been right in thinking that Damaris couldn't stay close to that soul if it resided in one of her enemies. She wanted to be near to it, watch over it, for reasons only Damaris knew. Maybe she longed for it, missed it. Maybe she regretted having given it up to become what she was today. As intelligent as she seemed to be, Damaris couldn't possibly imagine that she could ever have that soul back, so what was the next best thing?

What did that soul she no longer had the option to possess give her in return for her vigilance?

Another shot was fired behind him. Derek heard something heavy hit the ground, and he didn't turn around. He was entranced by the conversation between the two females in this alley, as well as the fact that Damaris had not yet gone in for the kill when Riley was less than six inches away.

"Tell me how to give it up," Riley said. "Make us a deal we can't refuse."

Damn it. No... Derek wanted to shout. This was a monster, and monsters didn't make deals. This was, in fact, the greatest monster of them all. No kind of deal existed that could justify her bloodsuckers being allowed to run amok in this city, or for her to have Riley.

When Damaris leaned closer to Riley, Derek managed to wedge his body between them. Damaris's anger was like an ice bath. Her dark eyes glared. But she did not go for his throat. She merely turned her head, as if to acknowledge the presence of a newcomer.

Derek heard a familiar voice cut through the dappled light.

"I'll take that soul, wolf, on my queen's behalf."

Chapter 37

Riley pressed herself to Derek as Damaris reacted to the voice that filled the alley with a swift turn that again left Seattle's vampire queen as misty and ill-defined as if the rawness of her anger had vaporized her.

Two more shots were fired. Riley heard Dale shout something, but for her, the moment seemed to stretch out in a kind of slow motion.

She heard Derek ask, "You again?" which led Riley to believe he had met this newcomer before. All she could concentrate on now was the fact that Damaris's talent for manipulating senses had robbed the good guys of a true target.

The new presence also carried the foul odor of a vampire. Riley tried to find it among the shadows as Damaris, moving like a black mist, cut through the alley to confront the vampire that had spoken in her stead.

The black-clothed, black-haired Prime now hovered

beside a white-faced vampire in a black coat. If Derek
had been right about vampires crawling up from the
grave, this one had died in his fifties, with stringy hair
and a lined face.

It was the vampire that had been watching her home.

The creature didn't cringe when Damaris faced it.
Nor did it turn away. It didn't seem to be afraid of anyone in the alley, including the powerful Prime.

Something new was going on, overshadowing Damaris's mission to extract an old and unusable soul from
the she-wolf she'd been stalking. Riley knew it, and so
did Derek.

Sensing movement from behind her, Riley jumped
to her left and was joined by Derek. The rogues were
on the move, only they weren't heading for her, Derek
or his packmates. The two big Weres were barreling
toward Damaris as if protecting her hadn't been their
goal, and they had come to fight her.

Derek muttered under his breath as he again placed
himself in front of Riley like a human shield. However,
no one was coming after her. Everyone's focus had
shifted to Damaris.

"It's a coup," Derek said, and she tried to follow that
thought to a logical conclusion.

"This was planned," Derek added.

Riley struggled harder to understand what Derek was
suggesting. The rogue Weres had been brought here
to help take down Damaris, and not anyone else who
showed up? That's why they hadn't attacked?

If that was true, then the old vampire now facing
Damaris might have been part of that plan.

The moonlight winked out, as if someone had hit a
switch, and the alley was thrown into darkness. Riley

felt the roughness of the wall behind her and expelled a breath when Derek jumped back.

She heard scuffling noises and a series of grunts before becoming aware of more heavy breathing beside her. The familiar scents of both Dale and Jared filled her with an odd kind of hope. She was alive. Derek was alive, and so were their friends. So far.

A harrowing, keening cry went up that sent her pulse soaring. Something wet splashed her face. Derek swore again and handed her the wooden stake. Then he, too, was gone, and Dale and Jared after him.

She was alone in the midst of a fight scene that was going on without her. She was supposed to be the grand prize. Maybe the white-faced vampire had lured Damaris here by dangling her old soul in front of her.

Derek had said this was a coup …

Sudden insight struck Riley as the events began to take shape in her mind. The white-faced vampire wanted to be Seattle's next Prime and was attempting to wrestle the title from the most powerful vampire Derek had ever heard of.

It seemed to Riley, as she stood there gripping the wooden stake, that Damaris must have won all of her battles in the past, because the vamp queen was lethally formidable.

More shots were fired. The growls Riley heard were exaggerated. Moonlight reappeared for a few seconds before the darkness returned again. Still, there had been enough light for Riley to view the scene.

Dale was crouched on one knee, taking aim at the last rogue Were standing. The two other rogues were lumps on the ground.

"So much for the muscle," Riley whispered as she pushed herself off the wall.

She didn't get far before her attention was drawn to Derek's voice, echoing from near the end of the alley. Though she could barely make him out, her eyes were beginning to adjust to the dark.

He was fighting the old vampire. Derek had taken on the black-coated bloodsucker by himself. So where the hell was Damaris, and why would Derek help her by ridding this alley of the vampire that was attempting to take her place?

Anger flared inside her as Riley left the temporary safety of the wall. Something flew past her that nearly knocked her back. Though it might have been a stray bullet, she was determined to get this over with, once and for all.

A strong hand stopped her from executing her plan. The icy grip on her arm instantly chilled her to the bone. A cold breath whispered in her ear, "They are fools to imagine I can't see what motivates them, and plan for that."

Shit...

The fox hadn't been outfoxed at all. And all of this, every last move, had been predicted by the one vampire able to do it.

Everything fell into place in Riley's mind. The old vampire had expected to lure Damaris here for the sake of the soul she coveted. That vampire had instigated a coup. Had tried to. And Damaris, queen for more reasons than merely being older and wiser, had seen it all, and had been prepared.

"Congratulations," Riley said as those icy fingers

scraped the hair away from the back of her neck. "You deserve the crown."

Numbness followed each touch of Damaris's chilled fingers. Riley shook, wondering when the bite would come to kill the wolf and steal the soul that had been hidden inside her.

Her grip on the weapon in her hand made her hand quake. Instead of speeding up, her pulse slowed down as she anticipated Damaris's final move. But this wasn't over yet, Riley's body told her. A tiny spark had ignited inside her, and that spark became a flare, then a heated lick of flame that seeped outward through her pores to counteract the numbness and the cold Damaris had caused.

The next whisper she heard was a combination of anger and surprise. In those few seconds of reprieve from the cold that had been about to overtake her, Riley whirled, raised the stake Derek had tucked into her hand, and brought it down hard.

It was no surprise that Damaris had anticipated that, too, and dodged the blow that could have, and should have, put an end to her.

Seattle's vampire queen reappeared by Riley's side— a ghostly apparition wearing a cruel smile, caught in another sudden ribbon of moonlight. Black eyes found Riley's. Pale fingers wiped away the wetness on Riley's face with a gesture that was obscenely intimate.

With another flare of heat-backed courage, Riley spoke. "I told the truth. I don't want that soul, even if keeping it would mean you'd lose the closeness to it."

Moonlight reappeared long enough for Riley to see the black eyes flash with an emotion that was unreadable. She went on as if she still had time for conversation.

"You told me you don't kill the people who house it. Is that true?"

"Why would I lie?" the voice of darkness replied.

The swish of Damaris's silk sleeve seemed out of place amid the chaos. The sounds of fighting hadn't ceased, though Riley had the sensation of being far removed from the battle, and in another space altogether.

"Then why am I still alive?" she asked, withholding another shiver as the vampire touched her hair. "I've been in Seattle for a while without realizing my heritage. You've had plenty of time to confront me."

Getting Damaris to answer that question would be a long shot. But she did.

"It was when you came into your heritage that things got tripped up," the vampire said. "Until then, I merely kept watch."

"It was you who placed that heritage in my lap by sending your vampires after me. Your vampires drove me into the arms of a Were."

"Not my plan," Damaris said. "His."

Riley didn't turn her head to look for the old vampire Derek had been fighting. "So, what now?"

"You must give it up. You are a wolf, an enemy, and can no longer sustain that soul. Nor can any usurper be allowed to control me through it."

Cold lips rested on Riley's face, next to her right ear. *This is it. The bite will come now*, her mind warned.

"It was a beautiful thing once," Damaris said. "Never pure, you understand, and yet it was mine to keep or share as I saw fit."

The bite had to come.

Damaris was toying with her.

"Nevertheless, I gave it up for love," the vampire continued.

Riley felt the tiny scratch of Damaris's fangs across her ear, and was determined not to faint.

"Which is what you must do, wolf," the vampire said. "Give it up for love."

The sting of those fangs sliding toward her neck made Riley's fingers curl. That's when she remembered the stake that was still clutched in her hand.

"If you believe that other vampire would be better in my place, you know nothing," Damaris said. "Blood will run on every street if I lose control. Rivers of it. There will be no reprieve from the horror those vampires will inflict."

"Yes, well, we can't see anyone getting the better of you, can we?" Riley dared to say. "So I doubt if that will happen. And I didn't have to give up my soul for the man I love. I only had to be willing to share it."

She didn't know how she could have moved when faced with such terror, but Riley pressed the sharp edge of the stake against Damaris's side without using it.

Something the vampire had said rang true, and that was about the threat this other vampire posed to Seattle and its inhabitants. Damaris could have lied about that, of course, but Riley had a feeling this vampire queen had been telling the truth...though the thought of Damaris, who everyone believed was evil incarnate, actually being the lesser of two evils here was beyond the realm of imagination.

"I refuse to die," Riley said, straining to hear what was happening outside of her little chat with Damaris. "I've only recently started to live, you see."

She continued in a rush. "The deal is this—you and I both live. The wolf in me will push your old soul out once I'm fully indoctrinated into the clan, and someone else will have it. I can feel it trying to get out. I don't want to keep it from you, and have no ulterior motive to do so. Until then, there has to be a way to end this. A truce."

A breath was necessary to get out the rest. "Take care of your bloodsucker problem and we can see this through. See if I'm right. Otherwise..."

Her voice faltered. She didn't have any threat that could top the closeness of Damaris's razor-sharp fangs.

Riley started over. "Call off your dogs. Help my pack here, and in return, I'll help you."

She pressed the stake into the black silk without causing a tear in the fabric, hoping that if Damaris was as smart as Derek said she was, the vampire would see the promise in the deal Riley had offered.

There was always the future, another alley and lots of dark, moonless nights if things didn't work out as planned. The vampires would keep killing. And Damaris wasn't really losing anything in postponing the use of those damn fangs.

The fangs moved again. Riley felt another brief sting as Damaris said, "You will owe me, wolf, if I agree."

"If I die here, that soul might die with me. My wolf might see that it never gets loose again."

As Riley saw it, time was up for negotiating with a vampire that actually had nothing to lose. She closed her eyes, willed herself to stillness and searched for the spark she knew was waiting for her.

That spark burst into bright flame that spread through her before Riley's next breath. She tore at her clothes, had a sensation of falling through space. Every part of her, from the roots of her hair to her toes, hurt with excruciating pain as her body convulsed.

The wooden stake made a hollow sound as it hit the ground. She no longer had the hands with which to wield it.

As Riley looked out from her new wolf eyes, and up at the vampire queen from her position on four legs, the thing she saw standing behind Damaris was what stole her next breath.

Chapter 38

Derek roared with anger over Damaris's closeness to Riley. He spun away from the cunning old vampire that had helped to set all of this in motion, and left the bloodsucker to his packmates.

He changed shape midstride as he sprinted toward Riley, letting his wolf out without worrying what Riley might think of this neat trick he hadn't shared with her. There was no moon to speak of, certainly no full moon, but it was going to take a fully wolfed-up Lycan to get that damn vampire queen away from the love of his life. And he was that wolf.

Riley shape-shifted as he closed in. Her gold eyes glowed in the thin beam of moonlight that swept over the alley. She had crouched, as if getting ready to spring at the vampire that had taunted her, and he couldn't allow her to make contact. Her crouch deepened when she saw him like this, and she issued a bark of surprise.

Damaris wheeled when his claws caught in her skirt, her dark eyes alight with anger. Derek didn't wait for the vampire to react. Before she could fade, disintegrate, or whatever the hell she was capable of doing to rapidly move from one place to another, he wound his claws into her hair and yanked her head back so that he could growl in her ear.

"Never touch what's mine."

Damaris's fangs were slender and needle-sharp as she turned to snap at him. In his current form, his canines also were lethal. With his tight grip on her hair, not even a vampire queen like this one could escape his wrath.

In seconds, his teeth were on Damaris's neck in what Derek assumed had to be a complete turnaround from her usual routine. Still, she was rumored to be the strongest of her kind for a reason, and she managed to slip from his grasp, leaving him with nothing but a fistful of her long black hair.

Oh, no you don't...

Again, he caught her silk skirt as she moved toward Riley, and he reeled Damaris back. Without a gun or a wooden stake, his hands and jaws would have to strike the necessary blow.

Damaris spun around fast and went for his throat, fangs gleaming. He held her off with the brute strength inherent in most full-blooded Lycans. She might have been angry, but his was the greater need to protect his own.

When Damaris began to fade away, Derek shook her hard enough to bring her back. She might have planned for that, too. Her fangs grazed his shoulder, cutting deep without doing any real damage. Lycans were far more resilient than most Weres. The wound had already begun to mend when he roared again, letting out more of his anger.

Her fangs skidded across his right cheek as she flexed her jaw. Even angrier now, he shoved Damaris to the wall behind them. As she righted herself, Derek pressed in for that last bite, thinking how ironic it was that a pair of sharp teeth was going to end this vampire's long existence.

He didn't take that bite, however, hesitating when a fresh streak of pain tore through the skin of his left thigh. Hell...had another vampire shown up?

Not a vampire...

Riley.

He hadn't hesitated long, and yet it was long enough for Damaris to move. She didn't go for him or retaliate for the rough and almost fatal treatment he had showed her. Instead, Damaris flew across the alley, pushed Dale and Jared from their battle with her pasty-faced adversary, as if both big Weres weighed nothing...and in less than five seconds, snapped the old vampire's neck.

The explosion followed. Gray ash rained down. And every Were in this damn alley, including Derek, stood there, gaping.

Riley wasn't sure if she had just doomed Seattle to an even darker fate or not. She remembered what Damaris had said.

If you believe that other vampire would be better in my place, you know nothing. Blood will run on every street if I lose control. Rivers of it. There will be no reprieve from the horror vampires will inflict.

Had that been a lie? Was it true that Damaris as queen kept vampire activity to a minimum?

She supposed they were going to find out.

A gloriously scary werewolf stood between her and the vampire queen that had effortlessly sent the traitor in her midst to a more appropriate afterlife. With that show of superior skill, strength and speed, every being here realized Damaris could have just as easily killed them all if she had wanted to...except maybe for Derek, who remained in his frightening new shape.

Gathering her courage while steadying herself on her four legs, Riley stood at Derek's side. After one brief glance up at him, she waited for Damaris's next move, hoping it wouldn't be to lunge toward the two Were males nearby.

When Damaris spoke, Riley held her breath.

"You can do it?" Damaris asked with her dark eyes on Riley. "Set the soul free? Use the wolf to do so?"

Riley hadn't exactly expected a thank-you for possibly saving Damaris from Derek, but these questions were unexpected, too. There was no way to answer, though, without human vocal cords, and Riley wasn't sure of anything, other than having just completed her second shape-shift.

She hadn't known that vampires and werewolves existed, and that she was part of the breed. She hadn't realized her mother and father had possessed so many secrets of their own that they hadn't shared, or that Derek did, too. Would foreknowledge of those things have changed this moment? Would it have sent her in another direction that might have kept her from meeting Derek and his pack?

She had nipped at Derek to stop him from killing Damaris, taking a chance that Damaris was right. She waited to find out if the vampire queen would accept the offer she'd been given.

Derek's claws stroked her fur. He was wary and ready to spring at the vampire facing them. He had faced vampires regularly and probably recognized an ill-gotten lull in the fighting that had taken place tonight.

Damaris, cunning, intelligent, might see Riley's hesitancy now in Riley not immediately responding to her questions.

Weres used telepathic channels to communicate, Derek had told her, but Derek's voice was also out of commission at the moment. So Riley spoke to Dale. *"Tell her I can't be sure. I can only promise that I will try to stand by what I said I would do. I want this as much as she does. Maybe more."*

Dale, with his eyes on Damaris and his finger on the trigger of the gun in his hand, repeated her message, out loud.

Damaris's dark eyes seemed to penetrate Riley's new disguise and see into the mind of the woman beneath the fur. Then, without another word, the vampire faded into her filmier form and wafted away on a nonexistent breeze.

Derek took hold of Riley's fur. He pulled her around to look into her wolfish face and sent a message of his own. *"What did you do?"*

"I made a deal with the devil," Riley messaged back.

"About that damn soul of hers?"

"That, and to keep more humans from being harmed."

Derek paused to consider what Riley had said. He couldn't really argue with her approach, seeing how

Damaris had not only rid the streets of one bad actor belonging to her nest, but had also left every Were here alive and without major injuries.

Riley had stopped the fight, maybe only for tonight, and yet who was to say? The damn Blood Knight that had faced Damaris in the past had also let her go. Either everyone had gone insane, had been bewitched by that vamp queen, or they saw something in Damaris that he didn't.

Eventually he'd find out the truth. But tonight his sole focus was on Riley.

Dale broke the tense silence. Covered in ash, he wiped off his shoulders and pointed to the ground where the shredded remains of Derek's clothes sat in a pile.

"We'll have to do something about that, boss," Dale said, taking in the extent of Derek's physical changes and how Riley was standing on her hind legs with her front paws carving fine red lines on Derek's chest.

"Unless you also can fly, looking like this will scare the pants off everyone on the street," Dale continued. "Because hell, you're scaring me."

Derek glanced down at himself, then into Riley's golden eyes. He saw no fear in those eyes. Riley Price had always been adventurous. She was the daughter of a Lycan cop and his Lycan wife. Could she accept his new semblance, the one that few had known about?

"It's all about secrets," he messaged to her, repeating a former sentiment. *"Too damn many of them."*

He added, alluding to the grooves she was accidentally making on his chest, *"And just so you know, that hurts."*

Riley growled and failed to move. Derek growled back with a force that ruffled her fur. Acceptance was a rare side effect of love. That whole love-is-blind thing was going on here, big-time.

He loved Riley with every patch of fur and every overstretched muscle currently covering his bones. And he planned to love her forever. Lycan love. Unrelenting and unstoppable.

What a pair they were. Two werewolves coded with different genetics, but Lycans all the same. The merging of their bloodlines would carry their rareness forward. Their offspring, if they were blessed to have some, would protect Seattle, just as their parents did, and his parents had done before him. Derek couldn't wait to get to that part.

Damaris was still out there, and real trouble had merely been postponed. Yet everyone here would live to fight another day. That was something. For now, it had to be enough.

As a wolf, Riley wasn't as delicate as she was as a human. She was actually quite menacing. Lucky for him, she didn't get that yet, and was relatively tame at the moment.

Now that those after-fight impulses were on him, Derek wanted her more than he ever had. The brightness of Riley's golden eyes told him she felt the same. They just had to get to a place where they could safely downsize and get on with more of the physical culmination of their love. Doubly seal the deal. Become as one. Forge another link in the chains that already bound them together.

"Yes," she messaged to him, as if she had heard every word of those thoughts and seconded them. *"Let's get to that."*

"Derek," Dale said from the periphery. "Time to go. I'll grab some clothes for you and…"

Derek wasn't listening, didn't hear the rest of Dale's sensible remarks. Riley was on the move. People or no people out there beyond the alley, she was heading for the street like a streak of lightning, leaving a trail of lush, fragrant wolf pheromones in her wake and growling comehithers to him every few strides.

"Hurry, werewolf. Catch me."

Swear to God, he had never been as happy as he was in this moment…

Give or take the next moment, when he'd catch up with her and get a start on that future.

* * * * *

We hope you enjoyed this story from

NOCTURNE™

Unleash your otherworldly desires.

Discover more stories from
Harlequin® series and continue
to venture where the normal and
paranormal collide.

Visit **Harlequin.com** for more Harlequin® series reads
and **www.Harlequin.com/ParanormalRomance**
for more paranormal reads!

From passionate, suspenseful
and dramatic love stories
to inspirational or historical...

With different lines to choose from
and new books in each one every month,
Harlequin satisfies the most voracious
romance readers.

SPECIAL EXCERPT FROM

⬧ HARLEQUIN
™

ROMANTIC suspense

*She's an American Special Forces soldier; he's an
Israeli commando. On a covert mission in Australia,
they have two weeks to stop a terror attack at the
Olympics...and fall in love. Let the games begin!*

Read on for a sneak preview of
New York Times *bestselling author Cindy Dees's*
Special Forces: The Operator, *the next book
in the Mission Medusa miniseries!*

Rebel asked more seriously, "How should a woman be treated,
then?"

Avi smiled broadly. Now they were getting somewhere. "It
would be my pleasure to show you."

She leaned back, staring openly at him. He was tempted to dare
her to take him up on it. After all, no Special Forces operator he'd
ever known could turn down a dare. But he was probably better
served by backing off and letting her make the next move. Not to
mention she deserved the decency on his part.

Waiting out her response was harder than he'd expected it to be.
He wanted her to take him up on the offer more than he'd realized.

"What would showing me entail?" she finally asked.

He shrugged. "It would entail whatever you're comfortable
with. Decent men don't force women to do anything they don't
want to do or are uncomfortable with."

"Hmm."

Suppressing a smile at her hedging, he said quietly, "They do,
however, insist on yes or no answers to questions of whether they
should proceed. Consent must always be clearly given."

He waited her out while the SUV carrying Piper and Zane
pulled up at the gate to the Olympic Village.

Gunnar delivered them to the back door of the building, and Avi watched the pair ride an elevator to their floor, walk down the hall and enter their room.

"Here comes Major Torsten now. He's going to spell me watching the cameras tonight."

"Excellent," Avi purred.

Alarm blossomed in Rebel's oh-so-expressive eyes. He liked making her a little nervous. If he didn't miss his guess, boredom would kill her interest in a man faster than just about anything else.

Avi moved his chair back to its position under the window. The hall door opened and he turned quickly. "Hey, Gun."

"Avi." A nod. "How's it going, Rebel?"

"All quiet on the western front."

"Great. You go get some sleep."

"Yes, sir," she said crisply.

"I'll walk you out," Avi said casually.

He followed Rebel into the hallway and closed the door behind her. They walked to the elevator in silence. Rebel was obviously as vividly aware as he was of the cameras Gunnar would be using to watch them.

"Walk with me?" he breathed without moving his lips as they reached the lobby. Gunnar no doubt read lips.

"Sure," Rebel uttered back, playing ventriloquist herself, and without so much as glancing in his direction.

It was a crisp Australian winter night under bright stars. The temperature was cool and bracing, perfect for a brisk walk. He matched his stride to Rebel's, relieved he didn't have to hold it back too much.

"So what's your answer, Rebel? Shall I show you how real men treat women? Yes or no?"

Don't miss
Special Forces: The Operator *by Cindy Dees,*
available July 2019 wherever
Harlequin® Romantic Suspense books
and ebooks are sold.

www.Harlequin.com

HRSEXP06191

Love Harlequin romance?

DISCOVER.

Be the first to find out about promotions,
news and exclusive content!

f Facebook.com/HarlequinBooks

y Twitter.com/HarlequinBooks

⊙ Instagram.com/HarlequinBooks

p Pinterest.com/HarlequinBooks

ReaderService.com

EXPLORE.

Sign up for the Harlequin e-newsletter and
download a free book from any series at
TryHarlequin.com.

CONNECT.

Join our Harlequin community to share
your thoughts and connect with other
romance readers!
Facebook.com/groups/HarlequinConnection

HARLEQUIN®

**ROMANCE WHEN
YOU NEED IT**

HSOCIAL2018